A MATTER OF JUSTICE

A GREY JUSTICE NOVEL

CHRISTY REECE

COPYRIGHT

A Matter Of Justice
A Grey Justice Novel
Published by Christy Reece
Cover Art by Patricia Schmitt/Pickyme
Copyright 2018 by Christy Reece
ISBN: 978-0-9967666-8-5

To obtain permission to excerpt portions of the text, please contact the author at Christy@christyreece.com.

A MATTER OF JUSTICE

Their past is complicated, their future is deadly.

She came from nothing and was no one until an evil man formed her into the perfect weapon, a beautiful creature of destruction. Capturing her prey held few challenges, until her target and her heart collided, and then the world came down around her. Irelyn Raine has worked hard to bury her past, but escape isn't always possible, especially when the one man she trusts above all others throws her back into the hell she swore she'd never revisit. Now Irelyn has no choice but to face down her demons.

Grey Justice lives by a standard few would approve or understand. Gaining justice for victims can be a messy business, and the outcome isn't always pretty. One woman knows all his secrets—the one woman who could break him. Irelyn Raine is his weakness and his strength, his shame and his redemption.

Someone else knows all their secrets, all their sins, and he'll use everything within his power to destroy what they've built together.

Surviving alone isn't possible, but can they find their way back to each other in time? Or will one of them be left behind? This time, forever?

No one escapes justice.

He who fights with monsters might take care lest he thereby become a monster. — Friedrich Nietzsche

What is done out of love always takes place beyond good and evil. — Friedrich Nietzsche

PROLOGUE

London, England

The trap was set. The prey had been lured. Now all he had to do was wait for the bait to lead them inside. He had looked forward to this day. Had put off the killing for too long. Life became busy, and there were more than a few irritants in his world. These two together had been just one more. He had tolerated them, but then they'd crossed a line, one he couldn't ignore. The time had come to end them.

They would be surprised, no doubt. He had chosen the bait well.

A slight sound outside alerted him that the finale was nigh. Moving the curtain only slightly, he watched the man and woman step up onto the small porch. The man wore tan pants, a light blue shirt, leather jacket; the woman was dressed in black slacks and a loose-fitting gray sweater. His eyes stuttered and stopped on the woman's face. She didn't photograph well, but in person she was really quite lovely. Thick, light brown hair just touched her shoulders. She had a stubbornness to her chin and an interesting little scar on her left cheek. He found the flaw quite intriguing. He would have liked to ask her how it came to be. Considering their lifestyle and career choice, he was sure the story would be quite entertaining.

Alas, he would never have the opportunity to ask.

The man beside her had the solid, lithe build of someone who could handle himself well. His dark blue eyes held a cold, ruthless quality, but when he looked down at the woman beside him, his entire expression changed, gentled. *Interesting.*

Andrew and Natalie Bishop had been a pain in his ass for several years. Still, he had steered clear of them...even admired them on some level. Their "white hat" mentality was wearisome but nevertheless harmless. Until it had ventured too far into his territory. His bank account had suffered somewhat, but the biggest sting was the damage to his reputation.

Had they known he would retaliate? Had they been on watch, waiting for him to strike? He imagined they had. They had been in the game a long time. They knew the risks. Knew what happened when one crossed paths with the wrong person.

They wouldn't expect this, though. Months had passed, and they likely had put his retaliation to the back of their minds. That's what made this one almost enjoyable. The surprise factor helped make this fun. Killing wasn't something he usually did for pleasure. There were much more pleasant ways to enjoy one's self. Killing was his business—a profitable one. These people had not only cut into his profit, they had embarrassed him. A double insult that he could not let slide.

He told himself those were the only reasons they had to die, but there was an inkling inside him that said it was more than that. A resentment, perhaps? An acknowledgment that they had made an impression in a way he never could?

No, he refused to even consider the notion. This was purely a business matter. Nothing more. She had done the job to his specifications, just like he'd taught her. To consider there had been a change in her because of them was intolerable. She was a good actress, and that was that.

The doorbell rang. He had thought about getting one of his female contractors to pose as his wife and play things out a bit. Rarely did he get a chance to playact anymore. But he had places to go and people to manipulate and destroy. Prolonging the inevitable would be a silly indulgence.

When the bell rang again, he went to the foyer and pressed the play button on the small recorder in his hand. "Come on in," a sweet female voice called out. "I'm just getting a pie out of the oven."

The house was small and cozy enough to make it seem as if the woman called out from the kitchen.

He stood at the entrance of the living room, scant feet away from the door, his gun pointed at the door. The moment they stepped inside, he would pop them, and that would be that.

The front door opened, slower than he'd anticipated. Stiffening, he cocked his head to hear any words being said. There was only silence.

Two things occurred that he should have anticipated.

From the back of the house, a young voice screamed, "No! Wait! Stop!"

The man and woman entered, their guns drawn. Had they anticipated the trap? Or were they just as wary as he always was? Even as he cursed his lack of foresight, he coldly and remorselessly planned his way out.

On high alert, he stepped sideways just in time to avoid

the first shot. If he hadn't moved, the bullet would have blown his head off.

He glared at the girl standing in the doorway of the kitchen. Light gray eyes, wide with horror, stared at him with a helplessness he usually enjoyed. Not this time, dammit. She would pay for her weakness and insubordination.

He should have seen this coming. Should have known she wouldn't be able to handle this. She had all the right qualities to be a female version of him. But she had one major flaw, one that might well be fatal. He might have a fondness for her, but that wouldn't stop him from teaching her a lesson she would never forget.

That would have to come later. For right now, he had the more urgent matter of staying alive. He turned his attention back to the couple now hunkered down behind a sofa in the sitting room.

"It's no use trying to escape, Bishop," he yelled. "You should've stayed out of my business."

No answer. How typically rude.

Glancing back at the girl, he waved her over. "Come here. Now."

The girl stood frozen in the doorway, her panicked eyes telling him shock would be setting in soon. He needed to act now.

"You know what's going to happen if you continue to disobey me, don't you?"

The words registered. He saw the panic turn to something else—obedience. She took a step forward.

"Leave the girl alone," Andrew Bishop shouted. "This is between us and you. She's not part of this."

"Oh, I beg to differ. She's the most integral part."

He was safe, hidden behind the thick wall. He couldn't see the man or the woman, but he knew where they were. He would keep a wary eye open for his opponents, but he focused most of his attention on the girl. She was his key to staying alive and his ticket out of here.

"Get over here. Now!" he whispered harshly.

She took another step forward. Shots exploded toward him. Pieces of plaster and shattered wood stung his face. Dammit, she would pay for that, too.

"Come here or else."

"No! You don't have to do this," Natalie Bishop screamed. "We can—"

He fired a shot toward the woman to shut her up. The girl might change her mind. She was a weak, malleable puppet, but dammit, she was his. He had created her and would use her for as long as he wanted.

"I said, come here!" he barked.

The quick shake of her head told him he was going to have to take a more direct approach. He blew out a breath. He hated to make concessions, even fake ones. He had no choice. He was as good a killer as there had ever been, but these two were almost as good. Two against one was not a fair fight.

He began to talk to her, whispering promises he would never keep. His voice was one of his most powerful attributes. Even when she wouldn't respond to anything else, his voice had a mesmerizing quality that never failed. He spoke low enough so only she could hear. His words were incessant as he repeated key phrases that would elicit a certain response. Each one penetrated her weak defenses.

She believed him. He could literally see her changing her mind as he continued his litany of persuasion. She took a step toward him, then another. Her movements were stiff and automatic, as if she were in a trance.

"No!"

The woman's shout was too late. The instant the girl was

close, he grabbed a fistful of hair and jerked her toward him. Wrapping his forearm around her neck, he put his mouth close to her ear. "Stay still, you little idiot, or I'll snap your neck like a twig."

The girl was stiff in his arms, but defiance vibrated through her body. Fury exploded. She would pay for her betrayal.

He and the girl were almost the same height, making her the perfect shield. He stepped out from behind the wall.

"Let the girl go," Bishop said in a quiet, moderate tone. "We'll all back away and forget this happened."

He almost laughed at the lie. Letting the girl go was not an option. He'd be dead the instant she was out of harm's way.

"That's not the way this game is played," he snarled. "Put your weapons down and the girl lives. That's your only option."

"The girl means nothing to you," the woman snapped. "We'll leave you alone. Just give us the girl."

"You're not hearing me. She is mine. Mine to do with as I please. However, I'll spare her life. All you have to do is drop your weapons."

"He won't kill me," the girl cried out. "Please. Just go! Get out of the house and—"

"Shut up," he snarled. Tightening his arm around her neck, he let her feel the impending threat. She knew he would kill her. She'd seen him do it to others.

She shifted slightly in his arms, relaxing a bit. Good, he was finally getting through to her. Now he just had to—

Agony exploded. He glanced down to see a knife sticking out of his upper thigh. The little bitch had stabbed him!

Ignoring the searing pain wasn't easy, but the anger helped. Game-playing was over. She would pay for her defiance, for the pain and aggravation she had caused. He wrapped an arm around her arms and then tightened the hold he had on her neck, cutting off her blood supply and ability to breathe.

She struggled vainly in his arms, fighting the inevitable.

"Stop it!" the woman screamed. "You're killing her."

"Put. Your. Guns. Down," he ground between clinched teeth.

"You kill her and you're a dead man," Bishop snapped.

"She'll be dead in less than a minute. Drop your guns."

The man and woman looked at each other. They knew there was little choice. Either the girl died, or they did.

As if they could read each other with their eyes, they lowered their weapons at the same time.

The girl was unconscious, but she would remain his human shield until this was over. She wouldn't die, but she'd suffer greatly for what she had almost cost him.

An ear-piercing blast exploded, as a bright, eye-searing light flashed. Temporarily blinded and disoriented, he held on to the girl and started firing as he limped to the door. The stun grenade had been a dirty trick. It wouldn't kill him but would definitely slow him down. They wouldn't shoot for fear of hitting the girl, but that didn't mean they wouldn't try to trap him.

The instant he felt cool air touch his back, he knew he was safe. Ignoring the pain in his thigh, he flung the girl over his left shoulder and ran down the steps and onto the sidewalk. Twenty feet away, he dared a glance back. They were still in the house. He could see them through the window. With a smile of triumph, he pressed a switch in his pocket and then took off running as hard as he could.

The explosion rocked the ground beneath his feet, but he didn't lose his balance. A block down the street, he slowed down and took in a deep breath. The house was engulfed in flames. They were dead. The job was done. They would never bother him again. It hadn't gone down as he had planned, but he consoled himself that the Bishops were out of his life, and that had been his intent.

The girl on his shoulder groaned softly. Good. She was waking up. When she was completely awake and aware of everything, he would make damn sure she understood the consequences of her disobedience. She would pay dearly for her betrayal.

CHAPTER ONE

Chicago, Illinois

The killer was good, she had to give him that. He stalked his prey with the prowess of a wild animal. Able to anticipate each move, he was one step ahead. He could strike at any time, but he liked to wait, to watch. The anticipation of the kill was the best part of the job for him. This was a well-known fact within the community. Some assassins killed for the thrill of taking a life. Most did the job for the money. And some, like him, enjoyed the hunt. Like a wild game of hide-and-seek or a cat stalking an unwary mouse. He played to win and he always won. He had once confided that the killing shot was a bit of a letdown. That was why he liked to draw out the hunt for as long as possible.

He was a skilled assassin.

She, however, was better.

Irelyn Raine stood in the darkened doorway of a bookstore. The thin coat she wore was lined so the cold, damp air wasn't a bother. She would stand here for hours if need be. She could see the young family quite clearly from here. They were having a nice meal at one of the window booths. The children, both girls, ages seven and nine, were coloring on the paper tablecloth while their parents had a quiet conversation. She didn't have to know what they were saying to know that they were enjoying each other's company. The tender looks they exchanged with each other, along with the affectionate way they touched, told her there was love. This was a happy, seemingly normal family.

They didn't know that someone wanted all of them dead.

Three tables to their right was the man who had been hired to make that happen. Family dynamics could be so odd. While some families loved each other with a fierce devotion, others did everything they could to destroy theirs. In this particular scenario, the reason was simple greed. The man's brother wanted their father's inheritance all to himself. The brother had been previously disowned, but their father's will stipulated that if no other family member was alive, then the entire fortune would be left to the disowned man. The father was ill. Little did he know that he'd set his son and his family up for death.

James Martin, aka Marty J, had been stalking the Worthingtons for five days. A ten-day time limit on the hit had given Marty time to enjoy the hunt. He wasn't in any hurry to do the deed. Irelyn didn't know the full terms of the agreement, but she anticipated that the hit would be all four at once. Taking them out individually was not only much harder to accomplish, the chances of getting caught were four times greater.

For more reasons than one, she wasn't going to let that happen.

Her eyes narrowed. Marty was talking on his cellphone, and even from here, she could tell he was angry. The stiffness of his body, along with his jerky hand gestures, told her that whoever he was talking to had made him furious. Then, as if a switch had been flipped, he shrugged, nodded, and then pocketed his cellphone. Irelyn knew in an instant that the hit would take place tonight. Whoever had been on the phone, whether his handler or the man paying for the hit, had likely indicated it was taking too long. Marty clearly hadn't wanted to end his fun, but pleasing the client came first. Along with a reputation for successful hits, repeat business was a must.

Marty stood and placed some cash on the table for his meal. He then walked out of the restaurant. She knew his process. He'd wait until the family left, follow them to the parking complex where they'd left their car, and pop them there.

She waited until the assassin was headed toward the parking garage before she stepped out onto the street. With some concern, she noted that Mr. Worthington was taking the bill from the waiter and handing him a credit card. She needed to take care of this before the family left the restaurant.

Staying close to the brick wall, she allowed the shadows to swallow her as she made her way to the garage. Her fingertips touched the grip of the gun in her pocket, its solidness a reassuring weight. Heaviness pulled at her with each step she took. She would do the deed, but she would never enjoy the moment. Never.

She slipped from the shadows and crossed the street at a run. Traffic wasn't heavy, and the streets were well lit. Getting back into the dark was a necessity. Marty wouldn't be expecting her, but he had been trained to be wary. Self-preservation was an integral part of being a successful assassin.

She entered the structure and stopped to listen. The Worthingtons had parked on the third level. That was where the hit would take place. Mr. and Mrs. Worthington were likely to be less aware of their surroundings when they were close to their car. Something about the reassurance of seeing their vehicle made people focus less on their surroundings and more on their destination. Pockets or purses were being rummaged for keys, and minds were occupied with getting inside the vehicle. The distraction was often the perfect opportunity to strike.

Her eyes searched for a trap. Just because she was good at tracking without being seen didn't mean she would ever take her talents for granted. She'd learned the hard way that letting your guard down for even an instant led to disaster. The ground level was filled with cars, but she saw and heard no one. Well-honed instincts warned her to be extra wary. Something was off. A stillness that shouldn't be there—a pregnant pause as if the universe held a collective breath. Even though she saw nothing out of the ordinary, heard nothing suspicious, she remained cautious.

Making her way to the stairway, she entered and then jerked to a stop. Marty stood on the fourth step, apparently waiting for her. "Why are you following me?"

She saw no weapon, but knew he could get to his gun in a flash.

Outrage flared in her eyes. "I beg your pardon. I am merely headed to my car."

"I saw you yesterday in the department store."

Dammit. She had thought he might have. He had been stalking Mrs. Worthington and her daughters in the store. And Irelyn had been stalking him. Mrs. Worthington had stopped at the cosmetic counter. Marty had been only a few feet away. Irelyn had been in the lingerie section several yards away and had thought herself well hidden. However, she'd glanced over at Marty, and for half a second, their eyes had met. She had looked away quickly, and when he had turned away without another glance, she had convinced herself he hadn't noticed her. Those were the kinds of mistakes rookies made, not seasoned professionals like herself. She'd dwell on that later. For now, she had a job to do.

"I have no idea what you're talking about, and I resent the—" Her eyes shifted to the top of the stairway. As she had intended, Marty made a fatal mistake and looked up, too. Irelyn pulled her weapon and fired. Two shots, one in the chest, one in the head. Neat little bloodless holes that belied the damage occurring inside the body. She caught him before he fell forward. Thankfully, he wasn't a large man, but he was a dead weight, and it took some effort to pull him down the stairs and into a small alcove on the other side of the railing, out of sight. A dead body on the stairs wasn't something the children needed in their heads. His eyes were already fixed in that death haze.

Pulling her cellphone from her pocket, she took several close-up photos. She'd email them later.

She heard a sound and peered out into the garage. The Worthingtons had just entered. The girls were giggling with each other, and Mrs. Worthington was laughing softly at something her husband said. It was a sweet sound of happy innocence, and one she had rarely heard.

Even though mistakes had been made, she was pleased with the night's outcome. The Worthingtons would continue on, never knowing how close they'd come to death. As soon as she returned to her hotel room, after she emailed the photos of Marty J's body, she would send a separate, anonymous message to the Worthington patriarch. He needed to know what his evil son had almost gotten away with. If the man didn't change his will, it would likely happen again. Hopefully, Mr. Worthington would take the free advice.

She walked out of the garage and back onto the street. The image of Marty's death mask would forever remain in her memory. Killing another human being, even one as vile as James Martin, was a nauseating, disturbing act. She might have been trained to be a killer, but she would never accept that she was one. However, she had made this bed and now she had to lie in it until she accomplished her goal.

If she lived that long.

CHAPTER TWO

Dallas, Texas

"The last one was found in a parking garage in Chicago. Two shots, head and chest."

Grey Justice studied the photographs before him. Five men, all skilled assassins, had been shot at point-blank range. The murder business was a dangerous profession, so the likelihood of an assassin getting killed wasn't uncommon. However, these five men had been killed within the last six months, and their deaths were not only mysterious, the hits were professional. It took a very skilled killer to take down another one. And he had intimate knowledge of one of the most skilled.

"You think she's responsible for all of them?" Nick Gallagher asked.

Over the past two years, Gallagher had become a close confidant. As a team leader, he had personal knowledge of every aspect of the Grey Justice Group. Grey had not only come to rely on Gallagher's good judgment and intellect, but he depended on his trustworthiness, too. When he'd asked him to investigate the murder of an assassin late last year, he had known he might find out things he didn't want to know. And now there were four more murders similar to that first one.

Aware that Gallagher's keen eyes were reading his every expression, Grey said quietly, "I don't know."

Irelyn was certainly capable of committing all of them. She had skills that would put the highest-paid contract killer to shame. But there was one thing she lacked…the one thing that made him doubt the evidence. Irelyn didn't have the heart of a killer. Beneath that beautiful, icy veneer was a warm, compassionate woman. Others might not see it, but Grey had firsthand experience. He knew Irelyn's heart.

A couple of years ago, another woman, looking almost identical to Irelyn, had been responsible for several kills. Ivy Roane had done her best to make others believe she was Irelyn and had almost succeeded. But he knew for a fact that Ivy Roane was dead. So was there another? Had infamous contract killer Hill Reed, with his bizarre obsession for Irelyn, created more than one knock-off?

His gut said no. This was something different. Something else was going on here, and Irelyn Raine was right in the middle of it all. If she had taken out these men, there was a reason. A damn good one. Question was, what?

"She's much better with a knife than a gun," Grey said.

"That's not exactly a reassuring vote of confidence."

Grey's smile was grim. "No, I guess not." He sighed. "Truth is, I don't know. She's got the skills, but…" He shook his head.

"The cameras haven't picked up anyone who looks like Irelyn," Gallagher said, "but you said yourself she's good with disguises. What we do have is proof that she was in the city when at least three of the killings took place." He held up a hand. "I know, I know. Not damning evidence but too damn coincidental."

"Different weapons were used for all five?"

"Yes."

"So…" Grey glanced down at the files. "These three here, James Martin aka Marty J, Marco Valenz, and Frank Seymour… They're the ones that we can place her in the same city when they were killed?"

"Yes. We can put her in Chicago around the time of Marty J's murder. She was in Toronto the week that Frank Seymour was found. And she flew into London two days before Valenz bought it."

Valenz, a low-level assassin, had been a particularly disgusting piece of work. For the past few years, he'd been trying to beef up his résumé by taking on jobs others might shy away from. Last year, he had been responsible for the deaths of two teenagers. A classmate of one of the teens, with more money than brains, had paid him to kill off his rivals for a particular girl. The kid had been found guilty of murder for hire, but Valenz had continued to evade capture.

By any decent person's standards, assassins weren't good people. However, many of them did have certain principles. Grey had always likened that mentality to how fellow criminals treated pedophiles and rapists in prison. Child molesters were considered the lowest of the low. Likewise, most assassins would not agree to kill a child. These three men—Marty J, Seymour, and Valenz—had all been exceptions. And that was why, even as much as he hated the thought, Grey knew Irelyn could very well be responsible for their deaths. Nothing could get Irelyn's ire up faster than the mistreatment of a child.

But if she did commit the killings, why? What was going on? She had to know she was setting herself up as a target. The community was cutthroat and ruthless, but they did take exception to someone systematically mowing down their own kind.

What the hell was she thinking? And how the hell was he going to be able to keep her alive when he couldn't even find her?

Calais, France
Sacred Heart Children's Home

"She's doing so much better than when she first came to us," Sister Nadeen assured her.

Standing beside the bed, Irelyn brushed back silky blond wisps of hair from the sleeping child's forehead. The unscarred portion of the little girl's face held a rosy pinkish color, consistent with a healthy child. The other side was a mass of scars that would never look normal. No matter how many surgeries were performed, Somer Dumas would never have soft, unlined skin. A boyfriend of the child's mother had seen to that.

"Is she eating better?"

"Much. She's found a few friends here." The nun smiled. "I even heard her giggle the other day."

Her chest tightened as her heart lurched. A giggle from this special angel would sound like music. Irelyn didn't know that much about Somer's earlier life, before the drugs had taken over her mother's mind and the abusive boyfriend had arrived, but she doubted the child had experienced many reasons to giggle.

She touched Somer's hand, noting how it grasped the teddy bear that Irelyn had sent her. "What can I do? What does she need?"

"She has everything she needs. Compared to how she looked when you brought her in, she's a miracle."

Irelyn agreed with that assessment. She had stumbled upon the little girl by accident. She'd been stalking a killer in Nice when she'd heard the soft whimpering. The child had been thrown into a dumpster. Irelyn had no idea who'd put her there or why. Her only focus had been on getting the little girl help.

Once the child had been treated, Irelyn had moved heaven and earth to get her away from that environment. It didn't take a psychiatrist to tell her she was projecting her own childhood onto the little girl. There were too many similarities to pretend otherwise. That didn't matter. This child would not fall into the hands of another monster. Not the way she had.

A few days after Irelyn found Somer, the little girl's mother had been found dead of an apparent overdose. No other relatives could be located. The child needed a family and Sister Nadeen had found the perfect one for her. A young couple had been on a waiting list to adopt for a long while. Though they had two other children, they wanted to add to their family by adopting another one. The adoption process would take a while, but once completed, Somer would have a new, ready-made family who would love and care for her.

Irelyn had researched the couple thoroughly. From all accounts, they were good people, but Irelyn would keep a careful eye on them just in case.

She took a step away from the bed and focused on Sister Nadeen. She had met the nun almost eight years ago. She was one of the few people Irelyn knew would never betray her. "I'm going away for a while."

"For how long?"

"I'm not certain. I just—" Irelyn swallowed, cleared her

throat. "You'll see she gets everything she needs? I've made provisions for her as well as the rest of the children. If you need something, email me at the regular address. I'll check it each day."

"I'll do that, but you've already been very generous." She took Irelyn's cold hand in her warm one. "Are you all right, my dear? You seem a bit pale."

"I'm fine. It's just a busy time for me, so…" She gave herself a hard mental shake. Sentimentality had no place where she was going. "You'll be sure to let me know if you or any of the children have need of anything?"

"Of course I will."

There was no use prolonging the event. Irelyn leaned over the child and pressed a kiss to her forehead. If she did nothing else worthwhile in this life, she was good with that. She had saved this last one, and that was all that mattered.

Giving Sister Nadeen one last nod of thanks, she turned and walked out the door. Spine straight, shoulders erect, chin held high, she focused on what lay ahead. The invitation she'd been working toward had finally arrived. And now she had one last thing to do before she accepted the offer. As hard as it had been to say goodbye to Somer and the other children at the hospital, this last goodbye would be a million times worse. But there was no choice. To do the thing she must, she had to sever every tie.

She had never been a fan of Friedrich Nietzsche and found it ironic that so many of his quotes fit her life. The clichéd if dire encouragement of his most famous one gave her an odd sort of comfort. *What doesn't destroy you makes you stronger.*

Irelyn was about to put those words to the test.

CHAPTER THREE

Dublin, Ireland

S he had never planned to return to this city. But, as she'd learned early in life, plans changed. You either rolled with them or let them roll over you.

Like so many things from her early childhood, the memories of living here were vague wisps of blurred features and images. She knew she was lucky in that respect. She had more than enough nightmares from the things she could remember.

She did remember terror and hopelessness. From her first breath, they had been with her. Some might say it would have been best if she had never had a second breath.

She sat at the window of the most exclusive restaurant in the city. From here, she could see a lush, lovely park. Children played with carefree abandon, while a mother, father, or nanny kept a careful, watchful eye. There was no hint of darkness or dirtiness. No shadow of danger. No one would guess that ten miles to the north, another story could be told. One of death, misery, and evil. She had once lived in the center of that darkness. She had escaped, but not without consequences, not without death.

Of her own choice, her own volition, she was returning to that darkness. The place where it had all begun. The very thought of going back created a knot the size of Texas in her stomach, but she had been working toward this goal for almost two years now. She could not back down now.

Today would be the final step. The most painful one she had ever made. But to do this successfully, she had no choice.

Shifting her gaze, she spotted a tall, well-dressed man striding down the sidewalk. He was too far away for her to see his face, but it didn't matter. She would recognize that purposeful gait anywhere. Some men walked to get to another location or escape where they had been. Grey Justice walked like he was on a mission, as if he could and would conquer worlds.

In many ways, he had. Whatever goal he set for himself, he achieved. Steely determination, combined with an uncanny ability to seize opportunities, had not only made him a wealthy man, but also one who was both respected and reviled.

She had loved and hated him for over half her life. Though, in her more honest moments, she could admit that the hatred was always at the edge of the overwhelming feelings she had for this man. Today, though he wouldn't like the news, she planned to sever the intricate ties that bound them together. It wouldn't alleviate the pain. In fact, ending their relationship would feel as though she had carved out her heart, leaving a gaping hole filled with nothing but dark emptiness. To not do it, though, would be even worse. To do this thing, to complete the task before her, she had to destroy their connection. It had to end...*they* had to end, here and now.

She felt him behind her. He confirmed his presence by

the touch of his hand on her bare shoulder. She resisted the temptation to close her eyes and relish the caress. If she was to succeed, she would have to shut down all the feelings and emotions. If he even suspected what was going on inside her, he would never accept the finality of her words.

She had placed her handbag in the chair to her right and a large shopping bag in the chair to her left. Anyone else would have taken the hint and sat across from her. Grey Justice wasn't like anyone else. Without a word, he lifted the shopping bag, placed it in the empty chair, and then sat down beside her. Irelyn restrained herself from releasing an exasperated huff.

"It's been too long, Irelyn."

"And some might say not long enough."

The smile he gave was a little whimsical, a little sad. "Not me."

"No, not you. Never you."

"I was surprised when you called." Blue eyes roamed over her face, and she knew he was searching for the answers to questions he hadn't yet asked. No one could read her like Grey, which was another reason she had to maintain her composure. He had to believe what she was selling.

"I thought it was time we had a face-to-face."

"That's an intriguing term for a lunch between close friends."

Friends? That word scarcely touched the complex relationship that she and Grey shared.

Before she could answer, the server came to their table and engaged Grey in a conversation. Appreciating the momentary reprieve, Irelyn took the opportunity to study him. With eyes a piercing midnight blue and a face that seemed carved from a master sculptor's talented hand, Grey was a striking man. His thick, coal-black hair was slightly longer than he normally wore it, almost touching his collar. That, along with the beard stubble and slight shadows beneath his eyes, told her he hadn't been taking care of himself as he should. That knowledge hurt. She knew she had caused him worry.

The waiter laughed at something Grey said, and she was struck as she often was by Grey's effortless charm. No one was immune, most especially Irelyn herself.

The famous Grey Justice was a well-known figure everywhere. Dublin was no exception. He would receive preferential treatment. Never because he demanded or really even expected it. Grey simply had a way about him that others responded to. She had watched, both mesmerized and occasionally amused, as they'd traveled the world and the famous Justice charm had opened doors as if he had some kind of magical key.

"Irelyn? Are you ready to order?"

Always prepared, she answered with a polite smile for the waiter, "Yes. The mushroom risotto, please."

She would wait until their meal ended before getting to the reason for their meeting. Grey had a tendency to forgo food if he became distracted. It was a little silly of her to want to continue to take care of him when very soon she wouldn't see him again, but that was the nature of their relationship. For almost two decades, they had been taking care of each other, seeing to one another's needs. Stopping wouldn't happen until that last sliver of thread was severed.

The waiter left the table, and Grey settled back in his chair. "How are you, Irelyn?"

"Good. Busy. But that's the way I prefer. And you?"

He cocked his head a little and then nodded as if acknowledging the more intimate discussion would occur after their meal.

Confirming her thoughts, he said, "I assume you heard that Ivy Roane is no longer a concern."

"Yes, I heard. I was sorry Jonah had to do the deed, but one less assassin is always a good thing, isn't it?"

"Indeed. Though I would have liked to have chatted with her a bit."

"Is that right?"

"She looked almost identical to you."

She tilted her head slightly. "Almost identical. Really? I wondered why she looked so familiar."

"Still playing games, Irelyn?"

"Always." The lack of humor in his eyes made her sigh. "It's obvious, isn't it? Since the first one didn't work out too well, he tried to create another Irelyn."

"And as we both know, there can only be one Irelyn."

"Yes. As you've said many times, one is more than enough."

"One is all I've ever needed."

She hated when he said things like that. It made her want to melt into his arms. To throw away every ounce of her resolve, forget about obligations and regrets. In Grey's arms, the world always faded away. It had been like that from the beginning.

This meeting needed to have the exact opposite effect. Changing the subject was her only defense. "And I saw that Jonah and Gabriella were recently married. They make a lovely couple."

"You know Gabriella?"

"Only from a distance. She seems delightful."

"She is. I had hoped you could come to the wedding."

"I was out of pocket, or I would have tried."

"Ah yes, out of pocket. Such an odd term for what you are doing these days."

"One term's as good as the other."

"Really? I think some are more appropriate than others.

Perhaps Lone Avenger. The Assassin of Assassins has a nice ring to it."

That he knew what she had done was no surprise. By necessity, she had not been discreet. Plus, Grey had informants all over the world.

"Hmm," she said as though in serious consideration. "I was thinking something pithy, like The Assassinator. Think I'll get some business cards printed up."

"What the hell are you doing, Irelyn?"

"I'm having lunch with you, Grey."

"Don't."

She was pushing him. Very soon, that charming veneer would crack, and the fury she could see hiding behind his eyes would erupt. Not that anyone but her would recognize it. Grey didn't show anger like other people. She'd only ever seen full-blown fury in him once. The night that had changed them forever.

She pushed the dark memories away. They would do nothing now but distract her from her main purpose. She allowed herself a slight smile, an elegant, feminine shrug. "I'm just doing what I was designed to do."

"You were not designed for this. You damn well know it."

Did she? No. She had indeed been groomed for this. Grey had done everything he could to change her life, to reverse what had been done. To help her overcome her past. But then that had changed, too.

"You, more than anyone, know that's not true."

She told herself to stop the direction of the conversation. He would blame himself, and that wasn't what she wanted. She was a grown woman, able to make her own decisions. Whatever she did, whatever her actions, she took full responsibility. She owned them, the good and the bad. Her past might have shaped her, but she was an adult. It had taken her years to acknowledge her choices and her mistakes. She wasn't about to let anyone else take the blame. Not Hill Reed, the man she had both reviled and once loved.

Most especially, she would not allow Grey Justice to take the blame. He had saved her when she had deserved nothing but death.

Out of Irelyn's view, Grey clenched his fist. Letting her see his pain would only make hers worse. He had told himself he wouldn't regret what he had made her do. Regrets were for those with choices. He'd had few choices since he was a teenager. The decisions he had made hadn't always been the right ones, but for him, they had been the only ones he could make. He lived by a certain code of rules. They were his rules and no one else's. But he had made a decision for Irelyn…one she never would have made for herself. He still couldn't say he regretted the decision, but he sure as hell regretted the hurt he'd caused.

Determined to get through to her, he faced her with the implacable truth. "I won't apologize for what I forced you to do."

"Forced?" Those fathomless gray eyes mocked him. "Do you really think you could force me to do anything, Grey?"

"No. I don't."

"Then you know I wasn't forced to do that either. As much as I hated you…as much as I despised the act, I knew it was past time for it to happen. He had outlived his usefulness to both of us."

Grey could regret every life he'd taken, but he damn well would never be sorry that Hill Reed was dead. There had been dozens of reasons to despise the famed contract killer, but Grey had had three distinct ones. He should have done the deed himself years ago. Not that it would have saved anyone's life. Finding an experienced killer was disgustingly easy. Reed had been a skilled assassin, but there were others just as good. So no, he wouldn't have saved anyone by ending Reed's life long ago, but no one had deserved to take the man out more than the woman across from him. The fact that she'd also happened to love the murdering bastard had been problematic.

"I'm sorry it happened the way it did."

"No, you're not."

He felt the stab to his chest, as if she'd used the stiletto knife he knew she wore in a sheath wrapped around her left thigh. She hated him for what had happened, even though she had accepted the inevitability of the act.

Their meal arrived before he could argue further. Not that arguing would do any good. Even when he'd made the decision to end Reed's life, he had known what it would cost him. He just hadn't known how damn bad it would hurt.

As they had thousands of times before, they put aside their differences to enjoy their meal. She did it for him. He knew that. Eating was sometimes a secondary priority when he had other things on his mind. Irelyn had always made sure, no matter what drama was going on in their lives, that he took care of himself.

They had been taking care of each other, in one way or another, for half their lives. He knew this woman better than anyone in the world. He knew the soft sigh she made just before she dropped off to sleep. He knew the nightmares she had about her past. He had held her as she had sobbed out her grief, her regret. He knew her phobias and her fears. And the many times she had cursed him.

She had fascinated him from the moment he'd met her. He had hated her, loved her, and cherished her for almost eighteen years. And without a doubt, he could spend a thousand more years with her and never tire of the multifaceted, fascinating woman that was Irelyn Raine.

They ate in silence for several moments. He would get nothing from her until they'd both finished their meal, so instead, he enjoyed watching her eat. She consumed her meal the way she did many things, with graceful gentility and efficiency. There wasn't an awkward bone in Irelyn's body, nor was there a wasteful one. In their early years, they'd gone days without much more than a bag of crisps and a bottle of pop between them. No matter how far they removed themselves from those old days, or how wealthy they became, neither of them would ever take a meal for granted.

He noticed she might have lost a bit of weight. Her face had the kind of bone structure that ensured she would be beautiful all her life, but it also had a tendency to be the first place weight loss showed.

She preferred dresses to pants. She liked the ease of movement if she needed to get away quickly. She also felt that hiding her weapon was easier with dresses. The knife he'd given her long ago was always strapped to her left thigh. On occasion, she wore a holster with a favorite gun on her right thigh. Although she was an excellent shot, shooting would never be Irelyn's thing. She claimed it was too impersonal, but that was an easy excuse. Her eyesight had once been impaired, so much so that they'd feared she would go blind. A surgeon had repaired her sight, but the memory of that impairment had a way of costing her when she needed her confidence. Hence the knife. A knife in Irelyn Raine's capable hands was the most lethal of weapons.

The dress she wore today made him think of cold, bleak winter. They'd experienced their share of brutal, bitter ones. He wondered if she had dressed with that thought in mind. She hadn't invited him to lunch in the city where she'd had her beginning for nothing. Meeting here in Dublin, she was making a point. The severe dress made a statement, too.

29

Irelyn didn't do anything by accident. Even the clothes she wore had significance.

He could read her moods and, more times than not, could predict what she was going to say. Today wasn't one of those days. Today, the secrets behind those stormy gray eyes were hers alone.

Noting she had finished her last bite of risotto, he took a swallow of water and said, "All right, Irelyn. Why am I here?"

"Considering that you've been stalking me for over a year now, I would think you'd appreciate an arranged meeting."

"Stalking you? That's a slight exaggeration, don't you think?"

"Perhaps. It doesn't really matter, does it?"

"You're right. You're here. I'm here. Let's talk. When are you coming home?"

She turned her gaze to the window. "I am home. Haven't you noticed?"

"No, you're not. Your home is in Texas."

"You don't get it, do you, Grey?"

"Apparently not. What is it you're trying to say?"

"Simply that I'm no longer part of your life. In Texas or anywhere else. I'm no longer a part of your life, period. It's over…we're over."

This wasn't the first time they'd had a discussion like this. Living in each other's pockets, as it were, meant they often had to take a break from one another. This was the longest break they'd ever had, though.

"We haven't had anything between us in almost two years. You're severing a tie that doesn't exist."

His words hurt her. She gave no discernible indication, but he could tell from the widening of those lovely eyes. He had said those words to get a reaction. He had expected fireworks, at the very least a denial. Instead, he got a hole punched in his heart.

She placed a ring on the table and pushed it toward him. He stared down at the thing, barely able to comprehend its reason for being there. The ring was a symbol of many things, one being their commitment to each other. That no matter what happened, no matter how far apart they were, they would always be, in some sense, together, connected. They'd exchanged rings several years ago, when things had been calm between them. There had been peace then. They had been working toward something worthwhile. And now it appeared she didn't believe in those things anymore. At least not with him.

He was surprised by how calmly he was able to say, "Why?"

IRELYN CONSIDERED HERSELF A GOOD ACTRESS. HAVING LIVED most of her life pretending to be someone else had trained her to handle anything with poise and confidence. But this? This was killing her. She couldn't let the pain stop her. Grey needed closure—he needed a way out. Severing their ties meant he could finally have a real life. And Irelyn? She would accomplish the goal she had set out for herself, and then she would see.

She told herself to get it done. Be quick. And, to have the most effective result, be cruel. "We've used each other as much as possible, don't you think?"

"Is that what we've been doing all these years? Using each other?"

"Haven't we?"

"No. But it's interesting that you see it that way."

She gave a twisted smile, knowing it wasn't her best, but right now it was all she could manage. "Let's not get maudlin. We're both adults. We knew at some point this had to end."

"Friendships don't always end."

"Friendship?" She forced a laugh and inwardly winced at the hollow sound. "Really, Grey, we're going there again?"

"What would you call it?"

"A mutually beneficial association that has reached the end of its usefulness."

Blue eyes pierced her, and she swore he could see through to her soul. Grey could read her better than anyone. If she didn't pull this off, he would never let up. And that would be dangerous. She would die before she let anything happen to him. This had to end now.

She took a breath and plunged the knife for a killing blow. "I've heard that cutting off the head of the snake is the best way."

"The best way for what?"

She shrugged. Dammit, couldn't he just let go? "To end things."

"And who's the snake in this particular scenario?"

"I think the past reveals that quite well."

Another piercing stare, this one with more than a little anger. He pushed his chair back and stood. "Very well." Picking up the ring from the middle of the table, he dropped it on an empty saucer in front of her. The clatter of platinum seemed to echo through the suddenly quiet restaurant. "Throw the damn thing away for all I care. Goodbye, Irelyn."

He walked away then. Irelyn stayed for several more moments, looking down at the small token of everything they had meant to each other. She should get up and leave. She still had so much to do. Instead, she stared at the ring, vaguely wondering why her vision was becoming blurred.

"Will there be anything else, ma'am?"

The polite question from the waiter at her side shook her from her frozen stance. She shook her head and stood. "No, thank you." She placed several large bills on the table and took a step away.

"Wait. Your ticket has been paid."

Of course it had. Grey, once again. She shrugged. "Keep the money for yourself."

She stepped out onto the sidewalk and, drawing in a shaky breath, refocused. It was done. The hardest part was out of the way. Now to move forward with the rest. The part that would most likely get her killed.

CHAPTER FOUR

Dallas, Texas
Grey Justice Building

"The Abernathy award ceremony is a week from Thursday. The coordinator called this morning to confirm you're bringing a guest. Is that right?"

The question shouldn't have caught him off guard. He had known about the event for months. The Abernathy Humanitarian Award was a prestigious honor. Even though he didn't seek the limelight and being rewarded for doing the right thing never really set well with him, he understood its importance. Garnering both publicity and additional funds for the Grey Justice Victims Advocacy Foundation was an important part of his everyday job. Just because he didn't like it didn't mean he wouldn't do it.

A few weeks ago, he had carelessly told Molly Evans, his executive assistant, he would bring a date to the event. Had he secretly thought that Irelyn would be back home by now? He rarely did anything without knowing why, so he wouldn't lie to himself now. Yes, he had expected she would be back home. He had hoped their meeting in Dublin last week would result in a reconciliation. Instead, it had split them even further apart.

"Grey? Is that right? You're bringing a guest?"

"No. Let her know I'll be solo."

Not by a molecule of movement did Molly indicate that she was disappointed in his answer. He felt her disapproval all the same. She wouldn't be the only person who blamed him for his and Irelyn's separation. Hell, he blamed himself, too. He'd handled things poorly. Instead of talking to her, trying to reason with her, figure out just what the hell she was up to, he'd stormed out of the restaurant like an arrogant ass. He should have stayed. Should have demanded answers. Irelyn always had reasons for what she did. Dammit, he should have found out what they were.

And why hadn't he at least warned her to be careful? At some point, she would face retribution. His heart skipped a long beat. Was that it? Was she trying to get herself killed? No, that wasn't it. Irelyn was too strong, too grounded to want to take the easy way out. There had to be something he was missing.

"Grey?"

"Yes?"

"She's never coming back, is she?"

Irelyn had made an impression on every one of his employees. She was both respected and revered. He doubted that she had seen that, though. Irelyn rarely went out of her way to impress anyone unless the act was part of the job. One of the many things he appreciated about her was her lack of artifice. Considering her beginning, or maybe because of it, she had a strong work ethic and a strict code of honor. Those two qualities hadn't always made her popular, but being liked had never been Irelyn's goal.

Aware that Molly was waiting for an answer, Grey gave

her the only one he could, vague though it was. "She's still got some things to sort out."

Molly nodded and went on to discuss the rest of this week's agenda. Grey listened, offering commentary when necessary, but his mind continued to review his last conversation with Irelyn. He should have asked more direct questions. Instead of pursuing the truth, he'd walked away.

In their years together, they'd hurt each other as much as two people could, but they had always made their way back to one another. This time was different, and he should have stuck around to find out why.

Gathering her notes and tablet, Molly stood and headed to the door. "I'll make the changes to your itinerary and send them to you for approval."

"Thank you."

She stopped midway and sent him a bright look. "I could call one of the modeling agencies to see if anyone is available."

It wouldn't be the first time Grey had escorted a stranger to an event. Up-and-coming actresses and models were always a safe bet. They appreciated the exposure, and he preferred an easygoing companion who had no illusions about a relationship.

"Stop trying to matchmake, Molly." He smiled to take the sting out of his words. As much as Molly wanted Irelyn to return, her primary goal was taking care of Grey, which lately had included matchmaking attempts. "Besides, going stag every once in a while is good for business. Keeps everyone guessing."

She gave him a quick smile before she walked out. The instant the door clicked shut, all humor left his face.

Swinging his chair around, he stared out at the massive city with its spiraling high-rises and mammoth buildings. He and Irelyn had come to Dallas with myriad dreams. Through hard work, perseverance, and the belief that what they were doing was right, they had succeeded. Even though their relationship had often been fraught with disagreements, their shared goals and incredible passion for one another had seen them through tough times.

Had she really decided to end them, or was something bigger going on? Dammit, why hadn't he ignored his bruised feelings and hurt pride and dug deeper? What was Irelyn really up to?

Hill House
England

IRELYN PARKED IN THE AREA DESIGNATED FOR VISITORS, BUT waited a moment before she exited the car. She had thought she was prepared, but the moment she'd driven through the familiar gates, a wild panic had surged through her bloodstream. One last and fierce lecture was needed before she walked through those doors again.

She noted that the place hadn't changed much, but she wasn't surprised. The new proprietor would want to follow in his mentor's footsteps.

The mansion had been aptly christened Hill House by its previous owner, Hill Reed. A gargantuan structure of brick, rock, and wood, built in the early twentieth century, the place had had a sad history long before Reed set his sights upon it.

A railroad baron from Nevada, newly married and with more money than he knew what to do with, had wanted to please his young English wife, so he'd commissioned the building of a massive home for her. Sadly, and Irelyn had always thought it to be a portent of what the house would eventually be, the baron and his wife never spent a night here. The ship carrying them to England had encountered a storm and sank. They had both perished.

The house had sat empty for years. When it had finally gone on the auction block, Reed had purchased it and the surrounding ten acres and turned it into a house of horrors.

Her return seemed almost inevitable. This place and what it stood for had profoundly affected her life. Returning to the scene of the crime was a fitting bookend. This had been her alpha and omega, her beginning and end.

She was here for two specific reasons. Irelyn didn't need to remind herself that staying alive was an important aspect of achieving both. She was going to have to act her ass off to get the job done.

Memories had to be put aside. All the hurt, anger, pain, and yes, even the joy, had to be dead before she walked through those doors. She had an agenda; she had goals. Those were the only things she needed to focus on.

Her mind, body, and heart once again in accord, Irelyn got out of the car. All emotions squelched, she looked up at the large structure with cool dispassion. At one time, she had believed it to be the most grand and beautiful place in the world. Now, she could see the flaws, the crumbling decay. Hill House would have been perfect as a mausoleum, or perhaps as a horror-movie setting.

Though it was still known as Hill House, the new owner had made some subtle changes. A new coat of paint here and there, new shutters on the third-floor windows. Nothing major, but enough to show that the murder house was alive and back in business.

With three full stories of red and brown brick, the mansion covered almost an entire acre. There were areas in the back where outdoor training took place, along with a large gun range. The majority of training took place within the walls, inside rooms where secrets were kept and a dark entity of evil coated the very air.

Located between two small villages about a hundred miles outside of York, the area surrounding Hill House was desolate and barren. It was the perfect location for evil to live and thrive, to replicate and destroy.

How fitting was it that one of its own would see to its destruction?

She walked up onto the porch, and the front door opened like magic. The man standing before her was a surprise. She hadn't expected Sebastian Dark to greet her personally. Before she could decide if that was a good or a bad thing, he held out his hand in a friendly, professional gesture. "It's good to see you, Irelyn. It's been too long."

To hear those words from him, the exact ones that Grey had greeted her with last week, was a bit of a jar. This man and Grey Justice had zero in common.

"I had hoped to be back sooner."

"Father would be pleased to know you've come back to us. Please, come in."

She took an inner bracing breath and walked into the hellhole she'd once called home.

Sitting at his desk, Sebastian examined the woman across from him. She was stunning, even more beautiful than he remembered. He hadn't seen her in person in years. She had changed significantly, but even back then, the beauty she would become had been apparent. She had definitely lived up to her potential, at least in that area.

He could definitely understand Hill Reed's obsession and why he had been unable to let her go completely. His fascination had been so great that he had even tried to re-create her in another woman. Sadly, Hill had learned that a replica could not replace the original. Ivy Roane had never lived up to expectations. If she had not gotten herself killed a few months back, Sebastian would have cut her loose or had her eliminated. She had once been a competent killer, but had allowed personal feelings to get in the way of doing her job. She'd become unhinged. Allowing emotions to infiltrate a job was the downfall of any hired killer. And that was why Ivy Roane was dead.

Another example of wrong-headed sentimentality was the woman in front of him. Hill Reed had possessed little softness. He had killed with admirable efficiency, trained with coldhearted focus, and manipulated with razor-sharp accuracy. He had been a master, one in a million. But this one woman had touched something inside Reed, where no one else ever had. Even after she'd gone off on her own, Hill had followed her progress.

Sebastian understood, to some extent, the obsession. With unparalleled beauty, she called to mind fairy-tale princesses. Her black designer dress gave nothing away, but hinted at the sleek, soft loveliness beneath the material. With flawless skin that glowed, ink-black hair so silky-looking it seemed almost unnatural, and eyes the color of a clear gray mist, her allure was understated, stunning in its simplicity.

She seemed remarkably unimpressed with her own appeal. Irelyn Raine knew who she was and what she wanted from life. As much as Sebastian despised her, he could definitely see why Reed had been so fascinated.

He was a little surprised to find himself attracted to her. He had a low libido and often went months without sexual release. Sex was a weakness—a weapon that could be used against you. When he did have the urge, he paid for the experience. Though he'd gladly offer to pay this woman for the use of her lovely body, he knew he'd end up with a bullet in his gut if he made the suggestion.

Hill had died almost two years ago without naming a successor. Sebastian believed he was the natural heir, but not everyone had agreed. The competition had been fierce and brutal, but he had won. During that time of uncertainty, many members had left, and Hill House had suffered greatly. Restoring it to its former glory and strength would take time and skill. Like any good assassin, Sebastian was a patient, methodical man. He had plans in place to make that happen.

It was time to fill the vacancies. And Irelyn Raine had made it more than apparent that she wanted to be one of his new hires.

"You have intrigued me with your escapades the last few months."

"That was my intent."

"Why?"

She arched a lovely brow but remained silent. Her self-control and poise impressed him.

"I was a little surprised to receive an acceptance to my invitation," he said.

"I find that hard to believe as I sent you numerous enticements."

The first email he had received had been a bit of a shock. The subsequent ones had been both illuminating and entertaining. Irelyn Raine was a skilled and inventive assassin.

"I'm interested as to how you chose your prey and why. Care to enlighten me?"

"I would think that's obvious. Killing an unsuspecting, untrained person is boringly easy. Taking out skilled killers requires extreme talent. I wanted to impress you, and I did."

"Why? You have no need for money."

"Nor do you, and yet here you are."

"Touché." He leaned forward and spoke softly. "But, you see, I don't have to explain why I'm here. You, however, are interviewing for a position within my house. You are required to answer the question."

"Of course." She shrugged. "I enjoy the work."

"You enjoy taking people's lives?"

"Some people's, yes. But what I enjoy the most is the chase."

It was a typical answer, and he found himself a bit disappointed. He had expected something less mundane. The woman was difficult to read—one of the many things she had learned from Reed.

"You already have an interesting life. You've attached yourself to a man who can give you anything. What more could you want?"

Not by any flicker did she indicate she knew of whom he spoke.

"This is the life I am meant to have. It's what Father wanted for me."

Though it jarred a bit to hear her refer to Reed as her father, he reminded himself that they were both playing a game. Irelyn Raine was not only a skilled killer, she was a gifted player.

"Yet, if my memory serves me correctly, you weren't very good."

"I believe I've demonstrated how much I've improved. Besides, you know our father never was one for compliments."

So she would play that card as well. That was good. He had quite a few cards himself to play.

"You do have a particular set of skills I could use."

"Such as?"

"We'll get into that after you've proved your proficiency."

"I haven't done so already?"

"No."

"What skills do you want me to show? And how am I to do this if I don't know what you're looking for?"

"You'll know, don't worry about that. My biggest drawback is in the area that concerned Hill, too."

"I've improved."

He liked that she didn't deny that there had been problems. "In what way have you improved?"

"In every way that counts."

"Be specific," he snapped.

"Very well. I don't allow emotions to get the best of me. Back then, I was a bit, shall we say, volatile. Father worked hard to rid me of useless sentiment. It finally took."

"That's good to hear. And you are willing to prove yourself again?"

"Of course."

"I won't be easy on you...not like he was."

By not even the slightest facial twitch did she reveal that she took exception to his statement. Sebastian knew what she had endured. Hell, he'd gone through most of it, too. All the training and discipline had been meticulously documented. Reed had been a stickler for detail. Everything, including the final day of her time here, had been recorded.

He had found the recordings when he had taken over Hill House and had been surprised not only by their sheer volume, but also the fastidious manner with which Hill had them stored. There was no doubt they were treasured memories. Then he'd realized it made sense. Reliving those moments had been an indulgence. Their father had rarely taken any time for himself. Recording his training methods had most likely been one of his few entertainments.

"Why didn't you return whilst Father was still alive?"

"I was more useful to him where I was."

"Then why come back here? You could be beneficial to me as well where you were. Or you could be independent.

Sell your skills to the highest bidder, keep all the money for yourself."

"My ties with Justice have been severed. We were beginning to bore one another. And the answer to the question of why I want to come back here is simple. I like the community."

Interesting that she had admitted breaking away from Justice. His intel had told him so, but he hadn't been sure. He would want, at some point, to revisit the reason behind that, but first things first.

"Provided you pass the fitness and skill tests, I'll take you on a probationary basis."

"How long?"

"Until I'm satisfied."

"I can give you a month."

For several long seconds, he held her gaze. She never blinked, and her expression never changed. She was quite determined, but so was he.

He would give her this concession, but only because it suited him. "We'll meet again in a month. If, after that time, I'm satisfied, we'll negotiate terms."

"Very well." She stood and waited for further instruction.

"You're staying at the Savoy?"

"Yes."

"I'll send over details for your testing."

"I had thought to stay here."

"Not yet."

She gave a solemn nod and walked out the door. He was once again struck by her beauty. She could have been anything—actress, model, and possibly the wife of one of the wealthiest men in the world. Instead, for reasons he wasn't completely sure of yet, the sinfully beautiful and multitalented Irelyn Raine had just agreed to be his newest assassin.

He leaned back in his chair, propped his feet on his desk, and smiled. The game had only begun.

———

AWARE THAT EYES WERE ON HER EVERY MOVEMENT, IRELYN walked out of the house with cool, confident elegance. Anyone looking would see a self-assured woman. One who could charm you with a smile one moment and slice your throat the next.

She was on the first floor, and while every room she passed held memories, none of them was of the dark, bitter variety. The third floor was where her horror lay. The one where punishments were meted out and certain kinds of training took place. Evil permeated the entire house, but the third floor would take every bit of her courage to breach. She had no choice. That floor held the key to everything.

She concentrated on what she had accomplished. Sebastian Dark had taken the bait. She had been sure he would, but it was nice to have that part out of the way. Proving herself was worrying, as she didn't know what the tests would entail. She had hoped the photographs she had sent would have been enough. What she'd said was true. Killing an innocent, unaware person was an easy feat. Taking out an assassin required an enormous amount of both skill and fortitude. Why, then, did she have to prove herself even more?

She should have known he'd want to play this game out. He was the new leader and was enjoying his moment of power.

The skill testing didn't concern her. Not only did she have the same ones from years ago, but they were much sharper now. Plus, she had several other talents. One in particular she wouldn't reveal until the right time and place.

Would he test her with a target to take out, or simply give her tasks to complete? She hoped it was the latter. If not, she would have to improvise and delay.

She'd remembered Sebastian Dark, but he looked nothing like her memories. Back then, he'd been known simply as Pippin, a short, skinny boy with bad acne, protruding teeth, and a weak chin. Sebastian Dark today was a tall, well-built man with perfect teeth and a flawless complexion. Even the chin had improved, though she suspected cosmetic surgery for that.

In some circles, Dark would be considered quite handsome. To Irelyn, he was nothing more than a means to an end.

The giant estate now in her rearview mirror, she drove down the long, tree-lined drive with a mixture of both elation and dread. From here, the mansion looked like just a mass of stone and brick, mortar and paint. But to her, it was so much more. This was the place that held some of her happiest moments as well as most of her nightmares. The place where she'd first learned about love and had become acquainted with pure evil.

There, she had learned that love could be twisted and wrong, manipulated. That it could be used to build up or destroy. Years had passed before the agony of those lessons had dimmed. Though she had replaced that darkness with light, there would be more than physical danger in returning to Hill House. Immersing herself in that darkness again would likely destroy the peace she had fought for so hard. To accomplish her goal, she had little choice.

Grey would be furious once he found out. She hadn't dared tell him. If she had, there would have been no stopping him from interfering. This was her battle to fight, her war to wage. Not his. Besides, there was always the worry that he could get hurt. When it came to protecting those he cared about, Grey Justice had no limits.

Ending their relationship might have torn her heart out of her chest, but anything bad happening to Grey would be a billion times worse. She had caused him unfathomable pain already. She would not be responsible for more.

This was her task to handle. One that Grey could never know about. At least until it was too late to stop her.

CHAPTER FIVE

Dallas, Texas

The event was finally winding down. For the last two hours, his smile had felt as wooden as the uncomfortable chair where his ass had gone to sleep. Being seen was often a drawback to being a high-profile personality. Most times, he dealt with it as just part of the job. Another one of the many things he missed about Irelyn. When she was by his side, he could always count on her for a droll comment or an amusing observation.

Dinner and the drawn-out speeches were now over. He'd delivered his short speech at the beginning of the night, but since he wasn't the only one receiving an award, others had spoken, too. Many of those had had much more to say than he had.

While most everyone else shuffled into the main ballroom where the orchestra was already playing a medley of popular hits, Grey headed toward the opposite end. He had been as sociable as he could force himself tonight. He was thankful he hadn't taken up Molly's suggestion that he bring a date. Idle chitchat was difficult enough. The need to be charming and pleasant to a date would have gone well beyond his capabilities tonight. There was only one woman he wanted at his side. And though Irelyn had made it more than clear that she didn't want to be with him, that didn't stop him from wanting.

As if fate had decided to torture him for his thoughts, he heard a soft voice call out to him, "Grey! Wait."

His heart double-timing, he whirled around and then huffed out an exasperated grunt. When had he become so desperate to hear her voice that he could mistake Lacey Slater's soft Texas drawl for Irelyn's lilting Irish accent?

His smile genuine, he held out his hand to Lacey, who looked lovely in a chocolate-brown, lace-covered gown that highlighted the golden tone of her skin and made her dark eyes sparkle. "I didn't know you'd be here tonight." His eyes roamed the crowd, looking for a familiar face. "Are you alone?"

She scrunched her nose up in a grimace. "Yes and no. My date decided that groping was acceptable first-date behavior. I was more than happy to send him on his way with only a few bruises."

"He hurt you?"

She laughed softly. "You know me better than that, Grey. He's the one with the bruises."

Yes, he did know she could take care of herself, but he had a particular soft spot for the youngest Slater. Not only was she one of the Grey Justice Group's best handlers, she was as genuine and upfront as anyone he'd ever met. She was also loyal to a fault.

"You need a ride home?"

"You read my mind."

"I was on my way out. Did you want to stay longer?"

"Not in the least. These kinds of events are so boring."

Her eyes glinted with laughter. "Guess I shouldn't admit that since you were being honored tonight."

His hand on her shoulder to steer her toward the exit, he laughed. "I happen to agree with you."

Several groups of people stopped them along the way. Some offered congratulations, a couple tried to engage him in conversation, and one sought financial advice. He handled each encounter as quickly and smoothly as possible. Much to the dismay of several, he never stopped moving.

There were more than a few speculative glances at Lacey at his side. Tomorrow's tabloid blogs would be rife with innuendoes and suppositions about their relationship. He couldn't care less about his own reputation, but exposing Lacey to more publicity wasn't something he wanted.

"There's going to be all sorts of speculation if we leave together. Sure you don't want me to find you another ride?"

"Don't be silly. After all the Slaters have been through, being in Grey Justice's company can only help my reputation."

"I'm not sure Eli and Jonah would agree."

"Ha. My brothers trust you much more than they trust me."

"They worry about you."

"They need to stop. Accepting that I'm a grown woman is taking them longer than it should."

Grey shook his head. "I think you made that point clear when you were Gabriella's handler. They saw you in a different light."

"Yeah, well, that light has dimmed in the last few months."

He handed the valet his ticket and walked with her over to a secluded corner. "What's going on?"

She grimaced. "It's nothing for you to be concerned about, really. They just won't stay out of my business."

"You mean your love life."

Lacey snorted. "What love life?"

"Kingston?"

The brief flash of pain in her eyes confirmed his thoughts. Wyatt Kingston was one of the most valuable and skilled freelance operatives Grey had ever worked with, but when it came to bullheadedness, he was on a whole different plane altogether.

"Want me to kick his ass for you?"

"Thanks. If kicking his ass could solve the problem, I would have done it long ago. It's his heart I'm having trouble with."

Lacey was wrong about that. Wyatt Kingston's heart was already taken. He was just too damned stubborn to do anything about it.

"He'll come around."

She shot him a curious look. "Not every woman will wait forever, Grey."

"What's that supposed to mean?"

"Just what I said."

Before he could delve deeper into her comment, a large, bony hand grabbed hold of his forearm. "Justice, we need to talk."

Instead of answering, he stared pointedly at the hand. His silence spoke volumes.

The hand was swiftly removed, and the man took a step back as if he feared physical retaliation. That wouldn't happen.

"We've said all we need to say, Morrissey."

"I know what you did. I know it was you."

"You think I'm going to deny it? I'm not."

"I'm losing everything because of you."

"Because of me?" Grey arched a brow, his look so arrogant, Caesar himself would've been impressed. "I don't believe I'm the one who stole millions of dollars from my employees' pension fund. You'll pay for your crimes, Morrissey, as you should."

"You think you're so above it all, don't you, Justice? I'll have you know—" He went to grab Grey's arm again.

"Don't even think about it."

The man quickly dropped his arm and backed away again.

"I suggest you find a ride home and sober up, Morrissey."

The man sent a self-conscious glance around the room, as if suddenly realizing he was attracting the wrong kind of attention.

"Is there a problem here?" One of the many security people had heard their exchange. He had a trained military look about him that said he could handle anything that came his way.

"No, there's no problem." Grey looked over at the angry man in front of him. "Is there, Morrissey?"

"No, no problem," he answered quickly.

The man nodded but didn't budge. Morrissey swallowed hard, glared at Grey, and then took another step back.

"Mr. Justice, sorry it took so long, sir." The valet ran toward him. "Your car is ready now."

Giving a nod of thanks to the young man, along with a hefty tip, Grey ushered Lacey out the door. Morrissey's burning stare as Grey exited made no impression. The man had bilked millions of dollars from his employees and had been caught. Justice wasn't always slow.

In a matter of moments, he and Lacey were settled in his BMW and headed out of the parking lot.

"That was intense back there," Lacey said.

"He's a sad sack." Grey shrugged. There was not much more he could say about the man. "Still living in the apartment on Tracer Avenue?"

"Yes."

Instead of turning right out of the convention center, which would have taken him back to his apartment, he went left to head toward Lacey's place a few miles from the city. He made a mental note to keep an eye on Morrissey. That much anger inside a bitter man had a tendency to erupt in unexpected ways.

THE SHOOTER QUICKLY AND EFFICIENTLY SET UP THE TRIPOD and rifle at the new location. When the call had come that his target would be taking a different route home, he hadn't been that concerned. Even though his job required careful planning, he wouldn't be very good at it if he didn't allow for last-minute changes or variances. In his estimation, if a man was willing to pay a million dollars for a job, he had a right to make a few changes. This one had required that he hightail it across town. He had been assured the target would be delayed, giving him the extra setup time. It had worked out well.

Setting up at night on a busy overpass with vehicles zipping up and down the road wasn't optimal, but he'd had worse conditions. Being seen was the biggest concern, but he was good at hiding in plain sight. Besides, people were usually so busy with their cellphones and their own issues, he was invisible to most of them. For the one or two who might notice him, he would improvise. His teacher had trained him to lie, manipulate, and, if all else failed, kill without remorse. He had been an excellent student.

This particular subject had been targeted several times in the past. All attempts had failed. This was the first time he'd been given the opportunity, and he wasn't going to fail. Grey Justice had finally pissed off the wrong person, and that person knew the organization to call to get the job done. The fact that he didn't know the identity of the moneyman worried him not at all. Receiving the agreed-upon amount when the job was done was his only concern.

Setup complete, he used the rest of the time to adjust the sight. A moving target was more challenging than a still one. With his last assignment a month ago, he was at twenty-three kills, and more than half of them had been moving targets. He prided himself on achieving his goals even when obstacles appeared. Targeting a black vehicle at night in dim lighting could be difficult, but he had made arrangements, ensuring his success. He'd have no problems spotting the BMW.

The passenger in the vehicle was of no concern. If anything, she added a bit more excitement to the mix. Her family had been targeted before, and there would be speculation that she was the target and not her companion. The thought of people scratching their heads, trying to determine who had been the real target was amusing. Not that it really mattered. Either way, they'd both be dead in the next five minutes.

THEY'D TALKED ABOUT EVERYTHING FROM WHO SHOULD HAVE been in the NBA playoffs to the new hairstyle Lacey's mother, Eleanor, was now sporting. He hadn't asked what she'd meant by her comment earlier, and it bothered him that he hadn't. Had she been talking about Irelyn when she said that not every woman would wait forever? What did that even mean?

He was known for his confrontations and blunt talk, so why the hell didn't he find out if she'd been talking about Irelyn?

"Has Irelyn been in touch with you?"

"Why would Irelyn contact me?"

"That's not an answer."

"Is this an inquisition?"

"Of course not. I just—"

The car in front of him abruptly switched lanes. Grey braked and swerved to avoid clipping its bumper. Bam! Fire and smoke exploded from under the hood. Grey slammed on his brakes, but the car didn't slow. He tried to steer toward the side of the road. Nothing.

"What's going on?" Lacey asked.

"I think someone took a shot at us. Brakes and steering are gone. I'm going to try—"

The concrete wall of the overpass loomed before them. Thrusting his arm out to protect Lacey as much as possible, Grey shouted, "Hold on!"

A split second later, the car slid sideways and slammed into the wall.

KNOWING HE COULD BE SEEN BY CURIOUS PASSERSBY STOPPING to gawk at the wreckage, he swiftly and efficiently packed up his gear. He'd missed his target. That was a first for him, and he was irritated. The small opaque sticker he'd placed on the windshield was invisible to the human eye until it came into direct contact with light. Headlights from surrounding vehicles had done their job, and he had spotted the sticker without any trouble. The headshot would have been perfect if Justice's car had not swerved.

He consoled himself that Justice and the Slater girl were likely dead from the crash. The money had been earned. But he prided himself on getting the job done in the specified manner. Instead, the bullet had penetrated something beneath the vehicle. He liked preciseness and predictability when it came to his job. This one hadn't pleased him at all.

Disappointment would be too strong of an emotion, but he was as close as he'd ever been to feeling it. He neither enjoyed nor hated his work. It was who he was, what he was created for. Nevertheless, as he headed toward the car he'd parked a half mile away, he acknowledged that the satisfaction of a job well done would not be his tonight.

CHAPTER SIX

Milan, Italy

Irelyn let herself into her hotel room. Four cities in eight days. She had known the test would be grueling, but she had to give Dark credit for being both creative and relentless.

Obscure clues to solve intricate puzzles. Hiding in plain sight while dressed in various disguises—so far, the mime had been her favorite. She had tailed various targets. And she had been tailed herself. She hadn't heard specific praise from Dark as of yet, but she felt quite pleased with her progress. Assassins had to be detail-oriented, masters of disguise, and skilled investigators. The slightest clue could ferret out the most elusive mark. She'd had no problem completing any of her assignments.

Placing her handbag on the dresser, she took careful note of the room. It was a typical hotel room, like so many she'd been in over the years. She was tired of them. Her soul longed to go home. She couldn't. Leading them there would be a disaster.

She had bought the property and house in Ireland on a

whim. Since she was the least-whimsical person she knew, purchasing it had been a surprise and one she had never regretted. It was a land of gently rolling hills covered in purple heather. A small stone walking bridge separated the house from the road. The locals even had a name for it. They called it the Place Beyond the Mist. She soon learned why. Mist from the river a half mile away often settled over the land, sometimes for days. The first time that happened, she had felt like a fairy sprite, hidden away from the world and all its woes.

The little house was nothing special. A two-bedroom, one-bath cottage made of stone, brick, and mortar, but it did have history. Over a hundred years ago, a young man and his bride had lived there, raised a family there, farming, living, and loving. Several families had lived in it since then. Sometimes, when she sat on the porch and the mist settled around her, she imagined she could hear their laughter.

There had been love in that house, and the moment she'd walked through that door, she had known she was home.

In that way, the place reminded her of Grey and their first meeting. She had been fascinated from afar, but when she'd finally gotten up the courage to arrange a meeting, there had been an instant connection. She had felt at home, at peace. She had never told him that. Their meeting hadn't exactly been a storybook beginning. Besides, revealing something so deeply personal to a man who knew every weakness and vulnerability she possessed was not a good idea.

Grey had never been there, and she had never told him about it. The cottage was her one place of refuge and peace. When she'd purchased it, she had thought to bring him there someday. That was no longer a possibility, but her heart often dreamed of it anyway.

With a huff of disgust, Irelyn pushed aside the memories. She had long ago learned that living in the past solved noth-

ing. The here and now was all that she had. And if she was to
do all that she had set out for herself, focusing on her regrets
would get her dead much sooner than she planned.

She'd had a long day, and tomorrow would not be any
shorter. With that thought, she went about setting the safety
measures that had kept her alive for this long. First, she thoroughly searched the hotel room. The number of people who
wanted to be the one to take her down had increased
dramatically in the last few months. As if she were some kind
of trophy animal. That would likely happen one day, but not
until she finished what she had started.

After checking for cameras, bugs, and explosives, she set
up her safeguards. Grey had been the one to teach her these
things. Before Grey, she had learned only how to pursue and
capture her prey. Grey had trained her how to stay alive.

Traps and countermeasures in place, she allowed her
muscles to ease a little. The last few days might have been
tiresome, but soon that would be over. Once she was fully
accepted by Dark, she would begin the real work.

She clicked on the television with the remote and scrolled
through the channel guide without interest. Noise to fill the
silence. Settling on a twenty-four-hour news station, she
slipped her shoes off and did a series of yoga stretches to
loosen her muscles even more. Her stomach growled,
reminding her that her breakfast of banana, grapes, and
energy bar was long gone. She had stopped at the market
before checking in and had exactly what she needed to make
a healthy and delicious meal. Problem was, she had no desire
to do so.

Sighing, she plopped down onto the edge of the bed and
faced the naked truth. She missed Grey. Oh, how she missed
him. From the little quirk his mouth would give when he
found something mildly amusing, to the slight growling
sound he'd sometimes make right before he kissed her. She

even missed his bad habit of leaving his damp towel in the middle of the floor after he showered.

Ending their relationship had been one of the hardest things she had ever done. It hadn't been a mistake, though. She had made enough of them to know the difference. Mistakes were the things that filled you with massive guilt, darkening your mind until no light existed. She lived with those mistakes daily, and that darkness always hovered above her.

No, saying goodbye to Grey hadn't been a mistake. Loving him wasn't a mistake either. She just wished both of them didn't hurt so very much.

Shaking off the sadness, Irelyn removed her clothes and stepped into the shower. The hot, steamy water should loosen her tired muscles and enable her to sleep. She never slept deeply while on a job, but she needed as much rest as she could allow herself.

She turned off her thoughts and enjoyed the luxury of the cleansing liquid. There were many things she would never take for granted and a hot shower was one of them. In their early years, when it seemed like the whole world was against both of them, cleanliness, like a good meal, had been a luxury.

She was stepping out of the shower stall when a breaking-news alert on the television caught her attention. Did she hear Grey's name mentioned, or was she missing him so much her mind had conjured his name?

Irelyn dashed into the bedroom. Standing in front of the television, still dripping from her shower, she stared at the screen. The over-polished, toothy reporter was giving information on an upcoming news story, but there was nothing about Grey. Had she just imagined it after all?

She clicked on another news channel and then another. Nothing. She was being silly. So what if they had mentioned

Grey's name? He was in the news all the time. Multibillion-dollar mergers and acquisitions were often big news items, and Grey was involved in many. It was probably nothing more than that. Still, she searched, returning to the same channel where she'd first thought she'd heard his name. Her breath caught when a photograph of Grey appeared on the screen.

"Repeating our earlier story: Billionaire philanthropist Grey Justice and an unknown companion were involved in a one-car accident this evening in Dallas, Texas. As yet, there is no news on their condition. The cause of the accident is under investigation. This is a developing story, and we'll keep you informed as we learn more."

She told herself it was a minor fender bender and nothing more. Just because the story had made international news wasn't that unusual. Everything was reported on these days, even the small things. She told herself she would know if something major had happened to him. She would know. Her gut, her heart, her soul would know.

Grabbing a burner phone from her stash, she punched in Grey's number.

"Justice," a voice growled.

Her breath caught in her throat, and it was several seconds before she could speak.

"Irelyn?"

She had called from a burner phone with an unknown number, but still he would know. That was just Grey.

She finally managed to speak. "You're okay?"

"Yes."

"What happened?"

"Rifle shot. Caused complete failure of steering and brakes. We hit a concrete wall."

"We?"

"Lacey Slater was with me."

"Is she okay?"

"No."

With that one word, she heard the fury.

"She's not—"

"She's alive. She's in surgery."

"I'm sorry, Grey. I know her family must be devastated."

"The prognosis is good, but recovery will take a while."

"And you weren't injured?"

"A bump on the head, a wrenched shoulder. Getting the bastard behind this will help."

This wasn't the first time someone had tried to kill him, but it was the first time she wasn't there with him to investigate. And to reassure herself that he was truly fine.

"Any idea who and why?"

"Not yet. You have any?"

"No." She frowned. Was he inferring she might have had something to do with the hit? "Grey, I didn't—"

"Hell, I know that, Irelyn. But you are associating yourself with that kind again."

She couldn't argue with the truth. "I can make some inquiries."

"No. Stay out of it. I have my people on it."

Yes, he would, and Grey Justice had a multitude of people who could and would uncover the culprit. He didn't need her.

"Very well. I'm glad you're okay. Please give Lacey my best. Goodbye."

"Wait! Irelyn!"

She disconnected the call on his curse and immediately dismantled the phone. She'd drop the parts in different dumpsters across the city tomorrow. But now she had a new worry. Someone was out to get Grey. Someone new? Or was this an old enemy? She should have heard the news. For obvious reasons, the assassin community was secretive to outsiders, but inside, there were rumors, speculation, and leaks. Her ears were always tuned to anything involving Grey. Why hadn't she known about this latest contract? More important, who was paying for it?

Dallas Memorial Hospital

CURSING HIMSELF FOR HIS BLUNTNESS AND SHORTSIGHTEDNESS, Grey hit redial. There was no answer and no voice-mail option. Irelyn had called him from a burner phone and had likely disabled it the moment she ended the call.

He was an ass and not proud of it. Irelyn rarely reached out to him anymore. Instead of declining her offer, he should have asked for her help. Not only was she a skilled investigator, he might have persuaded her to return to Dallas. But instead, he went into overprotective mode and rebuffed her offer.

No, he didn't want her involved, but he damn well wanted to know where she was and what she was doing. When had it gotten so messed up that he couldn't even talk with her without walking on eggshells? They had been together for so long, their communication had once been seamless. A subtle glance, a light touch, a lift of a brow was all that they had needed to convey their thoughts to one another. And when he'd been blunt, which was all too often, she'd given it right back to him. When had it gotten so complicated?

Hell, what was he thinking? *Irelyn* and *complicated* were synonymous.

He shook his head and regretted the movement. He was a little more banged up than he'd revealed to Irelyn. Slight concussion, badly bruised nose, and a cut on his forearm that had led to the need for a couple of pints of blood. That was nothing compared to Lacey's injuries.

He hadn't been unconscious long. Maybe a minute or two. People had been shouting at him when he woke—drivers who'd stopped to help. His brain had been addled a bit, but he'd had enough wits about him to turn to check on Lacey. Seeing the vibrant young woman unconscious and ghost pale had scared the hell out of him. When he'd touched her face, her skin had felt ice cold, and he'd been convinced she was dead. Thankfully, he'd been wrong, but she was gravely injured.

Things had gotten blurry after that. Paramedics had arrived. He and Lacey had been brought to the hospital, and while he could proclaim that he was the wealthy and powerful Grey Justice, medical professionals trying to save lives could care squat about his identity. As long as they saved Lacey's life, that was fine by him.

Grey's first call had been to Eli and hadn't been an easy one to make. No matter what anyone told him, he knew Lacey was fighting for her life for one reason only. She had accepted a ride home from a man whom too many people wanted to kill.

The entire Slater clan had descended on the hospital. While Eli and Jonah had cornered the doctor, their wives, Kathleen and Gabriella, had consoled Eleanor Slater. And Grey had been on the phone with his investigators. Whoever was behind this would pay.

THE LOCAL NEWS WAS FILLED WITH THE NEWS OF JUSTICE'S *accident*. The target was still alive.

A stinging punch of anger in his gut was his only emotion. Since anger would get him nowhere, he acknowledged his failure and moved on. Emotions were pointless. Cold, hard logic was his key to a successful termination. Emotions created chaos.

He entered a number into his burner phone. "I missed."

"That's unfortunate," a crisp British voice said.

"I'll get it done."

"I have no doubt."

"What's my time frame?"

"Three failed attempts will cancel the contract."

"I won't fail again." He ended the call on that bold statement. There was nothing else to discuss. He would get the job done the second time around.

Justice had proved to be an elusive target. More than one assassin had tried and failed to bring him down. Contracts had been dissolved, and lives had been destroyed. He didn't plan on being one of the casualties.

Having studied his subject, he felt he knew the billionaire as well as anyone did. But he'd had more than one reason to research the enigmatic philanthropist. Justice's longtime companion, Irelyn Raine, was even more intriguing. She wasn't the target, and by all accounts, the relationship between her and Justice had ended. Still, she fascinated him. He knew her, yet he didn't. He found himself wanting to know more. That was an oddity he refused to examine. He had little use for people and placed them in two categories: those who paid him to kill and those he killed.

He packed his small duffel bag and walked out of the hotel room. Even though he wasn't leaving Dallas as planned, he wouldn't stay here another night. Staying in one place too long invited curiosity and familiarity. Being forgotten or ignored was a plus in this business. His size and looks prevented him from blending into the background as well as some others. To compensate, he was extra wary, slipping in and out of his room at late hours. He always wore black or brown clothing and often changed his facial features with putty or enhancements. If more than one person was asked to describe him, no one would ever agree. He was that good.

As he made his way down the sidewalk, he glanced around at the people he passed. Did they realize death lived among them? Or did they go about their lives, unaware that the man next to them could, without remorse, end their lives? He wondered what that kind of naïveté felt like. From the moment of his birth, he had known only want and hunger and had been willing to do anything to get what he wanted. The day he'd been rescued was the day his life changed for the better, but he still felt the hunger and the want, just in a different way. He had wanted to devour. He had learned control and discipline, two things he hadn't had before. And he had been taught to destroy. The lessons had been harsh, but they had toughened him and made him into the ultimate killing machine.

He owed everything to the man who'd saved him, the man he had called Father. If he ever found the person responsible for killing Hill Reed, he'd take him apart, bit by bit, until not even the rats would want him.

CHAPTER SEVEN

Dallas, Texas
Offices of the Grey Justice Group

Grey stood at the front of the large conference room. The women and men who sat at the table were the heart and soul of the organization. He had a working knowledge of all the cases the team handled, but they were the ones who did the actual labor. Without them, justice, for many, would never be obtained.

Each person could choose his or her own case or have one assigned. One or two team members worked the case until justice had been served. On occasion, more people were involved, and yes, on occasion, laws were skirted or bypassed. Rarely did a case require significant laws to be broken. He might not be a stickler for following rules, but he damn well would not allow his people to put themselves or their families in jeopardy. He would take the fall before any of his people did. His neck was the only one he was willing to risk.

They were from all walks of life. College professors

worked right along with stay-at-home moms and dads, and fast-food employees worked beside CEOs of multimillion-dollar companies. Most didn't work for the group full time but worked when they could. They had myriad differences and experiences, but the one thing they all had in common was a fierce belief in fairness. Each one had experienced or seen injustice. Grey had recruited them, carefully vetted them. He would trust them with his life, but more important, he trusted them to accomplish what often seemed impossible.

His time was divided between his companies and his victims advocacy group, but he had multiple people who managed these interests. The Grey Justice Group was his passion. He had come from a long line of justice seekers. At one time, he had thought to ignore his heritage. Pursuing justice often led to heartbreak and even death. It certainly had in his parents' case. It hadn't taken long for him to change his mind. How could he live with himself if he allowed lives to be ruined or criminals to flourish? He couldn't—not when he could do something to stop it.

He had no superpowers, but he was a good judge of character. That, along with a keen sense of right and wrong, had guided him to his inevitable destiny. His parents would be in equal parts sad and proud that he had followed in their footsteps. They hadn't necessarily wanted this for him, but had trained him in case he chose this life.

He had made his choices and had few regrets. However, there were drawbacks.

"Thank you all for coming today. I know many of you have other obligations, so I won't delay any longer. As you know, last night an attempt was made on my life. Many of you know Lacey Slater. She was in the car with me and is in serious condition. The doctors expect a full recovery, but she has a long road ahead of her."

That Lacey had been injured because of him was something he deeply regretted. He should have found her another ride. No, he hadn't anticipated an assassination attempt, but in his line of work, it was inevitable. He wouldn't make the same mistake twice.

"Since the shooter's mission was not accomplished, I anticipate more attempts. When I started this group, I promised myself to put no one, other than myself, at risk. I haven't always been able to keep that promise. Several of you have faced danger and probably will again. But this situation is entirely different. Someone is personally targeting me, and I don't want anyone to get caught in the cross hairs. This is my battle to fight.

"Outside of this room, this group is known to only a few. I trust them, as I trust you. However, that doesn't mean someone can't or won't find a way inside. My primary concern is making sure all my employees stay safe. I'd like for all of you to give this some careful consideration. If you feel the need to back off for a while, I completely understand. I—"

"Excuse me, Grey. But I feel I need to say something before you finish."

Unsurprised by the interruption, but more than a little shocked at who'd spoken, Grey shifted his gaze to Mrs. Eugenia Wilcox. The elderly woman had been working with the Grey Justice Group for a little over a year. She was eighty-six years old, and although she was quite opinionated, she wasn't one to speak her concerns aloud in a large audience.

More than a little curious to hear what she had to say, he gave her a nod of encouragement. "Please do."

"I think we can all agree that we don't do this job because it's safe. We do it because it's the right thing to do. Some lowlife sleazebag is not going to stop me."

There were several "hear, hears," and then the entire room burst into applause.

Grey nodded his appreciation. "Thank you. I appreciate all of you and your work. Again, I don't believe anyone who works for any Grey Justice entity will be targeted, but take extra care just in case." He glanced over at Gallagher, standing a few feet away. "Nick is going to give you some safety tips and answer any of your questions. If you have any concerns, please don't hesitate to ask."

Grey walked out of the room, confident that Nick would give sound advice and alleviate concerns. The thought of another person being hurt because of him was a sickening prospect.

He went into his office and strode over to the far wall. He pressed a small panel, which opened to reveal an entry scanner. Placing his thumb on the pad, he heard a small click, followed by the door opening. Only his and Irelyn's thumbprints were coded into the system.

Once inside, he opened the laptop at his desk. He had five investigators digging into the assassination attempt, but that wouldn't stop him from doing his own research, too. Someone he knew, possibly did business with, wanted him dead.

Setting up for a kill took time. A skilled assassin could set up and tear down a shoot within a minute or two. However, the target had to be located first. He had gone in the opposite direction of his normal route to take Lacey to her apartment. Someone at the event had seen him with her and deduced that he was taking her home first. Additionally, this person or persons also knew where Lacey lived.

Grey wasn't naïve. Many people hated him. One didn't achieve money, influence, and power without making multiple enemies. And being someone who didn't put up with a lot of bullshit had landed him on several "least favorite" lists. How many of those people would spend the money to hire a professional hit man? Not that many, which made identifying the bastard a little easier.

In the past, he'd been targeted, but most times it had been by lowlifes who'd hired local thugs. This had been a professional. Just because the bastard had missed didn't mean he wasn't good at his job. Grey knew exactly what happened. He had swerved at the last moment. If not, he and possibly Lacy, too, would be lying in a morgue.

The assassin would search for another way to get to him, possibly using those he cared about to lure him.

Having acquaintances and contacts on both sides of the law had its rewards. One being that, in many things, he was in the know almost from the moment a decision was made. Few knew how high or how low his contacts stretched. Each had their advantages, but trust in them went only so far.

Over the years, he had found more people he could rely on. Some of them he could even call friends. But there was only one person he had total faith and trust in. He no longer questioned the oddity of that uncompromising faith. Irelyn Raine was many things, and loyalty was at the top of the list. Considering how they'd begun their relationship, she should be the last person he trusted. But Irelyn had proven herself a thousand times over. He no longer doubted her.

Irelyn.

Grey expelled a disgusted sigh. He'd messed up again. Instead of having a conversation with her, possibly getting her agreement to come home, he'd handled it wrong. His only thought was to protect her. Irelyn didn't do anything halfway. If she got involved, she wouldn't stop until the culprit was identified. And then, she would go further. It was the further part that bothered him. He'd do anything to protect her, including alienating her. But he'd hurt her again, and that hadn't been his intent.

Yes, he could call a half-dozen people who would tell him where she had been or where she was headed. A couple could even pinpoint her location right now. If it came to that, he would do it. Yeah, it'd piss her off, but when it came to her life, he didn't give two shits about pissing her off. A pissed-off Irelyn was a damn sight better than a dead one.

For now, he had an enemy to identify.

Sitting at his desk, he reviewed the names of the people who had attended the awards party last night. Grey judged that it was a good twenty minutes from the time he'd offered Lacey a ride home to when they'd left. Plenty of time for someone to notify the shooter so he could get to another location.

Just over five hundred people attended the event, not counting the wait staff. Most of them could be eliminated from the suspect list in a matter of moments, but that still left a lot of people to research. At the top of that list was Joe Morrissey. He'd been the one to deliberately seek Grey out. Had he done so with the intent to delay him? That was something he intended to find out.

Though Morrissey was at the top, he was just one of many who would need to be checked out. With a resigned shrug, he divided the names up and sent the lists to his investigators.

His personal cellphone chimed, and his heart went into overdrive when he saw the caller was Kathleen Slater, Eli's wife. Clicking on the answer icon, he said, "What's happened?"

"Lacey's awake."

Grey allowed himself a giant, relieved sigh. He had stayed all night at the hospital with the Slaters. The doctors had advised them that the surgery to repair her internal bleeding had been successful, but the next few hours would be critical. Lacey finally waking up was a huge step.

"Is she able to talk?"

"Not yet. She's still intubated and pretty groggy. They'll take the tube out soon, but said she'd be in and out of consciousness for the next twenty-four hours."

"How's the family holding up?"

"We finally convinced Eleanor to go home and rest. Jonah and Gabby are with her. Eli and I are heading home. We'll spend some time with the kids and then head back to the hospital."

"I'll come by this evening."

"Wyatt Kingston is here."

Her careful tone told him more than the words. Grey had called the man himself and told him about the accident. Even though Kingston had been in Frankfurt, Germany, Grey wasn't surprised that he'd flown home immediately. The on-again-off-again relationship between Lacey and Kingston was no longer a secret to her family. Not that it would have mattered. He knew Wyatt well enough to know that nothing would stop him if he thought Lacey needed him, including the disapproval of her overprotective brothers.

"Everyone getting along?"

"So far, so good. I think he's going to want to be in on the investigation."

"I'm sure he will. Thanks for the update. I'll see you soon."

Grey ended the call and leaned back in his chair. He was tired, but figured he had a few more hours left in him. He clicked on the list of names again, making notes as he went through them. Which one of them hated him enough to pay big bucks to take him out? There were plenty on the list who likely hated him, but who had taken it to the next level?

The intercom on his desk buzzed. He pressed a button. "Yes?"

"It's Nick. We need to talk."

"Be right out." He sprang out of his chair and headed to

the door. The instant he saw who was waiting with Nick, he knew he wasn't going to like the news. Charlotte "Charlie" Nolan was his top tech analyst. If she had something to tell him, he knew it was big.

"What's wrong?"

"Have you talked to Irelyn lately?" Gallagher asked.

"Yes. A few hours ago. Why?"

"She give you any indication what she's been up to?"

"Spit it out. What's going on?"

Gallagher shot a glance at Charlie. She nodded and said, "You asked me to keep an eye on Hill House. Let you know of any new activity."

"Yes."

"They've added a new assassin. Our sources say she's been working for them for a few weeks now."

An ominous dread filled him, and he knew the answer before he asked, "She?"

"Irelyn Raine is Hill House's newest assassin."

No one spoke for several seconds and Grey appreciated the silence. However, dropping a bombshell of this magnitude on him would require more than a few seconds of thought. That would have to come later. For now, he needed details.

"Tell me what you know."

"The new proprietor of Hill House is Sebastian Dark. Not much is known about him before he began his training at Hill House. We do know that he was a teenager when he arrived and has been a contract killer for a dozen or more years," Gallagher said.

"Hill Reed, the previous proprietor, died without naming his successor. Guess the asshole thought he'd live forever."

Grey had often wondered about Reed's shortsightedness of never designating his future replacement. Admittedly, the bastard hadn't planned on dying that soon—he'd only been in his early sixties. He definitely hadn't planned on being outsmarted and betrayed by one of the few people he still trusted. But having lived, eaten, and breathed death for so long, he should have been aware of his own mortality.

"After Reed's death, his assassins scattered like cockroaches," Gallagher went on. "The only ones left vied to take over Hill House. After several months and more than a few dead bodies floating in the Thames, Dark came out the victor."

Much of what Gallagher had learned, Grey already knew. Hill Reed's successor hadn't yet attained the status his predecessor had achieved. And likely never would.

It was a testament to Nick Gallagher's restraint that he could speak of Hill Reed in such a dispassionate tone. Mathias and Adam Slater had hired Reed to kill Thomas O'Connell, Gallagher's best friend and Kennedy's late husband.

Gallagher continued in the same even tone, "Rumor has it that Dark isn't the leader that his predecessor was. Doesn't inspire the following or have the training skills that Reed apparently possessed."

That was no surprise either. Not only had Hill Reed been a ruthless killer, he had been a skilled manipulator, a real-life Svengali who was a master at reading people and exploiting any detected vulnerability to gain what he wanted.

Grey had never doubted the existence of God, nor did he doubt the existence of the devil. He had seen evidence of both. Unfortunately, in his line of work, he saw evil much more often than good. In his expert opinion, Hill Reed had been, at the very least, one of Satan's most evil minions. He could not regret for one moment that the bastard was in hell where he belonged.

"How many assassins does Dark have in his employ?" Grey asked.

"Hard to say," Charlie answered. "Rumor has it that it's as many as twenty. Some say they've heard upwards of fifty, and one or two sources have said no more than five."

And now he had one more.

"Where do we go from here?" Gallagher asked.

"We wait. Watch it play out."

"Why would Irelyn associate herself with—"

Gallagher stopped when Grey held up his hand. Giving his tech analyst an apologetic smile, he said, "Charlie, while I trust you completely, I need to talk to Nick alone."

Giving both men a concerned glance, she stood. "No problem. Let me know what else you want me—"

"Just keep digging. The more we know, the better off we are."

"Will do."

Grey waited until the door closed and turned to Gallagher. "There are things you don't know. Things I don't have the right to tell you. And, admittedly, things I don't want you to know. But there's one thing I do know and want you to understand. I know Irelyn Raine, inside and out. I trust her with my life. I don't know why she's doing this, but I do know she's got a plan."

"A plan for what?"

He had no clue. Her insistence that they end their relationship had taken on a whole new meaning. Why hadn't he pressed her for more details? The excuse that she had hurt him was beyond ludicrous. His emotions were secondary to making sure Irelyn stayed safe. And now, for reasons known only to Irelyn herself, she was back in the devil's den.

Hell, Irelyn, what are you thinking, baby?

CHAPTER EIGHT

Minneapolis, Minnesota

I relyn paced the small confines of the hotel room. This was getting old and more than a little ridiculous. She had made her last handoff with the smoothness of a trained professional, but an amateur could have done the same thing with just as much success.

When Dark had told her she would be required to prove herself again, she'd expected anything from infiltrating corporations, to gaining top-secret information, to executing an actual termination contract. While she was pleased she hadn't been asked to kill anyone, the banal assignments were wearing on her.

At first, the tasks had been entertaining and interesting. The clues uncovered had seemed like mysteries to solve, and evading her tails had been challenging. Those jobs were a thing of the past. Her latest assignments had been as boring as watching grass grow.

She knew better than to complain. Dark was testing her patience, playing a power game. He could just as easily say she wasn't needed, and then all her work would amount to nothing. She had to get inside that house. To do that, she had to jump through every hoop, no matter how boring.

The traveling was getting old, too. Of course, one of the biggest reasons was because many of the destinations were places she and Grey had explored together. Few people knew that Grey Justice had a playful side, and when they went away together, he always found something delightfully entertaining to do. If there was a carnival in town, a play she wanted to see, or a street fair he thought she might like, they had always gone. No one knew her the way Grey did. And no one could ever take Grey's place.

That was another, even bigger reason she needed to get inside Hill House. The identity of the man or woman who had put out a contract on Grey could be within those walls.

Hill Reed had been a stickler for paper-only records. Every ounce of intel would be in the third-floor records room. Not only would that include every contract Hill House had ever accepted, but the room also contained something even more extraordinary. Few people knew that Hill kept records on contracts not associated with Hill House. His web of intel went far and wide. He'd been in the killing game for years and had known the who and the why of all the major players. Almost nothing went on inside the assassin community that Reed hadn't known about or kept a record of.

Sebastian Dark had worshipped Hill Reed, obsessively so. Changing a procedure that had been so much a part of Reed's core belief went against her profile of Dark. He would want to retain as much of his mentor's legacy as possible, and that included his most notable quirks. Whether Hill House or another assassin had taken the contract, the information on who wanted Grey dead could be in that room.

Problem was, the records room was behind secure,

locked doors. It would take stealth and cunning to get in there. But first, she had to actually get inside the house.

The phone in front of her chimed with a new text message. Irelyn tensed. This was the usual delivery method for her assignments. She had completed her last one two days ago and had been hanging around Minneapolis, waiting for further instructions. Where was he sending her now? She clicked on the message and had to blink twice to make sure she'd read the words correctly. But they couldn't be any clearer.

You've passed the tests. Time to come back home. See you Monday morning.

That was it? Was the probation period over, or would she be required to continue to prove herself? Either way, would she be allowed to stay at the house? Since that was her ultimate goal, she needed to do whatever was necessary to ensure that would happen. No matter what was asked of her, she had a plan and she needed to proceed.

Her luggage was already packed and ready to go. She could book a flight and be in Paris by tomorrow evening. There, she could regroup and recharge, ready herself for her meeting at Hill House on Monday.

Still, she hesitated. Even though she couldn't risk seeing Grey, there was someone else she needed to see. Someone she had hurt without ever intending to do so.

Question was, would she slam the door in her face, as Irelyn deserved? There was only one way to find out. She'd have to fly under an alias and wear a disguise, but that was nothing new.

Refusing to contemplate further, she took a burner phone from her collection. Accessing an airline Irelyn Raine had never used, she booked the next flight to Dallas.

CHAPTER NINE

Dallas, Texas

Kennedy Gallagher kissed her baby daughter's tiny foot and nibbled on her toe, delighting in the wonderful sound of baby giggles. Bath time was a treasured morning ritual.

Nick had left a few minutes ago, headed out of town for a few days on special assignment. Even though she missed him already, she had finally overcome, for the most part, the terror of watching him walk out the door. Losing Thomas, her first husband, so unexpectedly had left a huge amount of insecurity when it came to her loved ones. Each time she said goodbye, she was reminded that it could be the last time she saw them. Maudlin, yes, but overcoming the need to grab on for dear life had been a real struggle.

Thankfully, Nick, with his amazing ability to read her, understood. He called frequently throughout the day. He always seemingly had a reason, but she knew him well, too. One of the million reasons she adored Nick Gallagher was his incredible compassion.

Noticing that Isabella's eyes were fluttering sleepily, Kennedy picked her up and settled her in her crib. If she timed it right, she could do a load of laundry, put away the breakfast dishes, and get in an hour of research, too. Her job with the Grey Justice Group gave her the flexibility to complete her work in her time frame. Nap time for Isabella meant work time for her.

Just as she headed downstairs, the doorbell rang. Though her mind was on the various things she wanted to get accomplished, she never opened the door without looking first. She had been through too much, lost too much, to ever take anything for granted. Danger often lurked in the most unexpected places.

Her breath caught on a gasp as she peered through the peephole. There was no danger here, but shock momentarily froze her. The woman on her doorstep had long, honey-gold hair, wore dark-rimmed glasses, and had a sharp nose to go with her pointed chin. She would have been unrecognizable to almost anyone, but Kennedy had spent too much time staring into the mesmerizing gray eyes of Irelyn Raine not to recognize her.

Having her show up incognito was much less surprising than having her show up at all. She hadn't seen Irelyn in almost two years. Kennedy had once believed they shared a friendship, but after all this time, she had accepted that the other woman hadn't felt the same way.

She wasn't the best at hiding her feelings, so when she opened the door, she wasn't surprised to hear Irelyn say, "You have every right to be angry."

Shaking her head, Kennedy pushed open the screen door and stepped back, allowing Irelyn to step inside. "I'm not angry, I'm just—" She shook her head again. No, she wouldn't lie. "All right, I am angry, but mostly I'm hurt and confused. Where have you been, and why didn't you at least call and let me know you're okay?"

"I'm sorry." She gave a small smile. "I'm not used to people caring where I am."

"Even Grey?"

"Except for a few weeks here and there, Grey has always known my location."

"Have you seen him lately?"

"A few weeks ago." She glanced over Kennedy's shoulder. "Mind if we sit down?"

"Of course. Come in and have a seat. Would you like something to drink or eat?"

"Water would be good."

She led Irelyn into the living room and said, "Be right back."

"Kennedy?"

She glanced over her shoulder. "Yes?"

"Don't call Grey. Okay?"

"I won't, but don't expect me not to tell him when I see him. I don't keep secrets from my boss or my friends."

"I understand. It's one of the many reasons I've missed you."

Giving her a solemn look, Kennedy walked away.

IRELYN SETTLED INTO A CHAIR WITH A GIANT SIGH. ONCE SHE had decided to come here, she hadn't been able to get Kennedy out of her mind. Kennedy was the first and only real female friend Irelyn had ever had. She didn't waste time on regrets about that, but she did feel regret that she hadn't been there for her friend when she had needed her most. Kennedy had almost died at the hands of Adam Slater. Irelyn had been out of the country by then, coming to terms with what she had done—what she needed to do. She hadn't been a good friend to her only friend. Unfortunately, that wasn't going to change.

She gazed around at the organized chaos of the room. This was what a home was supposed to look like, from the comfortable-looking sofa that invited afternoon naps, to the basket full of stuffed animals and baby toys in the corner. Kennedy and Nick had made a home for themselves and for their daughter, filled with love, laughter, and all the things that went with having a family.

She had once ached for this beyond anything. She no longer thought about it. Wishing for something that would never happen was both pointless and a waste of energy.

"Here you go," Kennedy said as she returned to the living room. She handed a glass of ice water to Irelyn and then sat on the sofa across from her.

Irelyn took a sip of her water, surprised to realize she was nervous. Kennedy was so authentic and real…such a good person. Irelyn had rarely met anyone so genuinely fine. It was easier to deal with the fake and the feral—the ones who were only looking out for themselves. That was what she had been raised with and knew how to handle.

"Talk to me, Irelyn. Tell me where you've been, what you've been doing for almost two years."

Describing her life to Kennedy was not only impossible, it could be dangerous for her and Nick to know anything. No way was she going to put this family at risk.

"A bit of traveling."

"Traveling where?"

"Europe, mostly."

She watched as the other woman rose and came to sit on the arm of her chair. She should have known that Kennedy wasn't going to accept a trite, uninformative answer.

"Talk to me," Kennedy said. "You know you can trust me. I care about you…and I care about Grey. The attempt on his life has got everyone jittery. Lacey will be getting out of the hospital soon, but it'll be at least a month before she's able to go back to work. We're all on edge."

"But Grey is taking extra care, right? He's taking the threat seriously?"

"Of course he's taking it seriously. Someone tried to kill him."

She didn't tell Kennedy that attempts on Grey's life weren't all that uncommon. Grey was more than capable of protecting himself and usually handled the situation without police intervention. This time, because of Lacey's injury, that hadn't been possible. The assassination attempt had made international news, and the authorities, no doubt, were investigating heavily. That didn't mean, however, that Grey wasn't working on his own. His intel would reach farther and wider than anyone else's.

"I'm glad Lacey is on the road to recovery. I hope she'll come back to work for the Grey Justice Group. She's one of the best handlers we've…Grey has ever had."

Kennedy didn't mention the slip, but Irelyn cursed herself anyway. She was exhausted, and it was showing. She needed to do what she'd come here to do and get out. Her flight for England left in a couple of hours.

"Grey's not been the same without you."

Those words stopped her in her tracks, and another slash was added to a heart that had become much too vulnerable lately. In just a few moments of being in Kennedy's presence, she was a mass of emotions once again.

No, this couldn't happen. She stood. "I need to get going."

"But you just got here."

"I know…I just wanted to see you. I was in the States and…"

"And?" Kennedy said.

"Just wanted to say hi," she finished lamely.

"That's it?"

"That, and I also wanted to ask you to talk to Grey, convince him to take all precautions. Tell him not to trust anyone but his closest advisers. There could be moles or spies in the organization. Tell him—"

"Why don't you tell him yourself?"

Ignoring the question, she continued, "And tell Nick, too. He'll rein Grey in if he thinks he's putting himself too much at risk."

"We will all look out for Grey, Irelyn. But who's looking out for you?"

"I can look after myself. Just be on guard. Okay?" She took a step toward the front door.

"Wait. You can't leave without meeting Isabella."

It took extreme effort for Irelyn to say, "Maybe next time. I have a flight to catch."

"So you won't be seeing Grey?"

"No." Ignoring the hurt in Kennedy's eyes, she said sincerely, "I'm happy for you and Nick. You both deserve happiness. And congratulations on your daughter. She's a very lucky little girl to have you both as parents."

"Irelyn," Kennedy said softly, "why did you come here? Really."

She looked out into the neighborhood with its two- and three-car garages, manicured lawns, flower gardens, and young children playing hopscotch on the sidewalk. So lovely, so simple. So very far away from what she had known. What she was returning to.

"Irelyn?"

She shook herself and turned back to Kennedy. Getting sentimental would help no one. "Please, just make sure Grey understands that he needs to be careful. Extra careful. All precautions must be taken. He won't listen to me, but he'll listen to you and Nick. Whoever is behind this attempt won't stop until he's successful. Tell him. Okay?"

She walked toward the porch steps, her mind a jumble of emotions. There were many things she wanted to say to this woman she never planned to see again. If she said them, though, there would be more questions. Besides, it would be an indulgence. One she couldn't afford.

"Wait." Worry clouded Kennedy's lovely brown eyes. "Whatever happened between you and Grey...it can be fixed."

"No, it can't, but thank you for your concern."

"Nothing is irrevocable, Irelyn."

So much innocence and optimism in that statement. Another reason she admired Kennedy so much. She had gone through the darkest of the dark, but because of her strength and resilience, she had walked back into the sunshine. That took courage.

"Talk to Grey," Kennedy urged. "You can work things out. I know you can. He cares for you so much."

Irelyn knew that without a doubt. Hoping to convey her thoughts in a way Kennedy might understand, she said, "Have you ever played solitaire?"

Confusion flickered on Kennedy's face. "Yes, of course."

"Ever notice that with just one wrong move, you can lose the game?"

"Yes, but life isn't a game."

"Of course it is. Some people are just better at it than others. You and Nick, though—you're good at it. I'm really happy for you."

"Is that what happened? You or Grey made a wrong move? You did something you regret? He did something to hurt you? Whatever happened can be fixed."

"I can't fix what I did...some things can't be changed. They are what they are."

"What did you do that can't be fixed? What is it you think Grey can't forgive you for?"

"I killed his parents."

The words had spilled from her mouth before she knew she planned to say them. She didn't wait to see the shock and horror on Kennedy's face. She strode quickly to her car. Jumping in, she took off without a backward look. She shouldn't have said anything. Spontaneous outbursts like that were dangerous. They not only caused problems, they cost lives.

She blew out a cleansing breath. Okay, she had done what she came to Dallas to do. Now on to the next part. The part that would not only resolve her past, but would also save Grey's life. She planned to accomplish both, even at the cost of her own life. It was the very least she could do.

CHAPTER TEN

With a controlled violence, Grey pounded his fists into the taut leather boxing bag. The only sounds in the empty gym were the heavy thumps of his fists and the rasping breaths of a frustrated, exhausted man.

He threw one last punch and caught the violently swinging bag before it could come back and knock him to the floor. Grabbing hold with his arms, he leaned his face against the cool surface and breathed out harsh, heavy breaths. Beating the shit out of an inanimate object was a helluva lot safer but not nearly as satisfying as destroying the person who was trying to destroy him. It was, however, all he had right now.

The list of suspects was frustratingly long but they still had nothing concrete. He had enemies all around the globe. There were, however, only a few who would go to the trouble and expense to hire an assassin. Those few were being investigated thoroughly. While there had been some surprises, such as secret mistresses and illegal business practices, he had yet to uncover anyone who had recently hired a hit man.

Hunting took patience and skill. He had both. Grey might have been out of the game for a while, but he was no less prepared. Through the years, he had been the target of many. His skills were as sharp as ever. The contract killer would try again. And once again, he would fail. Grey would defeat anyone who threatened him and what was his.

The assassination attempt was no secret. There wasn't a media outlet on this planet that hadn't run a story, some more than one story, about the failed attempt on his life. He had turned down every recent interview request, which was frustrating. Discussing with the media the work of his victims advocacy group was usually a good thing. Unfortunately, the interviews now centered on the assassination attempt and speculation about who might want him dead. That was a conversation he preferred to have in private with his people and not the general public.

Everyone associated with any Grey Justice entity had been warned to be wary. He doubted anyone who happened to work for one of his companies was in danger, but caution was never a useless endeavor. He was concerned that those closest to him could be targeted. He cared about many, but there were only a few in his inner circle. They were the ones who could be used against him.

Irelyn was in that inner circle. Yes, she had chosen to end their relationship, but that didn't mean he'd stopped caring. He would never stop caring. He wanted to see her, talk to her. He wanted to know what the hell she was doing associating herself with Sebastian Dark and Hill House. Problem was, he had no idea where she was. She had gone dark this time—darker than she ever had before. He'd broken his promise to her and his own code of ethics and started looking for her again. She'd be furious, but having her hate him was nothing new. Damned if he'd have her wellbeing on his conscience more than he already did.

In the meantime, someone was out to get him, and he needed to find that person and fast.

"If you're tired of torturing that boxing bag, I'll be happy to go a round with you."

Wyatt Kingston stood at the doorway. The gleaming fury in his eyes belied the calm manner in which he'd spoken. Grey couldn't blame him. Lacey was doing better but she was still in a lot of pain. And Grey felt one hundred percent responsible. The life he lived called for enemies to want to end him, but he never intended for innocents to be hurt in the process.

"I would imagine you would like to do more than go a round with me."

"Not really. I'm saving most of my energy for the piece of shit responsible."

While he appreciated Kingston's words, he didn't agree. If he had found Lacey another ride home, which had been his initial thought, she wouldn't be going through hell right now.

"Have you seen Lacey today?"

The brief flicker of grief in Kingston's eyes was almost immediately replaced with fierce determination. "She's refused to see anyone but her family and you."

Grey wasn't surprised. Wyatt and Lacey's relationship had been volatile already. This incident hadn't helped.

"She'll come around."

"I know she will. In the meantime, my main purpose is to find the son of a bitch responsible."

That was no surprise either. Grey had more than a dozen people working on finding the bastard, but that wouldn't stop Kingston from doing his own investigation. Even though the man had headed up several missions for the Grey Justice Group, he wasn't a Justice employee. Wyatt, as the owner/operator of Kingston Defense, and his team often handled ops other defense and security companies deemed too risky or bordered on illegal. A few months ago, Wyatt and a few of his best had kidnapped Gabriella and Carlos Mendoza for the Grey Justice Group.

Though things had gotten complicated and dangerous later on, Kingston and his team had pulled off the abduction without a hitch. Carlos was now serving a long prison term for multiple rapes. His sister, Gabriella, had escaped a life of captivity and was now married to Jonah Slater, one of GJG's best operatives.

"We need a sit-down to share info."

Kingston jerked his head in a nod. "Why I'm here."

Grey grabbed a towel to wipe his face. "We can beat the hell out of each other another time."

Wyatt threw him a crooked grin. "You just don't want to be beaten up by an old man."

"Yeah, right."

Kingston was three years older than Grey's thirty-four years. Since he was in excellent shape and had more stamina than men half his age, Kingston's old-man reference should be laughable. It wasn't. Wyatt had started referring to himself as an old man after he'd met Lacey. Grey figured it was the man's way of reminding himself that she was way too young and innocent for him. Lacey, as usual, had a different opinion.

This newest obstacle certainly hadn't helped.

"Give me five minutes to grab a shower, and I'll meet you in my office."

With a grim nod, Kingston walked out, and Grey headed to his bathroom on the other side of his home. On the way, he pushed speed-dial for Nick.

"What's up?" Gallagher asked.

"Kingston's here at my apartment. Wants to go over the suspect list. You got anything else?"

"A couple more possibilities, but we're stretching."

And that was the problem. There were plenty of people to look at, but so far none of them looked viable. "Bring what you have."

"See you in fifteen."

Grey pocketed the phone, fighting the urge to throw it across the room. It had been a while since he was this frustrated. He'd learned early in life that losing his temper got him nowhere. Cool, calculated reasoning was his mainstay. Lately, though, his patience had been pushed to the brink.

Wyatt paced back and forth in Justice's office. He had almost nothing to go on and was relying on Justice to give him some leads. Once he got something concrete, nothing would stop him from hunting down and destroying the person behind this. He would have done this for Justice anyway, as the man was not only a friend but also his occasional employer. But that wasn't the biggest reason. He wanted to hunt down this bastard for Lacey.

Dropping into a chair, Wyatt closed his eyes in despair. He had let her down so much that he was sickened to even think about it. He couldn't get the guilt out of his mind. He had promised to attend the awards event with her and then, through sheer stupidity, had backed out. She'd ended up going with some creep who had made her uncomfortable, so she'd gotten a ride with Justice. Shouldn't have been a problem, except Justice had so many damn enemies. And because of that, Lacey had been injured in both body and spirit.

He would never forgive himself for letting her down, and right now all he had to go on was the hope of bringing the man responsible for the botched hit to justice. And after that? Hell, he didn't know. His reasons for not being with Lacey were as valid as ever. But to see her hurting and so damn dispirited tore a hole through that wall of self-protection he'd erected to deal with his emotions. From the moment he'd met Lacey Slater, she had penetrated every defense he'd ever put up. Without even trying.

"I called Gallagher," Justice said as he walked into the room. "He's got a couple more leads. Coffee?"

Wyatt appreciated his friend not questioning why he'd had his eyes closed with what was most likely a sad, defeated look on his face. His attitude wouldn't exactly inspire confidence, but if anyone understood his struggles, it was Justice. The man had endured a boatload of his own worries over someone he cared deeply about.

"Coffee sounds good."

"I spoke with Lacey's surgeon last night. He still thinks the prognosis for a full recovery is good."

"Yeah. Eli told me the same thing. The doctor also said a lot of it will have to do with Lacey herself."

"She'll come around," Justice assured him. "It just takes time."

Though he nodded his agreement, he wasn't as sure as Justice was. For as long as he'd known her, Lacey Slater had been one of the most optimistic and determined people he'd ever met. Her sheer energy and love of life had drawn him to her, but it was her unquestioning loyalty and incredible sweetness that made him long for her with an unending ache. He had stayed away from her as much as possible, but her tenacity and his fascination with her had gotten in the way of his resolve.

But now? Now she had told him to go away. Had even requested he be barred from visiting her in the hospital. There were ways around that, but still, the knowledge that she refused to see him tore through him like a machete. To know that her attitude was his own damn fault didn't help.

GREY HANDED THE COFFEE TO KINGSTON AND WALKED OVER to his floor-to-ceiling window. Dark gray clouds hovered like a thick, heavy blanket over the city, blending perfectly with the darkening storm inside him.

"Being in love is never easy." Grey murmured the words quietly, almost to himself, but there was a wealth of knowledge behind them.

"It sure as hell isn't."

At least Kingston hadn't denied his feelings. That was progress.

Before Grey could think of some encouraging words, which lately he had struggled with, Gallagher came through the door. Seconds later, his wife, Kennedy, followed him.

"I brought Kennedy along. I want to discuss another issue, too."

Grey knew exactly what that issue was. He also knew Kennedy and Nick had argued fervently about it. The surprise visit Irelyn had made to Kennedy had Nick in complete overprotective mode. As much as he understood Gallagher's need to protect his wife, Grey knew without a doubt that Irelyn would never harm her or any innocent. Her reasons for what she was doing were as mysterious as the woman herself, but he had learned long ago that he could trust her judgment.

"Let's talk suspects, then we'll go on to the other issue."

Both the Gallaghers nodded, but the mutinous expression on Kennedy's face and Nick's grim demeanor didn't bode well for a pleasant discussion.

"I sent an updated list to your tablet," Nick said.

Grey clicked on the link, forwarded it on to Kingston, and then reviewed the names. Many of their previous suspects had been eliminated. A few originals remained, and two had been added.

"Adam Slater?" Grey asked.

"That was my addition," Kennedy said. "I know he's a long shot since he doesn't have access to his money, but even locked up, he's found ways to hurt people."

"I don't disagree with your assessment, but why would Adam target me? We had few dealings before he was incarcerated and none since he's been locked up. As far as I know, he has no clue that I was one of the people who tried to bring him down."

"Because you're important to Eli and Jonah," Kennedy explained. "He may not know your involvement with bringing him to justice, but he's aware of a relationship between you and his brothers." Kennedy glanced around the room, meeting everyone's eyes. "We all know that Adam is evil enough to do this. Hurting his family, especially his brothers, would give him immense satisfaction."

Grey couldn't argue with her logic. Adam Slater, Mathias's oldest son, had been a chip off the old block. Though not nearly as intelligent or devious as his father, his self-absorption and coldheartedness made him just as dangerous and evil as Mathias had been.

"You're right. We already monitor him, but I'll make sure we delve deeper just to make sure he's not gotten back into the killing business."

"There's one more person I'd like to add," Nick said.

Kennedy's soft snort of disgust warned Grey about the identity of Nick's new suspect.

His brow raised, Grey asked, "Irelyn?"

"Yes."

"Nick, this is ridiculous," Kennedy snapped. "Irelyn would never hurt Grey."

"I know we'd all like to think that, Kennedy. The fact remains that she is an assassin."

"I know that's what you think, but there's got to be more than meets the eye here. She wouldn't—"

"You don't know what she would or wouldn't do," Gallagher said. "Just because she helped you when she worked for Grey doesn't mean she won't kill for money now. She's obviously dangerous, and I—"

"That's enough, Gallagher," Grey growled. "We've had this conversation before, and while I understand your concern for Kennedy, she is in no danger from Irelyn. I know for a fact that Irelyn would lay down her life for Kennedy…hell, for all of us, including you. I don't have a clue why she has associated herself with Hill House. I intend to find out the reason, but until then, know this. I trust Irelyn Raine more than anyone else in the world, period."

"And you're willing to gamble your life that she's not changed? Gone rogue?"

"Yes. Irelyn Raine is many things, but there's not an ounce of killer instinct in her."

"Then why the hell did she hire on as an assassin?"

Grey had racked his brain trying to figure out just what Irelyn had up her sleeve. She always had an agenda. A part of him feared exactly what that agenda entailed, but he knew to his soul it had nothing to do with killing innocent people. And though he was as far from innocent as a man could get, he also knew she would never physically harm him. Metaphorically tear his heart out of his chest? Most definitely. But never would she want to see him hurt.

"Again, I don't have an answer to that question." Grey glanced over at Kingston. "You have a unique perspective on this matter. You want to jump in?"

"Be glad to." Giving a half-smile, Kingston turned to Nick. "I met Irelyn almost seven years ago. I'd just gotten out of the military and was trying to reconnect with my daughter. She was ten years old going on thirty and resented every moment I wanted to spend with her. She agreed to come away with me if she could bring two of her friends.

"I took them to a beach resort in Florida. They went together to the bathroom on the beach and didn't come back. I went looking for them and…" He shook his head. "Scared the hell out of me. I was about to call the police when Irelyn showed up with them. She was working undercover to bring down a human-trafficking ring. She'd managed to sneak the girls out."

"Was this a GJG op?" Nick asked.

Grey smiled. "No. This was an Irelyn op."

There was so much people didn't understand about Irelyn Raine. She had saved lives so many times, and no one even knew she'd been involved.

"An Irelyn op?" Kennedy said. "So she was just doing this on her own?"

"Her main focus is child trafficking and child endangerment," Grey said.

"So what happened to the traffickers?" Nick asked.

"Took a few weeks more, but she was finally able to identify the head of the ring. All in all, eleven people were taken into custody. Seven children were saved and returned to their families."

"How did Irelyn keep from being outed?" Kennedy said.

Kingston gave a gruff laugh. "She's Irelyn."

Grey almost smiled. That was the answer to so many questions regarding Irelyn Raine. She was one of the strongest and most capable people he'd ever known. She had fascinated him the first time he met her, and years later, that hadn't changed.

"So you think she's infiltrated this assassin group as one of her undercover ops?" Kennedy asked.

That was his greatest fear and the likeliest answer. But there was so much more to this situation than met the eye. Irelyn's past and her present were now one. Grey knew to his soul there would not be a peaceful resolution.

"I do believe this, yes," Grey said. "I wish I could say why, but I don't know the answer. And I have been unable to locate her."

"Any chance it's related to the attempted hit on you?" Gallagher asked.

"That is a possibility."

"Then why didn't she warn you about it? Instead, she waits several days and then goes to Kennedy to deliver a message that you should be careful?"

Nick's distrust was understandable. As a former homicide detective, he had been trained to be suspicious. His anger was understandable as well. Kennedy's first husband, also Nick's best friend, had been killed by the very same organization that Irelyn had just joined. No one else knew about her past association with this group, and for now, no one would.

"That's another mystery I haven't solved, Gallagher. What I do know is Irelyn is not a threat to Kennedy nor to me."

An alarm chimed on his phone, and Grey glanced at the message. For the first time in weeks, he felt a lightening of his spirit. She had been located, and she was alive. All the other irritants, such as someone trying to kill him, were suddenly much more bearable.

"All right. Where does this leave us?" Kingston asked. "We have no solid leads and a thousand suspects? None of whom look all that viable."

"We keep looking until one pops," Gallagher said.

"There is another option," Grey said.

"What's that?" Gallagher asked.

"We lure the killer, take him alive, and make him talk. He can tell us who hired him."

"That's insane, Grey," Kennedy said. "There's got to be another way to find out who's behind this."

Both Kingston and Gallagher remained silent, but their expressions said they agreed. This would be the fastest way.

"Hired killers are remarkably patient. He'll wait as long as he needs. Damned if I'm going to hide from the bastard." Grey softened his next words. "I appreciate your concern, Kennedy, but I have the best people working with me."

Grey looked over at the other two men. "It needs to be soon, so let's start planning."

As they talked scenarios, Grey noticed Kennedy kept sending him odd glances. He knew she disapproved of the plan to lure the killer out, but her expression said there was more to it than that. He wasn't surprised when, after they'd settled on a plan, she said, "Grey, I'd like to talk with you alone for a few moments."

He glanced over at Nick, who looked at her curiously, which told him that she hadn't mentioned to her husband whatever was concerning her.

"Sure." He nodded at Gallagher and Kingston as they left the room. When the door closed behind them, he said, "What's wrong?"

She was silent for a few seconds, as if trying to figure out exactly what to say.

"You can ask me anything, Kennedy."

She released a drawn-out breath. "Irelyn said something when she left my house. I didn't mention it before, mostly because I really didn't know how. But I can't get it out of my mind."

Knowing Irelyn, who after all these years could still surprise him, he had no idea what she might have said. He gave Kennedy an encouraging nod and waited.

"She told me she killed your parents."

Of all the things he'd thought she might have told Kennedy, that was not even in his top one thousand.

"How on earth did something like that come up?"

"So it's true?"

For the first time in years, Grey found himself speechless. Why would Irelyn speak of something so private, so incredibly painful? He had been a little surprised at her unexpected visit to Kennedy, but he hadn't been alarmed. Irelyn had a special fondness for Kennedy, and since she had so few friends, he could understand her need to reconnect. But hearing what she had shared brought to mind a whole new possibility for the visit.

His mind scrambled to understand the nuances, and then, like a bullet, he zoomed to a sickening conclusion.

Surging from his chair, he strode over to where Kennedy sat on the couch. Taking her hand, he sat beside her and spoke with as much control as he could gather. "Tell me exactly what she said and the circumstances behind the conversation."

Though her eyes widened with alarm at his apparent urgency, she thankfully didn't question him. "We were talking about why she had come to see me. She didn't stay long…just a few minutes. She said she wanted me to tell you to be careful. That you wouldn't listen to her, but you'd listen to me.

"Then I told her you hadn't been the same since she left." She gave a self-conscious smile. "Sorry. That probably wasn't my place."

He couldn't argue with the truth. He was skilled at hiding his thoughts and feelings, but when it came to Irelyn, he had to work harder.

"What else?"

"I told her I was sure that whatever happened between you two you could work out. She said no, that she had done something unforgivable. I asked what it was, and she said she killed your parents. Before I could question her further, she jumped into her car and she was gone."

The fact that Irelyn had shared a secret that only the two of them knew about was beyond messed up. They hadn't talked about that fateful day in a long time. It had taken him a long time to forgive her, but it had taken even longer for her to forgive herself. Years of therapy and counseling had helped them deal, but he knew the cloud of that day would never completely disappear.

"Grey? Is what she said true? Did Irelyn really murder your parents?"

Kennedy was more than a valued employee, she was a dear friend. Still, talking about that time wasn't something he'd willingly do. Especially since he had more vital issues emerging, like just why the hell had Irelyn told Kennedy?

"Let's just say there's more to her statement than meets the eye. When you see Irelyn again, you can ask her to explain."

"All right. I will. Now tell me why you're so worried."

Another sign he wasn't doing well hiding his thoughts.

"It's just not something she talks about ever, to anyone."

"You think she told me for a specific reason?"

That was his biggest concern. Irelyn never said anything without a purpose. And for her to bring up the most painful moment in her life? Grey could think of only one reason, and it chilled him to the bone. Whatever she was setting in motion with this newest "job" of hers, she wasn't sure she would come out of it alive.

CHAPTER ELEVEN

Paris, France

Dressed in ripped jeans, black T-shirt, and black leather jacket, Grey blended in with the rest of the early afternoon crowd. The gray skies and icy-cold temperatures reflected his somber mood. He wasn't here for a pleasure trip. He was here to hunt down the elusive Irelyn Raine.

He knew Paris well. He and Irelyn had lived here for several years before moving to America. Since both of them spoke fluent French, the transition had been an easy one. Grey had been able to earn enough money to keep them relatively well fed. Irelyn had stayed at their apartment most days. She had finally stopped running away from him by then, but her reversal had been almost as bad as her fleeing. She had become so dependent on him, terrified that he would leave her alone. Looking back on that time now, it was almost impossible to equate the fragile, terrified young girl that Irelyn had once been with the incredibly strong and self-confident woman she was today.

He still remembered Irelyn's first show of independence.

It'd almost gotten both of them killed. They'd been running low on funds, and Irelyn, behind his back, had tried to earn money the only way she knew how. She had tried to con a guy out of a couple thousand euros. The man had realized her game and had almost killed her. Grey had arrived in time to save her, but it hadn't been easy. They'd both been battered but had managed to escape. The man, they'd learned later, was some local thug's muscle. Irelyn had chosen her target poorly.

Showing just how much grit and determination she had left inside her, she hadn't let that stop her from trying again. She had learned a valuable lesson when it came to picking the right target. Since Hill Reed had always chosen her target for her, she'd had little experience in discerning who would fall for her act and who would see through her. It wasn't the most ethical way to earn a living, but at that time, survival had been their most important goal.

Grey had fond memories of those days. Times had been tough, but they'd been fighting for a better future for both of them. Irelyn had eventually gotten a position as a shopkeeper's assistant and stopped her con games. Grey had worked two jobs and, in between those, studied his ass off to find a way to make more money.

By the time they'd left Paris, both he and Irelyn had been much more mature. They'd both been in their twenties by then and had seen so much of life, experiencing things most people never would in a lifetime. Their relationship had morphed from a wary dependency to full-fledged partnership. Shared goals and thirst for a better, more meaningful life had created an unbreakable bond. They'd found what they'd been looking for in America.

Leaving Europe had been the best thing for both of them. Getting as far away from their dark pasts as possible was the only way either of them would have survived.

"Pardon me, sir. Do you have the time of day?"

The man standing beside him was tall and lean, with a head full of silver hair and a twinkle in his golden eyes.

"Andre. Good to see you."

"And you. You look well. Except for that dangerous glint in your eyes."

"The glint is not for you, old friend."

"Ah yes, the lovely Irelyn has gone off the straight and narrow once again."

"No. Those days are long over. I'm concerned for another reason."

"Revenge, then?"

"Possibly."

"Why now?"

"That's something I don't know. I had hoped you'd heard something."

"Only that she's been trying to get back into the game. Odd way of doing so, as she's made herself a target. But our girl was ever the unpredictable one."

"No truer words. Any idea where she is?"

"Not a clue."

"I believe she's here, in Paris."

"If she is, she's keeping a lower profile than normal. I can ask around."

No. She would hear and be gone in a flash. She didn't want to be found, but he was determined to do just that and find out just what the hell she was up to.

"That's all right. I have a few more places to check."

"Irelyn has never been easy, has she?"

He smiled at the idea of anything with Irelyn being easy. "Never."

"But worth it?"

"Most definitely."

Andre held out his hand. "It was good to see you, my

friend. If I hear anything, I will alert you in the usual method."

Grey nodded. "Merci, mon ami."

In a way Grey had always admired, Andre disappeared into the crowd as if made of smoke. A magician by trade and thief by choice, Andre had learned to trick the eye at an early age. Andre was one of the first people Grey had met when they had first arrived in Paris. He was also one of the few from his old life who had never betrayed him.

Grey stood at a street corner and let his eyes roam. This beautiful, fascinating city held so many good memories. Irelyn had hated leaving. She'd made some friends here. Grey had hoped that if he couldn't find her, he could find at least one of her friends who might have seen or heard from her. Andre was the fifth and last of those friends. None of them had had contact with her in months.

She'd had an apartment here, where they used to live. He'd gone there yesterday and learned she no longer owned it. He'd been struck by how the area had improved since they'd lived there. Their rat-infested apartment building had been torn down and replaced with an elegant apartment complex and a small, upscale shopping center.

For a woman who claimed to have no sentimental attachment to anything, Irelyn was charmingly sentimental. The fact that she had given up the apartment bothered him. Was she cutting every tie she had with everything and everyone or just with him? Either way, that deep pit of dread inside his gut caved open a little more.

The light changed. He stepped off the curb and, along with dozens of other pedestrians, crossed the street. His eyes continued to roam as his mind searched for another way to find her. If he didn't locate her soon, he'd have to dig deeper. Whether Irelyn wanted it or not, she needed his help. Damned if he would let her down again.

He was about to cross over to another street when he spotted her. She was standing on a corner, looking directly at him. She wore a long-sleeved dark emerald sweater dress and three-inch heels. Her hair was pulled back into a chignon, highlighting her beauty. A small purse, large enough for her cellphone and possibly a small handgun, was wrapped around her shoulder. It took only a second to take in her appearance, but it was the expression in her eyes that held him mesmerized and unmoving. They gleamed with both fury and need.

His legs finally moved, and he went toward her. She remained at a standstill, waiting. When he was only inches away, he murmured softly, "It's about damn time."

"Why are you here, Grey?"

"You really need to ask?"

"You told me you wouldn't follow me. That you wouldn't look for me."

He glanced around. Having this conversation surrounded by strangers was one thing. They both knew how to convey a message without raising their voices. However, standing out in public when there were enemies about was another matter. Making it easy for a killer to strike was just damn stupid. Spotting a darkened alcove next to a gift shop, Grey took her arm and pushed her forward. Thankfully, she didn't seem inclined to protest.

When they were out of sight and had some semblance of privacy, he answered her question with one of his own. "What are you working on, Irelyn?"

"What do you mean?"

"You're cutting ties, saying goodbye. What the hell's going on?"

"I have no idea what you're talking about, Grey."

"Your apartment here in Paris. You let it go."

"How did you know I even had…" She shook her head.

"Never mind. That was a stupid question. You know everything."

"Not everything. Why did you tell Kennedy about our past?"

"It seemed the right thing to do."

"Why now?"

"She's my friend. She has a right to know."

"Know what, Irelyn? That you were once an assassin, or that you've become one again?"

Her smile was slightly twisted. "Apparently, you've heard the news."

"Hell yes, I heard. Did you think I wouldn't? What are you doing? Why would you even go near that place again? What are you—"

She took a quick step back, away from him. "This third degree is ridiculous, Justice. What I do and don't do is my business. Not yours. We've severed our ties. They need to stay that way."

"Like hell we have." Pushing her farther into the darkness, against a wall, he pressed his body against her and slammed his mouth onto hers.

HIS TASTE. OH, SWEET MERCY, SHE COULD NEVER FORGET THE taste of Grey. Sometimes, late at night, she would remember and she would yearn. It was weak of her, but she couldn't allow this opportunity to go by. Opening her mouth, she took him deep, gentling him and at the same time giving herself incredible pleasure. No one could kiss quite like Grey.

She heard a deep growl, and then he pulled her closer and gave her everything she needed. Grey was a generous lover— her pleasure was always his number one concern. The kiss was tender and passionate at once, stirring her desire and reminding her of the heat and the pleasure that were hers for the asking. She could have him anywhere at any time. Grey was that giving.

A warning alarm blared in her brain. No…just no. She could not do this. She had an agenda, and it could not include Grey. This moment of weakness had to end.

She pushed his shoulders hard. He didn't have to let her go. Grey was strong enough to keep her penned against the wall, but that was not his style.

His breath ragged, he leaned his forehead against hers. "Come home with me. Whatever you've got going, we can work on it together."

"No." Inwardly wincing at the weak, breathless refusal, she put more strength into her next words. "It's over, Grey. Stop following me. Stop digging into my life. Our relationship is over."

He took a step back, glared down at her. "So that's it, huh? I can just go about my business. Find another woman, marry, have children. We're through forever."

She refused to give voice to the screaming inside her at his words. Grey with another woman? Another woman's children? No. No. No. For as long as they'd been together, she had not once been concerned that he would stray. They had been many things to each other, hurt each other to the point of brutality, but never had she questioned his devotion or fidelity.

But she had ended it, hadn't she? Then she needed to live with the consequences, as painful as they were.

"Yes. Find a woman, marry her. Have children. Be happy. You deserve that."

He stared hard at her then. It took a massive amount of willpower to hold that fiery blue gaze without flinching. Without giving away the fact that she was bleeding inside.

Finally, he said in a gruff, thick tone, "And you, Irelyn?

You will find another man? Or have you already? Is that what this is about?"

She could make him believe her. If she told him she'd found someone else, he would likely let her go without another word. And while that was exactly what she needed him to do, there was no way in hell she would hurt him like that.

"No. There is no other man, Grey. But there needs to be. Don't you see? We need to get on with our lives."

"Don't give me that bullshit. We've been through too much together."

"It's not bullshit." She backed away slowly. "Goodbye, Grey. Have a good life. You deserve it."

"Walk away, Irelyn, and this is it. I won't try to find you again. I'm tired of chasing you."

"Good. That's the way I—" A lump was developing in her chest, threatening to envelop her throat and stop both her ability to breathe or to speak. She had to get this done and over with. Quickly.

"Have a good life, Grey. You are the best man I've ever known. You deserve every good thing." Unable to stop herself, she grabbed hold of his jacket, rose on her toes, and ground her mouth against his again. If she could have nothing more of him, then she would take his taste with her.

Before he could respond, she backed away completely and walked into the light, back into the milling crowd of strangers where she could be completely anonymous and alone. Grey didn't follow her. She knew he wouldn't. He had told the truth. He wouldn't chase her again. Wouldn't try to find her. This time, they were done for good.

Wrapping her arms around herself, Irelyn walked away for the last time.

CHAPTER TWELVE

**Hill House
England**

"I'm sure you remember this room. It hasn't changed since you were last here."

He was right. The room looked the same. She should know, since this particular one had been featured in many of her nightmares. This was the place where formal punishments were given. The area was large enough to hold a small group of people to witness the punishment, but not so large if Hill had wanted a more private setting. Dramatic in both color and design, the décor evoked memories she had spent a lifetime trying to forget. Hundreds of hours in therapy had eradicated the humiliation and excruciating pain, but no amount of therapy could wipe away the memory.

Only by reminding herself how far she had come was she able to act naturally. Dark had breezed through the first two floors with a minimum of detail. When they'd reached the third floor, where most of the horrible things took place, he had purposely slowed down, stopping at various areas to reminisce. The sparkling gleam in his eyes said he was enjoying himself immensely.

At the end of this long hallway was the place she wanted to go the most. He had barely mentioned the room as they'd passed, just making an aside that the records room was where it always had been. She had merely nodded and moved on, in no way indicating that what lay behind those locked doors was of utmost importance.

He had waited until the end of the tour to show this particular room. It was obvious he wanted a reaction out of her. Damned if she would give him any satisfaction. She was good at undercover, trained to hide and manipulate. This weasel, with his smarmy smile and wicked agenda, would not cause her to fail. This was the most important undercover mission she'd ever attempted. No way would she let the memories of horror stop her.

Using every bit of talent she had, she kept her expression free of the outrage and fury boiling in her blood. "It's a bit outdated. One would think we're still living in the twentieth century. Black and red are so gauche and passé."

His smile froze for an instant. "The classic look never really goes out of style, does it?"

"If you say so."

"You don't seem all that pleased to be back here. Perhaps this was a mistake."

"On the contrary, I'm extremely pleased to be back home. I'm just surprised that a man with your exquisite taste hasn't commissioned more renovations."

The smile became natural once more. Yes, she was playing him, and he knew it. As she'd told Kennedy, life was a game. She wasn't particularly good at certain parts. However, having been schooled by a master, she excelled in manipulation. But there was something else she needed to remem-

ber—that very same master had trained Sebastian Dark
as well.

"I am slowly renovating," Dark was saying. "I'm sure
you'll agree that, while our father was a bit old-fashioned, he
had exquisite taste."

This wasn't the first time Dark had referred to Hill Reed
as their father. The ploy was to remind her of their relationship. Their shared upbringing and just who had created
them.

"Besides, you'd be surprised at how slow to change many
of our members are. We remember and treasure the good
old days."

She didn't mention the absence of those members. The
house was virtually empty. Dark was having trouble gaining
the following that Reed had enjoyed. What he lacked in
assassins, he had made up for with guards. She had spotted at
least six so far.

The emptiness of the house was actually a disappointment. She had wanted to talk with Hill House members,
glean as much information as she could. The contract on
Grey Justice would be an exciting bit of gossip. In a relaxed
atmosphere, with a little alcohol, lips became looser, secrets
were shared. The likelihood of someone revealing the person
behind the hit was greater.

The fact that many in the community would want to kill
her wasn't a concern. Reed had employed a strict rule that an
assassin could not kill another assassin within five kilometers of Hill House. This place was to be a safe haven, while
the rest of the world was their killing field.

Had Dark adopted the same rules as well? From what she
could tell, he was doing his best to maintain Reed's
traditions.

Aware that he was waiting for her to comment on what
he called *the good old days*, she said, "Those were indeed good

days. However, if you need decorating assistance, I can recommend several excellent interior designers."

"Thank you, but I have everything under control." He waved a hand. "Shall we proceed?"

She would call this conversation a draw. The moment she'd touched down at Leeds Bradford Airport, she'd been under scrutiny. She was one of the best trackers in the business, which meant she knew when she was being followed. She had taken a roundabout way here. Having flown to and from Dallas under an alias, she had gone to Paris to grab her official go bag from her new apartment. She hadn't planned on seeing Grey. When she'd heard he was there, looking for her, she had been equal parts angry and excited. And the minute she'd seen him, she had wanted to throw away every bit of her resolve and return home with him. Thankfully, she had come to her senses before that had happened.

Only a few hours after seeing Grey, she had jumped onto another plane. This time as Irelyn Raine, resolved once more to see this through.

"Would you like to see where you'll be staying?"

Excitement washed away the sadness. *Finally.* This was what she had been working on forever. She was going to be able to stay here, get what she needed.

When she had lived here with Reed, a few of the older, retired assassins had made Hill House their temporary residence. Active assassins stayed here for training and between assignments, but never for very long. It was just as she had hoped—Dark was maintaining Reed's traditions.

They walked back down to the second floor, where he stopped at a door at the end of a corridor. "I thought you would enjoy staying in your old room."

Smiling, he opened the door wide. "Welcome home."

The room was just as she had left it. Reed's idea of femininity had been traditional, too. Varying shades of pink covered both the walls and the floors. As a child, she had thought her room was the most beautiful place in the world. She had never dreamed of having anything so fine or lovely. Looking at it now, with an adult's eyes and awful memories, she saw the room for what it was—a façade covering a multitude of sickness.

Her smile felt stiff on her lips. "It's just as I remember it. Thank you for allowing me to stay."

"You won't be here long."

He left it at that. Though she longed to ask how long she would be allowed to stay, she wouldn't. If Dark got the slightest impression of just how much she wanted to be here, she would be booted out immediately.

She would have to act fast. If she woke tomorrow morning and was told to leave, then all of her hard work would be for nothing. Once she had the information she'd come for, she would proceed with her second plan. It lifted her spirits a bit to think that, this time tomorrow, Hill House would no longer exist.

THE HALLWAYS WERE PITCH DARK. NO ONE SHOULD BE ABOUT this time of night. If they were, they were in places they shouldn't be. She would definitely fit that description. If caught, she would die. She didn't plan on getting caught.

Odd, really, that darkness could still bother her. Even after all this time, it was the one thing that could remind her of the past. The sheer emptiness, the terror of being completely alone. She had overcome much of what had been done to her, but that one aspect could sometimes plunge her back into those hideous days.

Reed had used the absence of light as punishment. Nothing had worked quite so well. Even beatings were preferable to being left alone in the dark. Lights had been turned off, bulbs removed, and the door locked. *Think about what you've done,* he would growl softly. And then he would whisper those awful, terrible words—the ones that would strike terror in her childish mind. That one threat would make her do anything to keep it from coming true. *Do it again and I'll leave you alone forever.*

In those first few years, she hadn't done anything bad. Basic childhood mess-ups that any sane adult would either ignore or send a child to stand in the corner for a while. A broken dish, spilled juice, not eating her peas and carrots. Anything he deemed an infraction was punished in this manner. The punishment had been effective. Eventually, just the verbal threat of being left alone in the darkness was enough to correct her behavior. He knew exactly how to manipulate her for maximum benefit.

Later on, the physical punishments had come. Not because she had misbehaved or had stopped being afraid of the dark. Punishment was followed by reward, again and again, until she would do anything...*anything* to prevent his punishment. She had often likened her behavior to a perverted version of Pavlov's famous experiment. She had practically salivated to not only avoid punishment but to receive affection. Like a well-trained pet or a puppet on a string, Reed had commanded, and she had followed those orders to the letter.

Until one day, she didn't.

After more than a decade of therapy, she understood more about the manner of man Hill Reed had been. On one hand, he saved her from certain death. He'd fed, clothed, and housed her. She had loved him with all the fervor of her naïve young heart, believing what she was receiving was love. He had abused and used her for his own evil works. Even as she hated the things he did, she had accepted them.

They were the norm for her, and she hadn't known anything different.

Then she had met people who showed her a different way of life. Goodness and light, justice and mercy. They were hers for the taking, but in the end, she destroyed those, too.

And now she was back in the heart of that hell, the place where it all began. But this was different. She was here on her terms, with one very specific purpose in mind. She would find the information she needed and deal with it. What that meant, she didn't yet fully know. She only knew she had to pursue this till the end. And if getting what she needed took her life, at least she would die with a clearer conscience and her soul intact.

As she crept through the darkness, she wondered about the ease with which she was able to penetrate the house. She wasn't egotistical enough to believe her success was all due to skill. Nothing worthwhile came without effort. No guards were about, no motion sensors activated. Why was Dark making this so easy?

Not that it mattered. Even if he was setting a trap, she had no choice but to take the chance. Getting to the records was her only goal. If that involved some risks, she was prepared. She had yet to demonstrate that she was better trained and more skilled than Dark could ever fathom. Whatever came her way, she could handle.

Though the mansion was enormous, the layout was simplistic. First floor held three parlors, a bar/clubhouse for social gatherings, a kitchen, and an enormous dining room. When Reed was alive, he had often held dinner parties for his elite assassins. She had never been invited, but she had heard about them. Considering that Hill House was so empty, she doubted that Sebastian threw many dinner parties.

Dark's private quarters covered the entire back part of the mansion, along with his private offices. The bedrooms and private apartments were located on the second floor, where she was staying. The third floor held the interrogation and training rooms, as well as the records room.

Hacking into computers was so much easier than breaking into a room filled with paper records. Hill Reed had known this. Though he had adapted the use of a cellphone for convenience, he had never embraced what he called the modern tools of communication. The more the world relied on technology, the more old-school he had become. She had teased him once that Morse code was next on his agenda, and he had laughingly described how Morse code and notes on paper napkins had been the only communication used in the successful killing of an entire family.

That conversation was the first time she realized how very much she hated him. Being able to discuss the decimation of a family with both amusement and pride, but not the slightest hint of remorse, made her recognize just how sick of a bastard her mentor really was. She had known he wasn't a good man and had fought the love/hate battle with him for years. But in that one conversation, she had accepted that her hatred of him was far greater than the minuscule amount of affection that remained.

She made it to the third floor without her flashlight. No lights would burn until six o'clock tomorrow morning. Fortunately, she knew this house so well that lights weren't necessary. Many nights, unable to sleep, she had roamed the halls. Insomnia had been a major problem back then. And now she realized how fortuitous her condition had been.

At just before three a.m., all was quiet. Even a death house had to sleep. Oddly enough, she was tense and nervous. Usually when she was on an op, she was able to shut down all nerves and do the job. Tonight felt off, but she couldn't put her finger on why. She consoled herself that once she was out of here, she would find a gym and work the kinks out of her body. A little one-on-one with a boxing bag and she would be fine.

She stood at the door to the records room, noting that the locks had been upgraded. Reed had used old-fashioned deadbolts, but Dark obviously felt the need for a bit of technology. She was grateful for that. Maintaining silence was of utmost importance. Cracking a passcode was not only easier than breaking a lock, it was also less noisy.

Half an hour later, she wasn't feeling quite as smug. Her handheld decoder was the highest-quality one on the black market. She had opened much more complicated locks. The delay was seriously cutting into the time she'd be able to spend searching. She had to—

The last digit lit up, and with an almost silent click, the lock disengaged. Her tension easing a bit, she twisted the knob and walked inside. The room hadn't changed much. The musty smell of old files blended with the lemon-scented air freshener someone had recently sprayed. Rows of filing cabinets were lined up against two large cream-colored walls.

One long summer, she'd been nine or so, Reed had still been trying to determine how he could use her best, and she had worked inside here for hours on end. Filing, alphabetizing, shredding. Nothing had been too menial. The work had been mind-numbing and boring, but not difficult. The small, enclosed space was what had almost driven her up the wall. When Reed had seen how she responded to confinement, he had exploited that weakness until she learned to control her reaction.

Even now, she could feel the walls closing in on her, but she pushed them back with disdain. She'd endured too much to allow a few walls to defeat her.

While that time had been torturous, she had learned an

enormous amount about how Reed conducted the business of killing. She would utilize that knowledge tonight.

Using a small pen flashlight, Irelyn eyed the labels on the file cabinets. Once again, she was glad that Dark wanted to follow so faithfully in Reed's footsteps. The labels didn't look like they'd been changed since she had worked here. She quickly located her personal file and pulled it from the drawer. Just shuffling through a few pages revealed that not only had Reed kept records of the ten years she'd lived here, but also after they'd reconnected years later. She would review and then destroy the pages later. For now, she was looking for a specific piece of intel.

She found the information on the third page. She stared at the words for several moments and was surprised that the lines became blurred. Getting emotional would not do a damn bit of good.

Emotions would have to wait. She had two more tasks to accomplish. The second file was right next to hers. Despite an inner voice telling her to get the hell out of there, she took a moment to flip through the pages. The photograph was expected—all personnel files carried one. What she hadn't expected was the visceral reaction. How had she not known? Why hadn't she remembered?

She flipped to another page and caught her breath on a soft gasp.

She had thought she was prepared for anything. Had believed that all the anger and pain had already been dealt with and put away. She had been wrong. Nothing could have prepared her for this new information. Sickness roiled through her stomach. It was a tragedy in the making. No way in hell this wasn't intentional.

Slamming the folder closed, she took both files and shoved them inside her jacket. She had everything she needed.

The urge to get out of this vile house and away from the decades of death and destruction was becoming imperative. She was across the floor and out of the room in seconds. She carefully closed the door and initiated the lock. No one would know until it was too late that the files were missing.

Her priorities had shifted. She had no choice but to get out of here as soon as possible. She would come back later and fulfill her second mission.

Anxiety that she might be too late mixed with bubbling rage, creating a mishmash of emotions. She had no time to process any of them. She had to get to Dallas and to Grey. She had to prevent this monumental travesty that had been set in motion.

"Find what you were looking for?"

She whirled. Benjamin, one of Dark's beefy guards, smirked down at her. Everyone, including the house servants, was trained to kill. Benjamin was no exception. His size alone would make most people run the other way. His arrogant expression said that he had every intention of doing what he was trained to do.

"What's going on?"

Another guard, Lionel, came up behind Benjamin. Though shorter and thinner than his counterpart, Lionel was wiry, without an ounce of excess fat. In her estimation, he was more lethal.

Both of them could kill without the slightest hesitation.

Inappropriate laughter burst from her. That one-on-one fight with a boxing bag would no longer be necessary. The fight she had been looking for had come to her. Now she just had to survive it.

Hoping they had more muscle than brains, she went for bravado first. Her brow arched with an arrogance she'd learned from Grey, she glared at them. "Can I help you?"

"Yes, you can tell us why you're sneaking around in the

records room," Lionel said.

"Sneaking? Excuse me? I have every right to be here. It's part of my new job. Did Dark forget to inform you?"

"Oh, he informed us all right. Said to keep an eye on you."

Though Lionel appeared to be the one in charge, Irelyn kept a wary eye on Benjamin as she said, "Then perhaps he just doesn't think you're important enough for updates. I assure you I have every right to be here."

A hint of doubt clouding his eyes, Benjamin said, "Maybe she's right, Lionel. I heard she was trained by Reed."

"Only one way to find out." Lionel pulled his radio from his belt.

In a flash, Irelyn double-kicked. The radio flew from his hand, and blood spurted from the nose she'd crushed. She took a step toward the door, then jerked to a halt when a hairy, muscular arm wrapped tight around her neck. Irelyn kicked back at her assailant, feeling a moment of triumph when her heel connected with a shinbone and she heard a grunt of pain. That brief flash of triumph disappeared when the arm around her tightened, cutting off her air. Lionel appeared in front of her. Blood poured from his nose, and murder gleamed in his eyes.

Wrapping her hands around Benjamin's arm and using it as leverage, she swung her legs up and kicked with all her might, focusing solely on Lionel's groin. His eyes rolled back in his head, and he dropped like a rock in front of her.

One down, one to go.

Still hanging on to the arm around her neck, Irelyn slammed her head back as hard as she could and heard a distinctive crunch. With a howl of agony, Benjamin dropped his arm. She sprinted for the stairway door. Halfway there, she found herself airborne and then slammed into a wall. Her shoulder hit first and then her hip.

Damn, that hurt.

She managed to land on her feet, albeit a bit wobbly. She whirled just in time to see Benjamin's giant fist barreling toward her face. Irelyn jerked back. Taking advantage of his forward momentum, she grabbed his arm and pulled hard. She barely got to enjoy the sound of the crash before he was whirling around and coming at her again.

Knowing it was now or never, Irelyn ignored the pain in her shoulder and hip and went after him full force. Double-kick to the groin and chest, whirl with a roundhouse kick to his belly. While he was still teetering on his feet, she went for a knockout kick to his head. She missed. One giant fist slammed into her jaw, and another grazed her ribs. She crashed into a chair, the backs of her legs taking the brunt of the impact.

Grinning, his face a bloody mask, he pulled his radio from his belt loop. "Dark's going to love this."

Irelyn sprang forward. Grabbing hold of his arm before he could press the talk button, she smashed both the radio and his own hand into his face. Heard another crunch. A broken jaw to go with his broken nose.

Benjamin tumbled backward, taking out the chair and the painting on the wall behind him on his way to the floor. She winced at the noise, but at least he wouldn't be waking up for a while. She spared a glance toward Lionel, pleased to see he was still lying on the floor, moaning with his hands covering his crotch.

She took no time to assess her own injuries. Doing so would acknowledge them, and she couldn't afford the weakness. Other guards, or Dark himself, would be here soon. She had to get out of the house before she found herself really outnumbered.

Dark would soon know her employment had been a ruse. He would know the files that were missing and why. She would soon have a price on her head, but that didn't matter.

Her only goal was to get to Grey before another attempt was made on his life.

She bypassed the elevator, opting for the stairway. It was easier to duck and run on the stairs. An elevator door opening on a load of firepower waiting for her was not a good idea.

Amazingly, she made it to the first floor without meeting anyone. Dawn was just starting to break, and she was living on borrowed time. She opened the front door and sprinted down the steps to the sidewalk. Heading to the back of the mansion, she went through the gate and into the woods. Her getaway car was hidden in bushes about two miles away.

Breath rasped from her aching lungs. She slipped and slid along the ground as she ran. Normally, she was surefooted and limber, but today she ran like an ox. She tripped over a tree root and fell face first onto the wet leaves. A part of her told her to stay there and rest awhile. No one was chasing her right now. She had time. But allowing herself to be seduced by exhaustion and pain was not an option. She had to get to Grey.

She pulled herself to her knees and then her feet. She knew she was bleeding somewhere, but she couldn't stop to find out where. Once she was safely in the air, she'd give herself a quick checkup.

Spotting the car in the bushes where she'd left it, she felt as though she could fly. Adrenaline gave her wings. She was only hours away from Grey. That was all she cared about.

CHAPTER THIRTEEN

Dallas, Texas

Lacey screamed her frustration. It was better than crying, which was what she wanted to do. According to her therapist, her physical therapy was going wonderfully well. She was young, healthy, and in excellent shape. That didn't negate the pain and frustration, though. Never again would she take for granted being able to walk with ease, much less run.

There was still the possibility of needing more surgery. And there was also the possibility of a permanent limp. Telling herself she was lucky to be alive, lucky she hadn't lost a limb—all those it-could've-been-worse scenarios went only so far. At the end of the day, she was still a woman on crutches, and she was pissed.

"You're the only woman I know who can be beautiful and angry at the same time."

She glanced over her shoulder and glared at one of the biggest reasons for her frustration. "Then you haven't known many women."

"Oh, I've known my share."

She turned back around, her hands gripping the rails so tight she thought they might break. She wanted to throw herself into his arms. She wanted him to kiss her until she couldn't remember her own name. She wanted him to love her.

"Why are you here, Kingston?"

"You won't return my calls or texts. I've been barred from visiting you like I'm some sort of creep."

"And yet here you are."

"Tell me what I've done, Lacey, to make you hate me."

Tears sprang to her eyes, and she was glad he couldn't see them. He'd know the truth then. That she hadn't stopped loving him. Would never stop. But things were different now.

"You haven't done anything. And I don't hate you."

"Then why don't you want to see me?"

Anger replaced the self-pity. She lowered herself into a wheelchair and whirled it around as fast as she could. "The question is, why do you want to see me?"

"What's that supposed to mean? I want to see you because I care about you."

"Really? Why now?"

"What the hell?" Golden sparks of fury gleamed in his brown eyes. Eyes she could easily get lost in and never want to return.

She pushed herself forward until she was right in front of him. "For almost a year, you've pushed me away, making excuse after excuse for why we can't be together. Showing up when you wanted to, but leaving without a backward glance when you got your fill. And now that I'm injured, you want to see me all the time."

"Is that what you think I've done? Walked away without a backward glance?" Leaning down, he gripped the arms of her chair and stopped within an inch of her face. His nose almost touching hers, he growled, "Every damn time I leave you, something inside me dies."

"Then why—"

"Because I'm too damn old for you, Lacey."

"You're not any younger than you were before, but somehow now you can't stay away from me. Is it because I may be disabled?" Tears sprang to her eyes, and she was furious with herself for showing her vulnerabilities, but when it came to this man, she was a mass of emotions.

"First of all, you're not disabled, nor are you going to be. And secondly, just what kind of rat weasel do you think I am?"

"Then, dammit, tell me, Kingston. Why have I suddenly become irresistible to you?"

"Have you thought that maybe it's because I realized that age is a trivial thing compared to living without you?"

"What?"

He went to his knees in front of her. "When I got the call that you were injured, I was thousands of miles away from you. I've never felt more helpless in my life. Not knowing if you were alive. Not knowing if I'd be able to get to you in time. I had hours of travel time to relive every moment we've spent together, and one thing became abundantly clear. If I ever got the chance to be with you again, I was never going to leave you."

"And it's not because—"

He pressed a finger to her mouth. "Lacey, sweetheart. Whatever your legs, arms, or any appendage you have can or cannot do is not why I love you."

"You love me?"

"From the moment we met."

She threw her arms around his shoulders and held him

tight. Wyatt closed his eyes again, this time in relief. He had almost messed everything up by being so damn stupid.

"Can you ever forgive me?" he asked.

She pulled away to beam at him. "If you can forgive me for being such a bitch to you."

"We'll call it a draw."

"Deal."

He kissed her then. The way he'd been dreaming about for what seemed like forever. Ever since he'd met her, he had felt the need to be careful, to not show her how much she meant to him. What a damned stupid fool he'd been. But not anymore. From now on, this beautiful, wonderful, incredible woman would know, every moment of every day, how much he loved her.

The kiss was sweet and then so passionate and deep they both lost their breath. Lips devoured, tongues tangled, and fire burned.

"Um," she gasped against his mouth. "Think we should go somewhere a bit more private?"

The need to be with her in every way possible was the only thing that enabled him to pull away from her and stand. He glanced around the room, more than a little shocked that there were several people in the room with them. He'd been so lost in her, his surroundings had disappeared. Though the other people were doing their best to give them privacy, he saw more than one surreptitious glance.

"Where to?"

"I'm staying at my mom's for a while."

He glanced down at her. "I need to be with you."

Loving the pink glow on her face, Wyatt laughed. Seeing his bold and courageous Lacey blush made his heart literally leap for joy.

"Wherever you want to go," she whispered.

Dropping one more kiss on her lips, he walked around to

the back of her wheelchair. Leaning over her, he growled in a low, soft voice, "We're going to my hotel room, where I'm going to make love to you until we can both barely move, and then…"

She tilted her head back to look up at him. "And then?"

"I'm going to start all over again."

"I love you, Wyatt Kingston."

"You'd better. I'd hate to be asking a woman who doesn't love me to marry me."

"Are you asking?"

"Oh yeah, I'm asking."

"Then I'm saying yes."

"Your brothers are going to kill me."

"No, they won't. They want to see me happy."

"Then they'll love me because I'm going to spend the rest of my life making sure that happens."

"Wyatt?" she whispered. "Push faster."

"Yes, ma'am."

Their hearts full, they sped down the hospital hallway toward a bright, beautiful future.

CHAPTER FOURTEEN

S he stood at the penthouse's private elevator.
Desperation and sheer bravado were the only things
keeping her upright. All she had to do was enter the number
into the keypad. No one but she and Grey knew the passcode. He wouldn't have changed it. There would be no need.
He would never keep her out of his life. It was always her
pushing him away. Every. Single. Time. Grey Justice was as
sure as the sunrise and, in every way that counted, the most
honorable person she'd ever known.

Pressing her forehead against the cool panel of the elevator, Irelyn took a moment to gather her strength. She drew
in a shallow breath and fought the dizziness and nausea that
had been her constant companions for almost thirty-six
hours of frustration as she'd tried to get home. Until now,
she had barely acknowledged their existence. Now that she
was finally here, ignoring them was impossible.

Grey wouldn't be here. It was the middle of the day. He
would be at his offices, either negotiating billion-dollar deals
or fighting for justice for an unknown victim. She would
have time to clean herself up, maybe grab a nap. When he

arrived home, she would be composed and back to her old self. She strived at all times to be the strong, competent, independent Irelyn Raine.

Yes, she would shower and change into one of her favorite dresses. Would have to be a long one, since she had more than a few bruises to hide. He wouldn't have given her clothes away, would he? The last time she'd been here, she hadn't thought to check. What about her porcelain clown collection? Would they still be here, or had he donated them to someone who wouldn't appreciate their beauty or understand the subtle meaning?

She drew away from the door and shook her head. Her thoughts were becoming chaotic, scattered. If she didn't get up to the penthouse soon, she would collapse on the shiny granite floor. Grey would be called, and he would discover just how weak she really was.

Ignoring the way her hand shook, she entered the five numbers and waited for the door to slide open. Nothing happened. She cleared the keypad and pressed the code again. Nothing. Bewildered, she stared at the damn thing, willing it to open the door. Why wouldn't the code work? She knew she had entered the correct numbers. Why did—

Realization hit, breath caught in her throat. The pain from her injuries was nothing compared to the searing ache in her heart. Grey had changed the code. She had told him they were over, and this time, he had taken her seriously. This time, he had set her free for good.

She needed to leave. Where would she go? She had money. She would find a hotel and…what? She needed time to think. She had come here for a reason. That reason still existed. What was it? Her thoughts blurred into myriad images and sounds. She told her legs to move, but for some reason, they weren't obeying. Her heart raced, and a staccato of harsh breaths left her lungs. In a distant part of her mind, she recognized an oncoming panic attack, but she was way past being able to talk herself out of it.

A ding sounded. The elevator door slid open. Grey stood before her. She told herself it was her imagination playing tricks on her. It wasn't really him. However, just in case, she put on her best fake smile and opened her mouth to say something witty and charming. She didn't get a sound out before black emptiness filled her mind, and she fell forward into nothingness.

GREY CAUGHT HER AS SHE FELL. HOLDING HER CLOSE IN HIS arms, he stepped back into the elevator. As it rose, he tried to assess her injuries. He had never seen her so pale. Had she been shot or stabbed? He couldn't see any blood, but until he could get her inside the apartment, he would rule nothing out.

The elevator opened. Grey strode through the apartment to Irelyn's bedroom. He pushed the door open with his foot and placed her gently on the bed. When he heard her groan, he began to breathe again. He'd honestly thought she might die before he could even get her this far. She looked that sick.

Knowing he couldn't do this on his own, he quickly punched the speed-dial for his on-call doctor and requested immediate help. Assured the man would arrive within minutes, Grey ended the call and began to assess Irelyn's injuries.

Her pulse was good, which was a tremendous relief. He removed her shoes, and as he moved to unzip her pants, he realized something shocking. He had removed Irelyn's clothes numerous times, but he had never taken pants off of her before. She always wore dresses or skirts, even when she was on a job. The only time he'd seen her in anything resembling trousers was when she wore workout clothing.

As he slid the pants down, he understood the reason behind the clothing, and his concern grew stronger. Her long, slender legs were a mass of bruises, scratches, and cuts. A particularly painful-looking bruise covered her right hip and upper thigh and she had a nasty cut on her left calf. As he continued on, anger blended with his concern. Whoever had done this to her would pay.

He unbuttoned her blouse and noted she had apparently received some sort of medical treatment for her injuries. A large bandage covered her left side at her waist. Not wanting to cause her pain by lifting her to take off her blouse, he pulled a knife from the sheath at his waist. He didn't usually wear one in his home, but he'd been headed out when he'd heard the alarm on the private elevator. He had barely believed his eyes when he'd watched on camera as Irelyn had entered the passcode. She had entered the right numbers but had forgotten to press enter. It had been obvious she was in severe distress to have forgotten something so simple. The instant he'd seen her pale, bloodless face and glazed eyes, his heart had almost stopped.

After cutting the blouse from her body, he was relieved to see that, though she was badly bruised, nothing seemed to be broken.

Grey pulled the covers over her naked body and leaned down to kiss her forehead. Her soft, silky skin against his mouth called to mind the thousand times he'd kissed her before. He wanted to be able to do that a million times more.

He tried to console himself that she had come to him. Out of all the places she could have gone, she'd come back home. That consolation went only so far. When she was well, would she try to run again?

Their lives had always been complicated. What had started off in deception and death had formed into an unlikely partnership. Between pockets of peace and happiness, their rough beginning had always hovered like a dark thundercloud over them. In their early years, while he hadn't liked it, he had understood her need to run from him. She had needed to prove to herself that she wasn't dependent upon him. She had fought long and hard for her independence, and while he had worried, he had understood her need to roam.

The ding of the public elevator told him the doctor had arrived. Turning away, he walked out of the room. It was time for Irelyn to stop running. When she woke, he would damn well get the answers he was looking for. And he would make sure she understood that running away would not solve their problems. Whatever her issues, they would face them together, just as they always had.

His heart lifted a bit at the thought of their forthcoming discussion. *Argument* was more like it, but that was fine with him. He enjoyed their verbal sparring and figured they were about even in their wins and losses.

This time would be different. No matter what, this was one battle he intended to win.

CHAPTER FIFTEEN

The moment she woke, the familiarity of scents and sounds offered immediate comfort. She could breathe easy once again—she was home. The pain still existed, but it was distant and nothing like the agony she'd experienced on the way here.

The trip hadn't exactly gone as planned. She had intended to drive to the train station in London, travel to Paris, and fly out of Charles de Gaulle Airport. That plan had been delayed for more than a day. She'd had no choice but to stop at a clinic in London. She'd chosen a free clinic, knowing they would treat her with a minimum of questions.

After the gash on her side and the cut on her leg were stitched up and bandaged and an ice bag was applied to her throbbing jaw, she'd felt almost normal. She hadn't been able to sleep. The feeling of having Dark and his minions on her tail had kept her awake and wary. Even when she was safely on the plane, headed to Dallas, she couldn't allow herself to rest. The closer to home she was, the more she'd dropped her guard and the worse she'd felt.

The instant she'd walked into the lobby of Grey's apartment building, everything had crashed down on her at once. It was only by sheer stubbornness that she had been able to walk to the elevator. She barely remembered what happened after that. She recalled a blurry darkness, and then out of that darkness, Grey appeared. The last thing she remembered were his eyes, blazing like blue fire.

She glanced around the bedroom, wondering where he was. How would he take the news of what she was keeping from him? He wouldn't like it, that was certain. She had to tell him. He had to know the truth, and then he would help her. That was one thing she should never have doubted. Grey would understand her need to right this wrong. She had worried he would see it another way. She was ashamed she'd even had that thought. She should have told him from the beginning.

"You're awake already."

Grey stood at the door. She couldn't read his mood. He was never easy to read, but that enigmatic expression appeared to be set in stone. She had hoped for a warmer welcome.

"Dr. Sanderson said you would be out for a long time. You're contrary, as usual."

He said the last part with a slight smile, and her muscles eased a bit.

"Dr. Bob was here?"

"Yes. You were unconscious."

"Guess I was sleepy."

"Sleepy?" The amusement disappeared, and she saw the burning anger beneath the façade. He came farther into the room, stood over the bed. "You scared the shit out of me, Irelyn. What the hell happened?"

She was torn between indignation at his autocratic tone and the knowledge that she owed him an explanation.

"I'm sorry I startled you. I—"

"Startled? Don't even—" He abruptly cut off his words.

Fascinated, she watched as he visibly controlled his anger. She had always admired that. When she was angry, she had to become someone else to regain control. Grey was never anyone other than himself, but his restraint was amazing. She had never known anyone more disciplined.

"How do you do that?" she asked.

"Do what?"

She shook her head. Exhaustion pulled at her, and her mind was still rattled. She had too much to tell him to get distracted.

"Never mind. I need to—"

"What you need to do is get some rest. You've only been asleep a few hours."

"Don't treat me like a child, Justice. This is too serious."

Despite his anger and worry, Grey couldn't prevent a smile. When Irelyn called him *Justice* in that crisp, slightly lyrical way of hers, she meant business. He had missed that.

"All right. But first, tell me who beat you up."

"Beat me up? Are you serious? I left two men unconscious."

"And those men would be?"

"Sebastian Dark's henchmen. Their names were Lionel and Benjamin."

"I think you'd better start from the beginning. But first, we take care of you." He lifted her gently in his arms, careful of her injuries.

"Where are you taking me?"

"To the bathroom."

Indignation flashed in her eyes. "Oh, for heaven's sake. Put me down. I can go to the bathroom on my own. I'm perfectly fine."

She obviously had no idea how she looked. She was modestly covered in a long-sleeved silk nightgown, so most of her injuries weren't apparent. The vicious bruise on her jaw was enough evidence that she was far from fine.

Ignoring her protests, he started toward the bathroom. When she struggled, he tightened his arms around her. "You can walk out of the bathroom under your own steam. For right now, be quiet."

Setting her on her feet, Grey inwardly winced when she hissed out a small sigh of pain. For Irelyn to show any kind of weakness meant she was hurting much more than she let on.

"Hurt?"

"It's manageable." She threw him a look that he was sure was meant to be haughty. "I can take it from here."

"Call out if you need me."

Grey stood just outside the closed bathroom door and waited to hear a thud telling him she had passed out. Yet, he knew she wouldn't. Irelyn was too damn stubborn to succumb to the normal human reaction to getting the hell beaten out of you. He hadn't lied. Her collapse into his arms earlier had scared the shit out of him.

Yes, he wanted answers. She was obviously ready to talk, and he was more than ready to listen. However, her health was his first concern. Dr. Sanderson had assured him that, while the gash on her side and bruised, battered body would be painful, the injuries weren't life-threatening. It was her obvious physical exhaustion that had him concerned. His recommendation of lots of sleep and good, nutritious food sounded simple enough, but with Irelyn, nothing was ever that simple. Nothing about her should surprise him anymore. Hell, he wouldn't be shocked if she walked out of the bathroom fully dressed and ready to leave.

This had to stop. Life was becoming more dangerous by

the minute. He needed to know she was safe, too. And dammit, he wanted her here, home with him.

The instant she walked out of the bathroom and he saw the look on her face, he knew that, at least for now, she would be staying.

"Let's get you back to bed."

She grimaced a smile. "I really do look like crap, don't I?"

"I guess it's all in your perspective. To me, you're lovely no matter how you look."

"You know that makes no sense, don't you?"

"How about we continue this conversation in bed?"

"Bed? Grey? Really?"

Laughing at her dry humor, Grey scooped her gingerly back into his arms. "I prefer you awake for that."

"I prefer me awake for that, too."

Settling her back onto the bed, he pressed a soft kiss on her head. "When's the last time you ate?"

"Not sure. I think I had a candy bar at some point."

"I'm bringing you a meal."

"But we need—"

"We'll talk after you eat."

She sighed and dropped her head onto her pillow. "No point in arguing."

"No point at all." He went to the door, but stopped when she called his name.

"I can't stay."

He walked out without answering. Arguing with her when she was at full strength was often infuriating and occasionally delightful. He didn't plan on having an argument about a sure thing. She was staying. Period.

IRELYN SCRAPED UP THE LAST BITE OF OMELET ON HER PLATE.
Amazing what a good protein-filled meal did for one's spirits. She swallowed the last of her orange juice and settled the
glass on the tray on her lap.

"Feel better?"

Grey had watched her eat every bite. She knew he was
worried about her. She'd been worried about herself. But
now she felt stronger. She had to tell him everything.

"Much better. Now we—"

Surprising her, he stood and removed the tray from her
lap. "Rest a bit more, and then we'll talk."

"I want..." She shook her head. In a matter of seconds, she
had gone from having a semiclear head and thinking coher-
ently to having no idea what she was going to say. Why was
her mind so muddled again?

"Rest, Irelyn."

She blinked up at him, noting how blurry he had become.
"You drugged me."

"Yes. Now, sleep. You'll feel better for it."

She wanted to shout at him for doing something so far
out of bounds. She wanted to cry, because she knew he'd
done it because he cared. She wanted... What was it? What
did she need to tell him?

"Dark. I have to tell you about..."

"We'll discuss him after you've rested."

Her eyes heavy with fatigue, she blinked to keep them
open. "Grey...no. Don't understand. I need—"

"Sleep," he whispered.

A soft, sweet darkness was closing around her,
enveloping her in a lovely velvety cloud. She was floating,
her thoughts peaceful, serene. Just before she drifted away,
she could feel Grey gently squeeze her hand, and she
managed to mumble, "Missed you."

With a soft press of his lips on her forehead, he answered quietly, "I missed you, too."

Unconsciousness claimed her.

CHAPTER SIXTEEN

Grey stood on the small stage of the beautiful old theater and looked out into the empty auditorium. Soon, the place would be milling with elegantly dressed men and women. The couples would appear as if they were wealthy and privileged and had nothing more on their minds than to enjoy an old classic movie while they sipped champagne and nibbled expensive hors d'oeuvres. No one would guess that beneath the veneer of elegance lay lethal, trained operatives. No one would guess that they were here to catch a killer.

And he, the überwealthy Grey Justice, superciliously proud of his newest acquisition, would greet those people as honored guests. His tuxedo had been designed by one of the leading new designers. No one would notice that some specific modifications had been made to his attire. His favorite Ruger and Ka-Bar knife were within easy reach, the SIG Sauer at his ankle one smooth movement away, and the Kevlar vest added only a slight amount of extra bulk to his frame.

Setting up his own execution had taken both skill and

creativity. Luring an experienced killer into a trap was difficult enough. Luring one you wanted to capture and not kill was even more of a challenge. Grey had known too many killers to not know how they thought. An assassin would much rather die than be captured.

A small smile of satisfaction curved his lips. Irelyn had once told him that no one could do arrogant quite as well as he could. To which he had laughingly replied that she could definitely compete with him. Through sheer stubbornness and dogged perseverance, they had both learned to disguise whatever was going on in their minds. The world would never know their true thoughts unless they wanted them revealed.

Irelyn. How he had hated leaving her. He wanted to be there when she woke, to talk with her. He needed to find out what had happened, who had hurt her, and why. He damn well wanted to make sure she didn't up and leave again. Unfortunately, he'd had no real choice. This sting had been days in the making and could not be canceled. It was a one-time opportunity to capture an assassin and find out who'd hired him.

He'd called Kennedy and asked her to come to the apartment. Having her there when Irelyn woke was the only thing he could think that wouldn't make her run. She would no doubt be angry, but at least she would still be there. He could handle her fireworks much easier than he could take her leaving him again.

He wanted this over and done with. He wanted weeks on end where it was just the two of them, talking, laughing, and loving like they used to. Everything had gotten too damn complicated. The important things had gotten pushed aside.

He wished he could pinpoint when their troubles started. They used to be able to talk about anything. Blaming it on their efforts to bring down Mathias Slater, or even Hill Reed reentering their lives so abruptly, would be too easy. Though that certainly had brought many things to a head. But there had been an awkwardness before all that happened. Whatever it was, he intended to find out.

But first, he had a killer to catch.

"We're all set."

Grey turned to Nick. Dressed in a dark gray tuxedo, Gallagher looked as though he had nothing more on his mind than enjoying an elegant evening out. The fact that his wife was not in attendance, and that he was armed to the teeth, would hopefully be missed by the assassin.

"Anything suspicious yet?"

"No. Everyone's milling around the lobby, laughing it up. If this asshole comes, he'll not be expecting that every one of them could take him down in an instant."

"Hopefully, it won't come to that."

"Even though our number one priority is keeping you alive, everyone knows their orders. Capturing the bastard is our goal."

"And if he or she doesn't show up, at least we'll have seen an excellent movie."

A lot of arm-twisting had been done to get this classic movie out of the vault, but Grey had insisted on this particular one. It was Irelyn's favorite—a Cary Grant romantic comedy that he hoped to show again under better circumstances.

Grey glanced down at his watch. "Let's get the party started, then."

Nick spoke into the microphone on his lapel. He was in charge of the operation and would call the shots. Since Grey was the target, he didn't want to appear to be overly concerned with anything other than making sure everyone had a good time.

The noisy chatter of dozens of excited theatergoers filled

the auditorium. Though the entire theater would hold just less than two hundred people, the balcony and box seats were closed off. All doors on the second floor had been locked, and guards were surreptitiously posted to ensure that the assassin could not get through. Limiting him in his effort to get to Grey gave them the ability to control his movements. If he was going to take a shot, there were only certain ways for it to go down.

Taking a measured breath, Grey positioned himself center stage to welcome his guests—and to make himself accessible for an assassin's bullet.

———

IRELYN WOKE GROGGY AND PISSED WITHOUT A CLUE WHY. ONE glance around the room and she remembered everything. *Justice.* He had drugged her. Even in their early years, when she had run away almost on a weekly basis, he had never done something so outrageous. Her heart told her he wouldn't have resorted to such drastic measures if he hadn't been so worried about her. Her mind told her that was not okay.

She shook her head to clear her thoughts. His arrogance would have to be dealt with later. For now, she had to tell him what was going on. He had to know, to take care.

Ignoring the multiple aches in her body, she sat up. No time for pain. Hearing a slight noise, she shifted her eyes to see Kennedy standing at the door.

Despite the dire urgency, Irelyn felt a lift to her spirits. "Hello there. What are you doing here?"

"Grey called me. He had to go out and wanted to make sure someone was here when you woke."

In other words, he wanted to make sure she didn't just up and leave. She never should have told him she couldn't stay.

"Did he go to his offices?" She glanced out the window, noting it was dark. Frowning, she saw the time on her beside clock. "He's usually home by this time."

"No, not his offices. He should be home soon, though. How are you feeling?"

Like someone beat the hell out of her. "A little sore."

"Grey said you're bruised from head to toe. That one on your face looks painful."

"I'm fine. There's nothing that won't mend."

"Would you like something to drink or eat?"

Under ordinary circumstances, her answer would have been yes. She was both thirsty and hungry. However, her concern for Grey overrode those needs. She had to talk to him...he had to know.

"If Grey's not at his offices, where is he?"

"He'll be home soon. No worries."

Her eyes narrowed. Kennedy was the most open and honest person Irelyn knew, and it was clear she was worried.

"What's going on, Kennedy? Is Nick okay?"

"Yes, of course. Or at least..." She shook her head. "I mean, yes, he's fine."

"What's happened?" Before Kennedy could deny that anything had happened, Irelyn quickly said, "It's important that I know. I didn't get to tell Grey why I came here. There are things he needs to know as soon as possible."

"Very well. He didn't want you to worry, so he asked me not to tell you, but you deserve to know. He wanted to be here when you woke, but he couldn't. He's set up a sting to catch the assassin who's been trying to kill him."

Ugly dread washed over her. "What kind of sting?"

"He bought an old theater. The old Dennison Theater on Fifth. It was going to be torn down, and Grey had it renovated. It's really quite lovely. It was built in the late 1800s and has been closed for about—" Apparently recognizing she'd gotten off track, she gave a small self-conscious smile. "Anyway, he thought this would be a good way to control the situation."

"How?"

"He invited only thirty or so people. Most of them work for the Grey Justice Group. All of them are trained. The plan is to capture this person. They'll question him to find out who's behind the contract on Grey."

It would not be that simple. It was never that simple.

Thankful she had been trained by the best to hide her thoughts, she nodded calmly. "That does sound like it would work."

"I'm just worried for Nick, but that's nothing new."

"He'll be fine. I'm sure. He's a skilled operative." She rubbed her stomach slightly. "You know, come to think of it, I am a little hungry. Is that offer of food still on?"

"You bet. Grey thought you might be a bit nauseated after the sedative he gave you. How about some chicken broth and crackers to start you off? See how that settles."

"Sounds delicious. Thank you." There was no need to explain that she was a vegetarian. She wouldn't be eating the soup.

Kennedy headed to the door, but stopped to look back at her. "I'm really glad you're back, Irelyn. Grey's not been the same since you've been gone."

With all the things on her mind, all the things that could go wrong, Irelyn gave what she hoped was some semblance of a smile. The instant Kennedy walked out, closing the door behind her, Irelyn threw the covers back and twisted around to get out of bed. She clenched her teeth against the pain, which only served to remind her of the bruise on her jaw. There was not one inch on her body that didn't ache. She could not let that stop her.

Broth would not take long to heat. She had to move fast.

Irelyn strode quickly to her closet and threw on the first thing she found. Black jeans, turtleneck sweater, and trainers were not her usual style—she wasn't even sure why she had them. Today, she was grateful she did. Hiding the bruises on her arm, legs, and neck would keep curious eyes away and wouldn't attract unwanted attention.

Opening the small safe in the back of the closet, she took out a gun, one of her favorite knives, and a burner phone. She crept past the kitchen, noting the quiet sounds of Kennedy preparing a meal for her. She winced with regret. Treating one of her few friends so poorly did not sit well with her, but she had no choice.

Seconds later, she was in the elevator, headed to the first-floor lobby. The instant she was on the sidewalk, she breathed a little easier. Even though it was pouring rain and the theater was several blocks away, she would still make better time on foot. Grabbing a cab at this time of night in this weather would be next to impossible.

She took a breath and started running. To the untrained eye, she was just another avid runner who intended to get her mileage in, lousy weather or not. No one could know that she had a life-and-death agenda ahead of her. Her number one priority was to keep Grey safe. But one additional item was on her agenda as well. His would-be assassin had to stay alive, too.

CHAPTER SEVENTEEN

She couldn't believe Grey had actually bought the
theater. It was even more beautiful than she had
dreamed. When they had talked about buying the place, it
had been her idea, not his. He had wanted to purchase an old
Victorian mansion a half-dozen blocks away and turn it into
a bed-and-breakfast. It wasn't as if they couldn't afford both,
but that wasn't the point. For the last few years, before things
went topsy-turvy on them, they had worked on a project
each year together. One year, it had been a small park and
playground. Another year, they'd purchased a run-down
diner and turned it into an old-fashioned ice cream shop. It
had been a hobby of sorts, and she had enjoyed every
moment.

Grey had been surprisingly and vehemently against
buying the old theater, pointing out structural issues, along
with a possible mold problem. She had wanted it because of
its romanticism and history, but had finally seen the wisdom
in not throwing money into a losing venture. They had been
on the verge of purchasing the Victorian mansion when
things went sour.

So why had he purchased the theater? And when had he bought it? She hadn't seen anything about its renovation online and had, in fact, assumed someone had purchased the property and demolished the building.

She would have to wait until later to get those answers. She was here for one purpose only and might already be too late.

No, she couldn't let herself think that. Yes, the event was apparently already over. A few people were slowly exiting the building. There were no police vehicles or any appearance of excitement, and she was taking that as a good sign. The assassin hadn't tried to strike yet.

On the way to the theater, she'd chanced a call to Grey. It had gone straight to voice mail, which didn't surprise her. Leaving a voice mail had been pointless. He wouldn't check for messages until this was over. And she didn't want him distracted anyway. She would have to fix this on her own.

If the assassin hadn't tried yet, he would likely see this as his best chance to strike. There would be a slight amount of chaos as theatergoers walked out of the theater. People laughing, not paying attention. She had experienced the same kind of training as the killer. They'd had the same teacher.

Oh God, why hadn't she known? Why hadn't she seen it?

She shook her head. She couldn't think about that now. She had to get into the killer's head. What was he thinking? Why had he waited? Where would he strike?

Wait for the right moment. Patience wins the prize, my dear.

How many times had she heard those words?

She crossed the street. She would mingle with the small crowd standing at the open theater door and then just slip inside, with any luck, unnoticed. She had tied her long hair back, and the black clothing hid that she was soaking wet. Hopefully, she didn't look too much like a drowned rat. If anyone did spot her, she would be recognized. Kennedy had told her only GJG operatives were attending. No one would think it strange for her to be there. No one would try to stop her. Grey would not have shared their problems with anyone, even his closest advisers.

"Irelyn? Is that you?"

That didn't take long.

Irelyn turned to Eli Slater, who was standing beside a stunning woman with auburn hair and the most amazing aquamarine eyes. Though she had never met Eli's wife, she knew Kathleen was a Grey Justice operative. She wasn't surprised they were both in attendance. Eli might look like a suave businessman, but she knew for a fact that he could handle himself as well as any operative.

"Hello, Eli. It's good to see you."

Instead of a warm greeting, Eli said, "Grey didn't tell me you were coming."

The words were innocuous, but his tone was guarded. Irelyn ignored the little stab of hurt. At one time, she and Eli had worked well together, but now he was looking at her with a wariness he'd never exhibited before. She knew she had only herself to blame. Her activities these past two years had been beyond questionable. He would know whom she'd aligned herself with, and he would wonder.

"I flew in just today. I didn't know about this little soirée until Kennedy mentioned it."

Both were truths, which she had learned was the easiest way to avoid trouble. Lying about the small things could cause major problems with the bigger things later on.

"It's been a while."

"Yes. Much too long." Wanting to get past the awkwardness and suspicion, she turned to Eli's wife. "You must be Kathleen. It's lovely to meet you at last."

Flashing her a beautiful smile, Kathleen didn't seem to have the same concerns as her husband. "It's wonderful to meet you, too. I've heard so much about you from Kennedy and Lacey."

"Maybe we can have lunch soon. Get better acquainted." She glanced around at the small crowd. "I'm looking for Grey. Have you seen him?"

"Do you know the reason behind this event?" Eli's voice held a tinge of suspicion.

"Yes. And I'm here to help."

"I believe Grey's got this covered."

That was what he thought, but he had no idea there was more to this than met the eye.

"I'm sure he does, but—"

"Irelyn, what the hell are you doing here?"

Bracing herself for his anger, she turned to see Grey standing in the lobby with that look on his face that could melt her like nothing else. Only Grey Justice could do furious and sexy with such elegance.

"I came to help."

He reached for her hand and pulled her close. "If you'll excuse us, Irelyn and I need to talk."

He gave her no time to do more than nod before he pulled her into a small, private corner.

"What are you doing here? You should be in bed."

"I couldn't stay there. And don't get me started on how furious I am with you. Dammit, Justice, you drugged me."

"I sure as hell did," he growled, "and I'd do it again if I had to."

"You had no right."

Grabbing her shoulders, he shook her gently. "Irelyn, only a few hours ago, you passed out in my arms, and then you threatened to leave. What was I supposed to do?"

"Trust me?"

"Trust you? You're asking a lot considering what you've been doing for the past two years."

Irelyn closed her eyes in frustration. They'd gotten completely off the topic. "We can talk about that later. I know why you're here. Kennedy told me what you have planned. I need to tell you—"

"Wait." He pressed his fingers to his ear, indicating he had an earbud and was listening to someone.

"You're sure?" he asked.

While she listened to Grey's one-sided conversation, her eyes swept the lobby behind them. While one part of her mind was taking in the beautiful interior, she was looking for a killer. There were about a dozen or more people in the lobby, and all were GJG employees. The assassin wouldn't strike here. Too many people to get in the way. He would want a more private place where he could do the job and then slip out without being noticed.

"I've got to go," Grey said. "They've caught him."

Relief made her already weak knees turn to jelly. She hadn't dared believe it could be that easy. "I need to go with you. I need to talk to—"

"No. What you need to do is go home and go back to bed. I can't believe you came here. You've got to be as weak as a kitten."

She didn't tell him that she was properly motivated. Ensuring he stayed safe would always come before her health. And this time, there was an additional reason she'd needed to be here.

"Grey, you don't understand. I need—"

"Irelyn, please." Surprising her, he leaned his forehead against hers and whispered, "Do this one thing for me. I promise that when I get home, we'll sort it all out."

"Okay," she whispered. As she watched him stride away, she huffed out a sigh. Arguing was pointless and would only delay him. She had come here for a purpose. It was imperative that she be there when they interviewed the assassin.

Watching him go up a small staircase, she followed Grey at a distance. When he walked out onto the stage, she was only a few steps behind. From what she could remember, there were offices on the other side. This was probably where they were holding the assassin.

A noise, softer than a whisper, sounded. The blood-red curtain covering the screen fluttered, and the muzzle of a gun appeared.

"Grey!" she screamed.

Pop. Pop. Pop.

Irelyn watched in horror as her worst nightmare came true. Grey fell forward as three bullets hit him in the back.

Please be wearing a vest...please, please, please be wearing a vest.

The assassin emerged from behind the curtain. His face devoid of all emotion, he ignored her as he walked to his prey. She knew the drill. He would take a headshot to ensure success.

Gun in hand, she called out "Kevin!"

The man jerked, as if surprised she knew his name. Recognition and something like amusement gleamed in his eyes. A small smile stretched his mouth into a smirk. The gun in his hand switched directions and was now pointing at her.

"Hello, Irelyn. Long time no see."

She lowered her own weapon and spoke softly, gently, "Kevin. You don't want to do this."

"Oh, but I do."

They froze like that for a moment. She searched for the right words, anything that would break through the years of training and abuse she knew he had endured. Familiar gray eyes stared into her own, and she swore she had made a connection. She gave him the only words she could come up with. "I'm so sorry, Kevin."

His head tilted, and confusion flickered on his face. Had she reached him? Would he—

As if he realized he'd shown a weakness, his face went blank once more.

Every instinct in her body told her to raise her own weapon. Instead, she stood frozen, watching as he steadied the weapon in his hand and aimed it, center-mass, at her.

"Irelyn!"

Grey's voice sent relief through her bloodstream. *Thank you, God.* He was all right.

Anger and something like betrayal flickered in Kevin's eyes. He whirled back around to Grey again.

"Kevin! No!"

"Stop!" several voices shouted at once.

The shooter looked around, saw five elegantly dressed people all pointing weapons at him. Shrugging, he held up his hands.

"Drop your weapon!" Nick shouted.

He dropped his gun.

"Now, put your hands behind your head, get on your knees."

He bent his knees, getting ready to kneel. In a flash, another gun appeared in his hand, and he shot at Grey.

"No!" Irelyn screamed as she fired her weapon. She didn't wait to see the man fall as she ran to Grey. Her eyes quickly roamed over him, searching for signs that he'd been hit.

Wrapping his hands around her waist, Grey whirled her around, putting her behind him. "I'm fine. I'm wearing a vest. He missed the second time."

Shivering in reaction, she peered over Grey's shoulder. Nick, Jonah, and Kathleen stood over the fallen man. She didn't need to ask if he was dead. She was a killer. She knew how to get the job done.

If she'd had more time, perhaps she could have winged him. Would that have made a difference? Assassins were taught to ignore pain, to do whatever it took to accomplish their mission. With his last breath, he would have taken another shot. But still her mind reviewed her choices. Would winging him have worked? She would never know. Her only thought had been to protect Grey.

"He's dead," Jonah said.

The man she had never known but had known all the same. Another person she should have been able to save and couldn't. Sadness as she hadn't felt in years swept through her.

Grey turned to her then, hiding her from everyone's eyes. "You're okay?"

"Yes."

He shook her shoulders slightly. "What were you thinking? He could have killed you."

She shook her head, unable to explain what had been going on in her mind. To describe the numbness that was spreading through her body.

"Irelyn?" His hand gently cupped her chin, tilting her head up. "You called him Kevin. You knew him?"

She nodded slowly.

"Who was he?"

"My brother," she whispered. "He was my brother."

CHAPTER EIGHTEEN

His hand on the small of her back, Grey gently ushered Irelyn into the apartment. She had been quiet since they'd left the theater. He knew she was in shock, exhausted and hurting, both physically and emotionally. He hadn't pushed her. She needed gentleness and care, not questions.

She pulled away from him. "I need to take a shower."

Intending to help her, he said, "All right," and walked with her toward her bedroom.

Without looking at him, she said in a too-distant voice, "I can do it. I'd...like to be alone for a while."

"Irelyn, look at me."

She raised her gaze then, and he felt a punch to his gut. The depth of pain in her eyes clawed at him. She had saved his life tonight and in the process had killed the only family she had.

"I'm so sorry." He had no other words he could say.

She nodded. "I know. I am, too." Clearing her throat, she darted a look to her bedroom door. "I'll be okay. Just need a moment alone."

"I'll make us some tea."

She didn't acknowledge his words, and he wasn't even sure she'd heard him. Her main focus was getting behind those doors so she could be alone. Before she disappeared into her bedroom, he said, "Thank you for saving my life."

The look she sent him spoke volumes, but her words almost brought him to his knees.

"I'd do it again if I had to." She closed the door.

He took a step toward the door and then made himself stop. Hell yes, he wanted to follow her. He wanted to hold her, comfort her, let her cry in his arms. But he also knew how important control was for Irelyn. He would respect her privacy for now.

He wasn't sure who needed to be held more, him or Irelyn. He could have so easily lost her tonight. She had stood there, motionless, watching as the shooter aimed directly at her. If Grey hadn't called out, the bastard would have killed her. He had no doubt about that.

He still didn't know how or why she thought the man was her brother, although he had seen a slight family resemblance, but it was obvious there had been no brotherly love for her.

Rubbing the tension at the back of his neck, Grey headed to the kitchen. While he prepared tea, he reviewed the night's events. They sure as hell hadn't gone down the way he had planned.

The assassin had waited until the movie ended. Grey had sat up front, alone, and waited. Apparently, the killer had been waiting, too. The man his people had caught and detained was no one other than a guy looking to see a movie for free. Little had he known that he had fallen into a trap set for an assassin. The guy had likely learned his lesson and wouldn't be doing that again.

Since it had obviously been a justified shooting—Grey had three holes in his tuxedo jacket and some ugly bruises on his back as proof—the questions from the police had been routine. The knowledge that someone had tried to kill him already had gone a long way in shutting down suspicion of anything other than self-defense.

Grey had left Gallagher in charge of cleanup. He had wanted to get Irelyn out of there as soon as possible. Though her answers to the police had been coherent and precise, he had recognized that she had put herself somewhere else until she could be alone.

Liberally lacing both teas with sugar and Irelyn's favorite whiskey, he carried two mugs to her room. He knocked, and after hearing her say, "Come in," he opened the door.

She was sitting on the edge of the bed, hair caught up in a messy knot. She wore no makeup and had on her favorite blue fuzzy robe. He found himself struck, as he often was, by her incredible, natural loveliness.

The droop of her mouth and her slumped shoulders told him something else. She was devastated. Though the heat of the shower had brought some color to her face, she was still too pale for his liking.

He handed her the cup of steaming tea, and then, pulling the chair from her vanity, he sat in front of her.

She stared down at the tea but didn't drink it, and Grey figured he knew why. "It's not drugged. Just added a bit of Irish to warm you."

She nodded and took her first swallow.

He waited till she'd downed several sips. When she settled the mug on the bedside table, he took that as a cue.

"Feel better?"

"A little. Thank you."

"Feel up to talking?"

"Yes. I guess I owe you an explanation. Several, actually."

"I want to hear it all." One particular question was

hammering at his head and his heart, and he had to know. "Why didn't you tell me?"

"I didn't even know I had a brother."

Coming from anyone else, that might have sounded strange. But he knew Irelyn's history. What she had been through. Not knowing she had a brother was completely plausible.

"When did you find out?"

"The night I killed Hill. He told me in a casual manner. As if it was just a bit of news I might be interested in knowing. As if it meant nothing."

"You don't remember him?"

"No. As you know, most of my life before Hill is just a blur of senses—smells, fear, hunger. I have no recall of a brother, or anyone else."

They had been down this road so many times before. He wished to his soul that he could change her past—give her some good memories. All she had was the horror of the truth. Purchased by Hill Reed from a drug-addicted woman who might or might not have been her mother. If Reed hadn't bought her, she would have likely died in the streets or been sold to another monster. Instead, she had been taken into a house filled with killers and thrown into another kind of hell.

"And Reed made him into an assassin."

"Yes. Just like me."

"No, baby, not just like you."

She looked at him then, pain so intense in her gray eyes they appeared almost black. "Why not like me, Grey? I am what he made me."

"You damn well are not. Let's not go down this path again, Irelyn. You left that life a long time ago."

"Did I?"

Grey rubbed his gritty eyes. Damn, he was tired, but he

could not let this go. She had killed her brother tonight to save his life.

"Are you sure Reed didn't lie?" The bastard had certainly been capable of it. From all he knew about Hill Reed, one of his greatest joys had been screwing with people's emotions and minds.

"That was my hope for a while, but the more I thought about it, the more I decided it wouldn't have made sense for him to lie. Yes, if he thought it would hurt me, or elicit a desired response, he would have. But that's not the way the conversation went. It was…" Her hands fluttered as she tried to explain. "It was just a little aside. Like an 'Oh, by the way, I stopped at the bakery and bought some bagels' kind of remark. Like it really wasn't that important." She shrugged. "I believed him."

"Did you try to contact Kevin when you found out? Try to talk to him?"

"No. I had no idea who he was. Didn't even know his name then."

"The bastard wouldn't tell you?"

"He didn't get the chance. He—"

"That's why you were giving him CPR."

"He dropped several bombshells in a row. Admitted he had nothing to do with Jonah's supposed death and told me my brother was working as an assassin for him." She shrugged. "I don't know if he would have told me his name. He probably wouldn't have if he knew how very badly I wanted to know."

"That's what you've been working on all this time. Why you killed those assassins. Why you wanted to get Sebastian Dark's attention. You needed to get back inside Hill House to find your brother."

"I knew Dark wouldn't let me in, especially not to stay there for any length of time. It was the only thing I could think to do to impress him, to get him to invite me to stay. I had to prove myself."

"And you couldn't kill any of his people since you didn't know which one was your brother."

"I couldn't have anyway. That would've just pissed Dark off. I tried to choose the most hideous killers."

"The ones who targeted children."

"Yes."

"Do you think Kevin recognized you?"

"I think so. He called me Irelyn. And I saw a glimmer of recognition, an acknowledgment maybe, of our connection. I think I remember him from my time at Hill House. I think I saw him. I don't know. I just don't know."

Grey closed his eyes. Shit, this was so messed up. "I would do anything to take away that pain."

"I know you would, Grey." She rubbed her forehead, and he noted her hands were shaking. She was on the edge.

"Do you want me to call Dr. Tobin?"

The therapist had helped Irelyn immensely and wouldn't be at all surprised to hear from her in the middle of the night.

"Why? So she can tell me again that I have nothing to feel guilty about?"

"He would have killed me, Irelyn. You saved my life. Do you regret that?"

"No. Of course I don't."

He had known the answer to that, but hoped to help her with some perspective. Even as volatile and unusual as their relationship was at times, he knew her feelings for him were deep. Their emotional bond had been honed by blood and death, but their relationship was also the truest, most honest one he'd ever possessed. Even in the midst of unimaginable pain, they had an unbreakable bond. She had tried to sever their connection, and now he knew why.

Everything was making sense again, but he couldn't get past one issue. "Why didn't you tell me? I would have helped."

"And that's exactly why. I just...I just..." She rubbed her forehead again. "I need some sleep. I can't think straight."

Meaning her defenses were down and she was likely to be completely honest. His head told him to push her and find out everything. Even though they had few secrets between them, Irelyn was so multifaceted that there were times when he had no clue what was going on in her beautiful head. His heart told him something else. She had been through too much. Hell, he still didn't know how she'd been injured. Cutting her some slack and letting her rest seemed a small allowance. He'd have to tear down the walls again tomorrow, but that was another day.

Standing, he reached for her mug on the nightstand. It was still half full, but it had hopefully given her a little comfort. She surprised him by grabbing his wrist. "Stay with me."

"I wouldn't have it any other way."

Grey returned the mug to the table and slipped off his shoes. He was in the middle of unbuttoning his shirt and stopped, struck by her sensual beauty as she slipped the robe off her shoulders. Other than those short passionate moments in Paris, it had been months since they'd kissed, even longer since they'd made love. He wanted her with a longing that went a million times past physical desire. That need would have to be put on hold. Holding her all night long had its own rewards.

The instant they slid beneath the covers, she went into his arms. Closing them around her, he held her gently, tenderly. Her body was sore, and her heart was broken. He wanted to fix everything in her life that had hurt her, but knew that was a useless want. So he did the only thing he could do. He held her, treasuring that he could.

CHAPTER NINETEEN

She couldn't sleep. Every time she closed her eyes, she saw her brother's body fall. Felt the kick of her gun as the bullet left the chamber. Saw the blood, felt the darkness of death enshroud her.

She'd finally found her brother only to end up killing him to save the man she loved. If it wasn't so damned painful, she might laugh. She was living her very own Shakespearean tragedy.

What she had told Grey was the truth. Hill Reed, killer and purveyor of all evil things, had told her about her brother that night. Though the manner of Reed's death had already been planned, she had come close to ending him in a different way. He had been the one to teach her how to shoot. It seemed only right that he should reap the rewards for all those painstaking lessons.

Of course, she hadn't done anything of the sort. Killing him in that manner would have completely spoiled their cover story. Minutes after Reed's death, his body had been wrapped and then loaded onto a van, ready to be transported thousands of miles away from Dallas. She also knew she would likely have hesitated at the last minute. If she had, Hill would have sensed that hesitation, and she would be dead instead. Hill Reed had never hesitated when it came to a kill, not even for someone he'd raised as a daughter.

She shifted slightly and felt Grey's arms tighten around her. She could have lost him. The fact that she had killed her brother to save him was the epitome of irony and the very definition of karma. But just because that was what she'd deserved didn't make it any less painful.

"Can't sleep?"

A wave of heat swept through her at Grey's sleep-gruff voice. No matter what the circumstance, Grey could move her unlike anyone else. She wanted nothing more than to sink into his arms and forget the world.

"Do you think what happened was karma?"

"Don't, baby. Don't go there."

"You have to admit it seems fitting. I took your parents, and now the only family I had left is dead because of—"

"Because you saved my life."

She rolled over in his arms and buried her face against his warm, hard chest. "Losing you would have destroyed me."

"Just as losing you would do the same to me."

She smiled against his skin. "We're joined at the hip…we two."

"Like two peas in a pod."

"Macaroni and cheese."

"Chicken and dumplings."

"I'm a vegetarian."

"Then you can be the dumpling."

She laughed through the threatening tears. This was an old game. Silly and frivolous, but it brought back good memories. She needed those memories tonight.

"I've missed you," she whispered.

"I've been here, waiting for you."

"You know why I had to leave."

His hands, large and more lethal than anyone could imagine, were gentle as he pulled her away from his chest. Even though it was still dark, the outline of his body was sizable and should have been forbidding. But it had been a long time since she'd been afraid of Grey. She knew he would never physically hurt her, even in his most fierce anger.

"After Reed's death, yes, I understood. But you were away too long this time."

"I didn't plan to come back."

"I know that, too. I just don't know why."

"Because I—" Articulating something that she barely understood herself was beyond her ability tonight.

"Can we talk about it tomorrow? Can you just hold me tonight?"

"Of course. Whatever you want."

Tears sprang to her eyes. Grey's tenderness was a well-hidden secret. Many people knew about his quest for justice and his resolve to protect the innocent. No one other than she knew about his gentleness and his romantic heart. His occasional silly side could have her in stitches. Multifaceted and fascinating, Grey Justice could infuriate her one moment and melt her heart the next.

The tears began to roll, and she didn't try to stop them. She rarely cried. In Hill Reed's world, showing vulnerabilities had equated to weakness. She had learned to control her tears. Grey was the only one she had ever allowed to see them.

Sobs built up until, finally, she let go. Burrowing into his warmth, she allowed the sadness to wash over and through her. For almost two years, she had focused on identifying and finding her brother. Just because she didn't remember him didn't mean she didn't want to meet him, get to know him. The moment his eyes, so very much like her own, had met hers, she had seen their emptiness. He had become a soulless creature, like so many of Reed's students. Could she have reached him? Saved him? She would never know.

"Shh. Irelyn, darling, I'm here. I'm here." Grey's soothing voice broke through, and she realized she was saying Grey's name over and over.

"It's so silly to cry over something I never even had. I just…" She shook her head. "I wanted to give him the same chance you gave me."

"I know, baby. I wish you could have, too."

"Let's not talk…not tonight." She put her mouth on his. "Tonight…just tonight. Let's be us again. Irelyn and Grey. Let the world disappear."

She could feel the controlled strength in him as he growled, "You're not too sore? I don't want to hurt you."

"You won't. You couldn't." Her mouth pressed hotly against the warmth of his naked chest. "I'm empty without you."

Propping himself up on his forearm, he said softly, "Then let's see what we can do about that."

Grey started out slow. His body, hard and throbbing, urged him to ignore everything other than the need for release. It had been so damn long, and he had missed her, missed this, so damn much. None of that mattered now. Irelyn was in his arms where she belonged. She needed him, his comfort, his strength. He would give her whatever she desired.

Gently, he kissed her neck, her face, tenderly exploring, always moving. Irelyn was a passionate, generous lover, but tonight he wanted her to lie back and let him give her the pleasure she deserved. He wanted the shadows in her eyes to disappear. He wanted to ease her heartbreak.

When she tried to put her arms around him, he pressed

them down. "Let me love you, darling. Close your eyes and relax. Let the world fall away."

He could feel the tenseness in her as she fought her natural instincts. She wanted to give, participate. He'd gladly accept her participation another time. Tonight was for Irelyn, for her pleasure. He wanted her to take.

Skin, hot and silky soft, fragrant from her shower, tasted sweet against his tongue. He started with a trail of kisses down her long, slender neck, then moved down her body, stopping at succulent sweet spots, nipping and licking. Gasping out breaths of arousal and need, Irelyn arched her body on a cry as he covered her nipple with his mouth and suckled hard. A hundred years, or a thousand, would never be enough time to spend making love to his beautiful, sexy temptress.

"Grey...I need..."

"Shh. I know what you need. Let me give you that." His mouth moved lower, loving her needy sounds. Her hands caressed his head, her fingers combing through his hair as she urged him on. He circled her belly button with his tongue, whispered against her warm, taut stomach. "I've missed you...your taste."

"Missed you, too. So much."

When he moved lower, she opened her legs with a welcoming sob. Glorying in her scent, her taste, Grey kissed then gently lapped at her. When he felt the surrender as her body gave itself up to the pleasure, he allowed himself to indulge. Thrust after thrust with his tongue until her body stiffened and she cried out his name.

He held her for a long while afterward, listened to the soft sounds of her sleeping, treasuring her.

Irelyn put herself at risk more times than he cared to remember. Most of the work she did with the Grey Justice Group involved strategic planning and training. She was an invaluable member of the group, and they missed her expertise. But Irelyn never felt like she was doing enough. From firsthand experience, she knew about abuse and neglect, of injustice. She often took it upon herself to right those wrongs, in her own way. He aided her when he could, always supporting her need to do more. But tonight, he could have lost her—that had come home to him more than at any other time. If he had, his life would never have been the same. Did she know that? Did she have any idea what she meant to him?

Exhausted in mind and body, he felt himself finally drifting off and tightened his arms around the warm woman beside him. She was home at last.

CHAPTER TWENTY

Alone in his study, Grey listened to the predawn quiet of the city he'd come to love and admire. When he and Irelyn had arrived in Dallas, they'd possessed little more than their dreams and the clothes on their backs. They'd both worked their asses off to create their empire. Even though the Grey Justice name was the recognizable brand, he would not have been as successful without Irelyn. She was a combination of intelligence, wisdom, and incredible strength of will. Through sheer perseverance, she had overcome so much.

He remembered their first meeting as if it were yesterday. He'd been all of seventeen, a little on the shy side, with a head full of so many dreams he could scarcely contain them. His parents had been the finest people he'd ever known, but they hadn't understood his need to break away from tradition. Generations before him had stood for justice and equality. To have their only son want to do something different not only bewildered them, it also frightened them. Breaking away from what they'd always known—duty, honor, and service—was foreign to them.

Looking back, he could understand their reservations, and he wished he'd been able to ease their concerns. He hadn't wanted to reject their core beliefs, he'd just wanted to go about them in another way.

If he had listened to his parents, followed their lead, they might still be alive. That hurt more than anyone could fathom. But he had wanted to go his own way, do good in different ways. In the end, they'd all paid a terrible price.

Irelyn, with her uncanny talent, had read him like the proverbial book. Even at fifteen, she had been a beauty. He had fallen hard, as had been the plan. He had been so easily manipulated, so transparent. So damn naïve. He had seen a lovely young woman who needed help and had been ensnared in her trap as effortlessly and quickly as a mouse.

His parents had fallen for her, too. Two people who had seen every trap and had survived the unimaginable had been duped by a fifteen-year-old con artist. Irelyn was just that good.

"Did you get any sleep?"

She stood in the doorway, an apparition and a dream. So many things had changed since that first meeting, but his fascination and need for her had never wavered.

"Some." He held out his hand. "How are you feeling?"

Not moving from the door, she shrugged. "Fine. A little tired, a lot sore. Nothing that a few days of rest can't fix."

She was back to being wary again. Last night, need and desire had consumed them, reuniting them in a tender reunion of both body and mind. He'd woken this morning, not physically sated, but optimistic that they were headed in the right direction. Apparently, she wasn't of the same mind.

And she was far from fine. Both the cut on her side and leg had required several stitches. The bruise on her face had darkened, as had the marks around her neck, indicating someone had tried to choke her. She had to be hurting. That pain was likely nothing, though, compared to the emotional trauma from last night.

He knew she had slept some, but she was still too pale. The ugly bruise on her jaw was a stark contrast against her ghost-white skin. Shadows lurked beneath her eyes, and her mouth drooped at the corners. He wanted to go to her, take her in his arms, and assure her everything was going to be okay. But platitudes were not his thing, nor were they hers. They dealt in reality. And the reality was, they had a huge chasm between them. The next few minutes were not going to be easy ones.

Wishing things could be different, he said, "We need to talk."

"I know. Mind if I have some coffee first?"

He stood and went to the coffee bar. "Want anything to eat?"

"No. Coffee's fine."

He'd make sure they both had something substantial later. For now, caffeine would have to see them through this.

She went to the sofa and eased down onto the cushion. Handing her a cup of coffee, fixed the way she liked it, he waited until she'd taken a few sips. In his opinion, springing hard questions on anyone without the benefit of caffeine in their system was barbaric.

When her eyes were a bit more clear, he said, his tone gentle but resolute, "All right, Irelyn. Let's talk. Why didn't you tell me about your brother?"

IRELYN TOOK ANOTHER BRACING SWALLOW OF COFFEE, A delaying tactic while her mind raced to pull herself out of the grief she'd woken with this morning. Grey would understandably give her only so much leeway.

Though her body still ached, her heart ached even more.

171

She had learned that some things take years to overcome. This would be one of those things. Not remembering that she had a brother was excruciatingly painful. Killing him was far worse. There had been no choice for her. Grey would always be her first priority. She only wished she had been able to save Kevin as well. But she'd seen his eyes. They had been as empty as those of Hill Reed, the man who made him into a killer.

Grey deserved answers to all his questions, but for the life of her, she was having trouble finding the right starting place.

"I'm waiting."

That icy tone helped. "Very well. What I did to Hill that night. What you insisted I do…I just…I couldn't deal with it."

"We've had this discussion before. I thought you said I couldn't force you to do anything."

Not a flicker of regret appeared on his face. She hadn't really expected one. Why would he regret something that should have happened years ago? Still, the knowledge that he wasn't the least bit sorry fueled her anger and her words.

"That doesn't mean I wasn't hurt or damaged by it, Grey. For heaven's sake, he was like a father to me."

"Bollocks," he snapped. "A father doesn't torture and cause pain, Irelyn. A father doesn't rape his child. A father does not make her kill."

"I know that. Don't you think I know that?" She sprang to her feet, started pacing. How could she explain something to him when she barely understood it herself?

"Hill Reed deserved to die. I, more than anyone, should have wanted him dead. And I did want him dead. I just—"

"What? Dammit, just spit it out, Irelyn."

She whirled around, intending to shout the truth at him, but her words came out as a hoarse whisper. "For the first time ever, you treated me like the killer he trained me to be."

Grey closed his eyes, and she saw the regret he hadn't revealed before. "I'm sorry for that. More than you'll ever know. It's definitely not what I intended. You have never and will never be the killer he tried to make you.

"I can only say this so many times, Irelyn. The man needed to die. And there's no one who deserved to do the killing more than you did."

"You knew all along that Reed had nothing to do with Jonah's supposed death. You knew he was still alive."

"Yes."

"And you didn't tell me. Why?"

"Because I knew you would find excuses to not go through with it." Before she could respond, he said, "Let me ask you this. Do you think the killing would have stopped if we had tried to have him arrested, tried the legal route?"

Of course it wouldn't have stopped him. They both knew that. Even if a prosecutor had been able to stay alive long enough to prove Hill Reed's guilt, the man would have continued to wreak havoc on the innocent. He had the money and influence to run a full-fledged kill factory out of a prison. Killing him had been the only way to stop him.

Apparently seeing the answer in her face, Grey continued, "The bastard needed to die before he could destroy more lives."

"You're right. I just…" She took a breath, continued pacing. "I had to get away from you. To mourn, grieve. To deal with the fact that I was so incredibly grateful that he was dead. And that I had been the one to kill him." She threw him a twisted smile. "Sorrow and elation are a tough combination to deal with."

"Did you talk to Dr. Tobin about it?"

She took a moment to be thankful that he didn't know that she had visited her therapist before she left Dallas that day. Sheila Tobin knew the truth of everything—the past and the present. Irelyn trusted her almost as much as she trusted Grey. That meant nothing when it came to Grey's need to know something. She'd often thought that Dr. Tobin saw her and Grey as one patient. They were that connected.

"Yes, I did. It helped to be able to articulate what I was feeling."

"You could have talked to me."

No, she couldn't have. She'd been too messed up at that time, and Grey would have been as implacable as he was now.

"I needed to deal with it on my own, in my own way."

"When did you decide you were going to find your brother?"

"From the moment Reed told me about him, I knew I had to find him."

"And you never thought to come to me? To let me help?"

"Help with what, Grey?"

"Finding your brother without risking your life. That's what."

"I didn't want to involve you."

"Did you think I would kill him?"

"I didn't know. I didn't want you to have to make that choice."

"You said last night that you wanted to try to save him, change him."

"It wouldn't have been impossible. You saved me. I changed."

"You changed yourself. Not me. You were never what Reed tried to make you. He might've damaged you, but he never corrupted your soul."

She wasn't so sure about that, but there was no point in going down that rabbit hole again.

"Kevin was—"

"Empty. You saw it, Irelyn. Don't tell me you didn't. His

eyes were as blank and soulless as a robot's. He would've killed you without hesitation."

She couldn't argue. She had seen that emptiness—and something else, too...something evil. He would have enjoyed killing her.

"I'm sorry you couldn't save him."

"Are you?"

"Yes. Despite our past, I would have liked for you to have family."

She knew that was true. Yet, she had doubted him all the same. Grey had a right to want everyone she cared about dead. How odd was it that he was the one she cared about the most?

"I shouldn't have doubted you. I just—"

"You stopped trusting me."

He said the words so matter-of-factly that anyone else would have thought it meant nothing to him. But she wasn't *anyone else*. She knew this man too well not to recognize his pain. Her distrust hurt him.

"Yes."

"What can I do to regain your trust?"

She wanted to say he already had. She wanted to take that grim look off his face, remove the darkness from his eyes. Lying to him, even to make him feel better, would be worse.

"I don't know."

He nodded. "Very well. While we work that out, I'd like to ask a favor. Stay with me, work with me to find out who's behind the attempts on my life."

That should be an easy promise to make. There was nowhere in the world she wanted to be more than with Grey. Whether she was here or somewhere else, her total focus would be on finding the person who wanted Grey dead. Still, she couldn't make the promise completely. Depending on what they found out, she might need to leave again.

"All right. I'll stay…for now."

Based on the relief on his face, he hadn't been sure of her answer. It hurt that there was this awkwardness and uncertainty in their relationship now. Even as much as they often warred with each other, they'd always communicated with ease. But their connection was damaged. They'd been struggling before that last painful break, when she'd ended Reed's life. Killing him had been the catalyst, but their troubles were brewing long before that.

She knew when it happened, remembered the day well. The saddest part was that he wouldn't remember. Out of the thousand things Grey did each day, this one hadn't even registered. To Irelyn, that one moment had defined who they were together and what their future looked like. Things had spiraled downhill after that.

Grey had no idea she was such a coward. If she had the courage he often attributed to her, she would have told him the truth and got it out there once and for all. Problem was, she knew he would confirm her deepest fear. So she had created this distance between them, and she saw no way out.

Pushing that pain aside, she asked, "So, what's the plan?"

"There's a meeting here at noon today."

"All right."

"Why don't you stick around the apartment this morning?"

"I will if you will."

The smile he gave her told her that had been his plan all along.

"Do you have a list of suspects you've been working with? I'd like to take a look at it, be prepared."

"I'll send it to you. But first, how about some breakfast? We both missed dinner last night."

"Sounds good."

Standing, he held out his hand. "Let's make it together, like we used to."

She accepted his hand and followed him into the kitchen. Nothing would ever be the way it used to be, but for now she would take what she could get.

CHAPTER TWENTY-ONE

Hill House
England

Sebastian smiled as the news reports from last night's event flashed across the screen. Just a scrolling ticker at the bottom, but that was to be expected. Grey Justice knew how to cover up his sins, even from the nosiest of media outlets.

It hadn't turned out exactly as he'd planned, but he'd take it as a win. Despite the death of one of his best contractors, everything was still on track. While Kevin's death was unfortunate, there were advantages. For one, it confirmed what he had known all along. Irelyn Raine had been on a fishing expedition when she had agreed to return to Hill House. She hadn't been looking to become a premier assassin, as she had claimed. She had wanted information. He had expected that was the case, but was disappointed all the same. Predictability was so passé.

She hadn't told him the truth. For that alone, he would cheerfully kill her. Yes, he told lies for a living, but that was

part of the job. Being lied to was a different animal altogether. He punished liars, and Irelyn would receive her
punishment in due time. She had so many sins to pay for,
and he couldn't wait to show her each and every one
of them.

But exposing Irelyn for who she really was wouldn't be
the only benefit. She had gone to *him*. To Justice.

A day of reckoning was coming for them both. Then real
justice would finally be attained. And he, Sebastian Dark,
would be the one meting out his very own brand.

Blood for blood.

Dallas, Texas

IRELYN HAD ATTENDED MANY GJG OP MEETINGS. SHE'D EVEN
headed up several of them. This was the first one in her
memory that she felt like an outsider. The hostility was
muted, but the suspicion was overt. They no longer trusted
her as one of their own.

She knew all six of them in varying degrees. She had
worked one-on-one with both Kennedy and Charlie. She had
become acquainted with Jonah Slater when he had worked
with them to help bring down his father, Mathias. Later,
when Jonah had been framed and imprisoned, she had
helped to try to free him. The fact that she had killed the
assassin who'd murdered his fiancée was a bone of
contention between them. He had wanted to do the deed, to
get his revenge. She took that opportunity away from him,
and he likely still resented her interference. She had no
regrets.

She didn't know Gabriella, Jonah's wife, nor had she
worked with Kathleen, Eli's wife, but Grey didn't bring

people into the group he couldn't wholly trust. She trusted his judgment.

And then there was Nick Gallagher. While everyone else had offered her a greeting or, at the least, a polite smile, Nick had done nothing but stare at her with suspicious eyes. Since he was a former homicide detective, the distrust was likely second nature for him.

She told herself the pain in her chest wasn't from hurt feelings. She didn't have those typical kinds of emotions. Nevertheless, she would be working with all of these people until the person behind the contract could be identified and dealt with. They might never like her or even respect her again, but they did need to trust her in this matter.

She waited until everyone was seated at the conference table and then stood. "I'd like to address the group before we begin."

Grey nodded his agreement. He'd recognized the tension, too. One of the many things she appreciated about Grey was his ability to stand back and let her defend herself, both physically or verbally.

"I know you're wondering where I've been and what I've been up to the last couple of years. I'm sure you've heard rumors and speculation. Some are true, some aren't. I won't go into a lot of detail except to say that not once have I betrayed Grey or the Grey Justice Group. Some of you might not approve of what I've done, but know this—there is no one more important to me than Grey. And nothing more important than finding out who is behind the attempts on his life and stopping him or her from succeeding."

This was the closest she'd ever come to sharing with anyone, other than Grey, how much he meant to her. She didn't expect to have to expound on those words, but wasn't really surprised at the next question, or who it came from.

"Stopping him or her how?" Nick asked.

Nick didn't try to hide his disapproval or distrust, and she wouldn't hide who she was. "Any way that's necessary."

"The way you stopped the man last night?"

"If necessary. Are you saying I shouldn't have killed him?"

"We wanted to capture him, to talk to him."

"Sorry, I thought saving Grey's life was a bit more important."

He ignored her sarcasm and continued, "I'm just wondering how likely you are to shoot first and ask questions later."

"Seeing as the man was about to shoot Grey, I didn't see an alternative."

"And the other ones you've eliminated over the last couple of years? Were they also not in a talkative mood?"

Explaining herself to anyone didn't sit well with her. She had shared more than she normally would have, but there was a limit. Before she could tell him that she was through justifying her actions, a surprising ally spoke up for her.

"That's enough, Nick," Kennedy said. "Irelyn has proven herself and her loyalty numerous times. You said yourself that she saved Grey's life last night. And what she has or hasn't been doing is her business, too."

"Maybe so, but she damn well owes you an apology for running out on you last night."

Eyes flashing at her husband, Kennedy shot back, "That's between her and me. I don't—"

"Nick's right, Kennedy," Irelyn said. "I do owe you an apology. I—"

Kennedy shook her head, gave her a warm smile. "We'll talk later."

"You called out his name."

"What?" The question caught her off guard. Turning away from Kennedy and her kind smile, she focused on Kathleen Slater.

"Last night. Things happened so fast, it was hard to process everything until later, but I heard you say his name. You called him Kevin. Did you know him?"

Kennedy's easy forgiveness didn't extend to the rest of the group. If she was going to gain their trust, she knew she would have to explain further. If she had to share more than she was comfortable with, that was her price to pay. There were still things she wouldn't tell. Revealing that the man she killed last night was her brother was one of them.

"Kevin was a member of an elite team of assassins trained by Hill Reed."

"The man responsible for Thomas's murder?" Kennedy asked.

"Yes. Hill Reed was a master manipulator and trainer. He trained dozens of killers. Kevin was one of them."

"And you know this how?" Nick asked.

She glanced over at Grey. The look on his face said she had his full support, no matter what she chose to share. Irelyn took a breath and answered, "Because I used to be one of them. Hill Reed trained me, too."

Under different circumstances, the silence in the room would have been funny. With the exception of Grey's, everyone else's expressions showed either shock or disbelief.

"You were an assassin?" Kathleen asked.

"No. At least—" She stole a look at Grey and then said firmly, "No. I'm not. But I did rejoin the association to root out some information."

"What kind of information?" Jonah asked.

That was going into territory she deemed none of their business. "Personal things. They're not pertinent to what we're talking about here. Bottom line, I am here to help. You may not like me or like what I've done, that's your prerogative. Either way, I'm here to stay until we find the person behind the contract."

Unable to stay seated any longer, Grey came to stand beside Irelyn. His natural instinct was to protect her. Defending her was as normal to him as breathing. He also knew she would want to handle the matter in her own way and wouldn't appreciate his interference. Irelyn could take care of herself, but that didn't mean he didn't want to butt in and defend her. His jaw was taut with the need to demand that they trust her as much as he did.

"In case anyone has doubts, I want to make my position perfectly clear." His eyes hit on everyone in the room, and then he centered his gaze on Gallagher. "I trust Irelyn, wholly, completely. In fact, there's no one I trust more." His eyes roamed around the room again. "Anyone here who disagrees with her working with us to find this person should feel free to leave. No questions asked. There are plenty of other projects to work on."

Everyone remained silent, including Gallagher. Grey hadn't expected anything different. Nick might have his doubts about Irelyn, but his loyalty to the Grey Justice Group and what they stood for was unquestionable.

"Okay. Now that that's settled, let's take a look at what we've got."

The lights dimmed slightly, and a large screen lowered from the ceiling. Thirty-six names appeared on the screen.

"We've narrowed the list down to these men and women," Kennedy said.

Still standing beside him, Irelyn nudged him with her shoulder, gave him a wry grin. "These are the only ones you've managed to piss off enough to want to kill you?"

He returned her grin. "I'm sure there are many more, but these are the ones who can afford to pay someone to do the deed."

"Our criteria was fairly broad," Kennedy said. "Any business or individual who had an association with any Grey Justice company where there might be bad blood or harsh feelings. We went back five years, as you suggested."

Grey nodded his agreement. If anyone was after him because of what they perceived as a bad or unfair deal, it would make sense that it was somewhat recent.

"And those are just the ones we know about," Charlie interjected.

"True," Grey said. "I'm sure there are three times as many who didn't show any outward resentment, but felt it all the same."

That was the nature of doing business. He never dealt unfairly with a competitor, but neither did he back away from doing what he thought was best for his companies. That didn't sit well with some people.

"I'm sure there are more," Grey added, "which is why capturing the hit man would have been our best bet."

"And that didn't happen."

There was no accusation in Nick's tone, but the message was heard nevertheless. Irelyn had killed the one man who might have been able to tell them what they needed to know. Grey wouldn't reveal that the man was her brother. If and when she wanted anyone else to know, that was her right.

Irelyn released a loud, exasperated sigh. "Oh, for heaven's sake, Nick. If I had wanted to betray Grey, wouldn't I have let the assassin kill him?"

Not bothering to wait for an answer, she stood and strode over to the screen. She was silent for several long seconds. Grey knew she had reviewed the list earlier and was likely gathering her thoughts as she culled the most likely suspects.

Because of the bruising and cut on her leg, she had made concessions on her clothing again today. Dressed in a pair of black straight-leg trousers and a thin light blue sweater, she managed to look both casually elegant and professional. The woman, more than the clothes, made that happen.

Feeling a bit on the smug side, Grey settled back in his seat to enjoy himself. This was Irelyn in her element. Where he knew the business side of things, could recognize trends, and knew a winning or losing venture, Irelyn knew people. She could read them, anticipate their actions. She wasn't a psychic, but she was as close to being one as he'd ever seen.

Much of her talent was a natural, God-given ability. Hill Reed had identified that gift early on, then whittled and honed it down for his own evil desires. But she was strong—much stronger than Grey in many respects. She had taken what Reed had taught her, cut the evil away, and through sheer determination, created something good and honorable.

"These three here." She pointed at a grouping of names. "They headed companies that merged the year prior to Grey's purchase. The top executive of each company was given only a meager severance package. When Grey took over, he repaired that retroactively." She turned back to the group. "They need to be removed from this list. They shouldn't be suspects."

Before anyone could comment, she went through the remaining names and gave her opinion on each one, showing not only her knowledge of the Grey Justice corporations, but also that she had intimate knowledge of each business deal.

Grey gazed around the room, noting both surprise and admiration. Even Gallagher seemed suitably impressed.

"These three, Bob Donaldson, Miles Petrie, and Joe Morrissey are the ones you should concentrate your efforts on," she said.

"Why those three?" Kathleen asked.

"What happened with them was while I was away. I wasn't involved in the meetings, so I don't know them. The rest in this bunch were pleased, satisfied. They may have not publicly proclaimed their happiness, but in private, they were happy with the deal they made with Grey. Some were even ecstatic." She threw Grey a laughing glance that looked so much like the old Irelyn, he literally caught his breath. "Remember Mr. Farnsworth, who kept sending you fruit baskets, chocolates, and champagne until you asked him to stop?"

Grey was so mesmerized and focused on Irelyn that he almost missed the shock in Gallagher's eyes. She rarely let down her guard to allow people to see the real Irelyn. He loved that she had allowed a crack in her armor long enough for others to see the woman beneath the veneer.

An unusual wave of longing hit him. He thrived on challenges, enjoyed the thrill of making deals in the business world and pursuing justice in his private world. But he wanted this over with. The threats would never go away completely. As long as he stayed in the public eye, he would always be a target. That was a risk he accepted. But he and Irelyn needed downtime—they needed time to be alone. She had said last night that she wanted them to be just Irelyn and Grey, just for a little while. He damn well wanted that, too.

He went to join Irelyn at the front of the room. "I agree with Irelyn on the three she's pointed out."

She glanced up at him. "Even though I wasn't involved in the meetings, I remember discussing both the Petrie and Donaldson deals with you before I left. I know nothing about Morrissey, though."

Grey nodded. "I thought it was going smoothly but the deal went sour a few months ago. I had the choice of backing out and letting a lot of good people suffer or doing a complete takeover."

"I remember reading about him," Kennedy said. "Didn't he use his employees' pension fund to buy his mistress a house in Italy?"

"He did that and much more. He's under indictment and will likely go to prison. But there were over four hundred employees who didn't deserve to lose their retirement."

Grey had no issues with letting an idiot run his own company into the ground for his own selfish desires. He did, however, have issues with others suffering because of one man's stupidity.

"You bailed his employees out," Nick said.

"Yes. That's not why he's pissed. He couldn't care less about them. He's furious because he knows I alerted the authorities that he was about to flee the country. He was arrested at the airport. He's out on bail now."

"So he's not angry about his business," Gabriella said. "He's angry that he got caught."

"And he holds me responsible."

"But does he have enough money left to hire a hit man?"

"Yes. He's hidden money all over Europe. That's for others to worry about. But I'm quite sure he's got enough to hire an assassin if he so desires.

"There's another reason he's at the top of my list. He stopped me at the Abernathy event. Insisted we needed to talk. Took me a few minutes to get away from him. That could've been a delaying tactic."

"So he might've stalled you, giving the shooter time to get to another location." Irelyn said.

It was a distinct possibility. Morrissey had little hope left. He would definitely serve time for his greed and heartlessness. What better way to get his revenge than to destroy the man he held responsible for his downfall?

"Let's keep our eyes open but concentrate heavily on these three for now. Kennedy, I'd like you take on Morrissey. Charlie, dig into Donaldson. And Gabby, see what you can find out about Petrie. Follow the contacts and the money."

"And if it's not one of those three men?" Kathleen asked.

"Then we come up with another way to find the culprit," Grey answered. "Assassins are patient by nature. Fortunately, the people who purchase their services aren't. We might have to force their hand again."

"What's the plan for you, Grey?" Kennedy asked. "Will you lie low until we can identify him?"

He'd given this a lot of thought over the last few hours. Irelyn likely wouldn't like his solution, but he wasn't going to let that stop him. She was putting on a good front for everyone, but she was still suffering, both physically and emotionally. Added to that was their need to reconnect. Her admission that she had lost trust in him hadn't been that much of a surprise. Her actions over the last two years bore that out. Knowing that and hearing it from her mouth were two different things. He'd felt as if someone had taken a machete to his heart. He wanted to regain what they had lost.

Refusing to even allow for an argument, he locked eyes with Irelyn as he answered Kennedy's question. "Irelyn and I are going away together."

He saw her surprise and figured she was about to give him a dressing-down for making that decision for her. He didn't give her a chance. Turning back to the rest of the group, he added, "I have a few things to take care of today. After that, I can work from a remote location. If anything urgent needs attending, Gallagher will be my liaison for all things connected to the Grey Justice Group."

He stopped talking and waited for an explosion. It never came. He looked back over at Irelyn and smiled. Her brow was arched, and her eyes gleamed with amusement, letting him know she recognized his highhandedness. She didn't say a word to refute him.

Feeling more optimistic by the moment, he glanced around the room. "Any questions?"

He waited a few seconds, and when no one said anything,

he stood. "Thank you all for your help. I know we'd all rather be doing something besides this. Hopefully, it'll get resolved soon and we can go on to more important things."

Charlie stood and threw the group one of her charming grins. "I'll be the brown-noser of the bunch and say something we're all thinking. There's nothing more important than protecting our boss."

The room exploded in laughter, lessening the seriousness of the meeting, ending on the right tone. He noted that Kennedy and Irelyn spoke quietly to each other for several moments, and then Kennedy hugged her before walking out of the room.

With the exception of Grey and Irelyn, the room was empty. Figuring she had waited till everyone left before she started arguing about going away together, he fired the first shot.

"You know as well as I do that you will be a target, too. Getting out of town and sticking together is the best way to ensure that we both survive."

"I agree," she said mildly. "While you're wrapping things up, I'm going to see Dr. Tobin. I have an appointment with her this afternoon."

Her agreement was almost too easy, but he would definitely not complain.

"Sounds good. Terrance can take you."

She nodded and walked toward the door, stopping at the entrance. "Grey, what you said about trusting me more than anyone. Is that true?"

"Do I ever say things I don't mean?"

"No."

"Well, then."

Biting her lip as if she wanted to say something else but couldn't, she merely said, "Thank you."

He had hoped for more, perhaps an assertion that she felt

the same way. He knew it wasn't going to be that easy to regain her trust. Time together would help.

"You and Kennedy get things ironed out?"

"I asked her to wait for me in the living room. I owe her an explanation and an apology."

"She's not angry with you."

"No, but that's because she's Kennedy. Nick, on the other hand, is furious, and rightly so."

"He's protective of her. It's what people who love each other do."

"Yes, I know." The look she gave him before walking out spoke volumes.

Grey blew out a huge, ragged sigh. Nothing with Irelyn was ever easy. And he was far from easy himself. Whatever was whirling around in that beautiful head of hers would eventually come out. He had days to make that happen.

A little smile tugged at his mouth. Damned if he wasn't feeling remarkably chipper for a man marked for death.

CHAPTER TWENTY-TWO

Irelyn settled onto a sofa across from Kennedy. She was nervous, which wasn't the norm, but this woman and her opinion meant so much to her. "I want to apologize for last night."

"You don't owe me an explanation or an apology, Irelyn. If I had been in your position, I would have done the same thing. You were trying to save Grey's life."

"Nick doesn't agree with you."

"You know how men are. He's just being super protective."

Yes, Grey was like that on occasion, too. *It's what people who love each other do.* The words he'd spoken before she'd walked out had almost stopped her heart. She had almost said things she'd never said before, asked questions she'd never had the courage to ask.

"Nick has every right to be angry on your behalf. Even if you don't want my apology, I do at least owe you an explanation."

"I understand why you did what you did last night. But I—" She waved her hand. "Look, if I'm out of line here, just tell me to mind my own business, but you said something when you came to my house that I can't get out of my head."

Irelyn didn't need to ask her what that was. She regretted that moment of vulnerability, but at the same time, she realized that saying the words had been oddly freeing.

"You want to know why I killed Grey's parents?"

"I want to know why you think you killed them."

Even now, knowing that Irelyn was a trained assassin, Kennedy didn't believe she could have done something so vile as to kill Grey's parents. For a moment, her mind wandered to what it would feel like to be that innocent and trusting. Though Kennedy's childhood had not been easy, she was fortunate to have had people in her life who actually cared about her well-being.

"Did you ask Grey?"

"Yes. He told me I should ask you. He said it's your story to tell."

Of course he wouldn't have told her. Grey would never reveal their secrets without her agreement.

She blew out a sigh, and her eyes went unfocused as she thought about what had happened to lead up to that fateful day.

"I was four or five years old when Hill Reed purchased me from my mother. I assume she was my mother. Grey and I tried to find her years later, but since I've never known my real name, it was a dead end from the start."

Her smile was twisted as she added, "Reed gave me my name. He said it was raining, and he was in Ireland, so it seemed to fit. The spelling came from a man who created my fake passport years later."

Realizing she'd gotten sidetracked already, she refocused. "All I knew was that I was warm and safe for the first time in my life. I had a soft place to sleep and food to fill my belly. I don't remember much about those days, before Reed, other than being cold and hungry. Reed gave me everything, and as he planned, I became totally dependent on him."

"He was a father figure to you."

Even now, years later, her stomach cramped when she thought about all the things Reed had been to her.

"Not in the sense that most people have fathers, but yes, that's true. But everything he did to me and for me had a purpose."

"Like what?"

"He was an assassin by trade. However, he was also the leader of a group of assassins. He took contracts for them, made assignments, took a cut for himself. In return, he provided training and support. Hill House is, or was, like a large club for assassins only. A few lived there, some only visited to socialize in a safe environment. All of them trained there. Hill Reed was considered one of the best assassin trainers in the business."

"He trained you to—" Horror flared on her face. "But you were just a baby!"

She smiled coldly. "That didn't happen until later. At first, all he did was make me believe I couldn't survive without him. That if he ever left me alone, I would die a horrible, painful death. By the end of that first year, I was wholly dependent upon him. I would have died for him."

"Was he at least affectionate toward you?"

It had taken her years to not shudder when she thought about Reed's idea of affection. "If it served his purpose, he could be kind. It wasn't until later on that he became brutally cruel. First, he won my affection, and then he used it against me."

"Did you have an education? Any kind of normal childhood?"

"Yes, to the education. No, to the normal childhood. Reed had specific plans for me, so he made sure I was well educated. I had tutors and teachers. A bizarre form of home-schooling I guess you could say."

"What about friends. Did you have any?"

"No. But it's not like I realized I was missing anything. Everything that happened seemed normal to me. I didn't know anything different. At least, not until…"

"Until?"

As clear as if it were yesterday, she remembered that monumental, life-changing moment when she met Grey.

"Did you know that Grey's parents were in the same kind of business as the Grey Justice Group?"

"No. Grey never talks about them."

"They were part of an organization called The Justice Seekers. It wasn't a government-sanctioned group, but they were able to get away with certain things an ordinary citizen might not."

"Is that how you two met?"

"Yes, but see…I was the villain in the scenario. Grey was my mark."

"Why?"

"Reed was contracted to assassinate an important government official. I didn't know the details, only that Grey's parents somehow thwarted the hit. It not only cost Reed a lot of money, it embarrassed him. His pride was bruised."

"And he used you to get to them."

Even though she was naïve in many ways, Kennedy had been around long enough to see where the story was going.

"They were too careful, too prepared, to be caught by Reed in a normal way. So, he decided to use their son instead."

"You lured Grey? How old were you?"

"I was fifteen, though I lied and said I was seventeen. Grey was seventeen… Actually, he wasn't Grey then. His name was Liam. His parents were Natalie and Andrew Bishop." She smiled and added, "You're the only one I've ever told that to."

"I wouldn't tell anyone."

"I know that. Anyway, I stalked Grey for several weeks, learned his routines. When I decided I knew what I needed, I went for him."

"How?"

"I knew the route he would take from his home to his classes. I knew the time. I simply arranged for a flat tire. Even back then, Grey was a knight in shining armor. He stopped to help.

"I guess you might say we had chemistry right off the mark. We started dating. He was..." Her heart lurched a little as she remembered. "He was both a gentleman and a gentle man."

"What happened?"

"Exactly what Reed and I planned. Grey and I dated for several months. He was a bit private, but I played him brilliantly. When he finally took me to meet his parents, I knew he was already half in love with me."

"You didn't...I mean, you wouldn't..."

"No, I didn't kill them outright. Reed wanted them for himself. I arranged for the meeting. They walked into a death trap that I set up."

"How?"

"I charmed them, just as I charmed their son. They believed I was neglected, mistreated. I came up with this elaborate lie that my parents were abusive, didn't care for me. It was a poor-little-rich-girl scenario, and I played it like I was born for the stage."

It still hurt to talk about it, but backing away from the truth never solved anything.

"I arranged for them to meet my so-called parents at my so-called home. The Bishops didn't say anything, but I got the impression they were going to ask if I could live with them. Grey would have been going away to university soon, and…" She swallowed past the giant lump in her throat and covered her awkwardness with a shrug. "They were just that kind…that good."

"What happened?"

"I realized too late that I couldn't go through with it. I screamed, tried to warn them. Reed wasn't having it. He killed them both."

"And Grey?"

"He was at school. The authorities called him."

"What happened to you?"

"Reed was furious. I was punished for my betrayal."

"Punished how?"

"He choked me until I passed out. When I woke, we were back at Hill House, in the training room."

"What did he do?"

"He beat the bottoms of my feet with several different instruments. I had been punished like that before, but not quite so severely. When he finished, he walked away. He knew I couldn't walk, so he didn't worry I would leave."

Tears shone in Kennedy's eyes. "How did you get away from him?"

"I waited until everyone went to bed, and then I crawled out of the house."

"Oh, Irelyn," Kennedy said softly.

She rarely thought about those horrific hours anymore. The pain had eventually gone away. She had healed. The pain of what she did to Grey and his parents was much less bearable.

"There was a telephone kiosk down the road. I called Grey, and he came to get me."

"You crawled all that way on your knees?"

"My knees. My ass. I would have crawled my way across England to get away from the bastard."

"Did Grey know what happened? About Reed? The setup?"

"Not until I told him."

"You could have lied."

"No, I couldn't. I was through lying. I was willing to take whatever punishment Grey wanted to give me. I deserved death. I deserved every hateful, hideous punishment he might want to inflict on me. Instead, Grey gave me a new life."

"He had to be furious with you."

"With me. With himself." She closed her eyes for a moment to refocus. Seeing his grief, knowing she was the cause, had been so much more painful than dealing with his anger.

"It couldn't have been that simple...that easy."

She smiled a little. "Nothing about Grey is simple or easy. You know, most people, if they live long enough, are given at least one defining moment in their lives. The moment when they choose a certain path or make a monumental decision that will change them forever. I was given that choice early in life. And I made the wrong one."

"You were a child."

"I was old enough to know the difference between right and wrong."

"But that was the problem. You weren't taught what was right and what was wrong. You were manipulated, brainwashed."

"Excuses can only go so far. Believe me, I've thought of all of them. Tried to give myself an out. Bottom line, I betrayed two people who did everything in their power to save me. They were the best people I ever knew, and I'm responsible for their deaths."

"Why did Grey do it?"

"What? Save me?"

"Yes. One would think he would want nothing to do with you."

"But that's Grey. I asked him why early, and he said it was what his parents would have expected him to do."

"Was that the only reason?" There was hesitation in Kennedy's voice as she continued, "Do you think he kept you close to punish you?"

"That might've been in his mind at the time. I don't know. On occasion, I felt like I was being punished, but that was more my guilt than any overt action from Grey. I think, more than anything, it was his way of dealing with the pain. As long as he focused on what he needed to do, he didn't have to deal with what happened."

"Was it rough? Living together, having this between you?"

"For a while, it was hell for both of us. He was never cruel. Angry and hurt, but never mean. We would go days without speaking."

"Then why didn't he just leave you? Or why didn't you leave him?"

"Because, for Grey, it was the right thing to do. And I left him plenty of times."

"You did? Why?"

"At first, because I hated myself so much. Could barely stand to look at myself, much less him. He would find me and bring me home, or I would come home on my own. I eventually stopped running."

She swallowed back a lump of emotion. Had she really stopped running? Every time she'd left him, hadn't she really been running away again?

"What about Hill Reed? Did he not try to come after you?"

"We didn't see him for a long time. We moved around a

lot. When we finally scraped up enough money, we moved to Paris. It wasn't until we came to Dallas and my name became associated with Grey's that he contacted me."

"I imagine both of you wanted to just kill him outright."

She wished she could say that was true. Even though it had been years since she'd seen Reed, and she hated him for all that he had done to her, there had still been that slightest smattering of affection she hadn't been able to deny. While her mind recognized him as a monster, her subconscious still had difficulty accepting him as one. That insidious thread that Reed so carefully weaved into her psyche had still existed.

"Grey believed Reed could be used. So instead of killing him, I reestablished a relationship with him."

"Wasn't that hard? I mean, he was a hideous person."

It had been hell. In the middle of that first meeting, she had excused herself, gone to the bathroom, and thrown up violently. A few minutes later, she had returned to their meeting, all smiles.

"I'm a good actress."

"So Reed never knew that Grey was Liam Bishop?"

"No. He would have had him killed. I made Hill believe I conned my way through Europe before coming to America and attaching myself to the wealthy Grey Justice. It's what he taught me to do, so he easily accepted it as fact."

"Was renewing the association worth it?"

"On occasion, he would drop bits of information that were helpful. In turn, I gave him little tidbits. Harmless stuff. I think, more than anything, he liked to think of our association as familial."

"It's so strange to be talking about this man," Kennedy said softly. "He was responsible for Thomas's death, and many others. Yet, to you, he was someone else, something else."

"No. He was a hideous monster. Period."

"Renewing your association must have been hard on Grey, too. Did he ever meet Hill in person?"

They had never even discussed such a prospect. It would have been disastrous. "Never. Grey's good at hiding his thoughts, but even he has his limits."

"How long did it take for Grey to forgive you?"

"You're assuming he has."

"Yes." She leaned forward. "Irelyn, you have to know how he feels about you."

Did she? Yes, she knew he cared. Even when he was at his angriest, that was never in question. And she knew he desired her. From their first meeting, they'd had a connection. They'd just been children, but even then there had been an amazing bond. Beyond a few kisses, they hadn't acted on those feelings. And then the world had crumpled, and other things, like staying alive and surviving, had taken precedence. It had been years before they made love the first time.

"I know he cares."

"*Cares*? Seriously? Irelyn, he's crazy about you."

She never had the chance to be a teenager giggling with a girlfriend over boys or crushes. And while she felt a little foolish now, she couldn't resist asking, "Why do you think so?"

"His eyes follow you. They light up when you talk. I can't believe you don't see that."

Maybe that was because she was too busy doing the same thing. When she was around Grey, everything and everyone often disappeared for her.

"And after you left, he wasn't the same. He became grim, almost reclusive. You're so good at reading people, I can't believe that you don't see it. He's in love with you, Irelyn."

Yes, she was excellent at reading people and usually good at reading Grey. If what Kennedy said was true, why hadn't he ever told her? Why were things the way they were between them?

"He's never said the words."

"Saying the words can be hard for some people. Have you said them to him?"

"No."

"Why not?"

Gut herself open and spill her feelings? She didn't doubt her courage and strength in other things, but when it came to her heart, she was a weakling.

"I guess I'm one of those people it's hard for. Besides, it's a little more complicated than just saying the words."

"No, it's really not, but it is scary."

Scary was a mild word for the panic ratcheting up inside her at the very thought.

"Until this is over, and the threat against Grey is gone, I can't think about that or the future."

"And when it's over?" When Irelyn didn't immediately answer, Kennedy added, "You gave me some great advice once. It helped save my life. So I'm going to give you some now. Don't be afraid to open yourself up and let Grey see your love for him. You deserve to be happy, Irelyn. And so does Grey."

CHAPTER TWENTY-THREE

Hill House
England

Dressed in black, Sebastian stood before the largest audience he'd ever faced. It had taken more than a little encouragement to get them all here. They were understandably wary. Assassins had a healthy sense of self-preservation, along with a high level of distrust. Being invited to an open-air event on such short notice would make the normal person somewhat curious. For an assassin, it made them deadlier.

He had implemented precautions. No one could get through the gates unless they relinquished their weapons. Some had refused, and he had let them know in no uncertain terms that they either followed the rules or they would not be allowed access to the party. Only two people had walked away. The rest, some throwing out a vicious curse or two, had surrendered their weapons.

Even dressed in elegant evening attire and without weapons, they were still lethal. An accomplished assassin didn't need a weapon to kill. A weapon was expedient. Skill and intent mattered much more than the instrument. Properly motivated, a man or woman could kill with bare hands or any innocuous object. However, taking their weapons should at least ensure there wouldn't be a bloodbath. There would be bloodletting tonight, but he was the only one who would have that privilege.

"Welcome, everyone, to my little soirée. I apologize for the short notice. However, I fully intend for you to be both entertained and enthralled tonight."

His eyes roamed around the small stadium. Reed had built this area for training and demonstrations. This was the first time it had been used as an entertainment venue. But even that would be educational. The assassin community had doubts about him as a leader. They needed visual proof of his strength and prowess.

With its leader having died without a successor, Hill House needed a strong, powerful leader to maintain its status in the community. Sebastian, along with several others, had campaigned to become the new head. Five assassins had placed their bids and proposals. At the time of Reed's death, Hill House had had twenty full-time assassins. After he died, several had gone off on their own, a couple had died, and one had been arrested and was now sitting on death row. Hill House had needed a strong leader to not only gather the remaining chicks and bring them back home, but to attract new blood.

Killing a competitor had been strictly forbidden to win the job, but everything else was fair game, including stealing or sabotaging contracts, as well as old-fashioned bribery. Sebastian had employed all of those tactics, plus a few only he knew about. And though it had been a close race between him and another assassin, Sebastian prevailed.

That should have been the end of it. Hill House should

have been thriving once more. But still there was resistance, doubt. Tonight's event should dissolve all uncertainty. Sebastian Dark was the new leader. After his performance tonight, he anticipated a deluge of requests to become Hill House assassins.

So far, everyone had behaved civilly to one another. They had eaten thousands of dollars' worth of caviar and foie gras while guzzling Dom Perignon like it was water. And now it was time for the main event. Time to show the prowess and stamina of Hill House's new boss.

The attendees had been ushered to the outside arena with almost no fuss. They knew tonight was about more than a social occasion. They were about to witness something phenomenal, something that few living people had ever seen. Sebastian Dark was about to reveal himself.

Nodding at the guards, Sebastian stood in the middle of the arena and waited for his first contestant to arrive. Three men would assist in showing his guests just how special Sebastian Dark really was.

The first one to enter was the guard who was on duty the night Irelyn Raine broke into the records room. Shuffling across the arena in leg irons, his arms cuffed behind him, he didn't look particularly impressive. That was not a problem. Physically fighting the man was not the goal. Assassins didn't have to be the strongest or the most lethal in hand-to-hand. Hill Reed had been a slender man of medium height, but his mastery had never been in question. And while Sebastian was much taller and more powerful-looking, proving his physical prowess was not the point.

Standing at just over six feet and weighing in at a meaty two hundred and eighty pounds, the guard had been slow in his pursuit of Raine. Though he had put out the alert the moment she'd run through the front door, his inability to capture her had earned his punishment. Because he had tried his best, Dark was taking pity on him. The other two wouldn't be so fortunate.

He picked up his preferred firearm from the table beside him, a Wilson Combat 9mm. Oddly enough, guns scared him. The blasts nauseated him, and even when using a silencer, he often lost his concentration because of the inane fear that the silencer wouldn't work. Only Hill Reed had known this and had, in fact, almost given up on him because of it. In his less-kind moments, he had even allowed some of the other trainees to use him as a target or punching bag. Out of sheer necessity and fear for his life, Sebastian had become an expert marksman. Though guns would never be his chosen weapons, showing his audience that he was proficient in using a firearm was a must.

The man, shaking and pale, was tied to a post. In a small bit of whimsy, Sebastian had instructed that the man have a red target tattooed on his forehead. Seeing it brought a smile to Sebastian's face, lightening his mood, easing his tension.

The length of the arena was thirty yards, which was a little longer than the average gun range. Hitting a motionless object was less of a challenge than a moving one. However, for demonstration purposes, this was perfect. He raised his weapon without further fanfare, aimed, and fired twice. The first bullet eviscerated the bull's-eye target, and the second bullet went into the man's broad chest, creating a nice, round, red complement to the hole in his forehead.

Sebastian didn't expect applause. That wasn't the reason for the exhibition, but when he heard a smattering through the small crowd, he couldn't resist a small bow. The lights were all on him, and the people were merely shadows, but he swore he felt their approval, admiration. Hill would be so pleased with him.

Without further aplomb, the carcass of his first prey was hurriedly removed, and the setup for the second demonstration commenced. Since it would take a moment or two, Sebastian took several sips of still water while he surreptitiously tried to overhear what his audience members were saying to one another. He could hear tittering and whispering. He knew they had to be impressed, but he wanted more. He wanted what Hill Reed had had. He wanted adoration and adulation. If he didn't already possess it after the first demonstration, the second would go a long way in achieving it. By the time he finished tonight, he would likely be a legend.

Two more men shuffled in, their chains and handcuffs clanging in a rhythmic noise that sounded almost musical. The first one was small, wiry, and mean as a jackal. Sebastian had seen him kill men twice his size without breaking a sweat. He should have been able to handle Irelyn Raine with no problem. Instead, he'd been found unconscious, with a lump on his head, a broken nose, and a severely bruised groin. She'd taken him down as if he'd been an amateur.

The second one was twice the size of the other one, but with a pea-sized intellect. Still, with his brawn, he should've been able to kill her with one sweep of a giant fist. Instead, she had taken him down, too.

They were both an embarrassment to Hill House and to Sebastian. Because of that, they would die together in Sebastian's favorite way.

Picking up his preferred weapon, Sebastian made a slow, 360-degree turn so everyone could get a good look at its beauty. Made of the finest leather, the whip had a distinctive characteristic. At the very end, a naked length of piano wire had been added, extending the whip to nine feet. There wasn't another one like it in the whole world. And no one could wield the whip so elegantly or masterfully.

Finding a weapon he could master had taken him years. During that time, Hill Reed had abused and used him in any way he saw fit. Later, Sebastian realized it had been his father's way of motivating him to prove his worth. It worked. Sebastian was determined to find a weapon he could master that would help him not only become a premier assassin, but also make his father proud. He found that in the bullwhip.

He became so adept that Reed commissioned this special whip just for Sebastian's use. It was presented to him on graduation day, which in the assassin world, was the day of his first contracted kill. That was also the day Hill had allowed him to choose a new identity. He had selected the name Sebastian Dark, which, to his mind, sounded both lethal and elegant. It fit his persona perfectly.

In a kill, Sebastian could wrap the whip around his target's neck from a distance. One swift jerk of his hand would break the neck. If Sebastian was in a special frame of mind, or even upon request, he would stand farther back and employ the wire. Not only would that break the neck, but the throat would also be sliced open. Sure, it was overkill, but sometimes that was what the client wanted. Sebastian lived to serve.

Tonight, he lived to impress. Nodding at the men who'd led his targets into the arena, they unlocked the shackles and cuffs and left. The instant his prey were free, they bolted toward the exit. Feeling as powerful as a god, Sebastian strode forward and swung the whip. It caught the smaller one, encircling his neck. With a swift, powerful jerk, Sebastian swept the man off his feet and then flung him to the ground. The pop of his neck was almost obscured by the audience's gasp.

Sebastian was unable to appreciate their awe. The big one changed course and charged him like an enraged bull. Startled, he backed up slightly and looked around. The man was getting too close for the whip to work. His mind in a panic, he picked up the gun he'd used earlier and unloaded the entire magazine into the giant's massive chest. The thudding crash of his big body echoed through the now silent arena.

His breath coming in gasps, Sebastian dared a peek at his audience. As he had instructed, the stadium lights had been turned on once the demonstration was over. He had anticipated seeing the awe and respect he deserved. Instead, he was stunned into immobility by their expressions. Boredom. He even saw anger in a few. No one seemed the least bit impressed with his power or expertise. Admittedly, the last kill hadn't gone as smoothly as he would have liked, but quick thinking had nevertheless ensured the kill.

Refusing to believe that he had not earned their admiration, Sebastian gave his most arrogant smile and bowed. He had learned bravado from a master. His head held high, he turned and walked out of the arena without a backward glance.

CHAPTER TWENTY-FOUR

Dallas, Texas

S he couldn't sit down. She and Dr. Tobin had been together for years. There wasn't a thing she didn't know about Irelyn and what she had done. Fortunately, the therapist was used to her rambling and walking at the same time, which was good, because Irelyn couldn't seem to settle in one place.

"He actually acts as if he really trusts me."

"And you don't think he's telling the truth?"

"Grey doesn't lie. If he said it, then it's the truth."

"Then what's the problem?"

She whirled around. "I'm afraid I'll let him down." She didn't add the word that they were both thinking. *Again.*

"Wouldn't it be wise to take what he says at face value? You haven't been the Irelyn he couldn't trust for a very long time."

"I know. I know. I just—"

"What's really bothering you, Irelyn?"

"I killed my brother last night."

The stark words hung out there like some kind of ugly, dark entity. Not many people could say that without getting at least a raised brow. Sheila Tobin was the exception. She merely said, "How did that happen?"

Irelyn told her everything, from how she found out that she had a brother, to how she'd gone about locating him. She held nothing back, including the men she killed to attract Dark's attention.

"Let's get back to your brother in a moment. Tell me about these men you terminated."

"They were assassins…killers. That was the only way I could get Dark's attention. He wouldn't have been impressed if I terminated an ordinary person. Killing a killer takes more skill."

"Would you have killed an ordinary person if it would have impressed him?"

"Of course not."

The therapist smiled. "Good. You need to recognize that. Now continue."

Irelyn frowned, distracted for a moment, and then said, "I killed them, and then Dark contacted me."

"Why are you avoiding talking about the men you killed?"

"What do you want me to say? They were bad men."

"Who were they, and what did they do?"

Talking about them in the abstract was so much easier than giving actual details. Of course, Dr. Tobin knew this and would continue to press until Irelyn acknowledged whatever the therapist believed she was avoiding. After years of therapy, Irelyn knew the drill.

She took a breath and began. She didn't bother to individualize them, as they had all been monsters. Instead, she told Dr. Tobin about their victims, families who were killed, the children massacred.

After all Irelyn had told her through the years, the therapist was almost immune to being shocked, but there was a definite glimmer of horror in her expression when Irelyn finished.

"So these men destroyed countless lives, killed innocent people, including children? And would likely have continued to do so if you hadn't killed them?"

"Yes."

"Does it help to know that you saved lives by doing so?"

It did and it didn't. Explaining that was impossible.

"I'm glad they can't hurt anyone any longer, but the sad part about this business is that someone will always take their place."

"What about the man you killed last night?"

"You mean my brother?"

"Did you have a choice?"

"No. He was there to kill Grey. If I hadn't pulled the trigger, Grey would be—" She couldn't even finish the sentence.

"You saved another life. This time, someone very important to you."

"Yes."

"Do you remember your brother at all?"

"Yes and no. As you know, what happened before Hill isn't clear or distinct. I remember vague impressions of people and events. I remember cold, hunger, fear. I don't remember any specific person, but I think I do remember him from Hill House. He was in training, too. I never talked to him, though."

"You trained together?"

"No. Hill was very specific about that. For the most part, I was kept separate from the others. I don't know if it was because I was special to him, or because I meant nothing."

"Does it matter?"

"No, I guess it doesn't. But now I'm wondering if it was

just a matter of practicality. Keeping us away from each other prevented any kind of bond."

"Or perhaps broke any bond that you already had."

"Yes."

"How do you feel about killing him?"

"He was going to kill Grey. I made the only choice I could."

"That's not an answer."

"It's the only one I've got right now."

Dr. Tobin occasionally pushed her for answers. Irelyn was thankful that this time she didn't. She had cried a river about it already. Tears hadn't helped, neither would words. It was done, couldn't be undone. She chose to focus on the one good thing about it all—Grey was still alive.

"You hadn't told me before today the things Reed revealed to you that last night. Why?"

Because there had been so much pain back then, so much to process. Killing the man she had both despised and loved. The breach with Grey she hadn't thought they'd be able to overcome. Learning that she had a brother, a blood relative, and finding out he'd been in the same house with her and she hadn't known him.

"It was just too much to deal with…to handle. I told you what I could."

"You're better now." Keen eyes assessed her. "Back in a good place again."

Irelyn almost laughed at the doctor's uncanny observation, because it was true. How screwed up did you have to be to have killed your only sibling the night before, to know that someone has a contract to kill the most important person in your life, and likely wants to kill you, too, and still realize that you are indeed in a good place? This was the most connected and grounded she'd felt in years. That was messed up.

"Grey and I were intimate last night."

"That hasn't happened in a while."

"No...not since...not since that night."

"The night you poisoned Hill Reed."

"Yes."

"I won't ask for details, but how was your connection?"

Amazing. Beautiful. Almost spiritual. All those things and so much more. Grey had touched her as if she were a precious gem. Tender, gentle, likely because of her injuries, but also resolute in his goal to give her the ultimate pleasure. It had been a long time since she'd felt so connected with him. She had wanted to give back, pleasure him, but he wouldn't let her. He had given himself without taking anything in return.

"Never mind," Dr. Tobin said. "I can tell by your expression that it was a good experience."

Relieved she didn't have to explain such an intimacy, she quickly answered, "Yes, it was lovely."

"So what happens now? Will you stay with him?"

"We're going away together until we can figure out who's behind this. Keeping him out of the limelight will ensure his safety."

"And what about your safety?"

"Well, sure, that, too."

"You don't really mean that, though, do you? Why is that, Irelyn? When are you going to realize that you deserve safety and protection, too?"

"Grey's the one being targeted, not me."

Instead of refuting Irelyn's words, Dr. Tobin tilted her head in that silent, confronting way of hers.

"Okay, so I'm probably on some hit lists, too. Either way, we'll both be out of the limelight. Grey's taking care of some business, but we're leaving tomorrow."

"Being alone with each other will give you a chance to

reconnect. Yet, you don't look very happy about it. Are you afraid you'll disclose more than you're ready to reveal?"

That and a thousand other reasons it was dangerous for her to be alone with him for too long. But she could not pass up this opportunity. It had been too long that it had been just the two of them together.

"I can't run away forever."

"Especially when you're running from someone you want to stay with forever."

Denying the truth would be futile. Dr. Tobin had a talent for seeing beyond the surface. Irelyn was excellent at hiding her deepest emotions, but from their first meeting, the therapist had seen beneath the façade that Irelyn showed the rest of the world.

She'd been so lost in thought, she hadn't realized the woman had sat down on the coffee table in front of her. In a surprising, unusual move, she took Irelyn's hand. "Perhaps it's time to reveal all, Irelyn. Lay it all on the table. Tell him what's in your heart. Perhaps it's time to put the past truly in the past."

GREY PUT HIS SIGNATURE ON THE LAST DOCUMENT HE intended to sign for a while. In the early years, he'd been a hands-on manager, but he'd learned that wasn't necessary when you hired the right people for the job. He had no concerns on that front.

He glanced at the clock on his desk. Terrance had called a couple of hours ago and informed him that Irelyn had gone off on her own after her doctor's appointment. Grey wasn't surprised. After a session with her therapist, she always needed solitude. The verbal spilling of guts wasn't easy for anyone, most especially a woman who kept most of her thoughts hidden throughout her life.

Besides that, Irelyn did not conform to other people's demands unless it suited her. She had left the apartment looking so different from the real Irelyn, he wasn't concerned that she would be recognized. And while he understood her need to be alone, he couldn't deny a tinge of worry. It was getting late. And while he told himself she would not renege on their agreement, the later it grew, the more concerned he became. What if she disappeared again?

Being uncertain in anything in his life wasn't a common occurrence for him, but Irelyn was a different entity altogether. Even though he knew her as well as anyone could, she was a law unto herself. He admired her tremendously, but she also drove him insane much of the time.

A soft chime sounded. Grey breathed out a quiet, relieved sigh and felt his muscles loosen. The private elevator was being used, which meant she was safe and home once again. Even though she had promised to go away with him, Irelyn wasn't always predictable. Especially not lately.

The office door opened, and a woman he wouldn't have recognized if he'd seen her anywhere but here appeared. She had iron-gray hair and wore thick, round glasses. Thick makeup, applied and shaded on the angles and planes of her face, added twenty years or more. A frumpy, threadbare coat and sensible shoes finished the disguise.

"How was your session with Dr. Tobin?"

"Same song, different day."

She came toward him, and Grey met her in the middle of the room. "Terrance called. Said you took off on your own."

"I needed some time. Was he put out?"

"Just concerned."

She held up the bag in her hand. "Maybe this will help. I stopped by Charlie's and picked up his favorite cookies."

In one move, he took the bag from her, threw it on his desk, and pulled her into his arms. "Have I told you lately how amazing I think you are?"

She smiled and wound her arms around his neck. "You're just saying that because you want a cookie."

"You read my mind so well." He leaned his forehead against hers. "I like this new look."

She brought her body closer, flush with his. "Is that right?"

"Yeah. Why don't you bring it with you?"

"Older women appeal to you now?"

"This one does."

"Oh yeah?" she asked softly. "Why's that?"

"Because I want you any way I can get you."

With the sweet groan that always drove him crazy, she pressed her mouth against his, and every problem, every issue disappeared. Irelyn was always able to do that to him. The moment her lips met his, he could forget everything. Devouring her luscious mouth, Grey tightened his hold, letting her feel exactly how much he wanted her.

Moments later, breathless and smiling, she pushed him slightly away. "I need to change clothes."

"While you do that, I'll order dinner. Anything in particular sound good?"

A wicked gleam in her eye, she whispered, "Something decadent and delicious."

"Decadent and delicious it is."

———

THEY ATE DINNER IN THE KITCHEN'S BREAKFAST NOOK. Because of its cozy size, it was Irelyn's favorite place to dine. While Grey chose the wine, she had selected their dinner music—soft, lyrical, distinctively Irish. The meal was from their favorite Italian restaurant. Mushroom ravioli for her, lasagna for Grey.

"It seems so quiet and peaceful tonight. No urgent phone calls, no major dramas," she said.

"Hopefully a sign of things to come."

"Where are we going? You didn't say."

"I thought the house in Colorado. The repairs are complete."

"Repairs? Did we have snow or wind damage?"

"Neither. You missed that particular drama."

"What happened?"

"Gabriella's grandfather, Luis Mendoza, happened."

"I thought he passed away."

"He did, but not before making her life a living hell, as well as destroying our home."

When she raised a questioning brow, Grey explained about Gabriella's abduction and how Jonah had hidden her away at their house.

"How did they find out she was there?"

"Never did learn that, but Ivy Roane was working with him."

"Poison Ivy. The woman definitely got around."

"That she did."

"So the house was destroyed?"

"Not destroyed, but definitely trashed. Little structural damage. They were looking for Gabriella, and when they couldn't find her, they moved on."

Taking one last bite of her truly excellent ravioli, Irelyn settled back in her chair. "Do you ever wonder what makes people the way they are? Some families are so strong and supportive of one another, and then there are those like Gabriella's who do everything they can to tear each other apart."

"It's been happening since time began. Remember Adam and Eve, Cain and Abel? Definitely dysfunctional."

"All because of evil. Do you think some people are more apt to be evil than others? That there's something inherently wrong with them at birth?"

"I don't know. I do think we all come to a point in our lives where we have to acknowledge what is right and what is wrong. And make a decision on which side of the fence we will stand."

"I've stood on that fence for a while now, haven't I?"

"No, Irelyn, you haven't been on that fence in a very long time. You just haven't allowed yourself to notice." He took her hand lying on the table and squeezed it.

"I told Kennedy about my past…about my training. About your parents."

"How did she take it?"

"Surprisingly well, considering."

"She's a compassionate person."

"Yes, she is."

"Any reason you shared that with her?"

"I don't know. I think… No, I *know* I'm tired of the isolation."

He lifted the hand he was still holding to his lips. "I'd say that's progress. Wouldn't you?"

Progress? Yes. Could she go further, though? Both Kennedy and Dr. Tobin had encouraged her to do so. Could she finally come clean with Grey once and for all?

GREY PICKED UP HIS EMPTY PLATE AND IRELYN'S ALMOST EMPTY one. He was pleased she'd eaten as much as she had. Last night when he was holding her, he'd noted her weight-loss. She had felt distinctly fragile in his arms. Days of eating regular meals and sleeping late would hopefully take care of that worry.

A soft hand closed around his wrist and he looked down at the lovely woman before him. He could stare into those luminous gray eyes forever and never tire of them. He also saw what she had tried to hide with cosmetics, fatigue and a lingering sadness.

"Why don't you go take a relaxing bubble-bath? I'll take care of the kitchen cleanup."

"Thank you. That does sound lovely. I'll wait up for you."

"No need. Go on to sleep. I still have a few things I need to attend to."

"But I—"

He pressed his fingers against her mouth. "We have a long day ahead of us tomorrow."

"Very well." She glanced around the kitchen as if somewhat lost and then gave him a careful smile. "I'll see you in the morning."

He nodded and watched her leave the room. As they'd eaten dinner, Grey had kept a watchful eye on her mannerisms. While Irelyn could hide a multitude of thoughts with a pleasant or bland expression, telltale signs of stress or exhaustion were often revealed in the way she moved or her hand gestures. Her session with Dr. Tobin had likely given her some relief and closure from last night's events but he knew she was still suffering. He intended to do everything within his power to ensure she had a chance to recover. And that was why he hadn't told her what was going on in his mind.

Today, when she'd been out, something had clicked in his head. He wanted some time to evaluate his thoughts. Bringing them up to her now would ensure only one thing. She would dive in with him. While he valued her opinion and would gladly accept her help, he would wait. There was no harm in doing a bit of investigating on his own. When he had more to go on, he would bring her in on his suspicions. Telling her now when he had nothing substantial would accomplish nothing.

Grey finished the quick cleanup, prepared their coffee for the next day, and then went into his private office. Shutting the door, he headed to his computer and the notes he'd made earlier. He still had no concrete reasons for his suspicions. For right now, they were mere wisps of ideas and thoughts.

Clicking into his private email account, he read answers to several emails he'd sent earlier. The more he read, the stronger his suspicions grew.

As the ideas coalesced and settled in his mind, Grey sat back in his chair and began to dig even deeper into the twisted and evil world of Sebastian Dark.

CHAPTER TWENTY-FIVE

I relyn zipped the small duffel bag and set it on top of the larger one standing at the bedroom door. It was only seven in the morning, but she was packed and ready to go. She'd woken just past dawn with an odd, almost panicky feeling in the pit of her stomach. She rarely had this feeling of impending disaster, so when she did, she took heed. Problem was, they weren't scheduled to leave until early afternoon. Grey had a couple of meetings he wanted to conduct in person. She knew if she told him she wanted to leave now, he would likely accommodate her, but she refused to give in to this silly premonition. The meetings were being held in his office here. He wasn't leaving the apartment, and no one could gain entry unless on the approved-visitors list.

She told herself the worry came from exhaustion. She was still battered and bruised. Plus, so much had happened over a short period of time, it only made sense that she felt physically drained. She hadn't slept well last night, had tossed and turned as nightmares dragged her through hell. She'd woken dry-eyed, with a throbbing headache. A hot shower and a bracing cup of coffee had helped, but she still felt washed out and ragged.

She also felt something she hadn't in a long time. Insecure and undesirable. Grey had turned her down last night. That had never happened. Even at their lowest, most-distant moments, they had always been able to connect physically.

She told herself it was understandable. He had a lot on his mind. Even though he could work remotely, there were a thousand things he needed to accomplish before their trip. It wasn't because he no longer wanted her.

When he had come to bed last night, she had turned to face him. Kissing his neck and his chest, her hands had roamed over him, letting him know how much she wanted him. Instead of reciprocating, he'd kissed her forehead and told her to go to sleep, that they had a long day ahead of them.

She had lain in his arms for a long time, bereft and rejected. And when she'd finally fallen asleep, nightmares welcomed her as an old friend.

He hadn't made love to her the night before that either. Yes, he'd given her unbelievable pleasure, but he hadn't taken anything for himself. At the time, she had believed it was because he feared hurting her, but now she wasn't so sure. Could it be that Grey had finally tired of her? After all she'd done, all she'd put him through, had he finally reached his limit?

"You're already packed?"

Startled, she whirled around. Grey stood at the door. Though his tone was mild, she heard the concern in his voice. Did he think she might be leaving on her own? Did he want her to leave? She hated this new insecurity, but couldn't let it go.

"Yes. I didn't want to leave it to the last minute."

"What's wrong?"

Hiding her worries from him was becoming more difficult. "Just anxious to get there, I guess."

"My last appointment had to reschedule. I came in to see if you wanted to leave earlier. Guess the answer is yes."

"Yes, please."

"The plane should be ready, but I'll call Lily and ask her to move up the flight plan. I—" Grey's phone buzzed with a text message.

"You get the text," Irelyn said. "I'll call Lily and—" She stopped, startled at the dark look on his face. "What?"

Instead of answering, he grabbed the television remote from the nightstand, pressed the power button, and switched to a local channel where a polished, appropriately serious reporter was saying, "Again, details are still coming in, but we can report that local businessman Joe Morrissey, president of Morrissey Industries, was found dead at his home last night. Cause of death has not been made public. Sources close to the investigation indicate the victim was killed yesterday afternoon in what may have been a stabbing. Morrissey was recently indicted on suspicion of embezzlement and fraud."

The rest of the news report was lost on Irelyn. Her heart was pounding with dread, and now she knew why she'd felt such trepidation earlier. How coincidental could it be that the man they'd suspected of hiring a hit man to kill Grey had been murdered?

GREY LISTENED CAREFULLY TO THE REPORT. HE'D LEARNED that first reports were often the closest to the truth. Irelyn stood beside him quietly, and he knew she was absorbing all the implications. They would need to talk, but for right now he wanted more facts.

The doorbell rang. He headed out of the room to answer it, assuming Irelyn would follow.

The security camera showed Gallagher's face, dark with concern and something else. The instant he opened the door, Nick said, "You heard?"

"Yes. Think it was a hit?"

"That's what my sources are telling me."

"Any suspects?"

"Not yet. I—" His eyes veered slightly as he looked behind Grey to Irelyn. "I'm sure there are more than a few people who wanted him dead."

"Is there something else you want to say, Nick?" Irelyn asked.

"No. Is there something you'd like to say?"

"That's enough, you two. Gallagher, have a seat. Irelyn, come with me."

Following Grey back to her bedroom, she waited until he closed the door to say, "Do you think I did this?"

"Why the hell would you even ask me that?"

"He was killed yesterday. I was conveniently absent for several hours. I could have broken into his home, killed him, and left without leaving any evidence behind. I'm that good."

"No, you're not."

"What do you mean?"

"Exactly what I said. You aren't good with break-ins. Yes, you can do great undercover work, and your disguises are both creative and excellent. But you're terrible at being covert. You're too loud. I think that might be why you were caught at Hill House."

She was so filled with ire at his insults, she completely forgot about her fear that Grey might think she had killed Morrissey.

"I'll have you know, I did not make a sound."

"You got caught, didn't you?"

"Well, yes, but—"

"But nothing, Irelyn. You suck at sneaking."

She was about to defend herself again when she noted his steady, unwavering expression. She dropped down on the edge of the bed and sighed. "You're deliberately pissing me off, aren't you?"

"Am I?"

"So you don't think I did this?"

"Of course I don't." He surprised her by kneeling in front of her. "Ah, darling." Taking her hand, he held it to his mouth, kissing it softly. "What's it going to take for you to trust me again?"

She tried to smile but was suddenly too tired to even try. "I guess we both need to work on the trust issue, don't we?"

"We've been battling it for a long while. I never let you forget where we started."

"It's not forgettable."

"No, it's not. But we move forward, or we don't move at all."

She straightened her shoulders, ready to focus on the here and now once more. "You think Morrissey's death has anything to do with you?"

"I doubt it. The man had almost as many enemies as I have."

She wished she could smile about that, as he intended. She couldn't. That just reminded her that someone hated him enough to pay a lot of money to have him killed.

"We're still going away?"

"Without a doubt. Why don't you call Lily and have her schedule our flight as soon as possible? I'll deal with Gallagher, and then we'll be on our way."

Colorado Mountains

THE HOUSE WAS LOVELIER THAN SHE REMEMBERED. SHE AND
Grey had purchased it several years ago, but had stayed in it
only a handful of times. Built with a combination of rock,
brick, and log, the small mansion stood like a massive
boulder on a small hillside. Surrounded by giant trees and
distant mountains topped with snow, it was Christmas-card
perfect.

"I'd forgotten how beautiful it is here."

As they carried their bags inside, Grey briefly described
the damage that Luis Mendoza's men had done, all in an
effort to find the man's granddaughter. Not because he loved
her, but because of his own selfish desires.

It no longer surprised her what people could do to one
another. When she was younger, she had thought she was the
rare breed and that other people had sane families and happy
lives. As she got older, she realized that there were more
sadists and evil people in the world than one could
ever guess.

She glanced over at Grey. He fought against that evil
every day. Most of the world knew him as a successful businessman and philanthropist, but only a few knew that he
actively sought justice for those who'd been denied. Even
fewer knew how lethal he was. To anyone who crossed him
or hurt those he cared about, he was a dangerous opponent.
And to Irelyn, who had met him at her most vulnerable, he
was the center of her universe. Grey was as constant as the
ocean and as steady as the mountains surrounding them. He
had seen her at her very worst.

Their relationship had changed over the years. Maturity
and wisdom had created a different dynamic. Their recent
division was the closest they'd been to losing each other.
She'd had her reasons for that separation, but it was clear

Grey did not agree. A discussion was coming. An open, throw-it-all-out-there kind of talk. They hadn't had one in a long while. She didn't look forward to this one, but it had to be done. Things needed to be said, grievances had to be aired. Secrets, lies, and half-truths were a part of a past she'd worked hard to escape. They might not survive the outing, but allowing anger to fester would only be worse. She owed Grey the truth, no matter how ugly and painful.

On the plane, they had sat together in silence, a lovely, quiet peace between them. Nothing was settled. She likened the mood to a dormant volcano—seemingly tranquil, but beneath it all were volatile emotions that could spew forth like molten lava, decimating everything in their path.

"Everything okay?" Grey asked. She'd been standing in the foyer for several moments, her expression distant, her thoughts obviously a million miles away. He wanted her back with him, totally focused on the here and now.

"Yes. Fine." She threw him a cool smile. "Just a bit weary, I guess."

Irelyn Raine had endless energy. Her stamina and endurance could put any champion athlete to shame. He knew she was still exhausted and hurting from the last few days, but he recognized the words for what they were. An evasion.

"The meaningless responses stop now, Irelyn. We've known each other too long to treat each other like polite strangers."

The distant expression disappeared and the look she gave him now could melt a furnace. That made him smile. This was the Irelyn he wanted to see. Fuming temper and all.

"Fine," she snapped. "I thought we'd give ourselves a few moments of peace before the fireworks begin."

"I've had enough of peace these last couple of years. We've been acting as if we don't want to offend one another. That shit stops. You've got things to say, and baby, I do, too."

"I'll go put on my boxing gloves and meet you in the gym. Is that what you want?"

"No, it's not. Stop turning everything into a battle. I just want the words from you, Irelyn. To know where you are in your head. What's going on in that beautiful, intelligent brain?"

"You're right. I'm looking for a fight."

"I'll oblige you in that, too, later on. For right now, I need words."

"Meet you in the den in fifteen?"

He felt a loosening in his muscles. "Deal."

She walked toward the stairway, her small bag in one hand. He waited until she was halfway up the stairs before he called out, "Oh, and Irelyn. Your bags go in the master bedroom, not the guest room. Understand?"

She looked over her shoulder, an unusual uncertainty on her face. "Where are your bags going?"

"Right beside yours."

Light entered her features, and her eyes heated with a sultriness that lifted his heart and made his body go hard in an instant. She repeated the words he'd said to her the other night, "I wouldn't have it any other way, Grey."

The moment she disappeared, Grey set to work. The next few hours wouldn't be enjoyable for either of them, but once they got everything out in the open, he hoped like hell their troubles would be behind them.

He told himself to ignore his all-too-accurate gut that told him no way in hell were they in the clear.

CHAPTER TWENTY-SIX

S he took the time to wash off the grime of travel. Grey
wouldn't hold her to the fifteen minutes. He knew
better than anyone that her outer appearance made a difference to her inner self. No matter how removed she was from
her old life, there was still the little girl inside her needing
approval. Wanting to look her best, to be the best. Beauty had
been a large part of her training. Luring men to their deaths
required certain prerequisites, including knowing how to
attract them. Ms. Watkins, former spy and retired assassin,
had trained her in all things related to her appearance and
using sensuality to lure her target.

From makeup and hair, to fashion and decorum, to
subtle, sensuous moves of her body to attract the eye. Ms.
Watkins's teaching methods had been as harsh as any drill
sergeant's, and her punishments had been fierce. But they
also had been effective. On occasion, Irelyn could still hear
her sultry, gravel-like voice say, "When one feels beautiful,
one can deceive the world."

Not that she was planning on deception tonight. Lying to
Grey wasn't something she took lightly, and it had been years

since she'd actively sought to deceive him. In the last few years, though, she'd developed a nasty habit of not sharing her thoughts with him. They had drifted away from each other. Even while she had recognized the symptoms of the separation, she had done nothing about them.

Standing in front of the full-length mirror in the large dressing room, she took in her appearance and felt herself settle. Yes, she did look nice. A maxi-dress the color of a quiet dawn over a field of heather was perfect for the occasion. The dress was loose enough for freedom of movement and had a clingy, silk-like material that felt lovely against her skin. She made a graceful turn and was pleased that the knife sheath attached to her left thigh wasn't the least bit visible.

Satisfied, Irelyn walked out of the room and into the master bedroom. When Grey had issued the ultimatum about her luggage, she had wanted to laugh with sheer happiness. Her fears and insecurities had been unnecessary.

"You look lovely." Grey stood at the door, waiting for her.

"Thank you. I feel lovely."

He held out his hand. "Are you hungry?"

"No. Not really."

"Me either. Come join me in the den. We can eat later."

She walked with him out the door and down the stairs. With each step, her nervousness increased. Risking life and limb was so much less terrifying than opening up and sharing what was in her heart. Even as much as she and Grey had shared over the years, she still felt astonishingly vulnerable

She could fool the world, but Grey was an exception to every rule where she was concerned.

He knew she was nervous and squeezed her hand several times as they headed to the back of the house and the small, cozy den. She felt a slight lessening of tension the moment she entered. A fire blazed in the hearth, and the lights were dim enough to not make her feel as though the spotlight was on her. An open bottle of her favorite wine sat beside two glasses.

Her nerves vanished like they'd been covered in a calming blanket. She settled on the sofa in front of the fire and accepted the wine Grey poured for her.

He poured a glass for himself and then sat down beside her. "I'll go first, if you like."

In their earlier years, this had been routine for them. Whenever they had issues or problems, they'd call a special "meeting of the minds" discussion. As time went by and life got busier, they'd gotten out of the habit. It felt good to be headed back in the right direction.

"Perhaps it's best if I go first, since I anticipate questions."

"All right."

"We started drifting apart, and I didn't know how to stop it."

"I think we got too comfortable. I took us for granted."

"We both did." She wasn't about to let him take all the blame on himself. "By the time the real trouble started, it was almost too late for us."

GREY NODDED, KNOWING EXACTLY WHAT SHE MEANT. HILL Reed's reentry into their lives had come without warning. Though Reed had on occasion contacted Irelyn, it was only once or twice a year. Nauseating, yes, but she had done her best to use the infrequent meetings to their advantage.

Life had gotten busier, more complicated. Both he and Irelyn had been focused on trying to clear Jonah and bringing down Mathias and Adam Slater. Hill Reed had exploded back into their lives with the killing of Thomas O'Connell, Kennedy's first husband. It had come as a complete shock to both of them. Grey hadn't handled things well.

"You started blaming me again."

He wanted to disagree, but he would not lie to her or himself. For years, Reed had been at the periphery of their lives. A dark, distant cloud they were both aware of, but did their best to ignore. That dark cloud had moved over them and settled in, almost destroying them.

"You're right, I did. It was wrong of me. Thomas O'Connell's murder brought back all the memories I'd done my best to push aside."

"The minute Reed reentered our lives, I felt us begin to crumble. And then—"

"You're still angry about his death."

"Angry? Devastated might be a more correct term."

"Are we going to rehash this? I—"

"You still don't get it, do you, Grey? For more than a decade, the man was the only father figure I'd ever known. Yes, he was hideous. Yes, he was a monster. And yes, he deserved to die. But killing him broke something inside of me."

Her words stabbed through him as he saw the event through her eyes. Hill Reed had tried to turn a small child into a killer. Irelyn had fought his teachings as much as she could, but his influence had been great. She had done things she hated herself for, would never forgive herself for. But Reed had also given her a home, food to eat, and an odd, if sick, kind of affection.

Grey had told her he forgave her, but had he really? By insisting she do the one thing Reed had never been able to get her to do, Grey, not Reed, had turned her into an assassin.

"I never completely understood how it was for you to kill him. That was damn selfish of me. We both knew the man had to be ended. After what he did to you, you deserved to be the one to do it, but I failed to foresee how that would affect you going forward and I'm very sorry for that."

He wasn't usually so inept at reading a situation, but he admitted to a total screw-up with this. His focus had been on finally ridding the world of Hill Reed, but he had missed the most important part. He had treated Irelyn as if she were a killer. She had fought so damn hard to overcome her past, and he had pushed all of that aside without an ounce of awareness of what it might do to her.

"I felt as though, after all these years, you were punishing me for your parents."

Was she right? Hell, *had* he been punishing her? Had he deluded himself into making the event into some kind of noble cause when instead it had been payback? The thought sickened him.

"Why didn't you tell me, Irelyn?"

"Because you were implacable, so determined. And as much as I hated everything about it, I knew it had to be done. Hill should have died long ago."

"Yes, he should have." Rarely tentative in any aspect of his life, Grey felt so now as he reached out and smoothed his hand over Irelyn's silky hair. Nothing in her life had ever been easy, and he'd expected her to do this incredibly difficult thing without considering how much it would cost her. He had known it might destroy their relationship, but he hadn't considered that it might well have destroyed her, too.

"I'm sorry. I should have been the one to do it. Not you."

"No, Grey. Please. Let's not do this again. What's done is done. Let's figure out a way to move forward."

"Can we? Move forward?"

"If you can forgive me for your parents, how can I not forgive you for this? Let's put the past where it belongs."

She was right. Rehashing the past would never push them

forward.

"Very well. Want to tell me what you've been doing for the last two years?"

"You mean besides trying to get back inside Hill House?"

As much as he hated it, he had to ask. "If I hadn't instigated..." He held up a hand. "I won't say *forced*, because as you've said before, if you had outright refused, I wouldn't have pushed it, but I did instigate Hill's death. So tell me, if I hadn't done that, would you have gone about trying to get back into Hill House by killing those assassins?"

"I don't know. Once Hill told me I had a brother, my sole focus was on finding him. And I knew the only way to find him was to get inside and find his file."

"And then when you found out I was your brother's next target?"

"I had to stop him, of course. If you're asking me if I regret shooting Kevin, I can only say I'm very sorry he's dead. But I could not let him kill you."

She hadn't needed to tell him—he had known that. Despite all the pain, sorrow, and anger throughout their life together, they cared for one another. Most would never understand their mutual devotion, but that was all right.

"Now I'm worried that all of that was too easy," she said.

Glad they'd gotten past the roughest part of their talk, Grey moved closer to her on the sofa. Only their shoulders touched, and that was good for right now. Her warmth beside him felt perfect.

"What was too easy?"

"Getting inside was tough, I'll admit. Even though those men were the lowest scum in the universe, and I don't regret their deaths, I hated what I had to do. If there had been another way—"

He squeezed her hand. "You would have taken it, Irelyn."

He felt her soft sigh before she answered, "Yes, I would

have. Other than to accept a contract for a hit, which I never would have done, taking out well-known assassins was the only way I knew to impress Dark."

She would need to tell him about them at some point. He knew that from experience. If not, it would eat at her soul.

"And then Dark's invitation came?"

"Yes. By courier, which is exactly the way Reed would have contacted me."

"How was your first meeting?"

"Polite, but with an edge. Like he was trying too hard, maybe. I remember him from the old days. Back then, Reed called him Pippin, said it sounded weak and that's what he was. I don't know how or why his name was changed to Sebastian Dark.

"He was small for his size, and Reed often allowed others to use him as a punching bag. As you know, Reed was good at finding what scared you most and using it to either punish you or reward you. Allowing others to beat him up was Reed's method of tough love. Dark finally had a growth spurt, and the beatings stopped, but that kind of pain never really leaves you."

Grey slid an arm around her shoulder and hugged her to him. Irelyn's training had been like that, and worse. It would never leave her, but damn, she was strong.

"How long were you there before you went for the files?"

"I had to do it the night I arrived. Dark made it clear I wouldn't be there long. I had hoped to insert myself back into the social scene there. I thought I could gather intel on who might be behind your contract. After I arrived, though, I realized that wasn't going to be possible. The house was almost empty. I think Dark's having leadership difficulties. He had plenty of guards, though. Looking back on it now, it was way too easy to get to the records room."

Considering she'd been confronted by two of those

trained guards, easy was definitely a relative term. He wouldn't even allow himself to think about what would have happened if she hadn't been able to get away.

"Maybe Dark's careless."

"No. He's calculating, meticulous…a perfectionist. And he's much more into technology than Reed ever was. He's got the money to have all the records transferred digitally, but he hasn't."

"So you think everything was a setup?"

"I didn't then, but I was so focused on getting what I needed and getting out." She shrugged. "That wouldn't have stopped me. I had to do it. In hindsight, though, I can see where so many things were too damn convenient." She raised her head and shifted slightly to look up at him. "So what's his reasoning?"

"Could he have wanted you to find your brother?"

"You mean in an altruistic 'let me reunite a family' kind of way? No, that's not Dark. He might be different from Reed in many ways, but he's just as evil."

"Maybe he wanted you to have to choose, me or your brother."

"Now that's something I could definitely see him wanting to do. But why? What's his endgame?"

"Who the hell knows? What I do know is that he's a dangerous psychopath who's not going to just stop on his own. If he wants to hurt you, he'll keep trying."

"I know." She dropped her head back onto his shoulder, pressed her face against him. "So what are we going to do?"

His chest went tight, and several seconds passed before Grey was able to speak. They were back to working together again, to being Grey and Irelyn, indomitable, inseparable. He had feared the gulf between them would never be bridged.

His voice thicker than usual, he answered, "We're going to do what we do best. We're going to stop him."

CHAPTER TWENTY-SEVEN

The meal was the best she'd eaten in a long while. Even though the food was just a simple broccoli and cauliflower casserole, she devoured her dinner like it was the most delicious of gourmet feasts.

She knew her enjoyment had more to do with the man she dined with than the taste of the food. Things felt right between them. There were still things to discuss, problems to solve, but for right now, she reveled in being with Grey once again. No secrets, no evasions.

They talked about nonconsequential things, nothing heavy or business related. He told her about the theater and what he had done to renovate it.

"But why did you buy it? I thought you were interested in turning that Victorian house you liked into a B&B."

His eyes glinted with laughter. "And that's exactly what I wanted you to think."

"But why?"

"I wanted to give it to you as a gift."

Her throat clogged, and unexpected tears burned her eyes. He had never given her anything like that. Jewelry, a first-edition book by a favorite author, a painting or work of art she had admired. He had occasionally gone whimsical and surprised her with something frivolous and silly. But this? This was beyond anything he had ever done.

"You had me completely fooled."

"The biggest problem was keeping it out of the news until I could get it finished. I'm sure the workmen thought I was the most eccentric of businessmen, since I asked them to only enter through the back and requested they not discuss the project with anyone."

Their projects each year had been one of their joys. She'd driven by the park they'd renovated on the way to her secret visit to Kennedy and had loved seeing children running and playing in an area that was once a mass of weeds and broken-down swings.

"I can't wait to explore it."

"I have a confession."

"What's that?"

"When we were walking through it that first time, I had my phone in my pocket recording the ideas you threw out. I wanted to get it as close to your vision of it as possible."

Touched and overwhelmed, she reached up and grabbed his face for a quick kiss. "Thank you, Grey."

"You're welcome." He glanced at her plate. "Finished?"

She nodded and picked up her empty plate. They carried their dishes to the kitchen and worked together to clean and straighten up. The coffee set for an early rising tomorrow, Grey held out his hand to her. She went into his arms, pressed her face against his chest.

"I can hardly believe we're here, together again. I never thought it would happen."

He squeezed her tight, dropping a kiss to the top of her head. "Nothing's going to pull us apart this time, I promise you that. Whatever troubles we face, we face together. No more secret missions, no more hiding. No more running. Understood?"

"Yes." She smiled up at him. "I love when you get all autocratic."

"I thought that was how I was most of the time."

"It is."

As far as she could remember, she had never told anyone that she loved them. She would tell Grey that she loved the things he did to her, the way he did something, but she never used those words in relation to how she felt about him. He hadn't either. Despite that, she felt his devotion, and she knew, without the words, how very much he cared. Could she take that last step and tell him what was in her heart? Were the words really necessary? Didn't he already know on some level? What if he didn't say them back? What if—

He must have felt her tension and uncertainty. "Slow and easy, sweetheart," he said softly. "It's just us. Grey and Irelyn, together again. Nothing hard about that."

She moved sensuously against his obvious arousal. "I have to disagree about that. Very hard indeed."

Issuing a sound between a laugh and a groan, Grey covered her mouth with his, and the world and all its problems fell away. Strong arms gathered her closer, and she lost herself in his taste, his passion, his need. This was the dream she often had about him. When she was in bed, alone, missing him so much her heart literally ached and her body felt so cold, yet so needy.

This was everything she craved, and more. This was Grey, wanting her, needing her. The heat from his hard body warmed her, his thick arousal pressing against her caused her heart to flutter. She felt empty and needed this man to fill her.

Clothes fell at their feet, and she didn't bother to notice if they were hers or his. She knew only that she wanted both of them naked and as close as two people could get. Grey's hands, rough and gentle at once, were roaming over her, leaving a trail of fire. His mouth continued to devour hers, and the slow burn of arousal began to flame out of control.

"Bed?" she gasped against his mouth.

"Don't think I can make it that far."

"Sofa… countertop. Floor." Laughing with sheer joy, she wrapped her arms around him, and then jumping a bit, she wrapped long legs around his waist. "I don't care where. I just need—" She broke off on a gasp as Grey entered her with one swift, hard thrust.

She sighed her contentment. "Yes. Exactly that."

Jaw clenched, his entire body rigid, Grey took two steps forward until he reached a counter. Cupping her ass slightly, he lifted her until she was at the exact level he needed. Then he could no longer hold on. She was all hot, sensual woman, and she was his. It had been so damn long since he'd felt anything this good, this right.

"Hold on. Okay?"

"Yes. All right."

Leaning her back against the counter, Grey slid out of her, groaning in ecstasy, and then plunged back in to the hilt. Irelyn's bare heels dug into his hips, urging him deeper. As he gave her hard, short thrusts, maximizing the pleasure, his mouth devoured her luscious breasts, suckling, licking.

Tension zipped up his spine. Dammit, not yet.

"Grey. Grey. Grey."

Her soft, lyrical litany of his name was his undoing. Unable to hold back, he pistoned into her, heat consuming, overwhelming, and then, with one last hard thrust, he growled her name as he exploded.

Holding her close, he felt her spasm around him, and he could barely keep himself from thrusting into her again. It'd been too damn long.

"Let's find a softer place for the next round."

"Next round? Oh, Justice, you are so the romantic."

"Ha. Give me about five more hours inside that beautiful body, and I might be able to squeeze out some romance. Right now, I feel like an animal in heat."

"Five hours, hmm?"

"Hours, days," he muttered against her neck. "I never want to let you go."

Pulling out of her was impossible. "Hang on." With that, he gathered her to him and headed out of the room and up the stairs. Since she nibbled on his ears and whispered hot, sexy little suggestions as he carried her, he figured she didn't mind his barnyard references.

Striding into the bedroom, he took her down to the bed and immediately began thrusting again. She was right there with him, taking him deep, urging him on with her hands, her words. He lost himself inside the only woman he could ever want or need in his life.

She was his Irelyn, now and forever.

HOURS LATER, SHE WOKE EXHAUSTED, SATED, AND WANTING more. Yes, she was sore. Grey had not been gentle, but that wasn't what she had needed. They had renewed a physical connection in the most elemental way possible. It had been raw, earthy, and absolutely perfect.

She smiled as she remembered some of his mutterings. Grey was the most articulate person she knew, but when it came to their lovemaking, he could make a caveman sound literate. And she loved every single utterance. The most controlled man in the world lost his head when she was in his arms. How could she not love that?

"Are you still breathing?" he asked in a gruff voice.

"Barely. How about you?"

"I'm considering it. Guess it's been a while for both of us."

Rolling over, she propped her chin on his chest. "You know what they say, abstinence makes everything harder."

"I think you mean absence makes the heart grow fonder."

She took him in her hand, caressed him till she felt that hardness begin to return. "I like my version better."

He hissed a soft sigh and arched his back. "Yeah, I see what you mean."

"I'm glad you missed me."

"You'll never know how much."

"Try me."

"I slept with one of your nightgowns beside me."

A wave of tenderness swept through her at his admission. Grey could often be romantic, but rarely was he sentimental. To have him admit something so mushy was so out of character.

"Did it help?"

"Hell no. I woke up craving you even more."

Her hand continued its caresses up and down his length. "How can I make it up to you?"

"You've made a good start."

"Let me see if I can help things along." She went to her knees and peppered kisses on his chest, whirling her tongue around a hard, male nipple. With each lick of her tongue or touch of her hand, his body went stiller, stiffer. Smiling at the effect she was having on him, she continued kissing down his body, stopping on occasion to lick at a spot, nibble another. By the time she reached the hard, male part of him, he was whispering curses, along with her name, and, if she wasn't mistaken, a few hallelujahs, too.

Having set the course and knowing torturing him would only mean torture for her, too, she delayed her play no longer. Leaning over him, she took him deep into her mouth, sucking hard.

With a harsh curse, Grey arched up, but Irelyn held him down and gave him her full attention. She loved his taste, his scent. She loved that this very male part of him had been inside her, had given her the most glorious pleasure imaginable. She loved that she could reduce this strong, beautiful man to mutters, grunts, and growls.

When she knew neither of them could handle another minute apart, she released him. Straddling his hips, she took his length into her hand and slid him inside her. Though darkness surrounded them, the lamp in the hallway gave enough light to see his beautiful face, the glittering of those cobalt-blue eyes, gleaming with heat, need.

She gasped when he grabbed her hips and held her like that. They stared at each other, connected, their bond both physical and spiritual. He was her Grey, she was his Irelyn. Everything they were, all that they were, was in their touch, their locked gazes, his body within hers.

And then everything accumulated into a massive rolling wave of ecstasy. Irelyn closed her eyes as she plunged into the deepest ocean and then was flung heavenward into the stars.

CHAPTER TWENTY-EIGHT

Hill House
England

Sebastian checked his email once more and fought an almost overwhelming urge to scream when zero messages were displayed. The day after his exhibition, he had sent queries to twenty-five of the more notable and up-and-coming assassins. He wanted a mix of experience in his stable of killers. They should have been beating at the door to be a Hill House member. And yet, not one of them had indicated the slightest interest in working for him. Some had answered with an outright no, a few had given vague excuses, and several had not even bothered to respond.

His event had backfired. He had thought he needed to show his expertise in killing to gain the respect of the community. Should he have explained things better? He hadn't considered his audience wanting to know why the guards were being punished. The men were simply props to display his talents, but perhaps his performance would have been better received if he had done a more thorough introduction.

Or perhaps it was something else altogether. Maybe killing wayward employees interested no one. Though the men had deserved the punishment, maybe he should have taken care of them in private. Had he, in effect, aired his dirty laundry?

He blamed his poor judgment on Irelyn Raine. If he had not been so focused on her, he would have realized his mistake sooner. She had taken his attention away from the more important matters of being the leader of Hill House. Like so many of her other sins, she would pay for this one, too.

He now had a new plan. One that would show his leadership abilities. Yes, he had impressed them with his skill as a bullwhip master, but they already knew he could kill. What they didn't know, what they needed to know, was that he could be a great leader, too. Just as great as Hill Reed.

And that was why he had ordered the killing of Grey Justice. It was actually a concession on his part, as he had wanted to go about that in another way, but no one but Sebastian knew this. This would work out just as well, though, as it would give his reputation the cache it needed. He would send some of his best men to take down the famous billionaire. The news would travel all over the world. The ordinary citizen would never know who was responsible, but the ones who mattered would know that Sebastian Dark had planned and instigated the bastard's death. They would be suitably impressed and realize he was the right leader for Hill House. Instead of him having to send out invitations, they would call him and beg to work for him.

Problem was, Justice had gone off the grid. Sebastian's sources had confirmed that his slut, Irelyn Raine, had returned to him. She was the one who'd taken down the assassin. The delight when he'd heard that bit of additional news had almost negated the aggravation of having lost one of the few assassins who'd still been loyal to Hill House.

But all of that would change once Grey Justice was dead. It would be the kill of the decade, if not the century. The famous billionaire, loved by millions and hated by millions, massacred in a hail of gunfire. It would all be very dramatic and Sebastian would make sure those that mattered knew exactly who had ordered the kill.

Justice wouldn't know what hit him. He was so damn arrogant and self-assured, he rarely went anywhere with bodyguards. Wherever he and Raine had disappeared to, he likely hadn't taken any with him. Yes, she was dangerous, but she could be neutralized quickly. He hoped she didn't die. Once they were located, he would give instructions that he wanted Irelyn Raine brought to him alive. He had plans for her. Big plans.

Having worked all of this out in his mind, he felt his tremendous burden lift. Yes, this would work out perfectly. Even better than his original plan for Justice. The famous bastard would be dead, and Irelyn Raine, the woman who had killed several from their community, would be at Sebastian's mercy. Once he finished with her, he would send a mass email, showing the woman groveling at his feet as he killed her. A fitting ending for a killer and a traitor.

And he, Sebastian Dark, would shoot to the top of the assassin world. A hundred years from now, people would still be talking about his conquests.

But first, he had to find his prey.

CHAPTER TWENTY-NINE

Colorado Mountains

Irelyn blinked her eyes open, not surprised to feel a smile on her face. She hadn't slept that well in years.

She stretched with that luxurious feeling of having nowhere to go and nothing on her agenda. This was a working vacation for her and Grey, but considering what she had been doing for the last two years, this felt decadent.

Grey was already up and most likely in the gym. She'd heard him wake just after dawn and then felt a kiss on her forehead. That soft, gentle caress had lulled her back into a wonderful, dreamless sleep.

She lay still for another moment and took stock. Last night had been as close to perfection as one could get. She and Grey hadn't talked like that in years. Even before their troubles had started, they'd gotten complacent. Who they were and what they were to each other were intertwined. Yes, they were individuals, but living with one another, working with each other, and sharing the same goals had created a unique intimacy. So much so that Irelyn hadn't thought anything could ever separate them. And that's where she had made her mistake. Taking anything so special for granted was a sure way to destroy it.

But now they were back, their connection as strong as ever. Last night, they'd not only recommitted their bodies, but also their minds and hearts. That was something she'd never take for granted again.

She wasn't avoiding the issue that had started the unraveling. She would mention it at some point, because it needed to be addressed. Whatever answer he gave no longer mattered. She had lived almost two years with this sadness hanging over her head. Had allowed it to weave a thread of uncertainty into their relationship. She would never allow that to happen again. Having been parted from him, with an ocean between them, she now knew what was important. She and Grey together, no matter how they defined themselves, was what mattered. The rest was merely semantics.

Physically sated and happier than she could ever remember, she also realized with glee that she was ravenous with hunger. She hadn't had much of an appetite for so long. She bounded out of bed, hurriedly showered, and dressed. While Grey finished up his workout, she would make breakfast.

As she walked through the house, she wondered how he felt this morning. He hadn't slept well, which was typical for him. Grey's restless mind always seemed to be working even when he was at rest. She knew he'd gotten up several times during the night to check on the alarms and safeguards he'd set. Once, she had thought to offer to do that for him, but had fallen asleep before she could get the words out. She was normally a light sleeper, but she had been through an emotional wringer, and the deep sleep had given her a much-needed reprieve.

She opened the refrigerator and perused the choices. Grey, as usual, had seen to it that her favorites were well stocked. She had adopted a vegetarian diet several years ago, and Grey always went out of his way to accommodate her.

Deciding that good nutrition could coexist with decadent and delicious food, she gathered the ingredients for blueberry pancakes. And though she wouldn't eat it, she took bacon from the fridge for Grey.

In the middle of pouring batter onto the hot griddle, she heard Grey's footsteps coming down the hallway and then stop. Music came through the speakers, and she smiled at one of her favorite songs. He knew her so well. Seconds later, sinewy arms wrapped around her from behind, and Irelyn melted into Grey's hard, warm body. These were the kind of moments she had missed.

GATHERING THE LOVELY WOMAN IN HIS ARMS CLOSER, GREY swayed with her to the music. Public displays of affection were not the norm for them, but when they were alone, touching each other came as natural as breathing.

He rubbed his beard-stubbled face against her silky-smooth cheek. "Good morning," he growled into her ear. "Did you sleep well?"

Her arms tightened around his, pulling him closer. Tilting her head back, she looked up at him. "Can't remember when I've slept better. In fact…" She turned in his arms and smiled up at him. "It was so delicious, maybe we can take a nap after breakfast."

This was the Irelyn he wanted to see. Free of shadows, free of doubts. "Come to think of it, I am a bit tired from my workout."

"Then you definitely need to get your rest." She stood on her toes and kissed him full on the mouth.

Grey deepened the kiss, devouring her luscious mouth, taking her breath into his body. Last night had been only a small taste of how he wanted to enjoy Irelyn. From the moment he'd met her, she had bewitched him. From the moment they'd first kissed, he had been hers.

The stench of overcooked pancake filled the air.

"Breakfast is burning," he muttered against her mouth.

"Um huh." Breathless, she nibbled at his mouth. "That's good. I—" With a gasp, she tried to pull out of his arms. "Breakfast is burning!"

Laughing, he reached behind her and turned off the flame. "Maybe we should take that nap now."

"A nap would likely improve my pancake-making skills, don't you think?"

"Let's find out." Scooping her up, he lifted her onto his shoulder and headed out the door. She was laughing so hard, she almost fell off twice before he made it into the bedroom. Throwing her onto the bed, he followed her down and began to strip her. By the time she was completely nude, the laughter had been replaced by sighs, moans, and groans. He loved every beautiful, sexy sound she made.

Starting at her feet, he kissed his way up her body. The bruises were fading, and the cuts on her leg and side were healing nicely. Amazing how someone so delicately feminine could be so damned strong. Women had fascinated him from a young age. They were all unique and so different from masculine, hairy, sweaty men. He loved their laughter, their shape, their softness…everything. But Irelyn? Oh, Irelyn was on another level altogether.

He wanted to savor every taste, remember every soft sigh. He wanted this to last forever. He wanted to hurry so he could start all over again. Soft, silky, fragrant deliciousness everywhere. Her inner thigh was so muscular, yet so soft. When his mouth touched her, she moaned, arching her back slightly. Knowing what she wanted, what she needed, knowing he needed it, too, he gently pushed her legs farther apart and put his mouth on her. Tasting the most feminine part of her, he reveled in her, lashing his tongue over her, inside her. Her body went rigid, and she screamed his name in a husky, sensual, sex-filled voice.

Though need pounded through him, he refused the urgency and continued up her body, stopping to lick and taste as he went. She had a small birthmark right under her left breast that was particularly sensitive. Knowing this, he tongued the area, relishing the little hissing sound she made. His mouth moved slightly, covering her breast, where he continued to taste, to suckle, to enjoy.

"Grey...please. I need you."

Lifting his head, he stared down at her. Beautiful, complex, fascinating, stubborn, strong. He could think of a thousand adjectives to describe Irelyn Raine, and he still wouldn't reach the epicenter of who she was. He had never known anyone like her, knew he never would.

"What's wrong?" she whispered.

"Absolutely nothing. I was just thinking about how perfect you are."

Myriad emotions flickered on her face as her eyes shimmered with tears. Her hand cupped his jaw, caressing him tenderly.

Dropping his head, he kissed her and then slid into her warmth. Gently, but with purpose, he withdrew and thrust again. When she wrapped her longs legs around his waist, showing him she wanted more, he was unable to slow his pace. He thrust again and again, setting them both on fire, and let it consume them as one.

———

THEY WERE IN THE MIDDLE OF DEVOURING WHAT SHE

considered the best pancakes she'd ever eaten when she gasped. "I can't believe I haven't told you about Somer."

"Who's Somer?"

"A little girl I found in Nice." She glossed over the details of how she had found the child, concentrating instead on describing her sweet personality and the injuries she had sustained from the mother's boyfriend. "She has an amazing spirit and is so sweet."

"I'd love to meet her. What happens to her when she's well?"

"A couple that Sister Nadeen is well acquainted with is going to adopt her."

"If they hadn't wanted her, would you have taken her yourself?"

Adopt a child? Her heart stuttered at the thought of being responsible for another living being—a child. For years, she had pushed aside that niggling need inside her. The longing to hold a child in her arms and know she was wholly and completely responsible for his or her well-being and care. It had once been a deep ache she had thought she had successfully squelched. She wasn't exactly mother material, was she?

"Hey, I didn't ask you to make you sad."

She shook her head, smiling. "I guess I never thought about it. My lifestyle, especially the last couple of years, certainly wouldn't be conducive to raising a child."

"That was then, this is now. Would you have considered it?"

This was the closest he'd ever come to talking about children with her. The nature of their work didn't exactly scream stable home environment for raising children. She had risked life and limb to save children. Had moved what seemed like insurmountable mountains to get them the care they needed, or a safe environment to live. Not once had she considered making one of them her own. And now? The idea of having a little one, or two, didn't scare her as much as she thought it would.

"That would be a huge step."

He took her hand, squeezed it gently "We've made big steps before. As long as we're together, we can do anything. Right?"

Together. Something like happiness settled inside her. Grey was right. They had come through every storm possible together, and they had survived. Once this final storm passed, they could move forward to something more. "Yes, I believe we can."

SHE WAS SITTING IN THE LIBRARY, SURROUNDED BY thousands of books. This was her favorite room in the house. Both she and Grey were avid readers, but the last couple of years, she hadn't had the time or inclination to lose herself in a great story. Today, she was reintroducing herself to one of her favorite classics, Louisa May Alcott's *Little Women.*

A part of her felt guilty. In between taking frequent breaks to enjoy their time together, Grey had been working. Normally, she would be doing the same, but she had been embarrassingly lazy since they'd arrived. Sleeping hours longer than she normally would, getting sleepier in the evenings before her normal bedtime, and taking frequent naps. Admittedly, many of those times had to do with having Grey around.

It was more than that, though. She hadn't realized that she had reached the peak of physical and mental exhaustion. She'd been living on nerves, not sleeping, eating, or taking care of herself like she should. She had thought Grey wanted to get away to get them out of harm's way, but looking back on it now, she knew that wasn't his biggest reason. He had known she had reached her limit.

In a way, it was hard to have someone know you so well…know you better than you knew yourself. Self-sufficiency and self-reliance were important to her peace of mind and stability. But she couldn't deny that having someone know her and care for her so much touched her like nothing else could. How many times had Grey set aside his needs for her own? Too many times to count. And it wasn't because he was controlling—although he certainly could be that. Neither was it because he necessarily thought he knew best. He did it because he cared.

Now that she was sleeping and eating better, her mind felt clearer, much less clogged. As she read, another part of her mind was left free to explore. Pieces began to fall together. Minuscule bits formed nuggets of information, leading to bigger clues. Faces and images appeared, conversations played through her mind, and she caught nuances she had previously ignored.

Grey walked into the library, and she almost pounced on him with her conclusion. "It's Dark. He's behind it all."

HESITATING, GREY ROAMED HIS GAZE OVER HER FACE AND then her body. They'd been here only a little over a week, but she was already looking remarkably better. Her face held a healthy glow again, her cheekbones didn't seem as hollow, and the shadows beneath her eyes had disappeared. She had even put on a couple of pounds. Her stamina in both the weight room and the bedroom was a testament to her strength and endurance. His mind eased that her recovery had been swift, but now he had a new worry.

"Grey?"

Aware that he had taken too long in answering, he nodded. "Yes, it is."

"You're not surprised. You already figured that out."

"It's the only thing that makes sense. Too many things kept going back to Dark's involvement."

"Why didn't you tell me?"

He cocked his head and gave her a raised brow. "What would you have done if I had?"

"I would have gone after him, of course. I—" She halted, laughed a little. "And I would have gotten myself killed."

"Yes. I knew the instant you figured it out, nothing would stop you from going after him. I couldn't risk that until you were well."

"So all that investigating that the Grey Justice Group is doing isn't really happening?"

"No, it's happening, too. I'm not arrogant enough to assume anything right now. I thought while you recovered, if something led us in another direction, we'd be better equipped to deal with whomever."

"But it's still leading you to Dark?"

"Without a doubt."

"What about Morrissey? Are there any leads on his murder? Could Sebastian somehow be involved in that?"

He was glad to be able to ease her mind about that. "I spoke with Gallagher this morning. One of Morrissey's former business partners was arrested and has confessed."

"That's a relief. I'm very sorry he's dead, but I am glad it's not related to us." She patted the open space on the sofa beside her and waited until he sat down. "But why is Dark targeting you? Why now?"

"I don't know. Maybe it's just a matter of bringing a little cache to his name. Maybe he's found out who I really am, though that's doubtful. There are only a few people left who have that knowledge."

"Do you think I brought this on? By trying to catch his attention to get back into Hill House?"

"Absolutely not. We know he's having issues getting assassins to come back to Hill House. This is likely his twisted way of trying to earn the community's respect."

"So what are we going to do about it?"

"What do you want to do?"

"I want to stop him, and I want to destroy Hill House once and for all."

The quickness with which she answered told him she'd been thinking about it already. And her answer didn't surprise him. He had known this day would come. He had thought about doing it himself. He certainly had the where-withal to destroy the place where she'd been abused and tortured. But he had waited, wanting her to come to that conclusion on her own.

He had forced the issue of ridding the world of Hill Reed. It wasn't in him to regret the man's death, but he damn well regretted what it had done to Irelyn, and to them.

A slender hand covered his own. He glanced down and marveled that something so lovely, so delicate-looking had the strength to fight such brutal evil. She was deceptively soft, deceptively fragile. There wasn't a weak bone in this woman's body.

Something settled within him, lessening his worry. They would do this, and they would win, because they would be doing it together.

"Then that's what we'll do." He squeezed her hand. "Together."

CHAPTER THIRTY

Hill House
England

"The intel is credible?" The question was rhetorical. Gibson would never dare come to him without verifiable proof.

"Do you remember Ivy Roane?"

How could he forget the woman Reed had created to ease his obsession with Irelyn Raine? The woman had been a pale imitation and a liability from the start.

"Yes, but what does Roane have to do with finding Raine and Justice?"

"She left detailed notes on all her contracts. The last one was the Mendoza and Bianchi debacle."

Debacle indeed. She had played everyone against one another, and in the end, everyone but the target had been killed, including Roane.

"Mendoza's granddaughter was hidden away in a house in the Colorado mountains. The house is owned by various shell corporations. Every time we uncover one, it leads to another one."

The people who worked for him knew that he was not a tolerant man. He had eliminated more than one employee for trying his patience. "Get to the point, Gibson."

The man's Adam's apple convulsed as he took a nervous gulp. "Yes, sir. It's a bit complicated, sir, but the point is, Jonah Slater is rumored to be closely associated with Justice. We believe Justice provided this place as a safe house to Slater and the Mendoza woman."

"And what makes you think Raine and Justice are there, in Colorado?"

Breathing a little easier, Gibson went on. "Justice has three houses in his name, Raine has two. They also have one together in Italy. There's been no activity at any of these houses, so we know they didn't go there."

"And?"

"When Justice's private plane left Dallas, the pilot had to file a flight plan. It's taken a few days to find someone to hack the records. We—"

"Gibson," he warned.

"Sorry, sir. Um." He looked down as if checking his notes. The man was a brilliant researcher, but had no stones when it came to this kind of work. Maybe he should just kill him right here, right now. Release a little tension. Maybe he should—

"They flew to Colorado, sir."

Thoughts of eliminating Gibson disappeared from his mind. In fact, he might just give the man a bonus.

"Send me the information. I'll take it from here."

"Yes, sir, thank you." The man practically ran from the room.

Sebastian waited until the door closed behind Gibson to do a triumphant fist pump. It was going to happen. Grey

Justice would soon have a new claim to fame. *Murdered billionaire.* It was going to be a spectacular takedown. While his people had been trying to find them, Sebastian had been busy planning. He was a detailed, meticulous—some might say anal-retentive—planner who left nothing to chance.

Justice would die, and Sebastian Dark would claim victory.

And then he could concentrate on something lovelier, something deliciously dark and deadly. He would have Irelyn Raine brought here, back to where she had begun. It was only fitting that the justice she so deserved be meted out here. He already had everything prepared. He just needed his unwilling participant.

Colorado Mountains

LYING IN BED WITH IRELYN, WRAPPED IN EACH OTHER'S ARMS, Grey stared into the darkness. Her easy, shallow breathing told him she was in a deep, dreamless sleep. That was a miracle in itself. Too many nights he had held her as nightmares overtook her, tortured her. They had lessened through the years, but on occasion, they would attack without warning. When he was with her, he could bring her back, ground her in reality. When she had been away from him, he knew she had battled them on her own. He didn't want that to ever happen again.

They had talked about the future, but only in abstract ways. He wanted something more, something different than what they'd had. Something concrete. What that looked like, he wasn't quite sure yet. He knew only that whatever she faced, whether it was a nightmare she needed to be woken from, or an endangered child she needed to save, he wanted to be with her.

This week had been a good start. It had been all about them, all about being together, working together. Tomorrow afternoon, they would go to the airport, where their plane would be waiting. They would fly into London, gather the supplies they needed, and then they'd move on Dark. There would be no going back.

Once they'd settled on their plans, they had agreed to let it go. Tomorrow would take care of itself. Tonight had been all about Irelyn and Grey. They had laughed and talked, watched a movie, ate popcorn, lay in front of the fireplace, dreaming and making love. It had been magical, beautiful. He wanted more of those moments. An eternity would not be enough. He wanted days on end of blissful—

A shrill alarm blared in the darkness. Grey and Irelyn sprang from the bed as one. No time for questions, no need to ask who or why. They had trained for this for years. It had been a while since they'd had practice drills, but he had no doubts about their preparedness.

"How much time do we have?" Irelyn asked.

"Ten minutes."

"You think it's Dark?"

"Does it matter?"

"No, guess not."

"Let's move, then." An unexpected anxiety hit him. He grabbed her arm before he could stop himself. "We can leave. We don't have to do this."

"Stop trying to protect me, Justice. I don't back away from a fight. And if you think I'd let you face this alone, you don't know me."

"Yes, I do, Irelyn. I always have."

Not waiting for a response, he went to the closet and pulled on a pair of black pants and a long-sleeved T-shirt.

Knowing she was getting dressed, too, he called out as he left the room, "Meet me in the sanctuary."

He ran down the hallway and took the stairs three at a time. Going to the back of the house, he keyed a code into the keypad next to the pantry door beside the kitchen. Another door swung open. He stepped inside, turned on the overhead light. They had named this room the very opposite of what it was. Weapons of all kinds covered the walls. Several steel chests held drawers filled with grenades, flash bangs, C-4, stun guns, and Tasers. A variety of handguns were within easy reach in a glass casing. A countertop displayed an assortment of knives.

There was no telling how many were coming, but they were prepared for an army. Their arsenal had been built over time, and it was a good one. Anything beyond a nuclear war, they were equipped and ready to engage.

He sensed Irelyn come in behind him. Turning, he took in her apparel, glad to see she had chosen to dress in a similar fashion, though she looked a damn sight sexier.

She gazed around the room. "You've added a few more items."

"Yeah." He threw a bulletproof vest her way and then slipped into one himself. Grabbing an HK237, he watched as she removed an M16 from the wall and handled the weapon like she'd been born with one in her hand.

A glance at the cameras showed the intruders' progress. Three large trucks were parked outside the perimeter. It was Dark's people. No one else would have sent this many men.

"Ready?"

He turned to face Irelyn, his warrior woman. She was dressed in black, her hair pulled back in a low ponytail, holding an M16, and he didn't think he'd ever seen anyone more beautiful or capable.

Though they had set up these safeguards in every house

they owned, he couldn't resist asking, "You know what to do if we get separated? Where to go?"

"Yes. And no heroics from you, big guy. Got it? We do this together."

He smiled. "Yes, ma'am." Grabbing her shoulders, he gave her a long, hard kiss.

She returned his kiss with equal fervor and then said softly, "Let's get rid of these bastards so we can go back to bed."

Grinning, he took two earbuds from a drawer. Handing her one, he inserted the other into his ear. "Sound check."

She gave a quick, affirmative nod and said, "Loud and clear."

There were so many things he wanted to say to her right now. There was no guarantee they would come out of this alive. They both knew that. Even though they'd faced this kind of challenge in the past, this one was more personal than any others. Dark was the spawn of Hill Reed and was just as evil. Ending him would put some finality to Irelyn's painful past.

Still, he couldn't just send her off without saying something. "Irelyn, you know that I—"

"Save it for later, Justice." Warmth turned her eyes a shimmering gray. "When I can fully appreciate it."

"It's a date."

Weapons loaded, they walked out the door together.

CHAPTER THIRTY-ONE

The battle had been a bloody one and it still wasn't over. Crouched on the floor behind the kitchen counter, Irelyn stayed on alert as she eased open a drawer. Feeling around in the dark, she grabbed hold of a kitchen towel. Shards of broken glass from a hallway mirror were gouged into her left arm and thigh. Most were superficial cuts on her arm, but her left thigh hadn't been so lucky. She could feel blood oozing down her leg from a large piece embedded in her skin.

She wrapped the towel around her thigh and tied it off. She was tempted to remove the glass but feared causing more damage. She'd wait until the fight was over. The hail of gunfire had finally stopped for a moment, and her ears were no longer ringing. Right now, there was only silence. She had taken three men out, but she was sure there were more. How many were left?

Where was Grey? In a hand-to-hand battle with one of Dark's men, she had lost her earbud and now had no way to reach him. Calling out to him would reveal their positions to the remaining men.

The last few shots had been in the den, close to the back of the house. She told herself they had come from Grey's weapon and that he was still alive, that he was okay. He had to be. Grey Justice was invincible. She had never known a cooler head or a better shot.

A noise hit her ears. Footsteps. Heavy-footed ones, their owner trying to be quiet and not succeeding, so she knew they didn't belong to Grey, who could be as silent as a panther. Scooting on her butt to the edge of the counter, she peered around the corner. Light from a flashlight appeared at the door. Irelyn didn't wait to see a face. She fired three rounds, heard a pained grunt and then a loud crash as a big body collapsed. She winced, knowing the statue of the goddess Diana that she'd purchased in Greece a few years back hadn't survived.

Again, there was only silence. She wouldn't wait much longer. She tried to reassure herself that Grey was okay, but an image of him bloodied and injured kept flashing through her mind. She needed to find him.

Long ago, she'd learned to block out physical pain, and it angered her that she had to grit her teeth to do so now. This was nothing compared to what she had endured in the past. Holding on to that anger, she got to her feet and crept toward the door leading to the dining room. Holding her breath, she stopped and listened intently. Other than the sound of the wind blowing through the broken windows, she heard nothing. She waited a few more seconds and then peeked out.

Death and destruction were all around. One man, dressed in black, lay facedown on the dining room table. Blondish hair stuck out of the end of his skullcap, reassuring her the man wasn't Grey. Another body lay crossway on the floor between the dining room and a small parlor. He was also dressed in black, but looked to be a mammoth size with a gut to match. Definitely not Grey.

Staying low, she ran to the next doorway, stopped, and listened. Still no human sounds. She looked around the door and jumped back. A man was rounding the corner. The barrel of his gun appeared first. Not one she recognized. She fired a shot. Missed. Rapid fire commenced.

Backing away, she ran back into the kitchen. Standing on the other side of the fridge, she weighed her options. She had four rounds left and then would resort to her secondary weapon, which had fifteen. Once they were gone, it was hand-to-hand with her knife until she could get back to the sanctuary and reload her weapons.

"Irelyn!"

Grey. A lump clogged her throat, and her eyes blurred. He was alive! And from the sound of his voice, he was also royally pissed.

"Yes?"

"You okay?"

"Yes. You?"

Instead of telling her he was okay, he shouted, "I have a question for you."

"What's that?"

"Marry me?"

Hidden in an alcove beside a bookshelf in the living room, Grey held his breath as he waited for the answer to the most important question he'd ever asked in his life. Proposing in the midst of a gun battle was not the most romantic way to go about such things, but for them, for who they were, this worked perfectly. He and Irelyn were the least traditional people he knew.

He should have asked her long ago and had no good

excuse for not making that last permanent commitment. They might have started in darkness, might have spent years fighting their way free of the pain, but she had brought light to his life, warmth to his soul. He could not imagine his life without her. If she said yes, he would spend the rest of his life making sure she knew that.

"Are you crazy?"

Her response was exactly what he'd wanted, with just the right amount of surprise, outrage, and laughter.

"Only about you."

Another bit of laughter for his cheesy answer, and then she shouted, "Are you all right? You didn't get hit in the head or something?"

He laughed. Only this woman could make him laugh in the midst of blood and death.

"No. I'm finally thinking straight. So what do you say?"

He held his breath, knowing she was probably both confused and scared. In all their time together, they had never talked marriage. Which was damn crazy. He had never wanted anyone but Irelyn.

"Irelyn?"

"You're sure?"

"Never been more sure of anything."

"Then, yes!"

Grinning like an idiot, Grey leaned against the wall and assessed his chances of getting out of here alive so he could marry his woman. He had disposed of seven intruders. By his count, there were at least two more in the house. One was upstairs, stomping around in a guest bedroom. As he'd hoped, the other one was now headed Grey's way. It would be the man's last mistake.

Footsteps above him indicated the other guy had heard him, too. One more check of his gun showed him what he already knew. Three rounds left. He'd gotten into a one-on-

one with one of the assholes and had dropped one of his weapons. Once he was out of ammo, the Ka-Bar knife would have to do the rest.

He glanced down at the blood soaked cloth he'd wrapped around his hand. Another casualty from the hand-to-hand battle. The guy had managed to slice open his palm. The pain was secondary to the aggravation of not being able to shoot with his dominant hand. He would make do but he was furious all the same. No way in hell were these bastards going to win.

He stood on the other side of the entertainment center. The instant the man entered, he'd be able to see him immediately. Grey leaned forward just a bit. Ah yes, he was coming and quite rapidly. One bullet should do the job. A grizzled-looking face appeared at the doorway. Grey took the shot but the guy ducked at the last second. Grey fired again, winged him on the shoulder but the guy kept coming. Firing his last shot, a hole appeared in the center of his forehead. He was dead before he hit the floor.

One down, one to go. He heard no more footsteps and figured the guy was waiting for Grey to make a move. Since he didn't want the man to go after Irelyn, Grey decided to oblige him. He took one step toward the door, and a shot rang out. Grey dropped to the floor. That shot hadn't come from the open door. Grey turned in time to see a man climbing through the broken window. Seemingly unconcerned about the shards of glass scattered across the floor, he came toward Grey with a wide grin on his face. There was no reason to wonder why. Grey was lying on the floor like a sitting duck. With only a knife, he'd never make the kill before the man blasted his head off.

Determined to not go to his grave while lying down, Grey sprang to his feet. Just as the guy went for the kill shot, a long, slender knife whooshed by Grey's head and embedded in the guy's throat. His gun dropped to the floor as he grabbed at his throat. The instant he pulled the knife free, blood gushed like a spigot had been turned on full force. The man collapsed inches from Grey's feet.

Turning, Grey stared at the lovely and lethal woman at the doorway. It wasn't the first time she had saved his life, but that might've been as close to death as he'd been in some time. "Whoever said not to bring a knife to a gunfight doesn't know Irelyn Raine."

They stiffened as the creak of a floorboard told them they weren't alone. The lone man upstairs was likely waiting to take them unawares.

"I'm out of ammo," Grey said softly. "You have any left?"

"Yes."

"Save it in case we don't have a choice. I'd like to have a talk with him. You go left, and I'll—" He broke off at the sound of an engine starting up and then a vehicle roaring away.

"Guess he changed his mind about staying."

"Think we're alone now?"

"Yeah. Except for about a dozen or so dead bodies."

Surprising him, she flew into his arms. "I thought I'd lost you."

"Not going to happen. At least for sixty or so years." He pushed her away to examine her. "Where are you hurt?"

"Most of them are just scratches and cuts."

He spotted the bloody towel at her thigh. "That looks a bit more serious."

"Probably needs a couple of stitches." She picked up his bloody hand. "This looks bad."

"A couple of stitches will take care of it, too." Before she could question him further, he pulled her back into his arms and held her tight. They hadn't come out unscathed, but considering what they'd been up against, he felt damn lucky.

She raised her head and looked around at the destruction. "Having a house with a lot of glass might not have been our best idea."

"Agreed. How about we get this place repaired again and sell it to someone who doesn't have a thousand or so enemies?"

"I'll miss it, but you're right. We need to move on."

"As long as we move on together."

"About the marriage thing." She chewed her lip, and uncertainty filled her eyes. "You were serious about that?"

"Never been more serious."

"But you said… I thought…" She shook her head. "Never mind."

"No. We don't do that, Irelyn. We say what's on our minds."

She sighed. "All right. Do you remember an interview you gave to that reporter a few years ago?"

"Seriously, Irelyn? I've talked to hundreds of reporters. How can I—"

"It was a television interview for *Dallas Talk*. The reporter asked you about your private life."

Having this conversation surrounded by broken glass, blood, and dead bodies felt surreal. If he hadn't recognized how important it was, he might have suggested they wait till later. But he saw the insecurity in her eyes. She had doubts, and he needed to address them.

"I vaguely remember. She got intrusive with her questions."

"Yes. She asked you why you've never married. Do you remember your answer?"

"No, I don't."

"You told her, 'Why would I want to get married?' You said you already had everything you could ever want."

"Irelyn…I—"

"Look, I know we've never been traditional in anything. Our lives are complicated and not what most people would call normal, but when I heard you say that, I realized that's the way you wanted it forever."

"You knew I was committed to you, and only you."

"I know. It just hit me that you didn't see us going beyond that to something more."

He barely remembered the interview, other than the aggravation at the too personal questions. But he could certainly see how a flippant remark might have been misconstrued, especially by the woman with whom he shared his life.

"That was a boneheaded answer to a reporter who should have known better than to ask. It was our agreement that she wouldn't ask personal questions, and I gave her an insincere, off-the-cuff remark. It had nothing to do with how I feel about you."

She gave him a self-conscious smile. "I guess I could have overreacted."

"Why didn't you say something before now?"

"I should have, but we were embroiled with what was going on with the Slaters."

Grey nodded, his understanding complete now. "And then Hill Reed exploded back into our lives."

"Yes. It kind of spiraled out of control after that."

"I'm sorry, Irelyn. I never want you to doubt me or my commitment to you, to us. In fact…" Using his uninjured hand, he reached into his pocket and pulled out the token of their long, complicated relationship.

They both looked down at the fragile silver ring she'd returned to him in Dublin.

"Oh, Grey," she breathed. "You went back for it?"

"You're damn right I did."

"I'm so glad. It broke my heart to leave it there."

"No more broken hearts for either of us. We've been through a lot together, Irelyn, but there's never been anyone but you. So, will you marry me?"

"Yes, oh, yes." She pressed her cheek against his chest and spoke the words he'd always longed for to her say, "I love you, Grey. So very much."

He closed his eyes. He had almost messed this up, but dammit, this time he would get it right.

"I love you, too. Never forget that."

She smiled up at him. "Irelyn and Grey, together again."

"Forever."

CHAPTER THIRTY-TWO

Twelve hours later, they sat together in the small hangar attached to the airport. Grey had managed to contact the local authorities and have the bodies taken care of with a minimum of fuss. Years ago, when they'd first built the house, she and Grey had made a point of getting to know local law enforcement. A mutual respect for each other had helped ease their way today. There would still likely be more questions, but thankfully, they had been allowed to leave.

Both she and Grey had been sewn up and bandaged at a small clinic. Most of their injuries had been superficial, but the gash on her thigh had required eleven stitches, and the cut on Grey's hand had required seven. All in all, considering what might have happened, she knew they'd gotten out quite well.

Lily, their pilot, was due to land in Colorado within the hour. They would then fly to England, where they would confront Sebastian Dark one final time. He would know by now that his plan hadn't worked.

Grey's eyes roamed over her. "How are you feeling?"

"Not too bad, considering."

"Lily should be here soon."

"Do you think we'll be able to fly out of here?"

A monster snowstorm was imminent for half of the state. Though they were in a small area specified for private air travel, a large group of corporate executives and their families were flying back from a retreat. Dozens of travelers milled around the terminal, their expressions varying from weariness to frustration. Parents, looking both harried and exhausted, tried to entertain young children as they waited to hear word about their flight. Getting out before the blizzard struck was a concern for everyone.

"If we can't, no worries. I've already booked a hotel room just in case. Lily's grandmother lives about fifteen miles from here. She'll relish being able to spend time with her."

"But—"

He squeezed her hand. "I know you want to go after him, but if he was going to rabbit, he's already done so. A delay because of this storm isn't going to make a difference."

He was right. Dark had to know that if she and Grey survived his siege, they'd come after him. If he went into hiding, it would be immediately after he learned his men had not been successful.

"You're right. Guess I just want it over with."

"Believe me, I do, too." He turned her to face him. "We'll get through this, just like we have before. We'll bring him to an end. And then we'll destroy Hill House."

"He'll be prepared for us."

"We'll be prepared for him, too. Trust me."

"I do."

A smile spread across his face. "Thank you. I won't ever take your trust for granted again."

"I think we've both learned a hard lesson."

"We've got sixty or so years to get it right."

That was the second time he'd mentioned the sixty-year

time span. Waking up with Grey Justice beside her for the next sixty or so years sounded like heaven.

Feeling more at ease, she stood and worked the stiffness out of her neck and shoulders.

"How the hell can someone look sexy after what you've been through today?"

She glanced down at herself. They hadn't wanted to delay their departure, so she had thrown on the first thing she'd come to in the closet. A long-sleeved red dress and black boots.

"I don't look like Santa?"

He gave a crack of laughter. "The sexiest Santa I've ever seen."

Grey, on the other hand, looked both sophisticated and as hard as nails. Dressed in jeans and a black turtle-neck sweater, he would fit in at the most elegant of restaurants and yet looked tough enough to take down an army of killers. He was the epitome of stylishly lethal.

An odd, dark, ominous feeling washed over her. Suddenly feeling chilled, she shivered.

"You're cold. Want some coffee?"

"Sounds perfect."

He stood and dropped a kiss on her forehead. "Coffee light with two sugars coming up."

She watched him walk away and, for some unknown reason, wanted to call him back. Another moment of fore-boding poured through her.

"Grey?"

He turned slightly. "Yeah?"

"Hurry back. Okay?"

He threw her a wink. "Be right back."

She watched him disappear into the crowd. The coffee line was likely backed up, and she doubted he'd return as quickly as he'd promised. Maybe she should have gone with him.

Shaking her head at her unusual anxiety she forced herself to sit back down on the cold seat. It was just the aftermath of everything that had happened. She had survived a gun battle and accepted a marriage proposal. That was enough to shake up anyone.

"Hello, Ms. Raine."

Irelyn stiffened at the crisp British voice behind her. She started to turn but stopped when he said, "No, just keep facing forward. We wouldn't want anyone to get hurt."

She took the threat at face value and did as he said. "How do you know my name?"

"Oh, I know many things about you, Ms. Raine."

Accepting the inevitability of whom this man was associated with, she asked, "What do you want?"

"Mr. Dark would like to see you."

"Tell Mr. Dark he can go fu—"

"Now, now. No need to be crude. He just wants a chance to chat with you."

"Considering the man sent several of his goons to try to kill me, why would I meet with him?"

"Hmm. Several reasons, actually. Do you see that charming young couple two rows over with the boy sitting between them?"

Irelyn's gaze went immediately to the small family. She had watched them a few minutes ago, enchanted by the dark-haired little boy's infectious grin.

Her throat dry as toast, she said, "Yes."

"See the spotted stuffed dog in his arms?"

"Yes."

"Now notice how one of the red dots isn't like the others."

Her heart stopped. A red dot was moving all around the dog and occasionally onto the child's arm.

"I'm not buying that anyone could have walked into this airport with a gun big enough to have a laser sight on it."

"That's a valid point. Would you like further proof? Perhaps a demonstration? Henre would be happy to oblige."

"Henre?"

"Henre Ballard. I believe you know him."

Yes, she knew quite a lot about Henre Ballard. If Dark had not contacted her when he had, to invite her to Hill House, Henre would have been Irelyn's next target. Ballard, like the other assassins she had killed, had a reputation for accepting contracts that included children.

"Yes, I know of Henre."

"Then you know he has no qualms about doing away with a child. But just in case you're not convinced that you need to come with me, take a look at the email account you use to communicate with Sister Nadeen."

Cold dread filling her, she pulled her cellphone from her pocket and clicked on the email account. She had one message from an unknown sender. There were no words, but the video attachment was more than enough. Sister Nadeen sat in a wooden chair. Her torso and legs were tied, but her arms were free. In them was a sleeping child, Somer Dumas.

It didn't matter how Dark had found out about them. Nothing mattered but saving them. "What do you want me to do?"

"Follow me."

She stood, noting that she could now see Grey standing at the coffee bar, waiting for his order. She had to leave without alerting him. If he saw her, he would try to stop her, or he would try to take down Dark's man. She couldn't take the chance. Sister Nadeen and Somer would die. She had no doubt about that.

With one last longing glance in Grey's direction, Irelyn walked through the crowded airport and out the door.

———

GREY WATCHED THE VIDEO FEED FIVE TIMES, ENSURING HE hadn't missed anything. Irelyn had left the airport with a man in a sheepskin jacket and sunglasses. He had worn a skullcap and kept his face turned away from the cameras, so identifying him using facial recognition would be tough. Irelyn, on the other hand, had looked directly at the camera and mouthed the word *Dark* right before she walked out the door. Seconds later, a black limo drove up and the back door had opened. The instant Irelyn put a foot inside the vehicle, the man with her had jabbed something into her neck. She had fallen forward and the car door had closed. The man then got into the front passenger seat, and the limo drove away. The windows were dark, the license plate missing.

When he had returned with their coffee and she hadn't been there, he had known something was wrong. Even if she had gone to the restroom, she would have texted him or called. Knowing every second counted, he'd run to the small security office and asked them to show him the video feed for the last fifteen minutes.

His cellphone buzzed. Grey nodded his thanks to the young security man who'd helped him and stalked out of the security area.

"What'd you find, Charlie?"

"Her phone is no longer active. I don't know if it's turned off or disabled."

"Can you access anything?"

"I didn't see any recent phone calls or texts, but I uncovered a couple of email accounts. They're old ones. Doesn't look like she uses them a lot. Most of it's junk mail, but she got an email about an hour ago that you need to see. I've sent it to you."

"Thanks, Charlie. I'll be back with you soon."

Clicking on the email, Grey watched the attached video. He already knew who was responsible for Irelyn leaving, and now he knew why she'd gone without a fight. He also knew one other thing—she was heading to her death.

CHAPTER THIRTY-THREE

Hill House
England

She was back where it had all begun, and she was in trouble. Big trouble. The last thing she remembered was stepping inside the back of a limo. When she woke, she'd found herself here, in the belly of the beast once more.

She knew she was in Hill House. Even though the darkness was so deep she could see nothing, she recognized the smell of decay. Oddly enough, she hadn't noticed that until she had come back. She suspected the stink had always existed. When she was a child, Hill House had smelled like home and safety. The adult Irelyn recognized the stench of death.

Her hands were tied behind her, and she was sitting in a straight-backed wooden chair. She closed her eyes and tried to envision where she was inside the house. The chilly air made her think she was underground. She knew there was a small wine cellar and basement that had rarely been used. The air didn't have the kind of musty, dampness one would associate with a basement, though. Actually, and she couldn't say why, she thought she detected a faint whiff of paint and turpentine.

Giving up on trying to determine her location within the house, Irelyn used her other senses. She was still wearing her dress, but her boots had been removed, and her feet were ice cold. The ties on her wrists and ankles were made of rope, not plastic. Rope would be hard to break.

She didn't know Dark's exact plan, but she had a good idea. Torture, then death. Why he hadn't taken that opportunity when she'd been here before was a mystery. Perhaps he would tell her before she killed him.

Someone who didn't know her history might laugh and call her delusional. She was sitting in the dark, barefoot and tied to a chair. But she had skills that weren't evident to the naked eye. Skills that Hill Reed had taught only her. She had never used them, never wanted to use them. She would gladly make an exception for Sebastian Dark.

So, unless Dark came in and shot her dead at point-blank range, she knew she would escape. What it might cost her in the long run could not be a factor. She would do what she had to do to not only save Somer and Sister Nadeen, but also herself.

It had taken her years to acknowledge that she deserved saving. If not for Grey's determination and perseverance, she likely never would have reached that point. He had saved her. Now it was up to her to save herself.

Wanting to get started, she yelled, "Dark! Come out and show yourself!"

Silence was her answer. That was no problem. She had good lungs and a strong voice. She set up a litany of insults and screams directed at Sebastian Dark. If he was listening, he was stinging.

Fifteen minutes later, she was rewarded. Lights exploded

around her, and agony burst behind her eyes. Blocking out the pain, Irelyn squeezed her eyes shut briefly and then reopened them. Dark stood before her. Dressed in his usual black suit and red power tie, he looked as evil as always.

"You are a loud one, aren't you?"

Ignoring her surroundings for the time being, she focused on the man in front of her. "Where are Somer and Sister Nadeen?"

"They're both safely back with the good sisters at the children's home."

"I want proof."

Dark smiled. It was ugly, vile, and evil all at the same time. "Understand that I don't have to do this, but just to show you I'm not without a heart…"

He nodded toward a wall. A giant screen dropped down, and then Somer, along with Nadeen, appeared.

"Irelyn?" Sister Nadeen said.

"I'm here." She glanced over at Dark. "I don't want them to see me like this."

"No worries, my dear. They can't."

"Are you all right, Irelyn? Did that man hurt you?"

"No, he didn't hurt me. Are you and Somer okay?"

"Yes. We're back home, safe and sound. We were both a little discombobulated for a while, but we're okay now."

Despite the circumstances, Irelyn smiled at the nun's word choice. Her penchant for English crossword puzzles often showed up in her conversations.

"I'm glad. I'm sorry for the trouble I've caused."

"You're sure you're okay? We—"

The screen went blank. "That's enough. You've seen that they're both alive. I don't hurt children or nuns."

Knowing he'd kill his own mother if it suited him, she didn't respond to his obvious lie.

Though it was painful to do so, she made herself look

around. The room was a large square and so intensely lit that her eyes watered. The only relief from the blinding white was the black television monitor and Dark himself.

She had never seen this room before, which reinforced her impression that it had been recently painted.

"I know you're redecorating, but I have to tell you I hate what you've done with the place. Quite unimaginative."

"It has its uses."

"Where are we? In the basement?"

"Actually, no. I added this little addition a year or so ago. I had it decorated just for special events. You're my first guest."

"That makes me feel all warm and cozy. What happens now?"

"We have a discussion."

"About what?"

"Don't you want to know why you're here?"

"Because you're a sick, twisted, perverted creep of a weasel who kidnapped a little girl and a nun."

Another smile, this one pure evil. "You think that's the worst thing I've done?"

She gave him a bored look. "I'm sure you think you're some sort of Big Bad, but you're nothing more than a slimy worm to me."

"Your insults won't change what's going to happen here."

"Then let's get on with it, shall we?"

"You don't want to know how I knew about the house in Colorado?"

For now, she was content to let him talk. His ego would be the death of him.

"You have little spies running all around the world. Information is easy to obtain if you find the right person and have a bit of money. So no, I'm not that interested."

"Very well, then. Do you want to know why I hate you so much?"

"Hmm. Let's see. Because I'm better than you? Because I was being groomed to be Hill's successor? Because our father loved me more than he loved you?"

All those things would slice into his insecurities, but her last statement would hurt him the most.

His face flickered with intense hatred for a moment. Then, as if a light switch had been flipped on, a triumphant and smug expression replaced the anger, preparing her before he asked the next question, "So tell me, how did it feel to kill your brother?"

"You did that on purpose, didn't you?"

"But of course. Though I would have been happy to have Kevin kill Justice, the way it worked out was much more satisfying. Poor little Irelyn having to choose between her brother and her lover. Oh how I would have enjoyed being there."

Allowing him to see her pain would only make his joy greater. She refused to give him an ounce of satisfaction. "I wish you had been there, too. Then I could have killed you as well."

His smile dimmed at her emotionless reply but he didn't let up. "You're not fooling me. He's the reason you broke into the records room. You wanted to find your brother. Maybe have a little family reunion. Instead you killed him."

Memories of that fatal moment would haunt her for the rest of her life. Damned if Dark would know that though. She snorted softly. "You really think it bothered me to kill another assassin? He was nothing to me. Just one more monster that needed to die."

"You think you're so tough, so smart. That you know so much. But you don't know anything. You don't even know why you're being punished."

"Is that what this is? Punishment?"

"It will be. But we learned from our wonderful father that

punishment does no good if you don't know the reason. You remember him, don't you, Irelyn? Hill Reed? The man you killed."

Okay, that surprised her. It was only thanks to the man she had killed that she was able to hide her shock. Only a handful of people knew what she had done. Who had ratted her out?

"You're not going to deny it?"

"Why would I deny something I'm so proud of?"

"For that alone, you will suffer greatly before you die." He came closer, stood in front of her. "Want to know how I know you killed our father?"

Since she really did want to know, and it was obvious he wanted to tell her, she remained silent.

"I knew he was having dinner with you that night."

"So what? That doesn't mean I killed him. If I remember correctly, he was found in a hotel in Luxembourg two days after our dinner meeting."

"Ah yes, all very mysterious. Nothing to trace back to you and Justice. But I know the truth. Want to know how I know?"

She sighed as if bored. "I believe you've already asked that question."

"Because Reed was going to kill you that night."

Another bombshell she hadn't expected, but it made perfect sense. Over the years, she had met with Hill for the occasional meal and a bit of information sharing. She had never revealed anything that couldn't be uncovered by a little legwork. In turn, she had gleaned information from him.

That last dinner, though, was set up for one reason only. She had arranged it to finally end Reed's life. And he obviously had been ready to do the same to her. She'd just gotten there first.

"He was going to retire, but wanted to tie up loose ends. You were a loose end."

She had to laugh. What a screwed-up life she'd lived.

"You think this is funny?"

"Well, yeah. Don't you? I mean, I go there to end him and get it done before he can do it to me. Neither one of us expects it from the other. My timing has always been a bit off, but I have to say, in this instance, it was impeccable."

"You'll pay for that, you bitch."

"Yes, yes. So you've said. I did the deed. What more is there to say?"

"For starters, how about you're sorry?"

"Sorry the perverted bastard is dead? Um, no, nope, and nada. Am I sorry that I was the one to kill him? Oh, hell no."

"You destroyed a great man."

"Are you still that delusional? He turned children into killers. He abused you, tortured you, allowed others to abuse you, and you can still say that he was a great man?"

"His methods of child-rearing might have been unorthodox, but they were effective."

"Child-rearing? He was a predator, a pedophile, and a killer. You should thank me for ending him."

"Thank you for killing our father?"

"He wasn't our father. He was a monster."

"Think so?" He walked to a digital keypad attached to the wall and pressed a button. "Maybe you need some reminding of how great a man our father was."

Five more screens appeared.

"Do you remember a television show a few years back called *This Is Your Life*?"

"No."

"Doesn't matter. Just thought it would help explain what's about to happen. I've worked night and day getting these in just the right order. I do hope you appreciate my hard work."

An image appeared on the first screen. The child was about Somer's age, maybe a little younger. She had long, stringy dark hair and a sallow complexion. She was bone-thin, malnourished. Her gray eyes spoke volumes of abuse, neglect, and hopelessness.

"Recognize this beauty?"

She couldn't look away if she tried. That damaged, lonely little girl still lived somewhere inside her.

"Amazing, isn't it? What was once the very image of pitiful and disgusting is now one of the loveliest women in the world."

As she continued to stare, photo after photo appeared. Most were of her in the same sad-looking green pants with yellow ducks and a dirty white T-shirt. She closed her eyes when several photos showed her wearing nothing at all.

Electricity shot through her body, and her eyes flew open. Dammit, the chair was hooked up to some kind of electrical current.

"That's so rude. I've prepared all these memories for you. You must see each one. If you don't, I'll be crushed."

"I know you're a sick, twisted bastard, but child pornography is low even for you."

"Oh my dear, this isn't pornography. This is art. Hill Reed was a gifted artist, and you were one of his most perfect creations."

She closed her eyes again, but remembered the shock and reopened them quickly.

Dark laughed. "You are a fast learner." He glanced at another screen. "We'll let those images remain and move on to other, more interesting things."

All of the screens began to display images and video of her life at Hill House. The sound was turned off, so she was at least spared hearing the treacherous voice of her former teacher.

She hadn't known he'd filmed their interactions. Yes, she had known that Reed had recorded some of her training. He had used the recordings on occasion to remind her of what would happen if she failed at a certain project he'd assigned her. The early ones were the most heartbreaking. They told the story of how a starving, neglected child had come to love her abuser. The bastard's manipulative, mesmerizing voice had practically hypnotized her, enthralled her. The food and warmth he had provided had done the rest. His training had been insidious, seeping into her mind, her heart, her very soul. By the end of the first year after her "rescue," she had been a willing participant in anything Hill Reed wanted from her.

Irelyn lost track of the time as the images played around her. She was so lost in the past, she wasn't even sure Dark was still in the room. Memories assailed her, and even as she told herself to fight them, they swamped her as she relived each day, lesson, and event that created Reed's perfect weapon. She could see, feel, taste everything. Affection, followed by mental, physical, and emotional abuse. Then, when he realized she had reached her limit, he would shower her with affection again. Special treats, toys, and clothes, anything a child could want. But she had sought his love and approval the most. Knowing he was disappointed in her was often more painful than physical punishments.

Sweet heavens, she had been so young and so damn malleable. To a child who had never known anything but hunger and pain, it had felt like rescue, like love. Her young mind had been the perfect training ground for Hill Reed's evil manipulation.

She drew in a ragged breath. She tried several times to close her eyes, to block out the more painful moments. The shocks pulsing through her body prevented her from escaping.

The chair she was strapped to moved in slow circles. Not fast enough to make her dizzy, but it enabled her to see each screen as her life played out. It was painful, demoralizing, and sickening to watch. The pitiful child who only wanted love, the budding teenager who wanted approval. He had played her like a master, and she had grasped at every straw and morsel he would allow.

The perverted bastard had even recorded the first rape. She remembered being frozen in fear. She'd been thirteen years old, a child blooming into womanhood without any idea what that meant. Even as she'd known what he was doing to her wasn't right, she had done nothing to stop him. Watching it now with adult eyes, she felt immense grief. The frightened child lay there, not knowing what to do, knowing what was being done to her was wrong, but still craving approval and warmth. That first time had hurt. She remembered the painful tearing, Reed's heavy breaths and grunts.

Nausea threatened and Irelyn swallowed back the bile.

Reed had told her that her body was a weapon and that someday she would use it to entice and secure her prey. But, that for now, her body was his to use as he wished.

The rapes had happened a handful of times, and afterward, he would hold her and whisper soft words of praise. She had craved that praise more than anything else on earth. She would cling to him, aching for what she had believed was love.

The beatings and torture had been horrific, but they almost seemed more bearable than those tender moments. Hugs, kisses, and verbal praise from a monster who'd doled out affection one moment and harsh discipline the next. She had learned to look for his approval in all things. She would have done almost anything for him.

And in the end, she had.

CHAPTER THIRTY-FOUR

Grey Justice Private Jet

The foul weather made a hellish trip even worse. It was damn dangerous to be in the air at all, and he'd told Lily he understood if she didn't want to take the chance. The look she'd given him had been his answer.

Getting approval to take off had been frustratingly slow. He had never bribed nor pleaded with more people in his life. It had taken almost an hour before he had worn them down.

Fifteen minutes later, after a harrowing, slippery takeoff, they'd been in the air. The flight was far from a smooth, direct one. Lily was doing everything she could to avoid the worst of the storm, and Grey trusted her enough to leave her to her job. Her co-pilot was just as able.

Grey spent most of that time on the phone, calling every person he knew in England. He had never felt this helpless in his life.

Irelyn Raine could handle herself against anyone,

including any trained killer. He told himself that she had a plan, that she would come out a winner. Problem was, Irelyn wasn't ruthless. Hill Reed had tried to destroy her humanity and turn her into an emotionless creature, devoid of feeling. He had failed. Irelyn led with her heart. Yes, she would kill when necessary, but she had something Reed had never been able to beat out of her. She had compassion. She would sacrifice herself, her life, to save another. He didn't doubt for an instant that she would do anything to save little Somer and Sister Nadeen.

He'd alerted the local authorities. Hill House was well known in all of England, but it had never been breached. Reed had known how to play the game of politics. As long as he wasn't blatant about what he did, he and his people were left alone to do as they pleased. It had taken no small amount of charm and bribery on Grey's part to get the police to go to Hill House to investigate. What they'd discovered was massively worrisome. She wasn't there. No one was there. The entire house had been searched, top to bottom. The place was empty.

Dark could have taken her anywhere, so Grey had feelers out all over the world. However, he believed the bastard would go home. Hill House was Dark's refuge. The connection that Dark and Irelyn shared was there, within those walls. He would go back at some point, and then Grey would destroy him.

He tried not to consider what she was going through, because he imagined only the worst. Sebastian Dark, like his predecessor, was purported to be a sadist. He would want to prolong his victim's agony and wouldn't kill her outright. A hideous thought, but grim, cold comfort was all he had right now.

They had come too far, overcome too much, to let it end this way. Not when they'd finally surmounted every emotional barrier. They were going to be married. He had told her they would be together sixty or so more years, and he was damn well going to keep that promise.

He would find her, he would save her, and then together, once and for all, they would destroy Hill House and all that dwelled within.

Hill House
England

GREY STALKED THROUGH THE MASSIVE MANSION, YELLING FOR Irelyn at the top of his lungs. He hadn't even considered using stealth. If Dark was here and heard him, he'd come out, and they would face off.

Footsteps sounded behind him. Gun drawn, Grey whirled in anticipation and then breathed out a frustrated sigh. Nick Gallagher and Jonah Slater. They had been waiting at the airport when he arrived.

"Anything?" Grey asked.

"No," Gallagher said. "I've searched the entire first floor."

He glanced over at Jonah, who shook his head. "Nothing on the second floor either. Half the rooms look like they haven't been occupied in years."

Grey had searched the third floor. From Irelyn's recounting, he knew the third floor was where her torture and training had taken place. It only made sense for Dark, who was trying so hard to emulate his mentor, to return with Irelyn to the place where his predecessor had been. So why hadn't he?

"Let's switch up. Maybe one of us will see something we missed the first time. I'll take the first floor. Gallagher, you take the second. Jonah, you're on the third."

In grim silence, they restarted their search. As Grey went from room to room on the first floor, a part of his mind noted surprise at the seeming normalness of the décor. Irelyn had never described the house, but in his mind, he had envisioned something between an old-time bordello, including red velvet curtains and cheap erotic art and a modern-day BDSM dungeon. He couldn't have been further from the truth. Admittedly, the décor held as much warmth as a funeral parlor, but there wasn't anything gauche or gaudy about it. Cream-colored walls, light beige area rugs, tan sofas and chairs showed that someone had tried, without much imagination, to make the place look the opposite of what it actually was.

The third floor was the complete opposite, though, and looked exactly as he'd expected. It was obvious that Reed had put more money and thought into that floor than any other part of the house. The reason for that sickened Grey.

Everywhere he looked—kitchen, parlors, what looked like a club room with a large bar and several poker tables, dining room, living room—every damn place was empty. He had pressed panels, pulled out drawers, pounded on walls, hoping that some kind of secret door would open to reveal a private area. There was nothing.

Filled with more frustration and worry than he'd ever had in his life, Grey returned to the foyer to see that Jonah and Gallagher had finished their searches as well.

"What now?" Jonah asked.

What now indeed?

"Let's search the outside perimeter. There're several acres of land attached. Maybe he's got another building somewhere."

Grey ignored the grim, doubtful looks that Jonah and Gallagher exchanged. They thought this was a hopeless endeavor. That wherever Dark had taken Irelyn, it was already too late to save her. He would damn well not accept that. Irelyn was still alive, he could feel it. They were connected in a way few could understand. He would not stop until he found her and brought her home.

There was no other option.

CHAPTER THIRTY-FIVE

Everything was going swimmingly, and he was enjoying every moment. That was one of the things his father had taught him. Savoring your successes was such an important aspect of the job. The life of an assassin was lonely, sometimes distasteful, but always interesting. Being in charge of a group of assassins wasn't nearly as enjoyable as being one of the ranks. He had responsibilities that he couldn't cast to just anyone. This had been one of them. Not that he would have wanted anyone else to take this over. This was a vendetta. Very personal. You didn't get much more personal than destroying the woman who murdered the most important person in your world.

Still, even as much as he had been looking forward to this event, he looked forward to its conclusion. He'd been working toward this day for so long. When he had learned of Hill's death, he had known immediately who was responsible. He hadn't shared that information with anyone else. This was his responsibility. As the leader of Hill House, he would see to the reckoning. Only Sebastian could avenge his father's death.

He realized that that was the main reason he hadn't been able to refill Hill House with the most-skilled assassins. His attention had been divided. Once this was over, the deed done, he could look forward to the future. Making Hill Reed proud of him had been a goal for as long as he could remember. Nothing would please him more than knowing that the woman who betrayed him had been destroyed.

The memories were getting to her. Her face was expressionless, but her pallor was almost as white as the walls that surrounded them. She was suffering, remembering all that had been done to her, all that she had been forced to do. The training she had endured, they had all endured, had been harsh but necessary. He was living proof of Hill Reed's brilliance.

Irelyn Raine, on the other hand, had been a failure from the start. She should have died long ago. By the time he was finished, she would be begging for death, pleading for him to put her out of her misery. She would be whimpering, speechless with agony, both emotional and physical. She would suffer, and then she would die.

The first phase was almost complete. She was almost ready for the second and final part of his punishment. She didn't know about his skills. Didn't know that he had talents she could only imagine possessing. He had intentionally made this room large enough to be able to use his bullwhip. First he would use it on her skin. That lovely unmarred body would no longer glow with good health. She would be hideous to look at and in extreme pain. Then he would deliver the coup de grace. The wire would wrap around her neck and she would beg for mercy an instant before he jerked the handle. She would die in both shock and awe of him. And on her final breath of life she would know that he had been the greatest, not her.

His eyes returned to the screens where Raine's early life

played out. Hill Reed had been a bit of a video hound. He had shelves of film he'd taken over the years. His training methods were works of art. Sebastian had watched several of the sessions. Many had involved people he had known. He had yet to watch recordings of his own training. His mind veered away from the thought of doing so. Those days were a blur to him, and the analogy that no one wanted to see how sausage was made worked for him. Especially when he was the sausage.

A time or two, he felt an odd, uncomfortable jolt, almost as if the electricity wired to the chair Raine sat in went through him. He had to look away from the screen and refocus. That didn't mean anything. Watching her suffer was the most important part anyway. He was merely saving his energy for the finale.

And that would be coming up very soon.

IRELYN DREW IN A SILENT BREATH. THE MAN STANDING A FEW feet from her had no idea of what he had done, what he had set free. Without a doubt, this was the most defining moment of her life. Irelyn had always thought that what she had done to Grey's parents had defined her, and now she realized she had been wrong. While that had been hideous and something she would regret for the rest of her life, that event didn't make her who she was.

Yes, the recordings were gruesome and vile. Nausea lay heavy in her belly, and she longed for a shower with an almost manic intensity. However, as she watched hour after hour of abuse, followed by repulsive moments of fake affection, something monumental happened within her. While she could cry for the abused little girl who had never known safety or love, she celebrated the woman she had become. For many, overcoming abuse like this would be impossible. It could have destroyed her, but instead, she had managed to escape, move forward.

And while watching all the vileness heaped on the fragile, vulnerable child she'd once been, she realized something else. Grey had given her a gift by allowing her to kill Hill Reed. By rights, he should have taken the opportunity himself. Hill Reed had killed his parents. Reed might have been a trained killer, but compared to Grey, he was ordinary. Grey could have easily taken the bastard down. Instead, he had allowed her to do the deed. He had known better than anyone what she had suffered at Hill Reed's hands. Grey had given her the gift of closure.

She hadn't seen it like that before now. Her feelings had been so mixed up, so confused. She had hated the monster that Hill Reed was, had mentally recognized his evil. However, the thread of affection that Reed had so carefully woven into her psyche had still existed. The hurt had been too deep for her to see everything clearly. But now, witnessing the abuse, seeing that fragile child so vulnerable, so scared, and seeing the evil gleam of delight in Hill's eyes, she was grateful she had been the one to destroy him.

Sebastian sat in a chair a few feet back. On occasion, he would make a nasty comment or laugh at something on the screens. His small mind could not begin to fathom what he had unleashed. He believed that witnessing her abuse would weaken her, possibly put her in a catatonic state where she wouldn't be able to function. It was all part of his plan of torture. If she hadn't wanted to keep her thoughts a secret, she would have laughed out loud. Messing with him was actually going to be fun.

While he was turned away from her, watching the images on the screen, she quietly studied him. The smug arrogance he'd started with had diminished considerably. There was now a slump to his shoulders and a slight tremble to his hands. Although none of his training had appeared on the screens, he was still affected by the memories nonetheless. He had endured much of the same torture disguised as training. She had been in some of his sessions and had witnessed his abuse firsthand.

She told herself she should feel sorry for Sebastian. She had escaped, he hadn't. Even though Grey had helped her, she had pulled herself up from the gutter. Sebastian could have done that, too. Instead, he had allowed evil to permeate his life. Not only had he killed innocents without compunction or remorse, he had kidnapped a child and a nun to use them in his sick game of revenge. So no, she had little pity.

Grey would be looking for her. Using every contact and calling in every favor, he wouldn't rest until he found her. She wanted this over before that happened. The fight wasn't Grey's, it was hers. She needed to end this, once and for all.

She focused her gaze inward. Sebastian thought she was looking at one of the screens where her abuse played out, but he was wrong. She saw far beyond that. She saw her strength, her purpose, and her destiny.

And she saw how she was going to kill him.

Most everyone within the community knew that she had been Hill Reed's favorite. Being a teacher's pet was not a coveted position, at least not at Hill House. Not only had Reed not treated her any better, but he had often been crueler and more profane in his punishments.

But there was something many didn't know. She had been destined to replace him. He had told her many times that she was to have been his successor.

For years, she had forced herself to forget his words. Forced herself to forget that Hill had seen something in her…something he identified with himself. The very thought that they had anything in common made her want to scream. But now, she allowed those memories to return, allowed those lessons to flood her mind. Hill had taught her all he knew about manipulation and coercion. He had controlled and directed his victims with words, and she had learned his methods. Drawing on all the things Hill had taught her, she would destroy Sebastian Dark, and he would never see it coming.

She started slow, almost conversationally. He wouldn't realize what was happening until it was too late to change course. When it was time, she would turn up the heat. Sebastian had made a fatal mistake. He had tried to use her past to destroy her, and instead, he had empowered her. Now the tables would be turned. She would use the very same things to destroy him.

"You know, Pippin, you weren't very good." Her mouth was dry, so her voice was low, huskier than usual. She would use that to her advantage.

SEBASTIAN JERKED AT THE SOFT, ALMOST INHUMAN-SOUNDING voice. He had thought she was well past being able to talk. "What did you call me?"

"Your name. That's what Hill named you."

He shook his head. "No. Hill and I agreed I could change it. He told me I wasn't Pippin any longer."

She smiled at him then, mocking and amused. "No matter what you named yourself, you were always his Pippin. His weak, malleable little boy who everyone beat up on. Hill and I used to make fun of you all the time. We would sit together at night and watch recordings of you and laugh and laugh."

"You lie!" he snarled. Pounding his chest with his fist, he shouted, "I am Sebastian Dark, owner and proprietor of Hill House."

She released a long, exaggerated sigh. "So very dramatic. No wonder Reed wanted to kill you, Pippin."

He was on his feet, stalking toward her before he realized it. Not only didn't she sound defeated, she was acting smug and confident.

"I told you not to call me that. My name is Sebastian Dark. And what you speak is a lie. They're all lies. I was one of Father's favorites."

"Really?" she drawled, her look almost pitying. "I don't know how many times I had to talk him out of killing you."

Could that be true? Everyone had known that Irelyn was Reed's protégé, his favorite student. She had inside information that others didn't.

"Remember how he would use you as bait? How he would allow everyone to beat up on you? He said he did that because you're a weakling, an imbecile."

No, he had put those days out of his mind. He wouldn't let himself think of them now. He couldn't. Reed would have chosen him as his replacement. If he hadn't died, he would have called a meeting and announced it to everyone.

As if she weren't tied to a chair, unable to move, as if she had no worries about her own safety, she continued to speak in a conversational tone. Sebastian stood frozen as he listened to her soft, beguiling voice. His father had used that same kind of coercion. The mesmerizing voice would creep into your mind like a slug slithered through the grass, leaving a trail of slime in its wake. That voice told him he wasn't good enough, that he would never amount to anything.

The words continued, on and on. Her voice went softer and lower. He leaned closer to listen. The voice enthralled, the words ripped and shredded. They seeped into every particle of his being, making him remember the pain and anguish. The humiliation and anger.

"Stop it!" Spittle flew from his mouth. "None of that is true! None of it. He loved me! I know he loved me best."

Her expression never changed. It was as if she were in a

trance, as if she were possessed by Hill Reed's spirit. Could it be Reed talking through her?

No. No. No. He shook himself. That wasn't possible.

"Stop it, you bitch!" He slapped her hard. The crack of his hand against her cheek echoed throughout the room. A blood-red imprint of his hand was the only color on her face. Yet, she never flinched, never moved. And she never stopped talking in that soft, insistent voice.

His heart pumped faster, and he could feel himself sweating as buried memories dug themselves out of their grave. All the hideous things he had endured. The torture, the deprivation, the beatings.

But no, no, no. All of that had been to make him stronger. To make him into the man he was today. He had once been Pippin, but now he was Sebastian Dark. He had overcome and conquered. He had excelled at everything Hill taught him. He was the best.

Slapping the bitch again, he watched blood spurt from her busted lip and felt intense joy. "You left him, and I stayed. I was his favorite, not you."

She acted as if he wasn't important, almost as if he wasn't even there. Her eyes were distant, blank. She kept repeating the same words, over and over, just like Hill had. And then he realized something strange and phenomenal had happened. The change had been so subtle, he didn't know when or how it happened, but she was now speaking in Reed's voice. That deep, resonating tone used to follow him into his dreams, creating nightmares that never seemed to stop.

Grabbing hold of her shoulders, he shook her hard. "Stop it!" he screamed.

She wouldn't. She wouldn't.

"You're nothing, you're no one. You can't fight, you can't kill. You're useless. I'm going to kill you, boy. I'm going to

301

take you apart, limb by limb, and let the buzzards feed on you."

He was crying now. He could feel the tears pouring down his face. "You love me. You told me I'm the best."

"You're weak, you're nothing. You can't even fight like a real man!"

"I can, too!"

"Prove it. Untie the bitch and give her what she deserves!"

Grabbing a knife from the table, he sliced the rope at her ankles and then her wrists. Before she could move, he knocked her to the floor with a resounding thud.

IRELYN LANDED ON HER FACE. BLOOD POURED FROM HER NOSE, and she vaguely wondered if it was broken. Pain didn't register. She jumped to her feet and whirled around, just in time to see a fist coming at her. She ducked, did a 360 turn, and then kicked with all her might. Dark flew across the room.

She straightened, preparing for another strike. He came at her full force, his face a red mask of fury. There was no holding back now. She had him exactly where she wanted. He was fighting his emotions more than he was fighting her. All the insecurities that Reed had instilled in him had taken over. When an opponent fought not to lose, winning was much easier. She was ready to destroy this bastard.

Fists flew and pummeled. Irelyn lost count of the times she fell to the floor or was slammed against the wall. Dark's eyes were wild and unfocused. He was not only fighting for his life, he was fighting for control of his mind.

They parted for a moment, their breathing heavy and rapid. Dark was sweating and bleeding. His nose was slightly askew from one of her first hits, and his entire body shook from fatigue. It was time to end it.

"Father would be ashamed of you, allowing a skinny girl to beat you up."

The instant the words were out of her mouth, she knew he would come at her full force and readied for the killing blow. The instant he struck, she would take him down.

That wasn't what happened.

The door behind him swung open, and without saying a word, he bolted before she could blink. Shocked, she was momentarily stunned into immobility.

The man had actually run from her?

She took a wobbling step toward the door, toward freedom. Her mind whirled as the pain she'd been denying made itself known. The fight had been a brutal one, and she had a sinking suspicion that she had more than a couple of broken bones. Her left arm in particular throbbed with a deep ache.

She had a choice here. Go after Dark and end him. Or she could do something that she had longed to do for so very long. She could destroy Hill House.

That choice was the easiest one she had ever made. Dark would have to wait, because she had a lifelong dream to achieve.

CHAPTER THIRTY-SIX

S tanding in front of Hill House once again, Grey felt a hopelessness growing within him. They had walked the entire perimeter. There had been several outbuildings, as well as some sort of small stadium, but they were as empty as the house. Defeat was not in his vocabulary, but dammit, this was as close as he'd ever been.

"She's got to be in there," he growled.

"Where, man? We've checked every damn nook and cranny at least a dozen times. She's not here, Justice."

Gallagher was right. They had searched every room numerous times. Had looked for secret passages and hidden doors. There was nothing. The place was a lifeless tomb and as cheerless as one.

Many times, he hadn't known Irelyn's whereabouts. She would disappear for weeks or even months. He had worried during those times, but not for an instant had he doubted he wouldn't see her again. This was the first time he wasn't sure. Dark had taken her somewhere out of Grey's reach, and no matter how much he reminded himself of Irelyn's strength and resilience, an insidious voice inside him was whispering that she was gone for good. He brutally fought that voice, refused to listen to its lies. Dammit, he would not give up.

He had a choice to make. He could return to his car and call, email, text his contacts. Begging, pleading, demanding that someone, somewhere, give him information about her whereabouts. Somebody had to know where Dark had taken her.

Or he could do what his gut was telling him to do. Go back inside that monstrosity and find Irelyn. She was here. Dammit, he knew to his soul that she was here!

He would not rest until she was found. And if she was no longer in the world?

Grey shook his head. No. He would not even allow that thought to enter his head. Irelyn would stay alive and come back to him. He had to believe that. He had no choice.

His cellphone buzzed. His heart in his throat, he pressed the answer key. "What?"

Kennedy's excited voice said, "We think she really is there, at Hill House."

"You found something?"

"Yes. An updated set of blueprints. They're only about a year old. Looks like Dark added several rooms in the basement."

He started running. "What part of the basement?"

"The northwest side. Looks like there's a door behind one of the wine racks."

He knew exactly where that was. He'd seen nothing that would indicate a hidden door, but that didn't matter. He'd tear down everything in the damn basement until he found it.

Pocketing his phone, he threw a glance over his shoulder. Jonah and Gallagher were right behind him.

"We've got a lead!" He turned back to the house. "Let's—"
His breath caught in his lungs. Was that smoke coming out of
a third-floor window? What the hell?

"Call the fire department!"

All questions of her whereabouts disappeared. Irelyn was,
without a doubt, inside that inferno. Grey jumped up onto
the front porch. Tendrils of smoke seeped through the
front door.

"Justice…wait!"

He didn't know who was yelling at him and didn't care.
Irelyn was in there.

"Put this over your head."

A wet cloth slapped into his hands. Still running, he
wound the material around his face, leaving an opening for
his eyes. He slammed through the door and was almost
knocked down by the heat and smoke.

"Irelyn!" he bellowed.

———

FLAMES LICKED AT HER BACK AS SHE RAN THROUGH THE LONG
hallway. She had mistimed how fast the fire would spread.
When she'd finally found her way out of the giant room
beneath the house, she'd found all the necessary require-
ments in the janitor's closet. Paint thinner, turpentine, and
matches. She'd started on the third floor. Throwing the flammable liquid into each room took time. Though her body
was telling her she was on her last reserve of strength, she
refused to stop. Her only focus, her only goal was to destroy
the place where nightmares were created. The instant she
saw the flare of the first flame, life and energy zoomed
through her. Feeling renewed, she ran down the hallway,
stopping at every other room to douse it with flammable
liquid.

She jerked to a stop at the punishment room. This was the one he'd used the most. It hadn't changed much. A mattress with heavy chains and handcuffs on each side. A table and chair where Reed would often sit and talk her through her punishments. A thick, heavy leather belt hung on the wall. It looked old and worn, and she remembered Hill using it on her.

Drawing in a shaky breath, she inhaled noxious smoke and remembered why she was here. This was not about going back, but moving forward. She doused the room, threw a match, and moved on. It was over, finished.

As fire consumed each room, she imagined she could hear the echoes of crying children calling out to her to help them. Even though it was too late for her and so many others, she could ensure that no child or adult would ever have to endure pain within these walls ever again.

She ran down the stairway to the second floor. Breathless, she stopped on the landing and considered her next move. Should she work her way through these rooms as well? She glanced up at the balcony of the third floor and, for the first time, felt alarm. Greedy red ribbons of flames were eating at the walls. The fire was spreading even faster than she had anticipated.

As though they wanted to escape, too, heavy smoke and flames followed her. The ravenous fire ate up the walls. Light fixtures exploded, raining glass. Exhaustion and grief pulled at her. From the second-floor, through the haze of dense smoke, she could see the giant foyer and the front door. She could make it. She had too much to live for to stop now. Grey was somewhere waiting for her. She had to leave. Now.

Irelyn took a step, and something slammed into her, knocking her legs out from under her.

Dark hadn't left after all. His red-rimmed eyes wild with fury, he glared down at her. "You bitch! You destroyed it all!"

She jumped to her feet and swung wide, her fist barely glancing off of his jaw. He pulled back and slammed his fist into her face. She felt herself falling, her arms wind-milling, looking to grasp on to anything. She landed on the hard marble surface of the first floor. She lay there, unable to move, unable to breathe. Dense smoke filled the air. She tried to cough, could find no air.

Her hazy, pain-filled mind told her this was a fitting ending. She had experienced agony here, but now she could be at peace. Hill House was no more.

She closed her eyes, imagined she heard Grey screaming her name, and she smiled.

THICK, BLACK SMOKE FILLED THE HOUSE, LEAVING NO ROOM for air. Grey held his breath. He couldn't see much, but he'd been through this house enough times to figure things out. He ran, shouting her name. The heat was becoming intense, but that would not stop him. She was here. She had set this fire, he was sure of it. But where the hell was she?

"Over here!"

He could see almost nothing, but he followed the voice. Gallagher was on his knees beside a prone figure.

Irelyn.

His legs could not move fast enough. He had to get to her.

"We've got to get her out of here!" Gallagher shouted.

Lifting her in his arms, Grey started running. Gallagher and Jonah were in front of him, clearing away obstacles. He ran onto the porch and then down the steps. The instant he was clear, he placed her on the ground.

She was a bloody mess. Covered in cuts and scratches from head to toe. Her left leg was twisted at an odd, painful angle, indicating multiple fractures.

Dropping to his knees beside her, he checked her pulse, relieved to feel the beat. Grey opened his mouth, and nothing came out. He swallowed, tried again. "Irelyn? Baby?"

Nothing. He leaned over her, realized she wasn't breathing. As Grey began CPR compressions, Gallagher kneeled down on the other side of her. They counted off thirty compressions together. Then, tilting her head back, Grey gave her mouth-to-mouth, keeping a careful watch on her chest. When it rose, he pulled away, was about to begin compressions again when he heard the sweetest sound he'd ever imagined. A cough.

"Irelyn?"

His heart stuttered when her eyelids flickered. She opened her mouth and then coughed violently.

"Take it easy, sweetheart. Help is on the way."

"Grey," she rasped.

Brushing her hair out of her face, he whispered, "Don't try to talk. Everything's going to be fine."

"Always getting…into a bit of trouble, aren't I?" Her voice was weak and raspy.

"You are that, my love."

A faint smile tugged at her mouth. "Love it when you call me that."

"It's always been true, even when I was too stubborn to say the words."

"Is it done?"

Grey raised his head and viewed the destruction. She had accomplished what she'd set out to do. Hill House was no more. The place where she'd known both pain and joy, where innocence was lost and the woman before him became a warrior.

"Yes, it's done."

"That's good, then. " She gasped, coughed, swallowed. "We…can be done with the past now, too."

No, there was one more thing to do, but he would take care of that himself. "We'll talk about that later."

"I think I may need a little help getting up."

Her face was coated with soot, grime, and blood. The red dress that had looked so lovely earlier hung in tatters. The cuts from all the glass that had exploded around her were too numerous to count. And he knew he had never seen anyone more beautiful or more precious. He loved her with endless abundance. His strong, courageous, beautiful warrior woman.

"Ambulance is here!" Jonah shouted.

Grey glanced up, spotted the vehicle zooming toward them. Though still worried, he felt almost weak with relief. If she was in any danger, the EMTs would know what to do.

Heavy footsteps ran toward him, and a voice said, "Step aside, sir."

Releasing her hand, Grey jumped out of the way and allowed the medics to attend her. Noise from the firemen working to put out the flames sounded in the background, barely penetrating his consciousness. His entire focus was on Irelyn and the medics working on her.

"We need to get her to a hospital."

Not bothering to see if they would protest, Grey ran with them as they rolled the gurney toward the ambulance and jumped inside with them. They were away in seconds, the siren blasting as they zoomed down the drive.

Her hand in his, Grey glanced out the back window to the burning house. Had Dark died in the fire? If he was still inside, he was dead now. But Grey was too well acquainted with evil to take the bastard's death for granted. Evil never died easy.

Irelyn moaned slightly, and Grey squeezed her hand, making sure she knew he was there with her. He would tend to Irelyn, ensure her safety and well-being. Once he was sure she would be okay, he was going on the hunt. If Dark was still alive, he would find him. And he would kill him.

CHAPTER THIRTY-SEVEN

Sitting in a chair beside Irelyn's bed, Grey held her hand, his fingers purposely on her pulse. He relished every beat. She was still unconscious. The doctors had warned him she might sleep for hours. Not only from the sedation from surgery, but also because her body was in desperate need of rest.

Her hand, like much of her body, was swollen with varying shades of bruising. He hadn't been able to talk with her about what happened, but it didn't take a genius to see that she had been in a brutal fight. His only consolation was that if Dark was still alive, he was hurting, too. And if he was alive, he had to know he was living on borrowed time.

"Hey, how is she?" Nick Gallagher stood at the door. His face was covered in soot, and he still wore the same fatigues he'd had on earlier.

"Unconscious, but the doctor said she should make a full recovery. She's going to be incapacitated for a while, though. The surgeon had to do some major repair work to her fractured leg. Other than that, she's got a broken right arm, her left shoulder was dislocated, and she has numerous bruises and a dozen or so stitches from all the glass cuts."

"She's damn lucky to be alive."

Yes, she was lucky, and so was he. The possibility of living without Irelyn wasn't something he ever wanted to face again.

"Where's Jonah?"

"At Hill House, working with the fire department. He checked in a second ago. Said they're still going through the debris, but so far there's no indication that anyone died in the fire."

It was as he'd figured. Sebastian Dark lived. "I'm going to kill the bastard."

"You stay with Irelyn. Slater and I have got this."

"No. Dark is mine. It might take a while, but I won't stop until I find him."

"Main thing is making sure Irelyn's okay."

"She won't be completely safe until Sebastian Dark is out of her life. I intend to make sure he never comes near her again."

"How can I help?"

"Dig as deep as you can. Once we get his location, I'll need you to oversee things at home till I get back."

Gallagher slapped him on the shoulder. "Whatever you need." He glanced down at Irelyn. "She's a fighter." His voice held admiration.

Grey's throat closed up, but he managed a husky, "That she is."

Gallagher headed toward the door. "Let us know if you need anything."

"Thank you. And give my thanks to Jonah, too." He looked down at Irelyn and cleared his throat of that uncomfortable lump. "She's more precious to me than I can say."

"I know how you feel."

As Gallagher walked out of the room, Grey realized he did know how he felt. A couple of years ago, Gallagher had almost lost Kennedy.

The incredible relief of knowing Irelyn was going to be all right was catching up with him. He was exhausted, but also jubilant. A few hours ago, he hadn't known if he'd ever see her again.

There were so many things he wanted to say to her, so many things he looked forward to sharing with her. Their life together had never been simple and probably never would be. Neither of them had easygoing, laid-back personalities. They liked to get involved, loved challenges, and enjoyed challenging each other. No matter what they faced, as long as they were together, they could conquer anything.

Exhaustion was weighing on him, but he had a couple of things to accomplish before he could rest. Standing, he pulled a burner phone from his pocket. Using code words and vague phrases he hadn't used in years, he texted people he hadn't heard from or seen since he and Irelyn had left England. Some would likely ignore his texts. Others might even use what he told them to hurt him. But he would use every avenue available. Irelyn would not be safe until Sebastian Dark was no longer breathing. Grey was going to do everything in his power to make that happen.

Satisfied he had done what he could for now, he returned to sit beside Irelyn. Taking her hand in his once more, he leaned his forehead against the cool, crisp hospital sheets. Closing his eyes, he allowed his thoughts to relax and roam. His mind played myriad images of his and Irelyn's life together, and then his thoughts went to the day when everything changed. Why his mind settled there, he didn't know. Why not go to the first time he met her, when he'd been so smitten by her beauty and incredible sweetness? Or why not the kisses they'd shared, the love they'd made, or the quiet times when all they'd had was each other and that had been enough? No, his mind veered toward that awful, awful day when the world as he'd known it had fallen away and only destruction lay before him.

What had started out as one of the best days of his life had turned into his worst nightmare. He'd been in his dorm room, packing and getting ready to head home. His finals were over, and he'd just received the news that he'd been accepted into MIT in the States. He had been practicing what he was going to say to his parents when the call came. Details blurred after that. He'd rushed to get home only to find that it was all true. His parents had died in an explosion. There had been only body parts to identify, but enough to confirm that they were indeed the remains of Andrew and Natalie Bishop. He'd been walking out of the morgue, his grief almost unbearable, when Irelyn had called.

"Liam? I need you. Please help me."

He'd recognized her voice in an instant and that she was in dire trouble. "What's wrong? Where are you?"

"I'm at a phone kiosk. I can't run. He'll find me. Please, Liam. I'm so very sorry, but you're the only one I trust."

He hadn't realized until later exactly what that meant. He knew only that he had to get to her. Were the people who killed his parents after her, too? It didn't matter that none of it made sense. He knew only that he had to act.

"Can you hide till I get there?"

"Yes. There's a church a couple of blocks away. I'll hide there."

The address she'd given him was about four hundred kilometers away. He didn't bother to ask why she was that far away. She needed him, and he would get to her. Four hours later, he had arrived at the church. His body was so tense with worry, his grief still so fresh and painful, he was surprised he was able to arrive so soon.

He parked in front of the church. It was going on three thirty in the morning, and no one was about. Thinking she would be inside the church, he had his foot on the first step when he heard her low voice cry out to him.

"Irelyn? Where are you?"

"To the right of you, in the bushes."

He ran toward her voice. He would never forget what he found. She was sitting with her back pressed against the cool brick of the building. She'd obviously been crying—her eyes were almost swollen shut. Her hair was matted, and she had a small bruise on her cheekbone and some bruising on her neck. Other than that, she looked amazingly healthy.

Asking questions would come later. They needed to get off the streets. He remembered holding out his hand to her and hearing her let out this tiny, little sob, as if she was doing all she could to hold back the pain. And she didn't move.

"Come on, let's go," he urged. "We need to get someplace safe."

"I can't."

"What do you mean, you can't?"

"I can't walk."

And that's when he realized that he'd shone his flashlight only on her face. When he moved the light lower, his heart almost stopped. Her knees were a bloody mess, almost like raw meat.

He knelt down to touch her, and she gasped. "No, please don't. They don't hurt that badly. Not really. It's just—"

He followed her gaze lower, and then he saw the real problem. If he thought her knees were bad, they were nothing compared to her feet. Bloody, swollen, most likely with several broken bones.

"Who did this to you?"

"Can we talk later? We need to get out of here before he finds us."

She was right. Questions would have to wait. He lifted her in his arms and quickly carried her to his car. He had expected her to cry out in pain, but that had been his first real inkling of just how strong Irelyn Raine really was.

The next few hours were again a blur. Since he didn't know who was after her or what was going on, he relied on his contacts. The Justice Seekers network penetrated every level of society. He got Irelyn into a small private hospital where a doctor examined her without questions. What Grey learned would haunt him till he died.

"Her feet have been beaten severely. I don't know what the monster used. Perhaps several instruments together. She's got three broken bones in her right foot, two in her left, including her middle toe. She has severe lacerations on both soles, which required stitches. It'll be weeks before she'll be able to walk without severe pain."

"What about her knees?"

"They were a mess, but once we washed away the blood and removed the broken glass and rocks embedded in her skin, they weren't as bad as we'd feared. No ligaments or tendons were damaged. She didn't say, but from what I can surmise, she crawled to escape. I don't know how far, but it had to have been some distance. She also has bruises on her arms and a few on her face. Looks like she was choked at some point, too." The doctor shook his head. "I cannot fathom the bastard who did this to her, nor can I fathom the agony that poor child has gone through. I hope, when you find him, you make him pay."

His mind was whirling with all that had happened. First, his parents and now Irelyn. What the hell was going on? He hadn't realized at the time that his nightmare had just begun.

The days following were some of the most difficult of his life. Burying his parents and taking care of Irelyn. She was in and out of consciousness for days. The doctor believed sedation was best for her, and he wouldn't argue. As long as she was safe, he told himself the questions could wait. He often wondered later if things would have been different if she had told him the truth immediately. Would he have saved lives or simply lost his own? He would never know.

More than a week passed before Irelyn could speak with any kind of clarity or coherence. He walked into her hospital room one day, and she was sitting up in bed. Her hair had been brushed, and there was the faintest glow of color in her pale cheeks. Her eyes, though, were dark with agony, but not because of physical pain this time.

"We have to talk," she said.

"Yes, we do. I want to know who did this to you. I'm going to—"

"No, not about that. About your parents."

"You know?" He hadn't planned on telling her until much later. She was fond of his parents, and they had loved her. He knew she would be devastated, but from the sound of her words, she already knew they were dead.

"The authorities have no clue who's responsible. I'm going to the police station later today to see if there's any news."

He didn't mention the people beyond the legal realm who were searching high and low for their killers. The Justice Seekers were almost as ravaged as he was by his parents' deaths and had sworn retribution on all responsible.

Irelyn didn't yet know about the secret organization his parents had belonged to, and he wanted to spare her that for now. She had been through too much already.

"I know who killed them."

He immediately assumed the obvious. The monster who had beaten her was also responsible for his parents' deaths.

"You saw his face? You can identify him?"

"I can take you to him."

"How? Where?"

"My home. My...my f-f-f-father killed them."

The words hung in the air for the longest time. He just looked at her, unable to comprehend exactly what she was saying.

"Your father killed my parents?"

"He's not my father, not really. He's the man I live with."

And then, like a deluge, the words spilled out of her, each one so horrific he wasn't sure he breathed during the telling. It had all been a setup from the beginning. Her meeting him, their getting to know each other. Their little romance was all a sham to get to his parents, to kill them.

He had brought Irelyn into their home, into his parents' lives. He was responsible for destroying two of the finest people he had ever known.

She begged, pleading for his forgiveness, but Grey walked out of the hospital room without saying a word. If he had stayed, he wasn't quite sure what he would have done, his rage was so great. He didn't stay away long, though. He needed details. He knew of Hill Reed. Knew all about Hill House or, as his parents had always referred to it, the murder house.

Andrew and Natalie Bishop had fought against Reed and his kind for years, but had never crossed his path until recently. Foiling the assassination plans of any killer was a dangerous endeavor. Doing so with a killer of Reed's reputation and a small fortune on the line was imminently even more so. His parents had been on the lookout, knowing he would seek revenge at some point. They had warned him to beware, that Reed might strike at him, too.

What they had never guessed was that Reed would go about his revenge in a different way, through a lovely young woman who seemed full of goodness and light. Deceived by beauty, they had all paid a terrible price.

Grey got the rest of the details from her and went to the Justice Seekers' council. When he revealed the name of the killer, they had raided Hill House. Only, the house was empty, and Hill Reed could not be found.

Unable to take vengeance on Reed, they instead sought justice through Irelyn. They wanted to use her to lure Reed out of hiding, or punish her outright. Grey refused to allow such a thing to happen. Yes, he was angry and hurt. He most likely hated her, but he would damn well not let her be used. She had been used enough.

He and Irelyn stole away in the dead of night. If the council had caught them, Grey would likely have died, too. The more zealous of the council members saw things only in black and white. It was during that time that he realized how justice had many different levels, colors, and shades. Allowing Irelyn to bear the brunt of what had happened would not solve anything.

For almost a year, they were on the run. She was still recovering, and they had very little money. He managed to find a few odd jobs to get them a place to stay and some food, but times were tough.

They didn't talk about what happened. Maybe if they had, things would have gotten better faster. He focused on survival, and she… Irelyn just existed. When he finally noticed how very frail she was looking, it was almost too late. She was fading away, day by day, while he was out working and trying to provide for them. He had a goal, but she had nothing but her guilt. And Grey had done almost nothing to help her deal with it.

He took time then to face his own anger and pain. Once he did, he was able to see beyond himself to Irelyn. Instead of lying about what happened with his parents, she had told him the truth. She could have come up with any kind of story about what happened to her, and he would have believed her. The truth had been almost unbelievable, so a lie would have been so much easier for her to pull off. She hadn't done that. Instead, she had told him everything, including all the ways she had deceived him and lied. There was no punishment he could mete out that was worse than what she was doing to herself.

He had made a decision then, one that set the course for their future. He vowed that they would put the past behind them forever, and they built a life together, one of purpose and meaning. But like the ugly little weasel he was, Hill Reed continued to haunt them. Even after death, the stench of his existence lingered. Sebastian Dark was the manifestation of that evil.

The hospital door swung open, and Grey was on his feet in a second, his gun in his hand.

"Whoa. Back down, buddy. It's just us."

Unable to believe his eyes, Grey stared speechlessly at the people standing at the door. Nick and Kennedy Gallagher, Kathleen and Eli Slater, Jonah and Gabby Slater.

Hell, how long had he been out of it? "What are you guys doing here?"

Kennedy was the first to move forward. "Where else would we be?" Surprising him, she gave him a hug and then looked down at Irelyn. "How is she?" she whispered.

Still trying to get his mind around the fact that half of the Grey Justice team had come all the way to England to be with them, he answered, "She's been unconscious since yesterday."

As they gathered around her bed, Grey fought a smile. If Irelyn woke up right now, she'd be either astounded or horrified. She had lived so long without anyone other than Grey getting close to her and had no clue how many people cared. No clue how many people treasured her.

"She came through the surgery just fine. Her leg was

broken in three places, so it'll take a few months before she's kicking ass again, but…" He cleared his throat. "She's lucky to be alive."

That was an understatement. Hill Reed had been a skillful and inventive torturer. It only made sense that his protégé would follow his example.

"She has a lot of bruising on her face."

That was mild compared to the bruising on the rest of her body. He had cared for Irelyn too many times not to recognize when she'd been in a bloody, physical fight. She could hold her own with anyone and, more often than not, come out the winner.

He shot a look at Gallagher. "Any word?"

"Not yet. We've cast a large net. Word is out in his community that he's a man marked for death. It's only a matter of time."

Grey nodded, knowing Gallagher was right. Dark could count down his time here on earth in days, if not hours.

The door opened, and one of Irelyn's nurses walked in. Her horrified eyes scanned the crowded room. "Only two visitors at a time," she barked. "The rest of you will have to go."

With amusement, he watched his friends gather like obedient children and single-file their way out of the room. Before going out with the others, Gallagher asked, "Anything you need?"

"Just having you all here is more than enough."

"We're staying at a B&B in York, and we have everything we need to work remotely. We'll spend twenty-four seven till we find the bastard."

Grey gave an appreciative nod and waited until the door closed before he retrieved his cellphone and checked his messages. He had received several replies, but only one gave him encouragement that he was on the right path. It was no surprise that it came from his most dangerous source. Turning back to Irelyn, he pressed a gentle kiss to her forehead. He hated leaving her, but he had a meeting, one that might either be his doom or his answer to finding Dark.

The Grey Justice Group didn't always color inside the lines, but there was always a concerted effort to avoid major illegalities. His operatives wouldn't agree with him, but he wanted to be the only one to take this risk. This was between him and Dark. A covert operation using some of the deadliest people in the world was the only way to get this done to his satisfaction.

For all the death and destruction he had caused, Sebastian Dark deserved every punishment known to man. For what he had done to Irelyn, the bastard would die.

CHAPTER THIRTY-EIGHT

Her first awareness that anything was wrong occurred when she tried to lift her arm. It felt heavy, cumbersome. Concern grew into panic when she realized one of her legs wouldn't move at all. Alarmed, she went for her knife at her bedside. Found nothing. It was gone. Grey had given her the knife, and she hadn't slept without it in years. Her heart raced at the implication. Dark still had her.

"Irelyn. Listen to me. You're fine." A soft light appeared in a corner, and big hands gently cupped her face. "Look at me, Irelyn. It's Grey."

The panic washed away. "Grey?" She blinked up at the hollow-eyed, beard-stubbled man. "What happened? Where am I?" She winced at how raspy her voice sounded, how dry her throat felt.

"I'll tell you everything, but first, do you want some water?"

"Yes," she whispered. "Thank you."

She heard the sound of water splashing into a glass, and then a small cup with a straw appeared. She took a sip and then another, finding instant relief.

"Not too much. Take it slow."

After another few swallows, she nodded her thanks. "Where are we? How did you find me?"

"You're in a private hospital in York. I found you at Hill House. Do you remember what happened?"

She closed her eyes for a moment, and everything flooded back at once. Anxiety slammed through her. "Sister Nadeen and Somer. Dark took them. Are they all right?"

"I called them. They're fine. Worried about you, but they're safe."

She took in a breath, hissed at the throb of pain that permeated her entire body.

"Do you remember what else happened?"

Yes, she remembered it all. Waking up in that hideous white room at Hill House. Dark had been standing, smirking. He had shown her recordings. They had fought and then…

Her thoughts grew hazy, and she frowned up at Grey. "Did I burn down the house?"

He grinned then, and despite feeling lousy, she felt her heart click up several beats at just how sexy he looked.

"To the ground. Flattened it."

Hill House was no more. Just that bit of news gave her a peace she hadn't felt in years.

"What about Dark? Did he die in the fire?"

"No. He's still out there."

She sighed. "I should have killed him when I had the chance."

"You feel up to telling me what happened?"

"Yes, but first, what's going on with my arm and leg? You said I had surgery. What for? Why is my voice so raspy? Why does my chest hurt? And why does my head feel like it's twice its normal size?"

As he told her about her injuries, memories of how she'd

325

received each one returned. The fight with Dark had been brutal.

"Wait." Irelyn held up her hand. "How'd I break my leg? I remember running through the house as I set it on fire."

"I think you must have fallen from the floor above. We found you in the foyer."

"Dark grabbed for me. I think he might have slugged me. I fell backward."

"Another one of the million reasons why I'm going to kill the bastard."

"I should have done it myself." She grimaced and shifted uncomfortably. "Poor execution leads to poor results. I could have come back later and destroyed the house."

"You had the chance to kill him, and you didn't take it?"

"Insane, I know. I just… I had a choice to make. Go after Dark or destroy the house." She threw Grey a wry look. "Guess I made the wrong choice."

"What do you mean, go after him?"

"We were in the midst of fighting, and he just turned and ran."

"Hell, Irelyn."

"I know. I know. I should have just gotten out. But I remembered seeing paint thinner and matches in the janitor's closet when I was there before. I couldn't resist destroying the house."

"You think you hesitated killing Dark because he ran from you?"

"Yeah, maybe so. I saw what I could have become if you hadn't saved me. He didn't have someone like you to lean on. If I hadn't had you—"

"I'm not going to take credit for something you did. You did the work, baby. Not me. I was just there to lend a hand and a shoulder to cry on. You made yourself into the woman you are today."

She wouldn't argue with him. Part of that was true, but she also knew that without Grey's support, she might have returned to the cesspool that Hill had created.

"So what's the plan? Do we have any idea where he's gone?"

"The plan is for you to recover. I've got a network of people looking for him. He won't stay hidden for long." Picking up her hand, he kissed it. "I thought I'd lost you."

"I'm sorry I had to leave that way." She told him about the men at the airport, about the laser light that had been focused on the little boy's stuffed animal. "I didn't know if it was really a gun aimed at him. Would've been hard to get one in the airport but crazier things have happened. He might've been bluffing but I just couldn't take that risk."

"Charlie hacked into your email account. I saw the video of Somer and Sister Nadeen, knew why you left. Took me forever to get clearance for Lily to take off. How did Dark get you to England so quickly?"

"I have no idea. As soon as I got into the limo, he knocked me out with some kind of sedative. When I woke, I was at Hill House."

"When I finally got to the house, and we couldn't find you, I almost went crazy."

The pain was there in his eyes. She had put him through hell.

"I'm so sorry, Grey. Apparently, Dark added new rooms. It was apparent that he's been planning this for a long time. He played us."

"How so?"

"He knew how Reed died."

"How the hell did he find that out? We vetted every single person involved."

"It wasn't any of our people. Reed told him he was meeting me that night." She hesitated to tell him the next bit of information, but they had agreed to keep no more secrets. "He was planning to kill me then."

"Reed was going to kill you? *Shit.* Then all of this *is* my fault. I was the one who insisted you make that appointment with him. If I hadn't had you set up that meeting, he—"

"Would have killed me at another time. He had apparently decided I couldn't be used anymore and would never return to Hill House. I know this seems crazy, but you saved my life by setting it up that way."

"I am sorry for the way it went down, but I can't be sorry he's dead."

"I'm not sorry about either one—that Reed is dead or the way it went down. If Sebastian did nothing else, he made me realize how glad I am that I was the one to kill Reed."

"How so?"

She told him about the recordings, about how they'd had the opposite effect on her than what Dark had expected.

"Seeing everything he did to me, all the horrendous things he put me through, I realized what a gift you gave me. You gave me closure." She smiled and added, "You gave me justice."

He kissed her hand again. "I love you, Irelyn Raine. I love you so damn much."

"I'll never tire of hearing you say that."

"Still going to marry me?"

"Absolutely. Once Dark is out of the way, nothing is going to stop us."

"I'll take care of Dark."

"That's not—"

He squeezed her hand. "Darling, you've done all the heavy lifting up until now. It's my turn."

"But—"

"No buts. My turn. You just get better. Understand?"

"I can't lose you, Grey."

"You won't."

"Promise?"

"Have I ever broken a promise to you?"

"No."

"I don't plan on starting now. We're in this together, Irelyn, for the long haul."

"The sixty-year plan. Right?"

Blue eyes gleaming with warmth, he leaned over and whispered against her mouth, "We'll renegotiate at sixty years."

"Deal," she said softly.

CHAPTER THIRTY-NINE

Sebastian looked down on the still smoldering ruins of his home. It was all gone. Destroyed. Decimated. Everything that Hill Reed had worked for, everything Sebastian had ever loved, was gone.

He couldn't even get close enough to pay his respects or say goodbye. Police barricades surrounded the estate, and at least a dozen guards stood around the perimeter of the once great mansion.

"Can you get any closer?"

"Not without attracting attention, Mr. Dark."

Sebastian nodded his understanding. He'd had to rent a helicopter and pilot to fly him over the estate. To everyone on the ground, he would just look like a curiosity seeker or perhaps a television news station gaining a different perspective of the famed structure. But in truth, he was almost as devastated as Hill House itself. His home. His property. His legacy. All gone.

She was responsible for all of it. She had never appreciated what Hill Reed had done for her. She had left, breaking Hill's heart. If that wasn't enough, she had murdered him in

cold blood years later. And now she had destroyed everything he had worked so hard to obtain.

She had survived the fire. He had watched her fall, but
had had to get out before he could confirm her death. He'd
hidden behind some bushes and watched Justice, along with
two other men, go into the burning building and bring her
out. The bitch should have died!

He should have made sure he'd killed her when he'd had
the chance. With one bullet to the head, he could have
stopped all of this from happening. Instead, he had allowed
her to get to him, to ensnare him. Looking back on it, he
realized she had employed the same tactics Reed had used.
Unlike Reed, who had employed those words only for guid-
ance and disciplinary love, she had used them to bring him
down. What a sacrilege!

If it was the last thing he did, he would make sure Irelyn
Raine paid for all her sins.

Then he would regroup and rebuild. He consoled himself
that Hill House had gotten old and had been at the point of
needing major repair work. The house might be gone, but
Hill Reed's legacy would live on. He would make sure of that.

He hadn't started anything yet, but he would soon. First,
he would rid himself and the world of two major pains in the
ass. Once Irelyn Raine and Grey Justice were finally dead,
then he'd get back to re-creating the life he was meant to
have. The one that his father wanted for him.

Sebastian Dark was not finished by a long shot.

London, England

GREY STOOD IN THE DARKNESS AND WAITED FOR THE VERDICT.
He had made his petition to the council. His arguments were

sound, his reasoning flawless. That didn't mean he would receive approval.

It would have been helpful to see their faces, to at least see that he was getting through to them. But this had been their way from the beginning. He knew most of these people, could picture them in his mind, but when in front of the council, one never saw their faces. It was, to him, a ridiculously archaic tradition but since he was asking for their help, he would play it the way they preferred.

"You look like both your parents."

Though he sounded much older than Grey remembered, he recognized the distinctive voice of Malcolm Cooke.

Grey acknowledged the statement with a nod. "I take that as a high compliment."

"It's too bad you didn't take after them in other ways."

"You believe I'm all that different?"

"You should have stayed here, carried on their legacy."

"Their legacy was gaining justice for victims. That's exactly what I do."

"Possibly, but not in the place of your birth. You could be here at this table, helping lead this group instead of coming here, as an outsider, requesting our help."

He was being baited. His reasons for leaving England were no secret to the council. They had tried to overreach their boundaries. Had wanted to use Irelyn without any concern or care for what she had endured. His first priority had been to protect her. That hadn't changed.

"The girl you wanted to use, to punish, has done your work for you," Grey said. "She killed Hill Reed, gaining justice for the deaths of my parents. She also destroyed Hill House, something you also never managed to do."

"Your arrogance is not appreciated."

"I speak the truth."

"The truth as you see it."

"And how do you see it?"

"That's enough." The new voice belonged to Aaron Finley and was so weak sounding it was almost unrecognizable. The Justice Seekers council consisted of five members, but only two of the original members, Cooke and Finley, remained. Both were elderly, but their philosophies on how justice should be attained were markedly different.

The quivering voice of the oldest council member continued. "Your parents were the finest of our group. We owe them a debt of gratitude, and I for one believe that should extend to their son.

"While it's true that Irelyn Raine contributed to their deaths, she has atoned for her mistakes. I, therefore, vote that we grant the petitioner's request."

Grey held his breath, waiting for the others to weigh in with their votes. He would find and destroy Dark either way, but the additional support might mean the difference between finding him next week and finding him in a year. He wanted this over and done with.

He breathed a little easier as, one by one, each council member gave his or her opinion of why they approved the request. The last holdout was no surprise. Cooke had been the one who had insisted all those years ago that Irelyn should be punished. He was also the grand high council and could, if he wanted, overrule the rest of the group.

"I am still not convinced that it's our place to intervene."

Holding his temper, Grey calmly explained, "You have a vested interest in destroying Sebastian Dark. While he doesn't have the following that Hill Reed obtained, he is wealthy enough to eventually gain that status. Killing him will, in large measure, destroy the legacy of Reed and the evil he perpetuated."

Again, there was silence. Finally, as if he was doing this for magnanimous reasons only, Cooke said, "Justice has and always will be at the core of our existence, but preventing further injustice is just as noble. Therefore, the petition is approved."

Grey nodded his appreciation and backed away. Irelyn Raine had destroyed both the man who killed his parents and the house he created. And now, his parents' legacy would destroy the man who tried to kill Irelyn. Life and justice had come full circle.

He would return to Irelyn assured that a vast network of people searched every corner of the universe. Also, when the time came, he would have the assistance of the deadliest of the deadly.

Sebastian Dark didn't know that a contract had been taken out on his life and that Grey Justice would carry that contract out to the end.

Dark's days were numbered.

CHAPTER FORTY

Eight weeks later
Dallas, Texas

"You're sure you don't want a large wedding?"

Sitting in front of a roaring fire, sipping a glass of Irish whiskey, and talking wedding plans with Grey was as close to perfection as she could imagine. She was still mending from her injuries, but each day she felt a marked improvement. A lot of that had to do with the man who sat beside her.

She shook her head, laughing at his question. "It *is* going to be a large wedding. We've invited half of Dallas."

"Yes, but we could invite the other half if you like."

"I think this will be more than enough." She glanced over at the table where the RSVPs were stacked. Who knew that almost everyone they invited would accept?

"You're not fooling me, you know."

"Oh yeah, how so?"

"You're enjoying every moment of it."

Another miracle she hadn't expected. The oh-so-private

Irelyn Raine was going to stand up in front of hundreds of people and proclaim her love. The wedding would be held just outside Dallas at a gargantuan estate owned by one of Grey's business associates. Though she had an amazingly efficient wedding planner, plus tons of ideas and suggestions from Kennedy, there were still hundreds of little details for her to decide on. And as usual, Grey had read her correctly. She was loving every moment.

Only one dark cloud remained.

"Are you sure we shouldn't wait until it's completely over?"

"Absolutely not. Dark is being surprisingly elusive. It could take several more weeks or months to find him. I don't want to wait any longer to make you mine."

"I was yours the moment I met you."

Pulling her closer, he said softly, "As I was yours."

Laying her head on his shoulder, she stared into the fire. Their journey had been a long, sometimes painful one. For many years, even as she acknowledged their bond could not be broken, she had never envisioned the happiness she would know. Accepting Grey's love and revealing her own had opened up a whole new world. The future was theirs.

She told herself there was no need to worry. Dozens of people—not just the Grey Justice Group, but also the network that Grey's parents had been a part of—were looking for him. There were rumors that even his own community had turned against him, that some were actively seeking to punish him for what they considered a stain on their community.

No matter where he went, where he tried to hide, he would be found by someone. She knew Grey wanted to be the one to find him, to end him, but in her heart of hearts, she wanted it to be someone else. Not because she didn't want Dark dead, and certainly not because Grey couldn't handle him. But the peace they had experienced lately felt so lovely, so perfect, she wanted to draw it out for as long as possible. Was that too much to ask?

Three Weeks Later

GREY WAITED BENEATH THE TRELLIS ADORNED WITH PINK ROSES and white daisies. His bride would be coming down the aisle soon. He'd never thought this day would get here. It seemed as though he had been waiting a lifetime to make Irelyn Raine his forever.

He wished everything could have been settled before this day arrived. She deserved to have this day free from worry or fear. He had done his best to keep the details of his search for Sebastian Dark to himself. On one memorable occasion, he had walked out of the room to take a phone call. That had been a mistake.

She had reminded him in no uncertain terms that they were partners in everything. Even now, he smiled at how he had gone about easing her anger. They had both been breathless and satisfied.

Dark would turn up one day and would die. Grey refused to put his life and their happiness on hold any longer. This day had been in the making for almost two decades. Damned if he would wait any longer.

Someone in the crowd laughed, and Grey glanced out at the audience. Irelyn had been right. It was a large wedding. Neither of them had a traditional family, but they were blessed with true friends who had become family. Those people, along with hundreds of others, had come to witness what many were calling the wedding of the decade. To him, it was the continuation of a partnership and the beginning of a beautiful life together.

He was pleased to see that Lacey and Wyatt, both looking tanned and happy, had made it back from their honeymoon in time to attend the wedding. Three weeks ago, Lacey had walked down the aisle unaided by crutches, to marry the man she loved. Though she was still going to rehab twice a week, her doctors and physical therapist had assured her of a full recovery. With Lacey's determination and Wyatt's devotion, Grey had no doubts about that.

The music, which had been a medley of his and Irelyn's favorite songs, suddenly changed. The crowd went quiet, and Grey got his first look at his bride. He lost his breath. He had seen this woman at her most beautiful, and still that could not compare with how she looked today. An ethereal glow seemed to surround her, and the small smile curving her beautiful mouth put Mona Lisa's to shame. In the depths of her lovely gray eyes, he saw every hope, every dream for their future. And his heart was at peace.

HER GOWN WAS ITALIAN LACE OVER IVORY SATIN. THE trumpet mermaid swirl at the bottom flared out into the slightest of trains, and she loved hearing the swish of satin as she moved. Her hair was styled in a loose braid, pulled away from her face. Grey had once told her the hairstyle reminded him of how she looked when they first met. Her jewelry was a simple silver locket that looked perfect with the V neck of the gown, and her earrings were two-carat diamond studs. On her right hand, she wore the silver ring Grey had given her years ago, a symbol of their unbreakable bond. She would soon wear a circle of diamonds that would symbolize their lifetime commitment on her left hand.

As she walked toward the man she loved beyond life,

she thought about fairy tales and happy endings. About glass slippers, castles in the air, and charming princes. She was living her very own storybook romance. But in every tale, there was always a threat of evil, that knowledge that no matter how much you pray for a smooth pathway to a happy ever after, something or someone could destroy it.

She wouldn't think about that today. For this moment in time, she would concentrate on what she had been given—a man who understood her and loved her just the way she was. What more could she ask?

It had taken them a long time to get things right. She had fought against happiness, thinking she didn't deserve it, but Grey had never given up on her.

Nontraditional, as usual, they had compromised on their wedding songs. She walked down the aisle with the soulful sound of Etta James's *At Last* soaring around her, which had been her choice. At the end of the ceremony, Grey's choice, John Legend's *All of Me*, would play. Both were powerful songs, and their beautiful words described so much of their love for each other.

She made it down the aisle without tripping and smiled her relief when Grey took a few steps forward and took her hand. Together, they walked to the minister waiting for them.

She turned to face her groom and counted herself fortunate that she was made of sturdy stuff, or she would have swooned. No male model, actor, or fairy-tale prince could compete with Grey Justice in a tuxedo.

"Hello, handsome," she whispered softly.

"Hello, my love."

"We are gathered today, in the sight of family and friends, to join these two people as one. Irelyn and Grey have written their own vows."

The minister turned to her first. "Irelyn, would you like to go first?"

She nodded and took a bracing breath. She had never made such a public statement of what was in her heart. More nervous than she'd ever thought possible, Irelyn raised her eyes to Grey's. When she saw the tenderness, the love, her nerves faded away. It didn't matter if she had an audience of a million, these words were for one man only.

"Grey, I loved you from the moment I met you, even though I had no idea what love really felt like. I loved you at fifteen when you were my knight in shining armor. I loved you when you forgave the unforgivable. Even when I hated and cursed you, I loved you. You never gave up on me, even when I gave up on myself.

"Thank you, my darling, for your bountiful love and tender forgiveness. For helping me become the kind of woman I can respect. I can never repay you for everything you've given me, everything you are to me. You are my life. You are my love. You are my everything."

More moved than he had ever been in his life, Grey had to wait a moment till the lump in his throat subsided. They had both wanted to write their vows, but they hadn't shared them until this moment.

He cleared his throat. "Irelyn, if I had all the words in the world to describe my feelings for you, there still wouldn't be enough to tell you how wonderful I think you are, or how very much I love you. Your courage and resilience amaze me. Your kind heart astounds me. Your beauty enthralls me. And your strength makes me stronger. You have my devotion, my fidelity, and my heart for all eternity. I would give my life for you. All that I am, all that I have, is yours."

The rest of the ceremony passed in a blur. Their eyes

remained locked, their unspoken words meant only for them. Grey came out of his trance when the minister said, "I now pronounce you husband and wife. You may kiss your bride."

A roar of approval swept through the crowd as their lips met for the first time as husband and wife.

CHAPTER FORTY-ONE

Four Weeks Later
England

Grey raised his binoculars and scanned the perimeter of the estate. The surrounding area was densely forested, providing the perfect cover. With him were five of the deadliest mercenaries in the business, sanctioned by the Justice Seekers for jobs such as these. This was not a Grey Justice Group operation. This was his mission.

The orders he had given them were simple. Take down everyone except for Sebastian Dark. The bastard was all Grey's.

The new residence was a much smaller version of Hill House and had been aptly named Dark House. The man had tried to emulate every aspect of Hill Reed, and this was just one more. Irelyn had pegged him correctly. He had no thought of his own that wasn't influenced by what Hill Reed had taught him.

It had taken too damn long to find him. And when he had been found, it'd taken weeks to study him. Others might have gone in and massacred the entire household. Grey could not do that. If Dark was copying everything that Hill Reed had done, that could mean he had brought children into the house. Damned if he would allow any other innocents to be killed or harmed because of this bastard. It might have taken longer than he liked, but at least he was now assured that the only people within that house were almost as evil as its owner.

Leaving Irelyn five days into their honeymoon had felt like he was flaying his own skin from his body. She hadn't wanted him to do this alone. Had tried to convince him that she should come with him, that they should do this together. He had never even considered her suggestion. Yes, she was more than capable, but this was his battle to wage. Sebastian Dark had tortured the woman he loved, had almost killed her. He had sent Irelyn's only brother to kill Grey, forcing her to make a heartbreaking choice. Dark had also been responsible for the accident that had almost killed Lacey Slater.

Sebastian Dark had to be stopped. If Grey didn't kill him, he would continue to copy Hill Reed. What he had told the council was true. Annihilating Dark would destroy Reed's legacy. All of that ended today.

They had been watching the house and surrounding area for weeks. From his count, twelve people were inside. The five that guarded the perimeter had already been taken out with one shot to the head each. The twelve remaining would be no problem for these men. Though he had worked with them over the last few days and had seen their humanity, Grey knew that when it came down to the actual job, they could be just as ruthless and soulless as Dark's men.

That worked just right for him. He wasn't here on a mercy mission. He was here, just as they were, to destroy.

Sebastian Dark was finished in the world of assassins.

Word was that he was considered a blemish on their community. All he had left was his money and his delusions.

He glanced at the men beside him. "Let's do this."

With the swift precision of expertly trained soldiers, three of them ran to the back of the house. Grey gave a nod to the remaining men, and they both took off running. One of the men placed C-4 on the door lock and stepped back. Grey checked his watch. They would go in four, three, two... he nodded. The door exploded, and they all ran into the building.

SEBASTIAN SPRANG FROM HIS BED. THE SMITH & WESSON M&P Shield that he had taken to sleeping with was in his hand in an instant. They were here. He'd heard rumors, of course. Just because he'd been banned from the community didn't mean he couldn't find out what was going on. Everyone, apparently, wanted him dead.

They could try to kill him, but they wouldn't touch a hair on his head. He had been planning for this very thing. He had more contingency plans than anyone could ever guess. He had money stashed all over the world. He had locations in both Europe and the US. He had an army to protect him.

He had no intention of dying, and the community that shunned him today would someday come crawling to him, begging for the chance to become a Dark House assassin.

He had made a mistake not following Reed in all things. But that would soon change. While others had been searching for him, he had been hidden away learning and planning. Reed had developed many of his own people by taking in children and training them himself. Sebastian had never considered such a thing, mostly because he despised the little buggers. But that didn't mean he couldn't work with them, teach them. He had been trained in that way. There was no reason he couldn't do the same thing. He would be the new Hill Reed. The children would revere and fear him, call him Father. And someday, they would kill for him.

Silly men might play their games, but Sebastian Dark would have the last laugh.

He ran to the control room next to his bedroom and switched on the video feed. There were only six intruders. His men would handle them without any problems. In fact, he was a little surprised that they'd been able to get near the house. When this was over, he'd have a very stern talk with the guards who'd allowed them to get this close.

It didn't really matter who was behind this raid. There were many who would pay for the privilege of taking down the infamous Sebastian Dark. Still, he couldn't help but hope that Justice and Raine were involved. He had been busy and put off going after them. He'd heard they'd gotten married, which made him want to kill them even more.

He pulled on his protective gear and armed himself. They would never make it to his private quarters, but it never hurt to be prepared just in case. He glanced back at the cameras displaying the inside of the house. Why was it so quiet? His men should be running through the hallways, shooting everyone in their path. What was taking them so long?

He switched camera views, and with each new scan, his concern grew. Several of his guards were lying on the floor. It was to be expected that he would lose a few, and that was no matter. He would get more. But where were the intruders? Were they dead somewhere else? It was as if they had been apparitions and had disappeared as quickly as they'd come.

What was happening out there? Should he wait here until the all clear sounded? Should he hide inside his safe room? He'd hired men to guard him, so it really wasn't his responsibility to check on them. He went to the door and chewed his lip in indecision.

He could hear his father's voice deriding him, telling him to stop being a coward, to go check things out.

He wasn't a coward. He wasn't.

Opening the bedroom door, he peered out into the hallway. A man lay facedown not five feet from his door. Blood pooled around his head. Again, one of his guards. Sebastian released a disgusted huff. *Imbecile.*

He was about to step into the hallway when something made him stop. Was that a shadow? Was someone coming his way? It didn't matter if it was one of his men, he couldn't take the chance. He fired several shots in the general direction and ducked back into the bedroom.

———

GREY NODDED HIS THANKS TO THE MERCENARIES WHO HAD helped him and watched as they walked out of the house, their job finished. In a matter of moments, they had achieved their objectives. Now there was only one target left, and he was Grey's to handle.

He headed down the hallway, toward Dark's room. The shots the idiot had fired had penetrated the wall. No one had been anywhere close. The man might not realize it, but he was spiraling out of control. Shooting and hoping to hit something was the mark of desperation.

Not only had Grey procured blueprints of this house, three days ago a tech security specialist had hacked into the security cameras. Grey had had the luxury of watching Sebastian Dark inside his home. He knew where he slept, what he ate for breakfast, and what he watched on television. Grey also knew about the secret room—the one that no one other than Dark was supposed to know about.

Stopping outside the bedroom door, Grey took a moment to listen. He heard what sounded like heavy breathing and then the sound of a door clicking shut. He smiled. The coward had gone into his safe room sooner than he'd thought he would.

Still cautious, Grey opened the door. Decorated in browns and charcoal, the room was as dark and depressing as a cave. The four-poster bed was unmade and had the look of someone who'd had a restless night. Considering the nightmares Irelyn suffered from, the thought of Dark having them made Grey feel better.

Seeing no one in the room, Grey went into the security room and pressed a red button on one of the control panels. A screen appeared with a keypad. He held his gun at the ready as he entered the sequence of numbers he'd seen Dark enter the night before. A second later, the door swung open on its hinges.

In a matter of seconds, Grey took in his surroundings. If his thoughts weren't as dark as the man he was hunting, he might have laughed. This was no safe room, this was a full-fledged apartment complete with a bed, entertainment center, kitchen, and bath. Dark was prepared to live here for months. That wasn't going to be necessary.

Bullets whizzed toward him, missing him. Grey didn't give him another chance. Firing rapidly, he ran toward the man he could see stooped behind a leather recliner. The thuds of his bullets hitting the leather echoed through the room.

Staying on his haunches, Dark half crawled, half scooted toward another barrier, this time a coffee table that he upended and hid behind. Grey kept moving forward, ducking behind various pieces of furniture for cover when necessary but never stopping.

"Don't come any closer!"

"Give it up, Dark. You're not getting away this time."

"How did you get in here?" He sounded both frustrated and furious.

"Guess your security isn't all it's cracked up to be."

Giving him no time to respond, Grey was on him in a second. Plucking him out of his hiding place, he jabbed his fist into the man's face, knocking him backward. With a roar, Dark came at him. Fists flew right and left, blood spewed, splattering the carpet and walls.

They dove into each other like feral animals, neither of them giving any quarter. Dark slammed a fist into Grey's mouth, and Grey returned the favor. Oddly enough, he was glad the man could fight. It would make taking him down all the sweeter.

Dark kicked out, grazing Grey's ribs with his steel-toed boot. Grey took advantage, grabbing the bastard's leg and twisting hard. He felt the pop and Dark howled like a banshee.

Dark dropped to the floor, scrambling backward on his ass. "You broke my leg," he screamed.

In his mind, Grey saw the image of Irelyn lying on the floor of Hill House, her leg broken because of this bastard. "Good."

Dark slid his hand into his pocket and a gleaming knife appeared in his hand. Backing up against the wall, he braced himself against it and stood.

"Come and get me."

Grey smiled. "My pleasure." Kicking the knife out of his hand, Grey moved on him faster, ruthlessly. Kick to the face, punch to the gut. Dark teetered, his balance off, his eyes glassy.

Grey told himself to finish it. No matter how pitiful and helpless the bastard appeared right now, the evil would never stop until he was dead. He raised his fist for the killing blow.

Slumping slightly, Dark looked away from him and cried out, "Wait! Please. It's not my fault. Hill made me this way. Just like he did Irelyn."

The words penetrated, striking Grey where he was most vulnerable. What Dark spoke was true. Irelyn had told him that he had suffered the same things she had endured. Sebastian Dark was a product of what Hill Reed had made him.

Grey hesitated.

In a flash, a small whip appeared in Dark's hand. He slashed out toward Grey, who managed to move in time to miss the brunt of it. Part of it still caught him on the side, leaving a stinging, bloody slice in his flesh.

"Son of a bitch!" Grey snarled.

The twisted smile on Dark's face was more evil than any Grey had ever witnessed. He might have once been an abused little boy, but he had developed into a man who had nothing but evil left inside him. Without a moment's hesitation, Grey grabbed the whip from Dark's hand and then slammed his head into the wall behind him. Dark's body slithered to the floor. His eyes were open, a surprised look frozen on his face.

Grey leaned over and checked for a pulse at his neck, his wrist. Assured that he was dead, Grey walked out of the mansion without a second glance. It was over, finished. The darkness that had stalked he and Irelyn for so long was finally over.

He could now return to the woman he adored, and their life could truly begin.

EPILOGUE

The Place Beyond The Mist
Ireland

She waited for him to come home to her. Before he'd left, she had told him about this place, had given him a detailed description. She wanted him to have an image in his mind, so he could know the peace that was waiting for him. She told him she would go back to Ireland and wait for him. It had been weeks, and still she waited.

Each morning when she rose, she would wonder if today would be the day. Others could have done this, she had told him, but he insisted this one was on him. She understood his need, but she worried. Oh, how she worried.

He had known of her concern, but she didn't tell about the terror. How could she? How many times had she disappeared and forced him to wonder and worry? Grey had understood her need to rescue, to make a difference in her own way. He *understood* her. Just as she understood him.

Their honeymoon had been a lovely, idyllic five days of bliss in Tahiti. It was to have been longer, but he'd gotten the call to leave. She had wanted to stop him, to beg, if necessary, but she hadn't. Never in her life had she sat back and let someone else fight a battle for her, but she had forced herself to do this for him. Grey needed this closure, just as she had needed the closure of ridding the world of Hill Reed.

He hadn't given her details before he left. Just that Dark had been located, and they were making plans to breach his house. It sounded as though he had found himself a new fortress. How many men were protecting him? How many men would Grey have with him? He hadn't volunteered the information, and she hadn't asked.

As she had every morning, she dressed warmly and took a steaming mug of coffee and a blanket out to the porch. She settled into the rocking chair and allowed the mist to envelope her. As it surrounded her, she imagined herself in a peaceful cloud that evil could not penetrate. She sipped her coffee, dreaming of the day she would see the tall figure of a man walking toward her. His dark head would rise above that mist as he came closer. And she would know that he had come home to her.

She hadn't expected to feel any different just because she was Grey's wife. She had already loved him, was already committed to him. Why would marriage be any different? She had been so wrong. If possible, she loved him a thousand times more than before they were married. That commitment, that bond, was unlike anything she had ever known. They were one.

Individualism was very important to her, and she didn't plan to give up who she was. Grey wouldn't let her anyway. But in marriage, she felt more of a connection than she'd ever believed possible. For a woman who had always been firmly grounded in reality, she had no explanation other than it felt almost mystical.

No one in Dallas knew what Grey was doing. Everyone

believed they were still on their honeymoon. Grey hadn't wanted any of his people involved, and she understood. Both Kennedy and Lacey had texted her, asking about the honeymoon, and she had been as vague as she could be without actually lying. If his people knew what he was doing, they would likely move heaven and earth to try to help.

So she waited alone, worry and hope her only companions.

She had so much to say to him, so much to tell him. And one very special surprise. He was going to be a father. Yesterday Sister Nadeen had called. The family that was to adopt Somer had learned they were expecting a new baby. Though they were heartbroken about the decision, they didn't feel they could give Somer the care and attention she would need or deserved. It had taken all of two seconds for Irelyn to tell Sister Nadeen that she and Grey would love to be Somer's parents.

There were issues to resolve, a process to go through, but Irelyn had no doubts that it would work out. She also had no doubts about Grey. He would be thrilled with the news.

Now if only he would come home to her.

Noting that her feet felt frozen and her coffee had gone cold, Irelyn stood. She would refill her cup, slip on another pair of socks, and return to her spot. She was halfway to the door when something stopped her. Had she seen a movement on the bridge, or was that just more mist coming to settle?

Her heart skipped a beat, and her breath left her lungs. No, it wasn't mist. It was the dark figure of a man walking on the bridge. Hurriedly, she put the mug down, dropped the blanket, and then jumped off the porch. Her heart racing as fast as her feet, she ran toward the man who was coming closer and closer.

Just where the bridge began, she stopped and waited. The

earth fell still around her. The mist parted, and she could finally see his face. Gratitude and unbelievable joy filling her, she ran into his open arms and sighed softly as they closed around her.

"Hello, my love," he growled softly.

"Hello, my husband," she replied. "I've missed you."

Pulling her closer, Grey held her close, absorbing her warmth. "I've missed you, too."

"It's over?"

"Yes, it's over."

She pulled away slightly to look up at his face. "And you're all right?"

"I am now."

She took his hand and pulled him forward. "Let's go home."

They walked together toward the cottage. She would ask him at some point to tell her what happened. He would need to share it, and she would be there to help him through it. But for now…for now, she would rejoice that the man she loved and adored was back home with her, safe and sound.

Grey and Irelyn together again.

At last.

DEAR READER

Thank you so much for reading **A Matter Of Justice, A Grey Justice Novel**. I sincerely hope you enjoyed Grey and Irelyn's love story. If you would be so kind as to leave a review at your favorite online retailer to help other readers find this book, I would sincerely appreciate it.

If you'd like to be notified when I have a new release, sign up for my newsletter.

http://authornewsletters.com/christyreece/

To learn about my other books and what I'm currently writing, please visit my website.

http://www.christyreece.com

Follow me on Facebook and on Twitter.

https://www.facebook.com/AuthorChristyReece/

https://twitter.com/ChristyReece

Wildefire Series writing as Ella Grace

Midnight Secrets, A Wildefire Novel

Midnight Lies, A Wildefire Novel

Midnight Shadows, A Wildefire Novel

ACKNOWLEDGMENTS

Special thanks to the following people for helping make this book possible:

My husband, for your love, support, numerous moments of comic relief, and almost always respecting my chocolate stash.

Keith Frost, for your expert advice on guns. Any mistakes are my own.

The amazing Joyce Lamb, for your awesome copyediting skills and fabulous advice.

Marie Force's eBook Formatting Fairies, who always answers my endless questions with endless patience.

Tricia Schmitt (Pickyme) for your gorgeous cover art.

The Reece's Readers Facebook groups, for all your support and encouragement.

Anne, always my first reader, who goes above and beyond, and then goes the extra mile, too. And also for giving me Irelyn's name.

My beta readers, Crystal, Hope, Julie, Alison, and Kris for their great suggestions.

Kara for reading a finished version and making excellent observations and for finding those things no one else found.

Linda Clarkson of Black Opal Proofreading, who, as always, did an amazing job. So appreciate your eagle eye, Linda!

Extra special thanks to Hope for your help and assistance in a multitude of things. Thank you for your generous heart and for keeping me on track!

And to all my readers, thank you for your patience. Your emails, Facebook, and Twitter messages about Grey and Irelyn's book were very much appreciated. Though their story was years in the making, I hope you feel it was worth the wait!

ABOUT THE AUTHOR

Christy Reece is the award winning, NYT Bestselling Author of dark romantic suspense. She lives in Alabama with her husband and a menagerie of pets.

Christy loves hearing from readers and can be contacted at Christy@ChristyReece.com.

DISCOVER THE EXCITING WORLD OF LCR ELITE

A WHOLE NEW LEVEL OF DANGER

With Last Chance Rescue's philosophy of rescuing the innocent, the Elite branch takes the stakes even higher. Infiltrating the most volatile locations in the world, LCR Elite Operatives risk everything to rescue high value targets. Unsanctioned. Off the grid. Every operation a secret, danger-filled mission. LCR Elite will stop at nothing, no matter the cost, to fulfill their promise.

RUNNING WILD
An LCR Elite Novel

He'll Stop At Nothing
To Protect The Ones He Loves

LCR Elite operative Aidan Thorne is dedicated to rescuing kidnapped victims from some of the most dangerous places in the world, but that will never stop him from hunting down a coldblooded killer. Child psychologist Anna Bradford is a temptation unlike any he's ever faced, penetrating the steely armor encasing his heart. Though he wants her with an unending ache, Anna's very survival requires Aidan to stay as far away from her as possible.

Understanding human behavior is Anna Bradford's profession. Aidan Thorne is a mystery she has yet to unravel. Her fascination for the snarling, often rude man is a battle she fights on a daily basis. Her head tells her to stay away, her heart tells her something different. When they join forces to help rescue a friend, Aidan finally allows Anna to see the man beneath the tough exterior. Falling in love with him was inevitable.

But someone is watching. He's been hiding in the shadows for years, waiting. The time has finally arrived. Anna Bradford will be his tool, his perfect weapon of revenge. She will be his masterpiece.

His worst fears realized, Aidan must now find a way to save Anna before the madman that destroyed his life once before lives out his ultimate fantasy.

CHAPTER ONE

Cali, Colombia

The bar was both sleazy and filthy. Smoke swirled through the big room like an industrialized bug fogger belching out its last toxic dregs. From the sticky fake-wood floor that hadn't seen soap and water in decades to the light fixtures with grimy coats of dirt and dead bugs, the ambience of Claudio's Cantina bellowed, *Enter at your own risk*.

Aidan figured it'd take at least a half-dozen showers before the stink left him.

Slouched in the corner, his back to the wall, he gave the appearance of being half wasted and all the way bored. He was neither. His informant was fifteen minutes late. Punctuality had never been a priority for Ernesto Diaz. Aidan had no illusions about the man. Though less corrupt than most in his business, if Diaz got a better offer, he'd sell out without a thought. Which was why Aidan was going to give the vermin only five more minutes to show. The back of his neck was getting that twitchy feeling, which usually meant trouble was brewing. Ignoring that twitch had once gotten him shot. He hadn't ignored it since.

He shifted in his chair, noting and appreciating the lack of pain. Three months ago, he'd been laid up with a broken leg. Weeks of doing almost nothing but waiting for it to heal had made him antsy and out of sorts. The minute he'd returned to full LCR duty, he'd jumped into the action as if all of hell's demons were on his ass. Too much time to think and remember. Too much time to regret. Nothing like staying on the edge of danger to help focus a man's thoughts.

In fact, he'd been so focused, that when he'd gotten the call from Diaz, he'd almost delayed the meet. After all this time with no viable intel, what was the point of rushing just to find out there was nothing new? After that thought, the inevitable guilt had followed. How dare he not follow up? Had he not made a promise? Had he not sworn that he would follow every lead, no matter how minuscule or far-fetched, until he found the murdering bastard?

So, despite the fact that Diaz was about as reliable as a politician and most likely had nothing new to tell him, Aidan had taken the bait.

His family thought he was certifiable. Not that they'd come right out and say it. His mother and father, ever supportive, just gave him that sympathetic, helpless look that basically said, *We're here for you, but we're completely lost on why you're not living up to your potential.*

His sister was a little more blunt. Last time he'd talked to her, they'd had a shouting match. She thought he was wasting his life and didn't mind saying so. He thought she was a nosy, opinionated buttinski who needed to stay out of his business. A day later, he had sent her flowers to apologize. She had sent him a bottle of his favorite wine. Both of them knew that all was forgiven.

To his family, it probably did look as though he was wasting his life. Or at least not living up to his potential. They had a vague idea of what his job with LCR entailed, but he did his best to shield them from the more hair-raising details. Rescuing kidnapped victims from the most dangerous places in the world was a far cry from the safe, secure world he'd left behind.

But that world stopped being safe and secure a decade ago. His family could stay in denial as long as they wanted. Aidan knew the truth. The monster was still out there. Watching. Waiting. Looking for his next chance to strike. Too many had paid the price for Aidan's carelessness. He would never let his guard down ever again.

Without moving a muscle, every inch of Aidan's body went on high alert. His eyes searched the reason for his unease. Detected nothing. Still, the hair on the back of his neck was screaming a warning. What the hell was going down?

"Let me go, you big gorilla! I don't want to go in here." What the hell?

A woman was shoved into the middle of the room. All eyes were on her, and almost every damn one of them had the salacious look of a predator about to pounce. This was not going to be pretty.

The room was too smoky to tell much about her, but that wouldn't matter to a bunch of drunk, horny, soulless men. Fresh meat had arrived in their vicinity, requiring no effort to obtain. The woman was in a shitload of trouble.

With a casualness in direct contrast to the circumstances, Aidan stood and eased himself over to the bar. Calling attention to his movements wouldn't be good for either him or the woman. He was her best chance to get out of here unscathed. If he was taken down, she was toast.

There were three men at the bar. An additional eight were at various tables. Four men had been playing pool. Two had been throwing darts. Of course, all activity had ceased. No one was doing anything now but staring at the woman and salivating.

Already trying to figure out which man he could pit against the other, Aidan leaned against the barstool and pretended to eye the woman just like everyone else. Acting as if he wasn't interested would call attention to himself, but in truth, he didn't bother to look at her. All other eyes were on their single target. Aidan's attention was on the safest way to get this woman out the door.

The music on the ancient jukebox ended. Since no one had bothered to pay for another song, silence filled the room.

"Look," the woman stated in a firm, no-nonsense way, "I'm just looking for my friend. If you've not seen her, that's fine. But I'm not going to stand here anymore. I'm leaving."

Aidan's involuntary gasp took in a giant gulp of smoky air, and he almost choked on the fumes. Probably would have if he wasn't in shock. His eyes finally settled on the woman, and even though his mind screamed a denial, he couldn't avoid the truth. Holy, holy hell. That was no girl, no mere woman. And definitely no stranger. That was the one, the only, Anna Bradford.

What the hell was she doing here? Most important, how was he going to get her out alive?

ANNA STOOD IN THE MIDDLE OF THE SMOKE-FILLED ROOM AND concentrated on acting tough and in control. She told herself she'd been in worse predicaments. A dozen bee stings in Arizona, a snakebite in Peru, and a severely broken heart in the ninth grade. Not to mention being kidnapped and tortured a few years back. She could darn well figure her way out of this situation. Admittedly, while all the men surrounding her looked as though they would murder their sainted granny for a dollar, she had learned to look beyond dirt and grime to the person beneath the surface. Out of all of these not terribly reputable-looking people, there had to be at least one with enough decency to help her get out of here.

So far, coming to Cali had been an abysmal failure. Counseling traumatized children was a challenge on the best of days. It was especially difficult when the parents of those children were less well-behaved than a one-year-old with diaper rash. But when the psychologist scheduled for the clinic had canceled because of a family emergency and Carrie had called her at the last minute, Anna had gotten swept up in the notion that if she didn't help, no one would. Now not only had she not helped a single child, Carrie was missing.

And to make matters a thousand times worse, Anna was now going to die a horrible death.

At that thought, her spine went stiff with indignation. She was most certainly not going to die today. She would simply explain what was going on to these men. Surely they had tender feelings for their mothers or sisters. She would just appeal to their human side.

Giving them the smile she often used to put a frightened child at ease, she stated firmly, clearly, "Gentlemen, I find myself in need of assistance. A friend of mine has gone missing. She's about five-feet-five, with blond hair and light green eyes. Her name is Carrie. Has anyone seen her?"

No one answered. Not even a headshake. She tried again. "I know if your mother or sister were missing, you'd want someone to help her. Wouldn't you?"

What came next burned her ears. These men were definitely not fond of their mothers or sisters.

She made a three-sixty-degree turn, looking for a friendly face. It wasn't to be found. Deciding a quick and graceful retreat was her best recourse, Anna started to back away. She took slow measured steps and began to feel optimistic. No one was coming after her. Maybe they were going to just let her—

She slammed into what felt like a brick wall. Heart thundering, her breathing almost to the point of hyperventilating, Anna turned around. Her eyes were on the level of a large, well-formed chest. The man stood before her like an immovable boulder. Tall, broad-shouldered, and so muscular that the sleeves of his olive green T-shirt were molded around his well-developed biceps.

Anna swallowed hard and finally found the courage to raise her gaze to his face. Beautiful, golden brown eyes, sensual, unsmiling mouth, sexy facial scruff. A wave of dizziness swept over her, and if he hadn't grabbed her shoulders, she would have keeled over at his feet.

Of all the gin joints, in all the towns, in all the world, why did she have to walk into his?

Casablanca was a million miles away. She was no Ingrid Bergman, and the man in front of her was definitely not Humphrey Bogart. Rick never would have glared at Ilsa like that.

"Having trouble staying out of trouble, Anna?"

"Hello, Aidan. It's nice to see you again. How are you?"

DESPITE THE TENSE SITUATION, AIDAN HAD TROUBLE KEEPING A straight face. "Only Anna Bradford could have two dozen salivating drunks surrounding her and act as if she's attending a Sunday social."

She lifted her chin. Such a lovely, stubborn slant. "Politeness never goes out of style."

"You think we could save the social niceties until after we get you out of here?"

Without moving her head, her gaze swept nervously around the room, the only indication that she was aware of the trouble she was in. Clearing her throat, she said, "I was just leaving."

"Very wise," Aidan said dryly.

Though he kept his eyes on Anna, Aidan was hyper-aware of everything that was going on around them. The three men at the bar were discussing their plan of attack. A half dozen other men were looking for their own chance to strike. The rest of them were hanging back. No doubt waiting to see what their friends could accomplish without them.

So for now, it was nine against two. Not the worst odds he'd ever faced. If he could get out of here without bloodshed, all the better. Protecting Anna was his priority.

She swallowed loudly. "Any suggestions?"

"Yes. Get ready to be offended."

Wide-eyed, she looked up at him. "What?"

He took advantage of her open mouth, swooped down, and slammed his mouth over hers. His tongue swept inside, and in an instant, Aidan knew the men surrounding them were the least of his troubles.

He'd dreamed about tasting her, and dammit, now he'd gone and done it. She was more delicious than anything he'd ever tasted in his life. He could stand here all day, drowning in her sweetness, savoring her flavor.

Oh hell no.

Before she could struggle or kick him in the groin, Aidan pulled away from her. Giving her no time to scream or slap his face, he scooped her up with one arm and threw her over his shoulder. With the other, he pulled his Glock from the holster on his thigh and glared around the room. And just in case they didn't get it, he shouted, "Mine! Anybody got a problem with that?"

Not waiting around for an answer, Aidan turned and stalked out of the bar.

Made in the USA
Monee, IL
29 September 2022

14868399R00225